# BLOSSOMING PATH

## BOOK TWO

# BLOSSOMING PATH

## BOOK TWO

Carlos Calma

Podium

# BLOSSOMING PATH

## BOOK TWO

# Preparation and Providence

No backing out now, Kai," I murmured to myself.

I glanced down at my hands, noticing the newly formed callouses along my knuckles.

Looked like I was becoming more of a warrior than I'd thought.

Tianyi, already awake and buzzing with energy, landed on my shoulder. Windy, curled up at the foot of my bed, stirred awake at the sound of my voice, its eyes blinking open to greet the new day.

With my iron staff in hand, I stepped outside into the crisp morning air, leaving Windy to continue bathing in the sun. The sect was quiet this early in the morning, and I only had a few hours before classes to get some training in.

"Let's start with a few basic drills," I said, focusing on the weight and balance of the staff in my hands. I began with slow, deliberate movements, practicing the forms I was familiar with.

My mind drifted to the upcoming trial. The thought of facing a third-class disciple was daunting, to say the least.

"So what if they have years of martial arts training under their belt? What does that matter in the face of unbridled talent like mine?"

I sighed, my shoulders drooping ever so slightly. That's enough of that. I'd better focus on the task at hand.

Shifting my focus to the Rooted Banyan Stance, I planted my feet firmly on the ground and tensed.

Maybe I couldn't outmuscle them, but there was definitely a way for me to outsmart them. And for that, I needed the capability to survive at least one blow against a third-class disciple.

Perhaps I should try my utmost to level up the Rooted Bayan Stance. I brought up the Interface to see the skill's requirements for evolving to the next step.

> *Next Stage: Deep Rooted Banyan Stance*
> *Requirements:*
> *Rooted Banyan Stance Proficiency—Level 10*
> *Accumulate 100 hours in the Rooted Banyan Stance.*
> *Sustain the stance without breaking for a continuous period of one hour.*
> *Develop a basic understanding of the principles of Qi defense.*

It didn't seem likely. My skill was still at the first level. The idea of holding myself in that stance for even a minute seemed impossible in my mind. But an hour?

Perhaps leveling it up would be enough to strengthen my defenses.

As the sun rose higher, I could feel the sweat forming on my brow, the physical exertion a welcome distraction from the swirling thoughts in my head. Holding the stance and maintaining flawless form took significant effort, even after all my practice. My reserves of qi diminished by the second.

After my energy bottomed out, I switched to polishing my forms. If I couldn't throw a proper punch or kick, I'd stand no chance against a cultivator.

My muscles ached, but it was a good ache, the kind that spoke of progress and hard work.

From the position of the sun, I estimated I'd have enough time to rest and recover before my first class.

I crossed my legs and began cultivating the Crimson Lotus Purification technique, circulating my qi throughout my body, and drawing in the surrounding energy with Tianyi's support.

Compared to when I was at home, the innate qi here was plentiful. I estimated that the energy I was able to collect while cultivating was at least double what I previously could.

I settled into the familiar rhythm of the Crimson Lotus Purification technique, allowing myself to be enveloped by the tranquility of the moment. I focused on my breathing, slow and steady, each inhalation drawing in more qi. I couldn't afford to rush it. The dangers of Qi Deviation were all too real—a misstep I'd experienced before.

Despite the urgency of my situation with the looming challenge with the Silent Moon Sect disciple, I knew I had to maintain my discipline. The temptation to hasten the process was there, a nagging impatience in the back of my mind. But I quelled it, reminding myself of the importance of patience in cultivation. After all, the strongest trees were those that grew slowly, deeply rooted in the earth.

The sun's rays began to peek through the foliage, casting dappled shadows around me.

Tianyi gently fluttered near, her delicate touch amplifying the effects of the Crimson Lotus Purification technique.

It was time for the second part of my cultivation technique—the purification process. I inhaled deeply, centering my thoughts, and prepared for the delicate task of refining the qi I had accumulated.

As if sifting gold from sand, I carefully separated the pure qi from the dross.

I imagined a filter within me, a sieve through which I passed the gathered qi. It was a slow, meticulous process, demanding my utmost concentration.

Though the rate at which I gathered energy was now doubled, one grain of sand still amounted to only two grains.

The purified qi was lighter, cleaner, and more potent, a fraction of its original amount but far superior in quality. As it settled into my dantian, I felt a surge of clarity and rejuvenation that lifted a weight from my shoulders. I opened my eyes, and the world seemed sharper and more vivid.

I could see why cultivators would spend years in seclusion. If going cross-legged and closing their eyes for a while made them stronger, it was no surprise. The longer I did it, the more I enjoyed the process.

"Thank you, Tianyi."

With a light pat, I signaled Tianyi to return. I stood up, feeling a newfound vitality coursing through me.

I returned to my quarters, where the little serpent awaited. It perked up as I entered, its eyes following my every move. I greeted it with a smile. "Hey, Windy. Miss me?"

It slithered over and coiled around my ankle affectionately. I chuckled as I bent to stroke its scales. "Looks like you're doing well," I said, pleased to see it thriving. As I watched its playful behavior, I mused aloud, "I wonder what gender you are."

My knowledge from the Interface flashed through my mind. As with many mystical creatures, a Wind Serpent's gender only became clear once it matured. For now, it remained a mystery, another layer of my serpentine companion's enigmatic nature. I shook my head to dismiss the thought.

Turning to Tianyi, I told her, "Instructor Xiao-Hu doesn't like you fluttering around the class. Stay here with Windy, okay?"

Her wings vibrated as if she understood.

After a quick farewell, I made a mental note to bring back some food for Windy. It didn't seem hungry now, but I didn't want to risk starving it.

After gathering my things, I headed to the alchemy pavilion. My steps were light, but my heart felt heavy. How would my classmates see me now? As a reckless upstart challenging a Silent Moon disciple, or as someone trying to rise above his station?

I cringed, remembering my words. What was I acting so cool and righteous for? If Wang Jun or Lan-Yin were here, they'd definitely poke fun at me.

As I neared the pavilion, I caught sight of a few older disciples milling around. Their glances felt like weights, each one adding to the burden of unease settling in my stomach. I quickened my pace, eager to escape their scrutinizing eyes.

"Elixir Synthesis," I reminded myself, trying to focus on the upcoming class rather than the whispers and stares.

I entered, the familiar scents of herbs and potions greeting me like an old friend. The pavilion was a sanctuary of sorts, a place where I could immerse myself in the art of alchemy, leaving the complexities of sect politics and future challenges at the door.

Taking a deep breath, I found my seat, arranging my materials with practiced ease. The classroom slowly filled, each student absorbed in their own pre-class rituals. None of them came forward to talk to me, which I was somewhat thankful for.

My mind wandered briefly to Windy and Tianyi. I hoped they were getting along, the former's playful nature meshing well with Tianyi's gentle demeanor. It brought a small smile to my face, a temporary respite from the nervous anticipation for the class ahead.

As Instructor Xiao-Hu appeared, his eyes met mine. Yesterday's events were still fresh in my mind. After lingering on me for a few moments, he surveyed the rest of the class and walked to the front of the room.

"Today, we'll be continuing where we left off, exploring the delicate balance of ingredients and the precise control of qi necessary to create potent concoctions. Prepare your cauldrons!"

When the class ended, there was a collective sigh of relief mixed with the clinking of glassware and the shuffling of feet. I packed up my materials, my hands moving automatically while my mind was still occupied with the nuances of today's lesson.

That's when Instructor Xiao-Hu approached me, his expression unreadable. "Kai, I need to see you. The sect leader wishes to meet with you."

My heart skipped a beat. The sect leader? Why would someone so important want to meet me? I tried to keep my expression calm, but I could feel the color drain from my face.

"Sure, no problem," I managed to choke out, though my voice sounded far from confident.

*All right, Kai. Peerless genius, right? You shouldn't be afraid of anyone or anything . . . Yeah, right.* The thought was meant to be empowering, but it sounded hollow in my mind. If I were truly a peerless genius, I wouldn't feel like vomiting right now.

I followed Instructor Xiao-Hu out of the alchemy pavilion, my feet dragging slightly. As we walked, the scenery changed, the familiar paths and buildings of the sect giving way to an area I hadn't been to before. The architecture here was grander while maintaining the sect's bamboo-and-wood aesthetic.

"What is this place?" I asked, my curiosity momentarily overtaking my nervousness.

"This is the Sect Leader Shaotian Ye's pavilion," Instructor Xiao-Hu replied, with a tone of respect that mirrored the grandeur of our surroundings.

I wondered if this sort of place was where the elders lived. Was a sect truly this wealthy? To have this sort of accommodation for all their elders?

As we approached the entrance, I couldn't help but feel small in comparison.

Gathering my courage, I followed Instructor Xiao-Hu into the pavilion. The interior was as impressive as the exterior, with elegant furnishings and natural touches.

As we walked down a long corridor, my apprehension grew. Meeting the sect leader felt more like walking into the lion's den. I took a deep breath, trying to calm my nerves. Whatever the reason for this meeting, I would face it head-on. After all, facing challenges was what cultivation was all about. Steeling myself, I prepared for the encounter.

# CHAPTER TWO

# Instructor Xia Ji

As I entered the office, the room's magnificence took my breath away. But it was nothing compared to the aura of the man behind the desk.

Sect Leader Shaotian Ye exuded quiet authority. His sharp features, thick eyebrows, and graying hair gave him a commanding presence. He looked about the same age as Elder Zhu. His deep, insightful eyes held a depth I couldn't begin to fathom.

I bowed, my heart racing. "Sect Leader Shaotian Ye, I am Kai. It's an honor to meet you." My voice trembled slightly despite my efforts to sound composed.

Sect Leader Ye nodded, his gaze appraising. "Rise, Kai. I've heard much about you lately."

Elder Zhu stood to the side. He gave me an encouraging nod, urging me to stand straight and face the sect leader with confidence.

"Your actions against the Silent Moon Sect have not gone unnoticed, Kai. However, contrary to what you might expect, it's not something punishable."

I blinked in surprise, the tension in my shoulders easing slightly. "Not punishable, Sect Leader?"

He snorted, a sound that seemed too casual to come from such an esteemed figure. "Elder Jun's posturing is of little consequence to us. In the grand scheme of things, he's a minor player, scrambling for a position he's ill-equipped to fill. His schemes are transparent and hardly a threat."

Inside, I was reeling. Elder Jun, who had loomed so large in my mind, was just an insignificant annoyance in the eyes of the Verdant Lotus Sect Leader?

The older man continued, "Instructor Xia Ji will be responsible for your training. Given the circumstances, we've decided it's best to prepare you thoroughly."

I nodded, absorbing the information. "Instructor Xia Ji. Understood."

"Tell me, Kai, do you have a background in martial arts?"

The question caught me off guard. I hesitated for a moment before replying, "My experience is limited, Sect Leader. I've only recently begun training this year, when the Heavenly Interface came into existence."

The powerful man nodded thoughtfully. "A solid foundation in both body and qi is essential before delving into advanced techniques. But that requires time—time we do not have."

He was right; I was a novice trying to prepare for a battle against a seasoned cultivator. The odds were not in my favor.

Shaotian Ye leaned back in his chair, his gaze still fixed on me. "First-class disciple Xia Ji is skilled in various martial techniques. Under her guidance, you will learn a series of techniques that will aid you in your upcoming trial. It won't be easy, but it's necessary."

I nodded. "I understand, Sect Leader. I'll do whatever it takes."

"Although this match is not directly linked to our Verdant Lotus Sect, since you are not a disciple, the outcome will nonetheless reflect upon us. The sect's reputation and influence extend far beyond our immediate members."

I swallowed hard, the gravity of his words hitting me. It was one thing to face a personal challenge, but now the stakes were even higher. My actions, my performance, would cast a shadow—or light—on the entire sect.

"The Verdant Lotus Sect will support you in this endeavor, Kai," he assured me. "We will ensure you have the resources and training necessary to make a respectable showing against the Silent Moon Sect, win or lose."

I nodded, my mind racing. The support of the Verdant Lotus Sect was both a blessing and a source of pressure. "Thank you, Sect Leader. I . . . I won't let the sect down."

My thoughts were a blur. Meeting the sect leader, learning this was Elder Jun's power play—I didn't know what to do.

My feet carried me to the training grounds. The air vibrated with clashing weapons and disciplined footsteps. Third-class disciples sparred outside, too immersed to notice me.

In the heart of the grounds stood Instructor Xia Ji. Standing at medium height, with piercing eyes and black hair neatly tied back, she radiated command and focus.

As I approached, her gaze landed on me, sizing me up. I clasped my hands together and bowed. I would give this my all! With a firm voice, I said, "Under the command of Sect Leader Ye, I am here to receive guidance from Instructor Xia Ji! Please teach me well."

Xia Ji nodded, stepping toward me as the disciples continued to hone their skills. "So, the foolish alchemist who bashed his hands into a pole is coming back. You picked a fight with the Silent Moon Sect? If there's one thing you have, it's guts. That's for sure."

"I will do anything you require of me! I can only hope my actions do not bring shame to the Verdant Lotus Sect."

"Elder Chen told me of the situation, as well as the conditions tied to your competition. With the sect leader's permission, I will be teaching you a martial arts technique. I trust that you have heard of our technique, the Lotus Palm?"

The Lotus Palm? I remembered the night I met Feng Wu, when he demonstrated the first stance. I'd also seen Li Na use it in our sparring matches—palm strikes and a sweeping low kick.

Even in the clearing where third-class disciples sparred, several used the style. It was easy to recognize, with its arcing blows and deflections that used the attacker's momentum against them. Truly an art of self-defense.

Having seen the Silent Moon Sect's forceful and direct movements, I concluded each sect's temperament was reflected in their martial styles. No wonder those guys were such aggressive jerks. What happened to the cultivator stereotype of having a "heart still like water"? More like a raging river!

Something like the Lotus Palm would perfectly suit me—a cool, calm, and collected fighter!

"Yes! I will work hard to learn the Lotus Palm!"

Instructor Xia Ji chuckled and shook her head. "No, you won't be learning the Lotus Palm. Do you honestly think you could learn an entire martial style in less than a month? And at a level where it's usable against a Silent Moon Sect disciple?"

Sweat beaded down my neck. I wasn't going to learn the Lotus Palm? Then . . .

The first-class disciple inclined her head toward the disciples sparring on the training grounds.

"The Lotus Palm differs greatly from the Silent Moon Sect's techniques. Their Twelve Form Harvest Moon controls the battle's tempo with simple, forceful moves. The Lotus Palm isn't effective against them, at least not at the level of third and second-class disciples." Her eyes narrowed slightly. "The Silent Moon's style is aggressive, but it's predictable once you understand their rhythm. You need a technique that can counter their brute force—something that combines the principles of hard and soft defenses. A technique that not only guards against their strike but also allows for a counterattack at the moment of impact."

"And what technique is that?"

Xia Ji turned serious. "It's a lesser-known technique within our sect called the Bamboo Reprisal Counter. Based on bamboo's ability to bend under force without breaking, it uses the opponent's energy to fuel your counterattack. However, to effectively use the Bamboo Reprisal Counter, you need to endure the strikes of a cultivator without faltering. This means intensive physical training to reinforce your body's durability. Are you ready for that?"

I nodded, my resolve strengthening. "Yes, Instructor. I understand and I'm prepared. But I do have a defensive technique of my own that I hope could be of some use for the battle. I was wondering if I could demonstrate it."

Xia Ji's expression shifted from amusement to curiosity. "A defensive technique of your own creation? Show me."

Centering myself in the training grounds, I assumed the Rooted Banyan Stance. My feet spread apart with knees slightly bent and body lowered, mirroring a sturdy tree. I tucked my arms and clenched my fists, poised yet relaxed. Taking a deep breath, I felt the qi rise within me, flowing through my veins. I channeled it to reinforce my muscles and bones. "Rooted Banyan Stance!"

Instructor Xia Ji struck swiftly and powerfully, aiming for my sternum.

The Rooted Banyan Stance held firm. My body absorbed the impact, dispersing the force throughout my frame. My feet dug into the ground, but I remained upright.

Her eyes widened in surprise, then narrowed in suspicion. "Impressive. You've grasped rudimentary qi defense similar to the Iron Palm Sect. How did you accomplish it?"

I released my defensive stance, feeling around my sternum but sensing no lasting damage. I hesitated for a moment but decided to tell her as honestly as I could. If I couldn't be up-front with them, who could I trust? It wasn't like I'd be saying anything wrong.

"My mentor . . . He taught me the basics of martial arts back in my village. As I continued my training, and with the help of the Interface, I gained an understanding of how to use this technique. I likened it to how the banyan tree near my village never wavered and incorporated it into the horse stance that I used for physical conditioning."

Incredulous, she laughed. "So, you came up with this technique?"

I scratched my head, suddenly embarrassed. "I wouldn't say that . . . It had more to do with my mentor's teachings and the Heavenly Interface. How could I say that I came up with it?"

It was genuinely how I felt. The technique was borne of my training with Elder Ming and the Heavenly Interface. Without either of them, I probably wouldn't have attained the knowledge for how to do the stance. It simply built upon what I'd already had to advance it to the next stage.

As she circled around me, her demeanor turned thoughtful. "Regardless, your Rooted Banyan Stance has merit, especially against straightforward, powerful attacks. But in your upcoming battle, you'll need more than just defense. Even if it's a singular blow, landing one against someone superior to you in both skill and physical ability isn't easy."

She paused, then continued, "The Bamboo Reprisal Counter I'm about to teach you will complement your Rooted Banyan Stance well. When an opponent's attack is absorbed by your stance, you can redirect that energy, countering with the flexibility and snap of bamboo. At such a close distance, most third-class disciples wouldn't be able to avoid it."

I listened intently as she explained the principles of the Bamboo Reprisal Counter. It was about the harmony of yielding and striking, a delicate balance between accepting force and redirecting it. *It shouldn't be too hard to learn, right?*

She smiled. "So, with that in mind, let's get you started."

# CHAPTER THREE

# Going Through the Motions

Argh!" I let out a disgraceful sound as another strike landed on my shoulder. Before I could wallow on the floor in agony, Li Na's palm came flying at me again.

Reacting instinctively, my body moved before my mind could catch up, arms raised and elbow tucked to block the incoming blow aimed at my liver. Despite my effort, she broke through my guard with ease and sent me sprawling on the floor.

"Get up! The Silent Moon Sect disciple wouldn't be holding back, nor would they be kind enough to let you gather your breath," Instructor Xia Ji barked, her eyes narrowing as she met my gaze.

A wave of frustration and helplessness washed over me. The gap between us felt like a chasm. Admiration and envy of her skill stirred within me, coupled with a burning determination.

I'd sparred with her before. It was playful, but after Instructor Xia Ji's instructions, she fought without holding back. I couldn't even use my Rooted Banyan Stance and had to withstand her strikes with just my body. The reminder of my gap from a third-class disciple humbled me. Every time I thought I knew how far behind I was, the gap seemed to grow.

Gritting my teeth, I dug my fingers into the dirt, stood up, and got back into my stance. My palms were slightly open in the beginning stance of the Bamboo Reprisal Counter.

I needed to calm my racing heart and frantic thoughts. Back home, when faced with difficult diagnoses, I relied on observation and analysis. I had to approach this challenge the same way. Focusing on Li Na's movements, I watched her body language, the subtle shifts, and the flicker in her eyes. I anticipated a kick aimed at my right flank and braced myself to counter. As she took the final step, I crossed my arms, tucking them to my sides and clenching my body.

But I was wrong. Her foot, swift as a striking viper, connected not with my flank but my head. I didn't even see it coming. A mere blur from my peripheral, and then the world spun.

The ground was cold and hard against my cheek. As I lay there, I felt a surge of anger at myself for not anticipating the kick.

I heard Li Na's voice, laced with concern. "Kai! I'm so sorry! Are you okay?"

Though I could say it was okay, I couldn't help feel a bit of resentment floating up in my heart. Why kick me in the head and *then* apologize?

Instructor Xia Ji loomed over me, her expression stern yet not without a hint of satisfaction. "The purpose of this practice is for you to get used to being hit. To anticipate and react. There's no doubt you'll get hit by the disciple you're fighting, but learning how to minimize the damage is integral if you want to achieve victory."

Her words sank in slowly. Li Na targeted my vitals at her top speed so I could learn the tell-tale signs of an impending strike. My mind raced with the implications of her words. To anticipate an attack was to understand it. And to understand, one must first experience it. I hadn't received much practical experience in that regard—aside from being whipped by a Wind Serpent's tail and being beaten by Elder Ming.

I knew that if I wanted to learn the technique, I'd have to learn how to anticipate where the strikes were going before they occurred as well.

But how?

Instructor Xia Ji's voice brought me back to the present. "Rest now, but be here at the same time tomorrow. Your training is far from over."

She barked out orders for the other third-class disciples to begin cleaning the training grounds. When Li Na turned to me, her eyes were fraught with worry and concern. "I'll help you to the dining hall. You should get some food and rest. Here." She lowered herself and offered her shoulder, then helped me to my feet. Her hands were so soft, it was hard to believe that she could produce so much force with them.

I winced, nursing several new bruises, and shook my head. "Thank you, Li Na. But I can make my way back home. I just . . . need some time right now, is all."

She looked at me for a moment but obliged and let me go about my way back home. I could feel her stare burning a hole in my back as I got farther and farther away.

As I trudged to the guest quarters, the sun setting and casting long shadows across the path, I couldn't help but think of Elder Ming. What would he say in this situation? Probably something incredibly wise and profound, leaving me just as clueless as before. He had a way of doing that, making me think deeper about every problem.

"I guess you'd tell me to 'embrace the pain as a teacher,' right, Elder Ming?" I muttered to myself, imagining his knowing smile. But this time, I was alone with my thoughts with no wise elder to guide me.

I wasn't some genius who could understand everything at a glance. I had to break it down, analyze each part of today's training. What had I missed? How could I have anticipated those strikes? These questions swirled in my mind as I cradled my injured body.

Before I knew it, I had made my way back to my room. Sliding open the wooden door, I was met with the sight of Windy sleeping peacefully, wrapped around the Beast Core of its predecessor. Tianyi made her way to me, her antennae twitching as though taking note of my disheveled appearance.

"It has been a long day. I think I'll just lie down on the bed for a moment. Sorry, Tianyi."

I stripped off my tattered robes. Fixing them wouldn't be a big deal. To some extent, all my clothes were banged up. I got dressed in the pristine white robes that the sect had graciously provided for me. Despite changing, I could still feel the dirt, sweat, and grime that clung to my body.

*I should go downstairs to the bathhouse. It's been a couple days since I last cleaned myself.*

As I closed my eyes, I felt the familiar thrum of Tianyi's powers circulating within me, her tiny body now perched atop my stomach. Was it just me, or were her powers getting stronger?

I opened my eyes to check her status, but nothing of note had changed. Yet my body was being repaired faster than before. The effects hadn't previously been this immediate. I assumed one of her skills had gone up a level or so.

In that regard, maybe it meant the same for me as well. There wasn't much change to my skills according to the Heavenly Interface, but wasn't I getting stronger, smarter, and more adept as the days passed?

Even if only a few numbers had changed, would the version of me that hadn't gone up against the Wind Serpents be able to fight the me of now? Could my previous self understand the concepts of alchemy as easily as I did now, even if what separated us was just a few levels between my mind and Nature's Attunement and Spiritual Herbalism?

In that sense, I wasn't even half as proficient with the Rooted Banyan Stance as I am now.

"You may be a genius, Tianyi, but I won't lag behind either."

She stopped her circulation of energy and looked at me in confusion. I didn't bother elaborating, going deep into my Memory Palace. Feng Wu's advice resounded within me. To use the Memory Palace technique as a mere knowledge repository was just the surface of its capabilities.

Amid the towering trees that contained all the knowledge I gained throughout my life, I stepped forward into a clearing of grass and *imagined*. Sunlight trickled through the canopy, casting patterns on the grass. The air was fresh, scented with earth and wildflowers. This sanctuary was where I could dissect and understand my experiences clearly.

In the center, I recreated the sparring scene with Li Na in detail: the hard-packed earth, the clatter of wooden swords, and the faint smells of sweat and iron. Even the slight breeze carried the scent of pine and distant cooking from the sect's kitchens.

There stood Li Na, as real as during our spar. I watched her intently, observing every movement—the tensing of her muscles, the shift in her weight, the narrowing of her eyes before she struck.

I replayed her palm strike at my liver. This time, my reaction was swifter and more precise. I raised my arms, tucking in my elbows, but with a crucial difference. As her palm neared, I twisted my hips, angling my body to reduce the strike's force. The impact pushed me back, but it was nothing compared to the pain I had endured during the actual match.

I was left incredulous, my heart pounding with excitement at the negligible amount of damage I had just taken. "I did it . . ." I whispered to myself, a smile creeping onto my lips. But my triumph was short-lived.

As I stood there in the midst of my Memory Palace, a surge of conflicting emotions washed over me.

What if this was just an illusion of progress? What if, in the real world, I couldn't replicate this success? These questions weighed on me, heavy and unrelenting.

The imagined Li Na was relentless, her movements fluid and unyielding. A kick, swift and powerful, was already arcing toward me. I was too slow to react this time, the blow landing squarely, jolting me out of the visualization.

"Argh! What the hell?!"

Unfortunately, the extent of my visualization seemed to encompass the sensation of pain as well.

"This Memory Palace technique . . . Sometimes it feels like my mind is working against me," I grumbled. It was a strange sensation, feeling both the thrill of success and the sting of failure within the confines of my own mind.

But then, as I replayed the scene of me successfully blocking the palm strike, a sense of revelation washed over me. The sensation of twisting my body, the exact timing of my movement, it all clicked into place. A breakthrough was at hand.

Eagerly, I stepped back into the clearing, my determination renewed. I imagined Li Na once more, her stance, her gaze, every detail vivid and clear. This time, I was ready. As she moved, I observed, picking up on those tiny cues that had eluded me before. The subtle tensing of her shoulders, the slight pivot of her foot. Each small sign was a precursor to her strikes.

I moved in tandem with her, my body responding almost instinctively. I blocked, dodged, and even started to anticipate her moves. Each successful defense bolstered my confidence, each mistake a lesson to be learned.

Sweat beaded on my forehead, not from physical exertion but from the intense focus required to maintain this level of visualization. I was no longer just a passive participant in these memories; I was actively engaging, learning, evolving.

As I continued, the boundary between reality and imagination blurred. The sensations became more tangible, the sounds more distinct. It was as if I were truly there, sparring with Li Na under the watchful eyes of Instructor Xia Ji.

Lost in this state of deep concentration, I honed my skills, pushing myself further than I had ever before. Each iteration of the spar was an opportunity to refine my reactions, to understand Li Na's fighting style better, to grow stronger.

Finally, as exhaustion began to set in, I stepped back, breathing heavily. My mind was a whirlwind of thoughts and emotions, but one thing was crystal clear: In my Memory Palace, I had not only relived the spar but transformed it into a tool for my growth.

With a deep breath, I opened my eyes, returning to the reality of my room. The sensation of the grass under my feet and the sun on my skin faded, replaced by the familiar surroundings of my quarters. Windy moved from its spot near the window to my arm, taking comfort in my warmth. Tianyi was still on my stomach, having finished repairing my body. I clenched and unclenched my fist, feeling the soreness and pain greatly diminish all over.

I was thirsty, but I couldn't move without waking up the two Spirit Beasts resting on top of me. I shrugged, deciding to stay in place and continue where I left off after some rest.

"I'll keep practicing, keep learning," I promised myself, determined. "Tomorrow, I'll be better prepared."

Settling down on my bed, I closed my eyes once more, diving back into the depths of my Memory Palace, ready to face whatever challenges lay ahead.

# CHAPTER FOUR

# Vanished into the Verdant

Instructor Xia Ji stood at the edge of the training ground, her eyes keenly observing Kai's every movement. The morning sun cast a warm glow over the field, illuminating the determination etched on the young herbalist's face. She had seen many students come and go, but Kai's progress, particularly since yesterday, was nothing short of astonishing.

He seemed more attuned, more responsive than the day before. His eyes darted keenly, tracking Li Na's every shift in weight, every minute change in her stance.

"Begin!" Xia Ji commanded.

Li Na lunged forward, her palm cutting through the air toward Kai. But this time, Kai was different. His body was moving even before Li Na's strike could reach him. He twisted his torso, aligning his body to diffuse the momentum of her strike.

Xia Ji's eyes narrowed, impressed. Kai was not just blocking the strikes; he was manipulating their flow, turning their force to his advantage. The foundation of the Bamboo Reprisal Counter. It was a technique that required acute observation and a deep understanding of one's own body and the opponent's movements. And Kai was executing it with a proficiency that belied his limited training.

*I thought it would take a week for him to understand it at this level . . . His responses are akin to muscle memory, but how could it have developed so quickly?*

For a full minute, the sparring continued, with Li Na unleashing a series of rapid strikes. Yet the fledgling alchemist managed to keep up, his body swaying and twisting like bamboo in the wind, never once getting knocked down.

"Enough," Xia Ji finally said, stepping forward. Both disciples halted, turning toward her with expectant eyes. She wiped a droplet of sweat from her brow, her mind racing at Kai's frightening learning speed.

"It's time we begin with the forms of the Bamboo Reprisal Counter," she announced, her voice steady despite the astonishment she felt.

Kai's eyes lit up with a mix of excitement and curiosity. Li Na retreated, giving them space.

Xia Ji walked closer to the teen, her gaze scrutinizing. "Your performance today has been commendable. However, there's much to learn. The Rooted Banyan Stance, while formidable in defense, restricts your movement due to the need to tense your body."

Kai nodded in agreement, his breathing still heavy from the spar. "Yes, Instructor. I've felt that limitation."

"The Bamboo Reprisal Counter, on the other hand, offers mobility along with the opportunity for a counterattack," Xia Ji continued, her hands clasping behind her back. "It's about blending the fluidity of movement with the strength of defense. Your key to victory lies in using these two techniques at the right place and the right time."

The herbalist stared back at her, his dark brown eyes unwavering. "Yes, Instructor Xia Ji! I understand."

"Get into your stance! We'll break down how the counter moves depending on the opponent's attack . . ."

I wiped the dirt off my sleeve, panting. The Bamboo Reprisal Counter was harder to learn than I thought, with multiple versions depending on how my opponent struck. It required flexibility, reflexes, and sensitivity to another's movements.

Engaging in a simple drill with Li Na, we tried to unbalance each other by pushing or pulling. Her reflexes were much faster than mine, her strength lying in her reaction rather than action. I lost count of how many times I fell, but her encouraging words helped me improve each time I got up.

After a grueling session of flexibility exercises, I was dismissed with sore muscles and an aching body. I collapsed by a tree, the cool shade a welcome respite from the relentless sun. Each breath I drew was a mix of pain and satisfaction.

"Here, drink this."

Li Na stood before me, extending a flask of water with a look of incredulity on her face. Her brows were furrowed, not with concern but with something akin to disbelief.

I accepted the flask gratefully, the cool liquid a balm to my parched throat. "Thank you."

"How did you get so good so fast?" Li Na asked, sitting beside me. Her tone was light, but I could sense the genuine curiosity behind her words.

I chuckled weakly, shaking my head. It was a nice compliment that lightened my heart, but I knew not to get excited. I was just happy that my progress looked like it was going according to Instructor Xia Ji's expectations. "It's not about being good. I just went over your fighting style again and again in my mind. I'm not some sort of genius, just observant and determined."

I knew it wasn't just about learning the technique or stance. It was about understanding Li Na's moves, habits, and tells. That's what made the difference in today's sparring session.

I lost count of how many times I reimagined the fight. Visualization in my Memory Palace was limited by my imagination; I couldn't capture her full capabilities. I could visualize her strikes' power and speed but not those of her other techniques. I couldn't mimic what I hadn't seen.

My success lay more in my familiarity with her style rather than my grasp of the technique itself. If I had sparred with a different disciple, I don't think I could've displayed even half of what I accomplished today.

Li Na seemed to ponder my words, her eyes studying me thoughtfully. "I don't know," she finally said, her tone playful yet serious. "Putting something you've learned into practice so quickly and effectively isn't something everyone can do."

I could only offer a shrug in response, my mind already wandering to other concerns. I hoped that being knocked around like this wouldn't mess with my memory. I still needed my brain for early-morning classes.

She stood up, dusting off her robes. "Come on, let's go to the dining hall. You need to eat."

Together, we made our way to the hall, the sounds of the bustling sect around us. Inside, the hall was filled with the aroma of freshly prepared meals, the clatter of utensils, and the buzz of conversation. We found Han Wei already there, his plate piled high with food.

"Hey, you two," he said us with a wide grin. "How'd training go?"

As they engaged in conversation about their day's activities, I ate quietly, my thoughts drifting. I glanced at the food, none of which would be suitable for Windy. I frowned, considering my options. There were no meat alternatives here, and I couldn't very well reveal Windy's existence.

A plan began to form in my mind. I would have to find food for Windy on my own, or perhaps make a trip to Crescent Bay City. But how long could Windy last? The thought nagged at me, a persistent worry amid the sea of other concerns.

As the sun began to set, casting a warm, orange hue over the sect, I excused myself and headed back to my guest quarters. Li Na and Han Wei bade me farewell. The walk was a time for reflection, for planning. I needed to find a solution for Windy, and soon.

". . . I mean, I'm not a sect disciple. I could probably head out tonight and get it as quickly as possible with Elder Zhu's permission."

The idea brewed in my mind for a moment.

Reaching the guest quarters, the fading sunlight cast elongated shadows across the wooden frame of the building. A sense of unease crept over me as I approached my room. I usually meticulously kept everything closed, a habit from my days back home where leaving a window open could mean a night filled with unwelcome insects. I opened the door, expecting Tianyi and Windy to awaken upon my arrival.

But the room was eerily absent, the window slightly ajar.

My heart skipped a beat. Tianyi and Windy. I pushed open the door, my eyes darting around the room. It was empty. The windowsill, where Tianyi often rested, was vacant, and Windy's usual coiled spot was just a patch of cold wood. A surge of panic rose within me, and my mind raced with terrifying possibilities. Kidnapping? An attack?

I rushed to the window, my eyes scanning for any signs of struggle, but there was nothing—no broken furniture, no scattered belongings. Even the treasured Beast Core lay by the bed, untouched.

I leaned out the window, looking down. The drop was about two zhang. Not lethal but certainly not a jump for the fainthearted. I pushed qi to my feet, the energy coursing through me, and leapt. The ground rushed up to meet me, but the qi cushioned my landing, leaving me unscathed.

A small clearing of grass transitioned into a forest, its trees standing tall and foreboding as the light dimmed. My instincts screamed at me to follow, to go deeper into the unknown.

The forest loomed before me, an impenetrable wall of shadows and whispers. As I ventured into its depths, the sounds of the night enveloped me—the rustling of leaves, the distant hooting of an owl, the subtle crackling of unseen creatures moving in the underbrush. The air was heavy with the scent of damp earth and the musky odor of wild foliage.

As I entered the forest, a thousand scenarios played in my mind. Had Tianyi chased an insect and gotten lost? Had Windy slithered out following a scent? Or was it something worse? My thoughts spiraled with fear.

The deeper I went, the more my anxiety grew. My imagination conjured every possible peril, from venomous snakes to predatory beasts. The memory of Tianyi's narrow escape from a crow sent a shiver down my spine.

Tianyi had a playful nature and a tendency to explore. Perhaps she had simply wandered off, and Windy, ever the curious one, had followed. I clung to that thought, willing it to be true.

I slowed my pace, taking deep breaths, trying to calm the storm within me. *Think, Kai. Where would they go? What would attract them?*

The forest opened up to a small clearing, the moon casting a soft glow over the grass. I paused, scanning the area. It was peaceful, serene—a stark contrast to the turmoil in my heart. I couldn't let my thoughts go wildly like this. I needed to calm myself.

I sat down, closing my eyes, focusing on my breathing. In, out. In, out. Gradually, the panic subsided, replaced by a quiet determination. I would find them. I had to.

I focused inward, trying to tap into the emotional bond I shared with Tianyi. It was a connection I seldom explored fully, its nuances still a mystery to me. The bond felt faint, a mere whisper in the back of my mind, which could mean two things: Either Tianyi was far away or she was calm, her emotions neutral.

I had to trust this slender thread of connection, assuming it would strengthen as I neared her. The Verdant Lotus Sect's territory blended seamlessly into the dense forest, a wild expanse unmarred by walls or barriers.

At times, the bond felt so tenuous, I feared it might snap, leaving me adrift in this sea of green. But then, a glimmer of satisfaction that wasn't my own surged through the bond. It was faint, like the touch of a breeze, but unmistakably there.

Encouraged, I quickened my steps, following the direction that seemed to strengthen the connection. I navigated carefully, mindful of roots that sought to trip me and branches that threatened to snag my clothes. The emotion through the bond was still faint, but it was more defined now, a subtle undercurrent of contentment that wasn't mine. I clung to it, letting it lead me, drawing me deeper into the heart of the forest.

As I moved, my mind raced with possibilities. What had drawn Tianyi and Windy out here?

The forest began to open up, the dense underbrush giving way to a clearer area. The dense underbrush of the forest gave way to a small clearing bathed in the silver light of the moon. There, in the midst of the serene night, I witnessed a display of nature's unspoken law—the hunter and the hunted.

# Snakes and Rats

Windy, with its snow-white scales, was in its element. The bamboo rat, with its light-green fur, stood no chance. It wasn't a struggle for survival but an act in the play of the food chain.

I watched in stunned silence as Windy struck with precision, coiling swiftly and biting the rat's neck. The rat's feeble defense was pitiful in comparison. It was over in a heartbeat, the hunter triumphant.

Part of me, the boy who had read countless tales, knew that Spirit Beasts weren't ordinary animals. They could utilize qi, with powers even cultivators struggled against. Yet, seeing Windy in action, I was struck by that reality anew.

"Shouldn't be surprised, really," I muttered to myself. "It's just nature doing its thing, and Windy's just . . . born strong, I suppose."

As I entered the clearing, Tianyi seemed to sense my approach. She fluttered down from a nearby branch, her delicate blue wings glinting in the moonlight. Her demeanor was that of a child caught in a mischievous act, the air around her charged with a feeling akin to an apology.

"Caught red-winged, huh, Tianyi?"

Her response was a gentle flutter and a small wave of guilt through our emotional bond.

Windy, meanwhile, continued its meal, unbothered by my presence. Watching the hatchling, a sense of calm washed over me.

Tianyi's wings brushed against my cheek, a soft, silent apology that I accepted with a nod. "You two really gave me a scare, you know? I thought I'd have to fight off a horde of demonic beasts to find you. Not that it would be a challenge, but . . ."

As Windy finished swallowing, leaving a noticeable bump around its serpentine body, I gathered both of my companions. It was time to head back.

"Let's head home. And no more unscheduled adventures, okay?"

The moon shone down on us as we made our way through the forest, a silent guardian watching over our return. With Tianyi's gentle fluttering and Windy's contented slithering, the night no longer seemed so ominous.

The journey back to the guest quarters was uneventful, but my mind buzzed with newfound realizations about Tianyi and Windy.

Standing outside the quarters, I gazed up at the window from which they had made their escape. It was a good two zhang high—not particularly daunting for me if I had some qi in my legs, but for the snake, it seemed an extraordinary feat to scale. How had Windy, with its tiny serpentine body, managed such a climb?

Setting them down, I looked at them with a mix of curiosity and admiration. "All right, show me how you did it," I said, gesturing to the window. "Up you go, as you would if I weren't here."

Tianyi, understanding my request, fluttered her wings and gracefully ascended toward the window, her movements as effortless as a leaf caught in a gentle breeze. Her delicate form glided upward, and she perched on the windowsill with an air of elegance.

Windy's approach, however, was a revelation in itself. It approached the wall, their small head tilting as if assessing the best route. Then, with surprising agility, the hatchling began to slither upward. Its movements were meticulous, precise and purposeful a skilled climber's, each inch of its progress marked by a calculated use of the slightest grooves and indentations in the wooden walls.

I watched, fascinated, as Windy slithered up the wall. The way it maneuvered its body, coiling and uncoiling, using every small advantage offered by the wall's surface, spoke of an intelligence I hadn't fully appreciated before.

Reaching the windowsill, it paused beside Tianyi. Then, with a dexterity that left me astounded, it used the end of its tail to nudge the window shut. It was a deliberate, thoughtful action, showcasing a level of understanding and intelligence that went beyond my previous assumptions about the Wind Serpent. I stood there, mouth agape, as the reality of their capabilities sank in.

"Well, I'll be," I murmured, a shocked grin spreading across my face. "Clever little one, aren't you?"

I couldn't help but feel a surge of pride watching them, these two remarkable beings that had chosen to bond with me. Well, at least one of them. Windy hadn't quite recognized me yet, going by the silence from the Heavenly Interface whenever I tried to summon its status like I did with Tianyi.

The adrenaline from my frantic search had ebbed, leaving me profoundly fatigued. Each step felt heavier, each breath more labored. The urgency was gone, replaced by exhaustion.

By the time I reached my room, I was bone-tired. The night's events replayed in my mind. Tianyi and Windy were safely back. Windy, indifferent to the night's events, was coiled around the Beast Core, digesting its meal.

Tianyi fluttered near me, her wings glowing softly. Through our bond, I sensed a mix of emotions: affirmation, mischief, and pride. It dawned on me; this wasn't their first venture out. Realization came in waves, not words.

"So, this has happened before, hasn't it?" I asked, half expecting an answer.

In response, Tianyi's wings fluttered softly, a sensation that conveyed affirmation. The tiny butterfly seemed to understand the gravity of my questions, her movements delicate yet expressive.

"And tonight, it just took longer to find something to hunt?" I continued, piecing together the story from her responses.

Tianyi confirmed with a gentle flutter.

"Did you ever help Windy with a kill?"

Her wings didn't flutter this time, and a firm feeling of negativity flowed. This back-and-forth conversation reminded me of the time I held out a book containing pictures of fruits and plants, showing Tianyi and trying to find out which she liked best.

I sat down, marveling at the situation. "Windy, you're quite the hunter, aren't you? Managing all this without needing Tianyi's help."

Windy, engrossed in the Beast Core, didn't react to my words. The hatchling's indifference was palpable.

"Listen, I can't stop you from going out, but we need to set some limits," I said, a plan forming in my mind. "I'll bring proper food for Windy. We'll establish a regular schedule for me to go out and bring back some meat and maybe a bit of alcohol. But that's if you cooperate."

At the mention of alcohol, Tianyi perked up, her wings fluttering in what seemed like excitement. She then turned to Windy, who continued to cradle the Beast Core, seemingly uninterested in our conversation.

Through a series of delicate movements and subtle shifts in her aura, Tianyi communicated with Windy. It was a silent conversation, but the understanding between them was palpable. Windy finally lifted its head, its gaze shifting between Tianyi and me. After a moment, the serpent seemed to accept the arrangement, its attention returning to the Beast Core.

"All right, it's a deal, then," I said, feeling a sense of relief. "We'll make this work. But no more secret nightly escapades, okay?"

Tianyi fluttered around me, her wings casting a soft glow in the dim room, a silent promise of cooperation.

Lying there in the quiet night, my thoughts drifted to natural instinct and talent. I watched Windy, content and with innate abilities for survival and hunting. It made me ponder my own cultivation journey.

I felt a twinge of envy for creatures like Windy, born with inherent skill and instinct. My cultivation path was full of hurdles. With a weak qi circulation system and a late start in martial arts, I faced a steep uphill battle, like scaling a sheer cliff—daunting and nearly impossible.

"If only I had started training when I was younger," I mused, a sense of regret weaving through my thoughts. I imagined a different life, one where I began my martial journey as a child. Perhaps then, I could have been like Li Na or Han Wei, naturally adept and confident in my abilities. Perhaps I could've been even stronger than them; I could've been able to challenge Feng Wu had I entered a sect at the same time they had!

Ah, that was ridiculous of me to say. It sounded wrong to even think about it. It denied their effort.

Reality was starkly different. My talent for martial arts was, to put it bluntly, subpar. It was a truth I had come to accept, albeit reluctantly. The realization of how much effort I needed to put in to even come close to people years younger than me was overwhelming at times.

It was in these moments of introspection that I summoned the Heavenly Interface, the system that had become my unlikely ally. The glowing interface appeared before me, its familiar presence a reminder of how far I had come. The skills and knowledge it granted me were more than just aids; they were the tools that leveled the playing field, giving me a fighting chance in a world where I was at a distinct disadvantage. Despite its silence now, I knew there was more to it. I shuddered to think what would've happened if I had kept talking against Elder Jun. Perhaps one of the third-class disciples would've turned me into a fine paste.

*Heavenly Interface: Kai Liu*
Perk(s):
Interface Manipulator—Allows manipulation of the Heavenly Interface and access to special features.
Race: Human
Vitality: Sufficient
Primary
Affinity—Wood
Cultivation Rank: Mortal Realm—Rank 3
Qi: Qi Initiation Stage—Rank 1
Mind: Mortal Realm—Rank 3
Body: Mortal Realm—Rank 2
Skills
Spiritual Herbalism—2 (. . .)
Nature's Attunement—2 (. . .)

> Reading—6 (. . .)
> Cultivation Techniques
> Rooted Banyan Stance—1 (. . .)
> Crimson Lotus Purification—1 (. . .)

I scrolled through the interface, taking in the skills and stats I had accumulated. Each number represented my journey and the effort I had poured into overcoming my limitations. The interface wasn't just a tool; it was my hope, my chance to carve my own path.

Despite my fatigue, a renewed sense of resolve filled me. I couldn't change my natural talent, but I had the Heavenly Interface. It was my bridge over the chasm of my limitations.

I pushed myself up and sat to meditate. The qi in the room, enriched by Tianyi's Qi Haven skill, felt denser. It was an ideal environment for cultivation, one I couldn't afford to waste.

Closing my eyes, I focused on my breathing, feeling the qi flow through my meridians. Each breath was a step forward, each circulation of qi a small victory. The challenges ahead were many, but with the Heavenly Interface and my determination, I was ready to face them.

As the night deepened, time and fatigue became inconsequential. I was a cultivator on a path of struggle, perseverance, and relentless growth.

The initial pessimism about my abilities began to dissipate, replaced by enthusiasm and determination. I smiled at the irony. Once lamenting my lack of talent, I now found pride in my journey.

"I might not be a natural-born genius," I whispered to the silent room, "but I am the genius of hard work."

I would work tirelessly, pushing beyond the limits set by my circumstances. Each step forward might be harder for me than for those naturally gifted, but that only made each achievement more gratifying.

It was as though the universe itself was conspiring to help me on my path, offering me tools and companions to aid me in my quest.

My story wouldn't be one of effortless victories but of hard-fought battles and hard-earned triumphs.

"I'll be a cultivator whose name will be remembered," I vowed, feeling the energy coursing through me, reinforcing my resolve. "Not because I was the most talented, but because I was the most dedicated. The genius of hard work—that will be my legacy."

And my legacy would begin with a glorious victory against the Silent Moon Sect!

# CHAPTER SIX

# Stiff Challenges and Softer Moments

Li Na's face was apologetic as she pulled on my arms. I bit my lip, letting out a low hiss of pain as my groin stretched just before the point of tearing.

"Five more seconds!"

Tears formed at the corner of my eyes. Was she pulling me even harder? *Hey! HEY! If you keep going, I can't be called a man anymore!*

But my mouth stayed shut. I knew that saying a single word while in this position was impossible. All I could let out were intakes of air, hisses so sharp, they would leave even Windy proud.

Finally, after what felt like an eternity, Li Na released my arms and I collapsed forward. Instructor Xia Ji gave a nod, a hint of amusement in her stern gaze, and dismissed us from practice.

"You know, Kai, for someone who wants to be a cultivator, you're pretty stiff."

I shot her a short glare, stretching out my legs, which felt like they were made of overcooked noodles. "Well, Li Na, not all of us have had the luxury of years of training to achieve such . . . elasticity."

Li Na's response was to demonstrate a perfect split, lowering herself effortlessly to the ground. "Actually, I've been able to do this since day one."

I groaned, half in admiration and half in self-pity. "That's just unfair!" I tried to stand upright, only to wobble and grab onto a nearby tree for support.

"Come on, Kai, don't be so hard on yourself," Li Na said, helping me up. "You're improving every day. And besides, you have your own strengths."

"Yeah, like being exceptionally good at complaining," I quipped, managing a weak grin. I straightened up, wincing slightly. "But you watch, Li Na. One day, I'll be just as flexible—and then we'll see who has the last laugh."

"I'll look forward to that day."

As we made our way back from the training ground, Li Na's curiosity seemed piqued. "How are your advanced classes going, Kai?"

"Oh, the Advanced Herbology class has been a real eye-opener," I began, feeling a surge of enthusiasm as I talked about my passion. "We're learning a lot about handling and growing qi plants. It's fascinating, really, how these plants absorb and store qi. It's like they have their own little cultivation journey. Instructor Xiao-Hu's very knowledgeable."

Li Na nodded, following along.

Encouraged, I continued, "And then there's my Array Formation class. That one's a bit more . . . let's say challenging. It's mostly independent study for me right now since I can't generate arrays like the other second-class disciples yet. But I'm getting closer to making a fully functional array. It's all about gaining more delicate control of my qi, which I hope will happen before the Grand Alchemy Gauntlet."

"Sounds like you're making great progress," Li Na complimented, and I could feel my cheeks heat up a bit.

"Yeah, well, you know me—the genius of hard work!" I said, puffing my chest. "I've even got a side project going on. I'm trying to make a hydrosol."

"Hydrosol?" Li Na's curiosity was clearly piqued, and I dove into an explanation.

"Yeah, it's like a distilled essence of plants. I've been learning how to use alchemical stills and making purified water. The idea is to soak gauze in this hydrosol, so it disinfects wounds and promotes healing. I'm hoping it'll help us heal faster from conditioning exercises and spars."

As I talked about the technical aspects of creating the hydrosol, I could see her start to glaze over slightly. I was rambling, wasn't I? I chuckled awkwardly, rubbing the back of my neck. "Sorry, I guess I got a bit carried away there. It's just really exciting stuff, you know?"

Li Na smiled a warm, amused smile that made her eyes crinkle. "It's cute how you get so engrossed when talking about the things you like, Kai."

My heart did a small flip. Was I going through Qi Deviation? Did she just call me cute? I felt a mix of embarrassment and a strange sense of accomplishment. I laughed, trying to play it cool. "Well, I guess when you're as brilliant as I am, it's hard not to get absorbed in your work."

As we reached the sect's dining hall, I felt a sense of lightheartedness envelop me. Li Na's presence had a way of making everything seem a little brighter, a little more fun. And her interest in my classes and projects? It was more motivating than any lecture or practice session. Han Wei wasn't here today, so we ate quietly together.

Leaving the dining hall with a skip in my step, I couldn't help but let my thoughts wander to Li Na. The way she had listened to me ramble about my classes, her smile . . . it was enough to make anyone's heart flutter.

Perhaps . . . ?

No, not perhaps! I was so tall and handsome, who wouldn't fall for me?

I put my hand on my head, feeling my face heat up. *Who am I kidding? It's best to expect nothing more. Just treasure the friendship as it is, Kai*, I reminded myself. After all, Li Na was a cherished friend, and that was more than enough. Besides, I had plenty of other things to focus on—cultivation, classes, and the looming challenge against the Silent Moon Sect.

Yet, deep down, a small seed of hope or doubt lingered, refusing to be completely uprooted. It was a foolish thing, really, but there it was—a tiny, stubborn part of me that wouldn't let go of the what-ifs.

I became acutely aware of the stares from the people around me. It felt as if everyone in the sect could read my mind. Embarrassed, I quickened my pace, eager to retreat to the sanctuary of my guest quarters.

Reaching my room, I took a deep breath, trying to settle the flurry of emotions that had unexpectedly bubbled up. I needed to refocus, to get back on track with my cultivation journey. That was my priority.

*Besides*, I thought as I opened the door to my room, *I've got Tianyi and Windy waiting for me. Who needs romance when you have a mystical butterfly and a Wind Serpent hatchling as your companions?*

Maybe one day, in the midst of all this cultivation and hard work, something more might just happen naturally.

For now, though, I had to prepare to leave for Crescent Bay City while there was daylight. They said I'd have someone escorting me, but Elder Zhu didn't really specify who it was. I'd find out when I met them at the entrance!

Master Qiang's rice wine, which I used as a treat for Tianyi, was starting to bottom out. Windy needed a ton of meat! I'd take this chance to grab everything I needed, and maybe a bite to eat. I'll treat whichever disciple is coming with me. The dining hall's food wasn't bad by any means, but it certainly got dull after a while.

"Tianyi, stay here! Windy, keep sleeping! No wandering, okay?"

My faithful butterfly companion acknowledged my request, and Windy, as usual, ignored me.

Aside from my bag and coin pouch, I don't think I needed anything. The trip would be short to avoid inconveniencing the disciple escorting me.

"Oh, I almost forgot!"

I opened the bedside drawer and took out a small jade amulet. Elder Ming's parting gift for me and a good-luck charm. I was too afraid to bring it with me on my daily routine, but it wouldn't hurt to wear it today, right?

Stepping out of the dining hall, my mind still replaying the conversation with Li Na, I made my way back to the guest quarters. The morning air was crisp, the sect alive with the sounds of disciples beginning their day. As I walked, I found myself deep in thought, mulling over the upcoming trip to Crescent Bay City.

*Really, who could Elder Zhu have arranged to escort me?* I pondered, the question nagging at me. *Han Wei, perhaps? Or maybe even Li Na?* The thought of Li Na accompanying me brought a foolish, shy giggle to my lips. The idea was exhilarating and nerve-racking.

Reaching the guest quarters, I quickly tidied myself up, my thoughts still circling around the possible escort.

With everything ready, I made my way to the stable where Elder Wen's horses were kept. The stable hands greeted me warmly, helping me get the cart and horses ready. Their efficiency and helpfulness made the task much easier, and soon I was leading the cart toward the sect's entrance.

"Hope you're doing well there. It's not too stuffy, is it?" I asked the pair. They whinnied in response. Unfortunately, I couldn't understand them like I did with Tianyi, so I had to assume it was a yes.

As I neared the sect entrance, a familiar silhouette leaned casually by the gate, piquing my curiosity. Who could it be? Though too distant to see clearly, their posture tugged at my memory.

*Could it be Li Na? Or Han Wei? Or someone I haven't interacted with before?* I wondered, the possibilities sending a wave of anticipation through me. Whoever it was, Elder Zhu had his reasons for choosing them, and I trusted his judgment.

The person from far away turned. It was a man, his broad shoulders showing through the green-and-white robes of second-class disciples.

As I drew closer, the details of the figure standing by the entrance became clearer. The unmistakable ponytail, a few stray strands of hair falling rebelliously, caught my attention immediately. A smile tugged at my lips. It was none other than Feng Wu.

They never told me he was back!

Something was off. Feng Wu's usual relaxed smile had a subtle frostiness, and the air around him felt less welcoming. It was a slight shift but noticeable.

Shrugging off my unease, I quickened my pace, eager to greet my friend. "Feng Wu!" I called out, a wide grin spreading across my face as I approached.

Feng Wu inclined his head toward me, his expression unchanging, that same upturned smile with eyes closed.

"It's been a while!" I exclaimed, reaching him with an enthusiasm that contrasted sharply with his reserved demeanor. "I didn't expect you to be my escort. How was your mission?"

He opened his eyes slowly, the frostiness in his expression melting into a more familiar warmth, but it wasn't as radiant as it used to be. "My mission went well," he replied, his tone clipped. "Elder Zhu's orders, as you may already know. Just got back and here I am, playing your chaperone to Crescent Bay City."

The change in Feng Wu's demeanor was subtle yet distinct, like a familiar tune played in a different key. As we began walking toward the sect's entrance, the atmosphere between us felt oddly strained, a far cry from our usual easy camaraderie.

"Haha," I laughed nervously, scratching the back of my head. "Sorry about that. You didn't even get the chance to rest at all."

"It's okay. I don't mind catching up. Are you ready to go?"

There was an awkward silence for a few moments as we walked out of the Verdant Lotus Sect. I was unsure what to say. But before I could speak, he turned to me again.

His gaze locked onto mine, piercing and inscrutable. "Kai," Feng Wu began slowly, his tone casual yet laced with something unreadable. "It seems a lot has happened at the sect while I was away."

I swallowed hard, my mind racing. Was he referring to the Silent Moon incident? My pulse quickened as I tried to gauge his thoughts behind those half-closed eyes. The way he studied me, it felt like he was sifting through my very soul.

"Yeah, y-you know, just the usual stuff," I stammered, attempting to sound nonchalant, but my voice betrayed a hint of nervousness. My palms felt clammy, and I resisted the urge to wipe them on my robes. "Training and whatnot."

Feng Wu's smile lingered, but there was an edge to it now, a sharpness that wasn't there before. He took a slow, deliberate step closer, reducing the distance between us. "The usual stuff, huh?" he echoed, his voice low and teasing, yet something in his tone sent a shiver down my spine.

"So, Kai," he said after a moment, "about you picking a fight with the Silent Moon Sect . . ." His words hung in the air like a guillotine ready to drop.

My eyes darted to look at him. There was still a pleasant expression fixed on his face, but it didn't convince me. A sense of dread settled in the pit of my stomach.

As the realization set in, I could only think one thing.

I'd really screwed up this time.

# CHAPTER SEVEN

# Silent Moon, Silent Ambitions

Past the imposing gates of the Silent Moon Sect, a path wound through formidable walls, each stone imbued with the sect's unyielding spirit. This well-trodden path led through meticulously arranged grounds, casting dancing shadows on the ancient cobblestones.

The walkway, lined with stern-faced statues of legendary warriors, spoke of the sect's storied past and its relentless pursuit of martial excellence. Here, the air was thick with an unspoken tension, a constant reminder of the sect's ethos, where strength reigned supreme.

Approaching the dining hall, the path's severity softened, giving way to a structure that, while simpler in decoration, held an air of solemn dignity. The tall doors of the hall stood ajar, inviting yet daunting. Inside, the hall was segmented into distinct levels, each a testament to the sect's rigid hierarchy.

At the lowest tier, tables for the third-class disciples were arrayed, their occupants visibly restrained in their demeanor, a mirror to their place within the sect. Above them, slightly elevated, the second-class disciples dined with a hint more ease, yet their eyes never strayed far from the lofty positions they aspired to reach. Higher still, the first-class disciples and the elders occupied their respective areas, each level an unspoken but clear declaration of power and status within the Silent Moon Sect.

In this place, where every stone and fabric spoke of discipline and dominion, the whispers of a daring challenge began to stir the air, rippling through the sect's carefully constructed order.

Among the throngs of disciples, a story was circulating—a tale about a bold herbalist who dared to challenge the sect over a Wind Serpent Beast Core.

Three of them, having just returned from the mission confronting the Verdant Lotus Sect, were particularly animated, their voices tinged with both excitement and disdain.

"Can you believe that audacity?" one of them, a tall disciple with a narrow face, exclaimed. "Challenging Elder Jun over a Beast Core!"

The others chuckled, their laughter echoing off the stone walls. "A mere civilian, an herbalist at that," snorted another, his eyes gleaming with mockery.

The two who hadn't been part of the mission leaned in, their curiosity piqued. "But the sect could've easily claimed it by force," one observed, his brow furrowed in thought. "Why show restraint?"

"It's the honor of our sect," declared the tall disciple, puffing out his chest. "We don't stoop to petty theft. We uphold principles, even when dealing with the likes of him."

Nods of agreement circled the table. "It's our strength and honor that makes us Silent Moon," another added, his voice firm with pride.

The conversation shifted as one disciple, a young man with sharp eyes, leaned forward. "But what does this herbalist think he's doing? Standing against the sect? It's like a moth flinging itself into the flame!"

Laughter erupted again, but it was laced with a hint of derision. "Exactly!" the first speaker said. "He's a fool, treating cultivation like a child's game. He has no idea what he's up against."

"He'll learn the hard way," said the disciple with sharp eyes, a cold smile playing on his lips. "In the Silent Moon Sect, strength is everything. He's just an herbalist, without the might of cultivation to back his challenge. He won't stand a chance."

In their words, the sect's ethos was clear—in the world of the Silent Moon, might made right, and those without it were nothing but fools playing at a game they could never win.

At that moment, a voice cut through the din from the elevated platform where the second-class disciples dined. Authoritative yet tinged with curiosity, it interrupted the third-class disciples' banter. "Is what you say true?"

They fell silent, glancing upward.

A figure emerged and descended the stairs, his presence commanding immediate attention. It was Xu Ziqing, known among his peers as the Azure Moon Marauder. Older than most second-class disciples, Xu Ziqing carried an air of experience. His beard, neatly trimmed, framed a face marked by sharp, piercing eyes that seemed to dissect the very air he gazed upon.

The third-class disciples rose in unison, their voices a chorus of deference. "Senior Brother Xu," they greeted him, their earlier bravado dissolving into a respectful fear.

Xu Ziqing nodded, acknowledging them with stoicism. "I overheard your conversation," he began. "This herbalist, he challenges the sect over a Wind Serpent Beast Core, you say?"

"Yes, Senior Brother," one of the disciples confirmed.

Xu Ziqing's eyes narrowed slightly, a flash of interest igniting in their depths. "And this herbalist," he said, his tone even, "what is his name?"

There was a momentary hush, the third-class disciples exchanging glances. Then, the one with sharp eyes who had returned from the mission, spoke up. "His name is Kai Liu, Senior Brother."

The name resonated in the air, striking a chord within Xu Ziqing. *Kai Liu*, he thought, the memory surfacing unbidden. He remembered Qingmu, the chaos of battle, and the young herbalist who had unexpectedly played a pivotal role. There was a vivid flash of that moment, when he had grabbed Kai by the collar and expected to see fear but was instead met with a burning gaze of defiance with eyes that did not belong to a weak civilian.

Xu Ziqing recalled how the boy had stood against the Wind Serpent, taking a brutal hit yet emerging alive, a feat that had demanded a grudging respect even from him. Those fiery eyes, they had told a story of unyielding spirit, a contrast to the often meek and compliant nature of those without cultivation.

As he stood there, the memory painting a stark picture in his mind, Xu Ziqing's gaze swept over the third-class disciples before him. They averted their eyes, unable to meet his intense stare. He felt something stir within him, perhaps disappointment. These disciples lacked that fire, that unspoken valor he had seen in the herbalist.

Xu Ziqing cut through the silence, deliberate and weighted. "Listen well. Your hubris may very well be your downfall. Should any of you be chosen for the sparring match against this herbalist, do not let arrogance cloud your judgment. Underestimate him at your own peril."

The words fell like stones in a pond, rippling through the gathered disciples. A hint of indignation flared among them.

"Senior Brother," one dared to retort, a challenge, "to suggest that a mere herbalist could even scratch us, that seems . . . disrespectful to our cultivation."

Xu Ziqing turned steely and firmly replied, "Take my advice as you will. It is merely a caution from someone who has seen more than you." With that, he turned, his robe billowing slightly as he moved away, leaving the third-class disciples in a huddle of confusion and wounded pride.

Alone with his thoughts, the man allowed a rare moment of introspection. *Kai Liu.* The name echoed in his mind, intertwined with the memory of those fierce eyes. As a second-class disciple, his path was clear, his duties defined, yet there lingered curiosity, an unspoken question about the herbalist who dared to challenge not just a mythical Spirit Beast but an entire sect.

As Xu Ziqing's steps echoed along the corridor, his thoughts delved deeper, past the immediate concerns of sect politics and power struggles. His mind wandered to the Heavenly Interface, a system that had intruded into their world mere months ago, bringing with it a paradigm shift in cultivation and martial prowess.

He recalled his own encounter with the system. It had presented him with a quest, a challenge that had pushed him beyond his limits, allowing him to refine his swordsmanship and break through a plateau that had long hindered his martial arts advancement. The experience had been transformative, giving him a small but profound insight into his swordsmanship.

As he contemplated Kai Liu's rapid ascent, Xu Ziqing wondered if the herbalist had been touched by the Heavenly Interface's power. Kai Liu's mental fortitude, despite his humble background and lack of formal training, was striking. Could the Interface have played a part in forging such resilience?

Xu Ziqing mused over the possibility of the Interface synergizing with Kai Liu's innate qualities. The boy's unexpected growth rate, his ability to stand tall against overwhelming odds—it was a pattern that resonated with the stories of quests and trials bestowed by the Heavenly Interface to his fellow disciples.

Perhaps Kai Liu wasn't just a beneficiary of random luck or willpower. The Interface might have recognized something in him that even seasoned cultivators had overlooked. If true, Kai Liu's potential was more than a fleeting anomaly; it could signal other civilians accessing skills and resources previously limited to sects, heralding a change that could ripple throughout the Jianghu.

As Xu Ziqing continued his solitary walk, these thoughts lingered. The possibility that Kai Liu could surpass his junior brothers added a layer of complexity to their upcoming confrontation.

In a world where strength was the ultimate currency, such unpredictability was both a threat and an exhilarating unknown.

*But while the Interface can level the playing field, it is not a panacea for weakness nor a shortcut to true mastery.*

He himself had harnessed its power, channeling it to enhance his already-formidable skills. The quests and trials had sharpened his techniques, yes, but it was his years of disciplined training and unwavering dedication within the Silent Moon Sect that formed the bedrock of his strength.

A cold, pragmatic part of Xu Ziqing acknowledged the potential threat Kai Liu represented. Bolstered by the Interface, the boy could one day rival or even surpass the sect's disciples. However, he was not one to yield to potential threats or rest on his laurels.

*Let the boy have his Interface,* he mused, his pace resuming its steady rhythm as he approached the heart of the sect. *I, too, have access to this tool, and I will not allow him, or anyone else, to outpace me.* The resolve in his heart was a steel blade, unsheathed and ready. The sect had taught him that strength was paramount, and he would not be bested. Not by Kai Liu and not by Feng Wu or anybody else.

As he traversed the sect grounds, the atmosphere shifted. The narrow pathway, flanked by ancient trees, led to the regal training grounds, where the air thrummed with practice and discipline.

Clad in dark blue and black, disciples moved with precision, their actions a dance of strength and control. Instructors stood elevated on platforms, their sharp eyes missing nothing, a constant reminder of the sect's hierarchy.

Xu Ziqing moved past them, his gaze lingering momentarily.

Deeper into the center of the sect, the ambiance grew heavier, the air thick with the scent of ancient wood and whispered secrets. Here lay the elders' quarters, a cluster of imposing structures that stood as silent guardians of the sect's wisdom and power. The buildings cast long shadows that stretched across the cobblestone paths.

His mind wandered back to the task at hand—a mission bestowed upon him by one of the elders. The memory of the elder's grave voice was clear.

*Your loyalty to the sect is unquestionable, Xu Ziqing. But tread carefully. Elder Jun is not a man to be taken lightly. He is as cunning as he is powerful. Watch him but do not let your guard down.*

Approaching Elder Jun's courtyard, he scanned the area with practiced ease. Blossoming trees and carefully arranged stones created an illusion of serenity, but like everything in the sect, it was a facade, masking the true nature of what lay within.

A third-class disciple, absorbed in tending to the plants, looked up, his eyes widening in recognition. "Senior Brother Xu." He bowed deeply.

Xu Ziqing nodded, his expression unreadable. "Take me to Elder Jun," he commanded, leaving no room for hesitation.

The disciple led him through the courtyard, into the heart of Elder Jun's residence. The interior was a display of wealth and taste.

As they moved through the opulent halls, Xu Ziqing's thoughts briefly returned to Kai Liu. It was a curious turn of events that the herbalist's brazen challenge had provided him with a valid pretext to observe Elder Jun's movements closely. He could not help but feel a grudging respect for Kai's unintended assistance.

They reached the inner chamber, where Elder Jun was said to spend most of his time. The disciple hesitated, then knocked gently on the massive wooden door.

"Elder Jun, Senior Brother Xu Ziqing requests an audience."

The door opened slowly, revealing the chamber's interior. Elder Jun, seated at a large desk cluttered with scrolls, looked up. His eyes, sharp and calculating, fixated on the Azure Moon Marauder.

"Ah, Xu Ziqing. What brings you to my quarters?" Elder Jun asked.

"Elder Jun, I wish to speak of the forthcoming challenge against the herbalist, Kai Liu. I intend to witness his defeat personally," he stated with feigned eagerness.

The elder remained composed yet interested. "And why does this particular challenge pique your interest, Xu Ziqing?"

"This herbalist is the same one I encountered during our mission in Qingmu. I find it necessary to see him crushed to satisfy a grudge," he said with pride and resentment.

Recognition flickered across Elder Jun's face. "Ah, the Qingmu incident," he recalled, understanding dawning on him. "Very well. Your request is granted. Witnessing the outcome of this challenge could indeed be . . . enlightening for you."

Xu Ziqing nodded but hid his true intentions. "Thank you, Elder. I shall not take this opportunity for granted."

Elder Jun's lips curved into a smile that unspoken thoughts behind it. "Think nothing of it, Xu Ziqing. It is my duty as an elder to aid our disciples in their endeavors," he reassured smoothly as he watched Xu Ziqing with interest. Seizing the moment, continued pointedly, "Before you go, I have a question for you. It is always enlightening to understand the perspectives of our promising disciples."

He then turned to the third-class disciple who had accompanied Xu Ziqing and politely dismissed him. "You may leave us. Close the door behind you."

The disciple hastily exited, closing the door with a soft click. The atmosphere in the room became intimate.

As the door closed behind him, Xu Ziqing felt the weight of his mission bearing down on his shoulders. In a place where strength was everything, and secrets were currency, every step was a dance on the edge of a blade. He was ready for it. After all, in the Silent Moon Sect, it was the only way to survive.

# CHAPTER EIGHT

# Feng Wu's Return

As Feng Wu's question about the Silent Moon Sect hung in the air, I felt a trickle of sweat slide down my back. The way his eyes crinkled at the corners told me he was more amused than angry, but still, I couldn't help but gulp.

"Ah, you heard about that, huh?" I tried to chuckle, but it came out more like a strangled squawk. "I might have . . . slightly, possibly, maybe . . . gotten into a tiny bit of trouble. But who hasn't, right? Even someone like you must've got into something like this before."

His smile widened, though it no longer reached his eyes, which sparkled with a mix of mischief and reprimand. "Kai, Kai, Kai," he tsked, shaking his head. "Nobody gets into trouble like you. I leave for a few days, and you decide to take on a whole sect?"

I scratched the back of my head, offering a sheepish smile. "Well, you know me. I never back down from a challenge. Even when maybe, just maybe, I should."

He shook his head, but I could see his smile warming, a hint of the old Feng Wu resurfacing. "You never change, do you? Always jumping headfirst into the fray."

"Hey, I like to think of it as being proactive," I said in defense of myself, still grinning despite the situation. "Besides, it all worked out in the end, didn't it? I'm still alive, not reduced to a paste on the sect grounds."

His laughter was genuine, and he clapped me on the shoulder. "Only you, Kai. Only you could stir up trouble like this and come out smiling. Just be careful, all right? We can't have a rising star like you getting snuffed out too soon."

I nodded, lightening up. Feng Wu's easygoing nature had always been a comfort, and even now his words put me at ease. "I'll be more careful. I swear it on my honor as the genius of the realm, Kai Liu!"

He raised an eyebrow, his smile turning into a smirk. "On your honor as the 'genius of the realm,' you say? So I take it that everything you say from this point on is a lie, then."

I feigned offense, puffing out my chest slightly. "Of course not—I stand by my word! And for the record, it was more of a misunderstanding than an actual fight."

Feng Wu grew serious. "All right, Kai. Let's hear it, then. What exactly happened? Tell me everything."

After I finished explaining that day, he shook his head in disbelief, running a hand through his hair. "I heard most of it from Elder Chen, but hearing it from you . . . it's no less surprising. You have a knack for turning even the simplest of situations into an adventure."

I shrugged sheepishly. "I guess I have a flair for the dramatic."

The man looked at me with both exasperation and admiration. "That you do, Kai. Just remember to be careful. You're making a name for yourself here, and not all attention is good attention."

I nodded, taking his words to heart.

Feng Wu patted my back, his typical calm and composed demeanor returning. "Good. Now, let's get going. Crescent Bay City won't wait for us, and I'm sure you have a long list of things to get."

As we walked along the path leading out of the Verdant Lotus Sect, I found myself opening up to Feng Wu about the cascade of events following my impromptu challenge to Elder Jun: my meeting with his sect leader, Shaotian Ye . . .

"You met with the sect leader? I suppose he left quite the impression on you, didn't he? I still remember the first time I saw him during my initiation into the sect."

. . . And my training regime that I'd been grinding away at.

"Instructor Xia Ji . . . She's a taskmaster. Good. You need someone who won't go easy on you."

"It's been brutal, Feng Wu. Early mornings, late nights, nonstop drills. But I've learned so much. I've been focusing on the Bamboo Reprisal Counter, trying to get it just right."

Feng Wu shook his head in mock dismay. "The Bamboo Reprisal Counter? Unorthodox. Although I trust Instructor Xia Ji's judgment. But I'm glad you're taking it seriously."

I laughed nervously. "Well, I've got no choice, have I? I have to land a single hit on that third-class disciple. Just one hit and I win."

Feng Wu sobered. "That was smart, setting the challenge that way. But, Kai, I don't mean to offend you, but you need to be realistic. Going against a third-class disciple in a full sparring match, especially with a Beast Core at stake . . . you don't stand much of a chance."

For a moment, I was tempted to mention that the challenge wasn't entirely my idea. If it weren't for the Heavenly Interface, I don't think I would've proposed something so bold in front of a sect elder. But I bit my tongue.

"I know, Feng Wu. I'm under no illusions here. But that's why I'm focusing on strategy and technique. They're underestimating me, and I want to take advantage of it. Do you remember your advice regarding the Memory Palace technique?"

A flicker of recognition appeared in his eyes. "Yes, I do."

"Well, I used it to visualize my training, just like you told me," I said. "I've been using it to analyze my memories and think about what I could've done better."

He nodded in approval, and I continued.

"It helped against my sparring with Li Na, how to read the signs for when she'd strike. Although it hurts whenever her visualization manages to hit me, it's really helped me build up my confidence in real life."

"Impressive. I'm surprised you were able to— Wait." Feng Wu suddenly raised an eyebrow. "Pain in your visualization? That's unusual. Most cultivators can't replicate sensations accurately in mental exercises. Are you saying you actually feel pain during these visualizations?"

I nodded, aware now of how strange it sounded. "Yeah, it's weird. The pain isn't real, of course, but it feels incredibly vivid, almost like actual combat. I don't do it at will; it just happens."

The man fell into a contemplative silence, his gaze distant. Then he spoke again. "That's quite extraordinary, Kai. I've practiced various visualization techniques over the years, but never heard of such a thing. Even in my own Memory Palace, I can't replicate the sensation of pain like you can. Are you sure that's the case?"

I chuckled, trying to lighten the mood. "Maybe it's because I read too many tales and fictions as a kid. My mind's probably overactive from all that imaginative stuff."

The man still seemed lost in thought, and I couldn't help but wonder if my abilities were as peculiar as he made them seem.

As the silence stretched on, my mind wandered back to my Essence Extraction skill. It was another ability that baffled me at times. I could extract essences from plant matter with ease, but when it came to metals or living beings, the skill was utterly ineffective. Was it another quirk of the Heavenly Interface?

"Kai, have you considered that these unique aspects of your abilities might be influenced by the Heavenly Interface?" Feng Wu finally spoke, echoing my thoughts.

I nodded slowly. "I have, actually. It's like each ability comes with its own set of rules or limitations. It's helpful, sure, but sometimes it feels like I'm only scratching the surface of what's possible."

Feng Wu looked at me with a hint of admiration. "You're adapting well, considering how recently you've been exposed to all of this."

"Thanks. I really appreciate hearing that."

The rest of the journey passed in comfortable silence, our minds elsewhere. As we approached Crescent Bay City, the bustling energy of the marketplace and the scent of street food filled the air, pulling me back to the present.

I turned to him, my spirits lifted by the lively atmosphere. "Let's go shopping first!"

Feng Wu smiled, his earlier pensiveness replaced by his usual calm demeanor. "Let's see what Crescent Bay City has in store for us. Why don't we visit the Azure Silk trading Company's shops? You're bound to find better deals there."

Accepting his suggestion, we headed to the center of Crescent Bay City. Despite having seen it before, the city's vibrancy left me in awe.

I instinctively scanned the crowd for Silent Moon Sect disciples in their dark blue uniforms. Thankfully, I saw none, and a wave of relief washed over me.

The disciple led me to a bustling courtyard, the heart of the city's market. Rows of stalls and shops, some under elegant pavilions, filled the expanse. The air was rich with the scents of spices, herbs, and street food.

I looked around, slightly overwhelmed by the sheer number of shops. "How do we find the Azure Silk Trading Company here?"

Feng Wu pointed toward a few shops with a specific marking on their signages. "See those symbols? That's the mark of the Azure Silk Trading Company. Any shop with that emblem is affiliated with them."

I followed his gaze and noticed several textile shops sporting the same symbol. It was a delicate, intricate design that couldn't be missed if you knew what you were looking for.

"Do you get a discount as a disciple?" I asked, curious.

The green-eyed man shook his head slightly. "No, not personally. But the Verdant Lotus Sect has an agreement with them. We receive a twenty percent discount on our purchases due to our long-standing relationship."

I couldn't hide my dismay. "Really? Why don't I have something like that?" I sighed but then shrugged it off. "Well, can I use your discount, then? I need to stock up on a few things."

He nodded, a slight smile on his lips. "Of course you can use my discount. Consider it a perk of being accompanied by a Verdant Lotus disciple."

I grinned at him, feeling a rush of gratitude. "You're the best, Feng Wu! I owe you one. How about I treat you to lunch at whatever restaurant catches your eye?"

He chuckled, the familiar ease between us returning. "I'll hold you to that, Kai. But first, let's take care of your shopping."

Feng Wu elaborated as we strolled through the lively market, "The Azure Silk Trading Company is renowned for their textiles. In fact, our Verdant Lotus

Sect uniforms are supplied by them. They're known for their quality and durability."

His words sparked an idea in my mind. My current robes, though functional, were starting to show signs of wear and tear. And honestly, they lacked a certain . . . flair. "You know, I've been thinking about getting a new set of robes. Something in maroon, my signature color. It's time for an upgrade."

Feng Wu nodded in agreement. "A wise choice. Good robes not only offer protection but also represent your identity as a cultivator."

We entered a textile shop adorned with the Azure Silk Trading Company's emblem. The interior was a haven of luxurious fabrics and elegant designs. I was quickly attended to by a courteous shopkeeper, who took my measurements with a professional eye.

As the shopkeeper brought out various shades of maroon fabric, Feng Wu stepped forward, flashing his lotus charm. "This young man is an esteemed guest of the Verdant Lotus Sect."

The shopkeeper lit up with recognition and respect. "Of course, honored disciple. We're always pleased to serve the Verdant Lotus Sect."

I couldn't help but feel a bit like a celebrity under Feng Wu's wing. As I tried on the new set of robes, tailored to fit me perfectly, I admired my reflection in the mirror.

As I turned and admired myself, I immediately noticed their comfortable fit and the quality of the maroon fabric, a practical yet stylish shade that complimented my complexion. The material felt durable and light, allowing ease of movement—essential for my cultivation practices. Simple but elegant, the robes were accented with subtle patterns that added a touch of character without being ostentatious. Looking in the mirror, I felt a quiet confidence; these robes were a fitting upgrade from my old attire.

Now I truly looked the part of a cultivator!

However, when the time came to settle the bill, even with the discount, the price made me wince internally.

*These robes better last me a lifetime*, I thought, handing over the payment. *I need to be more careful with my spending. Can't get carried away, even if I am in Crescent Bay City. Meat for Windy, alcohol for Tianyi!*

Stepping out of the textile shop, I couldn't help but feel a twinge of buyer's remorse. The robes were exquisite, yes, but the cost . . .

We continued our stroll through the bustling streets of Crescent Bay City. My mind was still reeling from the purchase when a sudden collision snapped me back to the present.

"Oh, pardon me!" I exclaimed as I bumped into a hooded figure. I reached out instinctively to steady them.

But the figure steadied themselves and then turned to face me. They pushed back their hood. My heart skipped a beat. It was her—the mysterious woman who had tried to buy Tianyi back at the Spirited Noodle. She recognized me.

"You," she said, her voice low. "The boy with the Azure Moonlight Flutter. Where is it?"

# CHAPTER NINE

# Meat, Wine, and Hooded Rivals

You're the girl who tried to steal Tianyi!" I pointed at her, my finger shaking slightly.

She looked affronted. "How rude! I was offering to purchase the Spirit Beast! A disciple of the Whispering Wind Sect wouldn't resort to such lowly tactics, especially against a peasant fool who can't recognize a pearl even if it was in their palm."

Her words stung, but I stood my ground. "A pearl? Tianyi is my companion, not some trinket to be bartered."

The woman's eyes narrowed, her lips curling into a smirk. "Companion? A beast like that is wasted on someone like you. You probably don't even understand her true value. I collect Spirit Beasts for breeding, and a female Azure Moonlight Flutter is a rare find. I need her for my work."

I felt a surge of protectiveness for Tianyi. "Well, she's not for sale. And calling me ignorant won't change my mind."

Feng Wu, who had been silently observing the exchange, gave me a subtle nod, a silent message of support.

The woman huffed, her frustration evident. "You're squandering a great opportunity here. I am the future head of alchemy at the Whispering Wind Sect. My favor is not a boon to be taken lightly."

"You're an alchemist?" I asked. "I'm an aspiring alchemist myself."

"You? Are you planning to participate in the Grand Alchemy Gauntlet?"

"That's right, and I'll be sponsored by the Verdant Lotus Sect."

Her eyes narrowed further, her gaze now icy. "You think cultivation and alchemy are mere games to be played? Just because the Heavenly Interface appeared, you believe you stand a chance?"

"Why do you all think I'm taking this as some sort of game? Is it because of my status?" I demanded, my voice rising. *What is up with cultivators thinking everyone is below them?*

She looked at me as if I had said the most foolish thing in the world. "It's not about status. It's about resources, proper guidance, years of dedication. You're like a child hitting a tree with a stick and calling it martial arts training. You're disregarding the real work that goes into mastering alchemy."

I opened my mouth to retort, but the words tangled in my throat. I was flustered, insulted by her disdain, and struggling to articulate my frustration.

Feng Wu stepped in, his voice calm but firm. "That's a narrow view of alchemy," he said. "The study and practice of this art aren't limited to prestigious sects alone. There are many paths to mastery, and each cultivator's journey is unique."

The woman scoffed, unimpressed. "You speak of ideals, but the reality is different. The Grand Alchemy Gauntlet isn't a playground for amateurs. It's a serious competition where only the most talented succeed."

His demeanor remained unshaken. "And who's to say Kai won't be among them? The path of cultivation is full of surprises, and dismissing someone's potential based on their origin or status is a mistake."

*That's right, Feng Wu! Speak your profound words!*

I nodded, bolstered by his intervention. "He's right. I might be new to this, but I'm not clueless. I've been training hard, and I plan to give it my all. Your skepticism won't deter me. Don't be too hurt when I leave you in the dust!"

She raised a sculpted eyebrow that arched elegantly above piercing dark blue eyes that seemed to scrutinize my every word. A hint of a smirk played on her lips, only slightly obscured by her hood. "Overshadow me? You're amusing, at least. Let's make a wager, then. If you truly believe in your abilities, put your Azure Moonlight Flutter on the line."

My heart skipped a beat. "No way!" I blurted out, louder than I intended. I could feel Feng Wu's hand gripping my shoulder in a terrifyingly gentle manner. The message was clear:

*Think before you leap, Kai.*

The woman let out a derisive snort. "Coward. Can't even back your own words with action. Don't heed my advice at your peril. You'll regret underestimating the Jianghu." With a swirl of her cloak, she turned and disappeared into the bustling crowd of Crescent Bay City.

I let out a sigh of relief, feeling the tension drain from my shoulders. "That was close . . ."

Her words echoed in my thoughts, haunting me with their stinging truth. The path of cultivation was fraught with uncertainties, and facing the elite of the Jianghu, I felt a pang of insecurity.

I looked at my hands, the same hands that had wielded techniques and brewed concoctions all these years, and wondered if they were enough. The seeds of doubt planted by her disdain began to grow.

Standing amid the bustling streets of Crescent Bay City, I felt smaller than ever. The path ahead seemed shrouded in mist, and for the first time, I questioned not just my ability to navigate it but whether I belonged on it at all.

Feng Wu released his grip, chuckling softly. "You have a knack for attracting interesting characters, Kai. But remember, wagers and taunts are a part of the Jianghu. You must be cautious with your words and promises. Especially with someone like her."

"You recognize her?"

"She's part of the Lian clan. They all have white hair and blue eyes. They've been a cornerstone of the Whispering Wind Sect for generations. It's no wonder she carries herself with such . . . unwavering confidence."

I nodded, mulling over Feng Wu's words. "Unwavering confidence, huh? That's a polite way to put it. She was downright arrogant!"

"Arrogance often comes with power. In the cultivation world, power can justify many things like that. The Lian clan has immense resources and influence. They're renowned for their expertise in alchemy, and to them, purchasing a Spirit Beast, no matter the price, is trivial."

"So, they just throw their weight around because they can?" I asked, my curiosity piqued.

"In a manner of speaking, yes. Their status and wealth grant them certain liberties. But that comes with great scrutiny. The Lian clan, despite their privileges, are bound by the expectations and traditions of their lineage and sect."

"Sounds suffocating."

"It can be," Feng Wu agreed. "But it's also a life of luxury and opportunity. Cultivators from powerful clans have access to resources and training that others can only dream of. It shapes their worldview, their aspirations, and even their attitude toward others."

"I guess that puts things into perspective," I said, feeling a bit more understanding toward the woman from the Whispering Wind Sect. "Still, it doesn't excuse her trying to buy Tianyi like she's shopping for groceries."

Feng Wu laughed. "No, it doesn't. But it's important to understand where she's coming from. In the world of cultivation, understanding the background and motivations of others can be as crucial as mastering a new technique. Knowing your opponent, in alchemy or in combat, gives you an edge. And in your case, it might help you navigate any further negotiations or confrontations with her."

"Navigate and negotiate. I can do that," I replied, glancing briefly at the spot where the mysterious alchemist had vanished. "But seriously, what is it with cultivators and their love for gambling? It's like every other story I heard growing up. Some cultivator wagers their left pinky toe to impress a jade beauty, get whacked, then lose it in their hubris. Do you, O Wise and Venerable Feng Wu, also have a secret penchant for high-stakes gambling? Should I be watching my back in case you bet me in a cultivator card game?"

Feng Wu raised an eyebrow, a playful smirk dancing on his lips. "Kai, if there were such a thing as a cultivator card game, I assure you, I'd be the reigning champion. But fear not, I only gamble on sure things. Like your potential, for instance."

"Well, that's a relief. I mean, if you're betting on me, you must be the most risk-averse gambler in the cultivation world."

Feng Wu chuckled. "It seems the stories you read are where your imagination comes from, Kai. But you're not entirely wrong. Cultivators, by nature, are driven by ambition and the pursuit of strength. It leads some to take . . . unorthodox paths."

"Yeah, 'unorthodox' is one way to put it," I mused, my tone light but thoughtful. "Growing up without cultivation being a big part of my life, all this did seem like just fun and games. You know, the kind of stuff that makes a good story but you never expect to see in real life. But now, being in the thick of it, it's like living in one of those tales."

He nodded, mulling my words, amused. "The books you speak of do interest me. Do you know the authors who're writing them?"

"You know, most of the books I've read were by a guy named Liang Feng," I began, trying to sound nonchalant. "But between you and me," I continued, leaning closer to Feng Wu as if sharing a state secret, "I suspect this Liang Feng is also behind several other books under different pseudonyms. The writing style is far too similar, and they all harp on the same themes."

Feng Wu seemed intrigued. "That's quite an observation. What makes you so sure?"

I shrugged, feeling a bit self-conscious about my theory. "Just a hunch, I guess. The way he describes martial arts techniques, the philosophies behind cultivation, even his characters' quirks—it's like he has this unique fingerprint that's hard to miss once you've read enough of his work."

"Interesting," Feng Wu mused. "Perhaps you have a talent for literary analysis as well as alchemy and cultivation."

I chuckled, shaking my head. "Doubtful. I just read a lot. Speaking of which, we should probably get moving. It's getting late, and we still have a lot to buy. The shops will be closing soon."

As we weaved our way through the throngs of people, my mind drifted back to the confrontation with the hooded girl from the Lian family.

Her arrogance, her outright dismissal of my abilities—it irked me. But Feng Wu's words lingered in my mind, painting a picture of a world shaped by power, status, and expectation. Was she just a product of her environment? Was her disdain for me, a novice in the grand scheme of things, justified in the context of her upbringing?

I glanced over at the second-class disciple who seemed lost in thought. "Hey, Feng Wu," I started hesitantly, "do you think she's right? About me not standing a chance in the Grand Alchemy Gauntlet, I mean."

He turned to me, contemplative. "Kai, in the path of cultivation, nothing is certain. Your journey has been unconventional, to say the least. But that doesn't mean you're doomed to fail. What matters is your dedication, your willingness to learn and adapt."

His words were comforting, but the seed of doubt planted by her still lingered. I knew I had a lot to learn, and my path was fraught with unknowns. But Feng Wu's faith in me bolstered my resolve. I wouldn't let her or anyone else dictate my worth.

As we continued our errands, picking up cuts of meat, and a particularly expensive bottle of lychee wine for Tianyi, Feng Wu finally commented on my purchases.

Feng Wu cocked his head. "Kai, you do realize that bringing such . . . earthly indulgences into a Taoist sect like ours is seen as . . . Well, let's just say it's not exactly in line with our principles."

I could practically feel the eyes of imaginary elders boring into me, judging my every move. "I, uh, have faith in me, Feng Wu?" I offered weakly, trying to sound confident but probably failing miserably.

He chuckled. "I trust you, Kai, but you must understand why I didn't flaunt the sect's symbol for a discount this time. If the elders caught wind of me buying alcohol and meat, especially in such quantities, I'd be spending several days in the penance hall."

I grimaced, realizing how ridiculous and disrespectful my actions must have seemed from an outsider's perspective. "Right, I didn't think that through. But I promise, there's a good reason for it. I just can't reveal it yet."

Feng Wu sighed, still smiling. "All right, I'll trust your judgment. But you better have a good explanation ready. Now, that meal you promised . . ."

"You're the veteran, Feng Wu. Lead the way!"

He put a finger to his chin, considering the options before his eyes lit up. "There's a restaurant called Cloudrift Pavilion, if you're partial to seafood. I usually go with their Cliffside Bamboo Shoots. The view is amazing, especially at nighttime. Does that sound satisfactory?"

With the moon casting its light over our heads, we set off for Cloudrift Pavilion. Despite the oddity of the situation, his easygoing nature and willingness to go along with my unorthodox methods were a reminder of why I valued his friendship so much. It was like having the older brother I never had.

Little did he know, the real surprise was yet to come. And I couldn't wait to see his reaction when I finally revealed Windy. For now, though, I'd enjoy the moment, a lighthearted break in the grand scheme of things.

# CHAPTER TEN

# Windy's Revelation

As we arrived back at the Verdant Lotus Sect, the clock had long since passed midnight. The faint light from a few strategically placed lanterns flickered gently, creating dancing shadows on the ground. It was a scene of peaceful beauty, but my mind was anything but calm.

I picked up the neatly packaged bags containing the results of my shopping spree—lychee wine, slabs of meat, and other assorted items—feeling a growing sense of unease.

*Bringing these into a Taoist sect's premises . . . What was I thinking?* I tried to convince myself that they likely didn't hold guests to the same principles as their disciples, but the thought did little to alleviate my anxiety.

Feng Wu seemed to sense my discomfort and slowed his pace to walk beside me. "You know, the elders might be strict, but they're not unreasonable. They understand that guests have different customs and needs."

I glanced at him, trying to find reassurance in his words. "Yeah, but meat and wine? It's not exactly the kind of 'different customs' that would go unnoticed here."

He laughed softly, the sound echoing in the quiet night. "True, but remember, you're here as a sponsored participant for the Grand Alchemy Gauntlet. And as long as you're not openly flaunting these items or disturbing the peace of the sect, I doubt there will be any issues."

As we neared the guest quarters, the silence of the night was comforting, the soft sounds of nature blending with our footsteps. The occasional creak of a bamboo stalk or the distant hoot of an owl added to the night's ambiance.

Finally, we reached the guest quarters, the familiar structure a welcome sight.

"We made it," I murmured, more to myself than to Feng Wu.

As we walked up the steps, I grinned at him. "You won't believe what you're about to see."

I opened the door, and revealed what I had been hiding all this time.

Tianyi perched by the windowsill with Windy. As I approached, Tianyi fluttered over while Windy, waking up, gazed at me and Feng Wu. The snake eyed Feng Wu cautiously but relaxed upon seeing Tianyi interact with him.

The butterfly landed delicately on Feng Wu's nose, greeting him. Feng Wu smiled warmly. "Tianyi, you look healthier than ever," he said softly. Tianyi fluttered her wings in response, pleased with the attention.

Then his gaze shifted to Windy, whom I had been so anxious to introduce. "And this must be the new addition. It has pure white scales with a bluish sheen. An aberrant?"

I couldn't hide my disappointment at Feng Wu's lack of surprise. "You're not shocked? I thought revealing Windy would be a big moment."

"Kai, I've known you long enough to connect the dots. It was unlikely you'd buy raw slabs of meat for yourself to enjoy. But, I must admit, it is truly a remarkable creature."

I sighed, accepting that maybe my expectations for a dramatic reaction were a bit too high.

"Well, anyway, I've named it Windy."

Feng Wu nodded approvingly. "Do you know the gender yet?"

"Not yet. They have to mature before I can tell," I explained. I opened the pack containing the meat and alcohol and poured out some of the lychee wine for Tianyi to enjoy.

Turning my attention to the raw meat, I realized I needed to slice it into more manageable chunks for Windy. My herb-cutting knife lay on the table, but it was too dull for the job. "Feng Wu, I could use some help here. I need to slice this meat, but my knife isn't going to cut it—literally."

With a flick of his wrist, his bladed fan snapped open, revealing the gleaming razor-sharp edge. He had expertly chopped it within seconds.

"Thank you," I said, genuinely impressed by his deftness.

I offered some sliced meat to Windy, who cautiously slithered forward to inspect it. After a moment, it began to eat, its tongue flickering in and out. As Windy nibbled on the chunks, I noticed a slight grimace with each bite. I realized that Wind Serpents like Windy were probably used to consuming whole prey, with skin and bones providing nutrients that meat alone couldn't give.

"This is only a stop-gap solution to keep Windy from starving," I mentioned to Feng Wu, feeling a bit guilty. "But to keep them truly happy, I'll need to provide whole prey. Chopped meat isn't ideal for snakes."

I grimaced, remembering their little escapade. "Letting them out to hunt is risky, and they've already escaped through the window to hunt before. It's nothing short of a miracle we haven't been caught yet. I wouldn't want to find out how one of the disciples would react to a Spirit Beast wandering on sect premises."

Stroking his chin thoughtfully, Feng Wu nodded in understanding. "It is indeed a risky situation. Why don't we reveal Windy's existence to the elders? If they're aware, you won't have to tiptoe around the sect to feed them."

I hesitated, the idea of revealing Windy to the elders filled me with unease. "I'm not sure about that," I said, my voice laced with reluctance. "I don't know how well it'll be taken, and I fear for Windy's safety. What if the Silent Moon Sect were to hear of them?"

"Trust in the sect, Kai. We can keep a secret. Besides, they can help ensure Windy's well-being and perhaps even provide a safer way for them to hunt."

Pushing these doubts aside, I focused on the immediate concern. "All right, I'll show Windy to Elder Zhu and the others after my classes and training tomorrow."

It was the least I could do. They'd invested so much into me, so how could I not reward them with my trust? A relationship required investment from both sides.

*Perhaps it's for the best*, I mused internally. *The Verdant Lotus Sect has been a sanctuary for me. They've shown nothing but kindness and understanding. It's time I trust them with this part of my journey.*

"Kai, I know you're worried," Feng Wu calmly. "But remember, the elders have seen many unusual cases in their lifetimes. Your situation with Windy will be handled with care and wisdom."

"I'll trust the sect," I finally said, more to convince myself than to reassure Feng Wu. "Hopefully, they'll understand and help find a solution for Windy's feeding situation."

Feng Wu smiled, his confidence unwavering. "They will, Kai. You're not just a guest here; you're a part of this community now. Your concerns are their concerns. I'll help set up the meeting, just do what you need for your classes."

I bowed my head in thanks. "Thank you Feng Wu, you're a lifesaver."

Soon after, Feng Wu left, leaving me with much to think about.

As I prepared to retire for the night, my thoughts kept returning to Windy and the impending conversation with the elders. Keeping Windy a secret wasn't sustainable; the sect's resources could provide a safer environment and help me understand the hatchling better.

I settled down to rest, but sleep eluded me. To ease my restless thoughts, I meditated, focusing on calming my mind and cultivating my energy. The gentle rhythm of my breathing brought tranquility, slowly fading my worries.

The next afternoon came quicker than expected. After finishing my last class, I received a notification.

---

*Reading has reached level 7.*

Alchemy Array Crafting was my hardest class by far. Whether it was my lack of qi or ability to operate it, Instructor Fei Ni knew I would have to dedicate my time to understanding the theory and practicing my qi control before I could wield even the most basic arrays. I suppose my efforts have finally bore fruit after reading so many books on the topic.

After a strenuous training routine with Instructor Xia Ji, I felt physically and mentally exhausted. However, the thought of meeting with Elder Zhu reignited my energy. I returned to the guest quarters, picked up Windy and Tianyi, and let the serpent hide within the sleeves of my new robes.

I approached Elder Zhu's office with Feng Wu following closely behind. In the sleeve of my robe, Windy remained hidden, obedient but clearly curious about the world outside.

I raised my hand to knock on the intricately carved wooden door. The door swung open silently, revealing Elder Zhu sitting at his desk, surrounded by piles of scrolls.

"Elder Zhu." I greeted him with a bow, feeling a mixture of respect and nervousness.

The elder looked up from his work and smiled warmly at me. "Ah, Kai! It's good to see you. How have things been going? And what brings you to my office today?" His voice was gentle, yet there was a hint of curiosity in his tone.

Taking a deep breath, I carefully revealed Windy, who was hiding in my sleeve. The small Wind Serpent peered out, its blue-tinged white scales shimmering slightly in the light of the room.

Elder Zhu's eyes widened in surprise, and for a moment, he looked genuinely stunned. "This . . . is a Wind Serpent hatchling!" he exclaimed, leaning forward for a closer look. "Remarkable. Where did you come across such a rare creature?"

I shifted uncomfortably, aware of Windy's curious gaze moving between Elder Zhu and me. "I found an egg in Qingmu shortly after our ordeal with the Wind Serpents," I explained, carefully watching his reaction. "I've been keeping it until it hatched."

Elder Zhu nodded thoughtfully, still fixed on Windy. "I see. And you've been taking care of it ever since?"

"Yes, Elder," I replied. "I've been feeding it, but I'm concerned about its diet and well-being. That's why I wanted to talk to you. Is it all right if I continue to feed Windy here? Is there a way we could procure some sort of food for Windy? I'll be willing to pay for all the costs related to the expense."

"It's not common for someone to care for a Spirit Beast, especially one as rare as a Wind Serpent. But given the circumstances, I see no reason to object. We can arrange for appropriate food for Windy."

"There's no issue regarding feeding Windy meat? I mean, this is a Taoist sect, after all . . ."

Elder Zhu shook his head gently. "In Taoism, it's about following the natural way, the Tao. Feeding a snake its natural prey aligns with this principle, as it maintains the balance and harmony of nature."

I let out a sigh of relief, grateful for his understanding.

"But, Kai, do you have some special affinity for Spirit Beasts? This is quite unusual. First with Tianyi, and now . . ."

I shook my head, bewildered by the turn of events. "No, Elder. I don't think so. It's just a matter of luck that they came to me."

"Hmm," Elder Zhu hummed, his eyes twinkling with interest. "It's rare for one to bond with not just one but two Spirit Beasts, especially of such distinct natures. Tianyi and now Windy. You might have an innate talent for this, Kai. Perhaps it'd be prudent to do some research."

His words left me pondering. Could it be just luck, or was there something more to my connection with these Spirit Beasts?

The elder's gaze shifted, becoming more contemplative as if weighing his next words carefully. A silence fell between us, filled only by the faint rustling of scrolls and the distant sounds of the sect.

"Kai," Elder Zhu finally said. "I've been observing your progress since you arrived here. Your dedication, your ability to overcome challenges, and your unique bond with Spirit Beasts . . . All these factors have led me to a decision."

I tensed up, sensing the gravity of what was to come. Even Feng Wu, who had been quietly observing, looked interested in the sudden shift in conversation.

"I'd like to offer you the opportunity to join the Verdant Lotus Sect as a third-class disciple," Elder Zhu announced, his eyes locked onto mine. "One apprenticed to me."

The words hit me like a wave. Shock, happiness, anxiety—a whirlwind of emotions swirled inside me. My mind raced, trying to process the magnitude of Elder Zhu's offer. Feng Wu's surprised expression mirrored my feelings.

A part of me longed for Elder Ming's guidance at this moment, wishing he were here to help steer my decision. I even hoped for some indication from the Heavenly Interface, but it remained silent as if affirming that this was a decision I had to make on my own.

*Elder Zhu as my mentor . . . Joining the Verdant Lotus Sect officially . . .* The thoughts tumbled through my mind. The opportunity was enormous, yet so were the implications. Would accepting change the course of my path? What would it mean for my future?

I bit my lip, gathering my thoughts. Elder Zhu waited patiently, his expression kind yet expectant. Feng Wu's seemed filled with both pride and anticipation.

Finally, I looked up, meeting Elder Zhu's gaze. My heart pounded in my chest, but my voice was steady. "Elder Zhu, this . . . this is a huge honor. I'm grateful, truly grateful, for the opportunity. I . . ."

# CHAPTER ELEVEN

# The Verdant Lotus Sect's Proposal

As the moon hung full and luminous in the night sky, I found myself enveloped in tranquility. Nestled away from the daily bustle of the Verdant Lotus Sect, this place became a sanctuary where my thoughts and movements could flow unimpeded.

The night set the perfect backdrop for my training routine. I was already fatigued from my morning and afternoon classes, but it helped to keep my mind elsewhere.

Tianyi and Windy were strewn about the clearing, exploring to their heart's content while I started with slow, deliberate punches, each one more precise than the last, feeling the power coiling and uncoiling in my muscles.

As I moved, my mind couldn't help but drift to Elder Zhu's offer. The weight of it hung in the air, as tangible as the mist that sometimes settled over these grounds at dawn.

*Elder Zhu as my mentor . . . Joining the Verdant Lotus Sect officially . . .* The words echoed again in my head.

It was an honor, no doubt, a recognition of my efforts and potential.

But with this honor came a tether, a commitment that went beyond casual learning. It meant embracing the sect's ways. My heart ached slightly at the thought. Since childhood, I had been enthralled by Liang Feng's written works of the wandering cultivator—free spirits roaming the lands, their destinies firmly in their own hands. That world of escapism had been a beacon in my younger years, a dream that had felt so distant yet so alluring.

I paused, taking the time to clench and unclench my fist to keep it from wavering.

To be part of the Verdant Lotus Sect, to be under Elder Zhu's guidance . . . It offered a path of growth, stability, and respect. Yet a part of me yearned for the uncharted path, the freedom to explore and grow in the unpredictability of the world outside a sect's walls.

I gazed up at the moon, seeking its silent counsel. It was then that I found myself transported back to that pivotal moment, the turning point that had brought me to this solitary practice under the moonlit sky.

"I . . ."

In Elder Zhu's office, the air had been dense with the weight of my decision. Feng Wu stood beside me, a quiet pillar of strength. My heart pounded in my chest when I faced him.

"Elder Zhu, this honor . . . It's more than I could have ever imagined. But I must respectfully decline. I'm deeply grateful for your belief in me, but my path . . . I believe it needs to be one of self-discovery, away from the structure of a sect."

Elder Zhu's face had remained impassive for a moment, then softened with understanding. "Kai, before you finalize your decision, consider what being part of our sect entails. Beyond the prestige, it's about the protection and resources we provide. With the Silent Moon Sect's growing animosity, our support could be invaluable to you. And think of the knowledge we freely share with our own, knowledge that we would hesitate to impart to an outsider."

His words echoed in the chambers of my mind, intensifying the turmoil within. The lure of safety and knowledge had been tempting, almost overwhelmingly so. My resolve wavered. But a deeper voice within me whispered of freedom, of uncharted paths that I yearned to tread. It was a voice that spoke of dreams nurtured since childhood, dreams of a life unbound by the strictures of any single creed or sect.

With a heavy heart, I responded, "I understand the gravity of what I'm relinquishing, Elder Zhu, and it pains me to refuse. But my long-term goals . . . I don't believe they align with remaining within the sect. I seek a journey filled with unpredictability and learning that only the open world can offer."

Elder Zhu then regarded me for a long moment with respect and unspoken disappointment. "I see. The Verdant Lotus Sect values the freedom of its disciples, even if it means letting them go. You have our blessings, Kai. The Tao teaches us the beauty of letting things be. Nonattachment is a principle we hold dear. You have done no wrong in following your heart."

Feng Wu's reaction had mirrored Elder Zhu's: respect and slight sadness. "Choosing to join a sect is no light matter," he had said. "I respect your decision, Kai. It takes courage to follow your own path, especially when it leads away from the safety and resources of a sect."

I nodded, feeling a bittersweet mixture of relief and regret. Elder Zhu's offer had been a beacon of security, a fast track to cultivation knowledge and protection against external threats like the Silent Moon Sect. The thought of turning it down was daunting. I was stepping away from a path many would covet, venturing into a world where I would have to rely solely on my own strength and wits.

Had I been being naive, romanticizing the life of a solo cultivator? The sect offered a wealth of knowledge and a network of support that I was now choosing to forgo. The risks of walking the path alone were many, and the journey would undoubtedly be more challenging.

Elder Zhu's voice pulled me back from my thoughts. "Kai, remember that the Verdant Lotus Sect will always regard you as a friend. Our doors will remain open should you ever seek guidance or respite."

"Thank you, Elder Zhu. Your understanding means more to me than I can express."

Now, back in the clearing, I resumed my martial arts routine, each motion infused with a newfound sense of clarity and purpose.

I had made the right decision for me. Yes, the allure of being a recognized disciple under Elder Zhu was tempting, but my heart lay in a different journey—one of freedom, exploration, and self-discovery.

Once I got my bearings and established a strong foundation, I'd travel throughout the Tranquil Breeze Coast, and when I finished that, I'd head to the world beyond this province! Jade Mist Valley, Crimson Flame Peaks, the Emerald Spirit Forest! There were so many places I'd heard about only through hearsay or rumor, and I wanted to see it for myself.

As I moved, my mind spun with ideas of how I could maintain a close relationship with the Verdant Lotus Sect and give back to the community that had given so much to me. Perhaps as a wanderer, I could bring back treasures and knowledge from other faraway regions to the Tranquil Breeze Coast.

The idea excited me. It was a way to stay connected to the sect while following my aspiration. I could venture into the unknown, learn from the vast world, and return with rare herbs, unique cultivation techniques, or even tales of uncharted lands.

"Kai, the rising dragon, flying free across the lands where no young master would dare," I said, trying to inject some humor into my thoughts. Yet, amid this self-assurance, a whisper of doubt crept in. I stopped my movements, standing still in the moonlight, feeling the cool light wash over me. I looked up at the stars, imagining my parents somewhere among them.

"Mother, Father," I whispered, my voice barely more than a breath in the night air. "Am I making the right choice?" The question hung in the air, unanswered.

I didn't expect a reply, nor did I truly believe one would come, but voicing the question felt right. It was a connection to them, a way to share my doubts and hopes. Only silence greeted me, the eternal quiet of the night. I sighed with relief and lingering uncertainty. "Time will tell, I guess."

I turned my gaze back to Tianyi and Windy. Watching them brought a smile to my face. They were reminders of the paths I had already taken, the choices I had made that led me to them.

My thoughts shifted to the immediate challenges ahead. The wager with the Silent Moon Sect was looming, and the Grand Alchemy Gauntlet was an opportunity I couldn't afford to mess up. Otherwise, I'd be proving that girl from the Lian family right! And that would never happen. Both required my full attention, my best effort.

The night wore on, and as my training session came to an end, I felt a sense of accomplishment and clarity. I had made a choice, one that felt true to me, and now it was time to follow through with action.

I whistled softly, calling Tianyi and Windy back to my side. "All right, you two, playtime is over. Let's head back."

Tianyi landed gracefully on my shoulder, her delicate wings fluttering softly, while Windy coiled around my arm, its scales cool against my skin.

The path I had chosen wasn't the easiest, but it was mine, and I was determined to see where it would lead me.

I settled Tianyi and Windy in their respective resting places, ensuring they were comfortable for the night.

Sitting down at the edge of my bed, I took a moment to reflect on everything that had happened. The path of a cultivator was never easy, filled with challenges and decisions that could change the course of one's life. Yet it was also a path of incredible growth, discovery, and most importantly, the freedom to choose one's destiny.

As I lay down, closing my eyes, the events of the day replayed in my mind.

"Tomorrow is another day," I murmured to myself, feeling peaceful despite the uncertainty of the future. I drifted off to sleep, my dreams filled with visions of distant lands, untold adventures, and the endless possibilities that lay ahead.

Time flowed like water, and the leaves transformed from a vibrant green to a rich tapestry of reds and golds, signaling the deepening embrace of autumn.

There was a crispness to the air. With each falling leaf, I found myself more immersed in my cultivation journey, embracing the lessons and challenges that came with each new day.

I was sparring with Han Wei, who volunteered to help me prepare for the duel against the Silent Moon Sect's disciple. As we circled, I compared his style to Li Na's. Her movements were graceful and fluid, while Han Wei's were powerful and focused on palm strikes.

We exchanged strikes, testing each other's defenses. Han Wei favored palm strikes over leg sweeps, unlike Li Na, giving me a slight advantage since I was more prepared for his approach.

As we sparred, I found myself recalling the teachings of Instructor Xia Ji, blending her advice with my own instincts. The Bamboo Reprisal Counter seemed like the perfect response to Han Wei's aggressive style.

I bided my time, waiting for the right moment. Han Wei launched a powerful palm strike toward me. I moved with the blow, using his momentum against him. I twisted my body, ready to deliver a precise kick to his midsection.

*BAMBOO REPRISAL COUNT—*

But just as I was about to connect, a voice called out, "Kai Liu!"

I halted mid-strike, pulling back at the last second. Han Wei stumbled forward, caught off balance by stopping so suddenly.

Turning toward the voice, I saw one of the sect's messengers approaching with urgency. "Lady Xiao Yun has arrived and is expecting you."

I clasped my hands, bowed to Han Wei, and then turned to Instructor Xia Ji. "Instructor, may I have permission to leave training early? I have something I must discuss with the Azure Silk Trading Company."

Instructor Xia Ji glared at me, but I could tell there was no heat behind her stare. "Such a distracted trainee, how will you stand a chance against the Silent Moon Sect like this? Go! However, don't think you can skip out like this tomorrow."

"Many thanks, Instructor Xia Ji. This humble disciple shall never forget the grace you've shown me."

Han Wei perked up, wiping the sweat off his forehead with a grin. "Disciple? Everyone's already heard about your refusal to join the sect. You can't take back words so easily, you know."

I groaned internally. Li Na and Han Wei never let me live it down after learning what happened from Feng Wu. "No, I just wouldn't want to be considered a junior to you and Li Na. Both of you would certainly use your seniority as a way to exploit me."

Reaching down into my pack, I retrieved the new robes I'd bought from the textile shop at Crescent Bay City. If I were to meet Lady Xiao Yun, I'd need to look my best.

"Thank you for waiting, sir," I said to the messenger. "Could you show me where she is?"

"Of course, please follow me," the messenger replied with a polite nod.

As I trailed behind the messenger through the sect's premises, I couldn't help but reflect on how much my life had changed. Just a few months ago, I was a simple village herbalist chasing butterflies, and now I was walking through the halls of the Verdant Lotus Sect, meeting with the daughter of a prominent trading company.

We arrived at a meeting room, where Lady Xiao Yun was seated elegantly alongside her two attendants, Mei Liling and Liang Chen. I recognized them immediately—they were the ones I had negotiated the finer details of my original contract with.

I greeted them with a respectful bow. "Lady Xiao Yun, Mei Liling, Liang Chen, it's an honor to meet with you again."

Lady Xiao Yun smiled warmly. "Kai Liu, you've . . . grown since we last met."

I scratched my head, slightly embarrassed. "Well, I don't think I've gotten much taller," I replied, trying to deflect my nervousness with humor. I guess those tofu and vegan diets at a Taoist sect really did wonders for the growing body.

She laughed softly, like the chime of small bells. "Not in height but in presence. You carry yourself differently now, more like a cultivator than a simple herbalist." Her hair was pinned up neatly, adorned with small jade ornaments that shimmered in the light. Her eyes, sharp and intelligent, seemed to miss nothing.

Her attendants, Mei Liling and Liang Chen, were equally well dressed, though their attires were more subdued, befitting their roles. They sat attentively, one holding a scroll and the other with a writing brush and inkstone at the ready.

"Thank you, Lady Xiao Yun," I said, feeling a bit more at ease. "I wanted to discuss the final shipment of our contract. It's ready to go. But more importantly, I'm interested in what direction we're willing to go forward in the future."

She nodded, her expression turning to one of keen interest. "Of course, Kai Liu. We've been impressed with the quality of your products and the efficiency of your deliveries. Especially despite the . . . *rumors* we've heard concerning your situation."

Did the Silent Moon Sect leak out the fact they made a wager with an herbalist? How did it reach the Azure Silk Trading Company, of all places?!

I listened attentively, already having my plan and answer prepared. However, it was crucial to hear what they had to offer before putting my plan into action.

Mei Liling carefully placed a scroll on the table, unrolling it to reveal the contract extension paper.

"We are prepared to offer an extended contract," Lady Xiao Yun continued. "We're also interested in any new herbal formulas or discoveries you might have. The market is always looking for innovations."

I nodded, looking down at the written contract they offered.

It was time to implement my plan.

"I'm grateful for the opportunity to continue our partnership. However, I have a proposal that might benefit us both even more . . ."

# CHAPTER TWELVE

# Contract Complete

You've piqued my interest," Lady Xiao Yun said, her eyebrow arching gracefully. "Please, share your proposal."

Taking a deep breath, I gathered my thoughts. "Lady Xiao Yun, your offer is generous, and I'm grateful. But I propose we wait to seal our pact until after the Grand Alchemy Gauntlet."

"A bold suggestion, Kai Liu. How does this benefit the Azure Silk Trading Company? We thrive on certainties, not gambles. What's to say this delay won't be our loss?"

"I understand your concern, Lady Xiao Yun. My aim is to elevate both my standing and the company's. A strong showing at the Gauntlet by someone under your patronage will draw attention and enhance your prestige. My success would position us to negotiate a better deal reflecting my enhanced status. It's an investment in potential higher returns for both of us."

She studied me for a long moment, her expression inscrutable. "Your confidence is commendable, but what if your performance falls short of expectations? The risk for us is not insignificant."

I met her gaze firmly. "I'm fully aware of the risks involved. But I also know my capabilities and the effort I'm willing to put in. It's a calculated risk, yes, but one with the potential for significant rewards."

Lady Xiao Yun leaned back, her fingers tapping lightly on the armrest of her chair. The room fell into a thoughtful silence, only broken by the soft rustle of scrolls being shifted by her attendants. "Your assurance speaks volumes. Yet, should the winds not favor us, the gamble could tarnish more than just silver."

Holding her gaze, I let my resolve shine through. "I'm not blind to the stakes at play, nor am I a stranger to the weight of expectations. If you place your trust in me, there is no doubt in my mind that I can be of great value to the Azure Silk Trading Company."

I hoped my request didn't come across as too forward, but I trusted in the strength of my conviction.

After a moment, she nodded, her lips curling into a smile. "Very well, Kai Liu. We'll await the outcome of the Gauntlet. We're intrigued to see how you fare."

Relief washed over me, and I bowed slightly. "Thank you, Lady Xiao Yun. You won't regret this."

With the meeting concluded, I assisted in loading the crate of my goods onto the horse-drawn carriage outside. The crate was heavier than it looked, but I managed to secure it firmly in the carriage.

As I straightened up, wiping the sweat from my brow, Mei Liling approached me, holding a small, intricately designed charm. "Lady Xiao Yun wishes you to have this," she said, extending the charm toward me.

Taking it in my hands, I examined the item. "What is this?"

"It's a charm that will grant you a small discount at any of our branches in the Tranquil Breeze Coast," Lady Xiao Yun explained, stepping closer. "Consider it a token of our faith in your potential and a symbol of our continued interest in your endeavors."

"Thank you, Lady Xiao Yun. I'll treasure this."

As they departed, I received a notification from the Heavenly Interface.

> *Quest: Contract Fulfillment (Production) has been completed.*
> *Due to your status as Interface Manipulator, your rewards will*
> *be adjusted accordingly.*

One of my oddest quests so far. I wondered what it had in store for me.

> *You have now gained access to the feature Binding Oath.*
> *Binding Oath—A feature that allows cultivators to create and enforce*
> *agreements or promises through the Heavenly Interface.*
> *Upon drafting an agreement, both parties must agree to the terms.*
> *Once bound, the penalties for breaking the oath are enforced*
> *by Heaven's Will.*

As the carriage disappeared into the distance, leaving behind a trail of dust, my focus shifted to the new notification from the Heavenly Interface.

The explanation sent a shiver down my spine. "Enforced by Heaven's Will"— the phrase was ominous. I had heard tales of cultivators suffering dire consequences for breaking heavenly oaths, their cultivation bases crippled, or worse, meeting untimely ends shrouded in misfortune.

This is a scary feature! I don't think I want to use this. Unless I came across a powerful cultivator and had to twist his arm into teaching me or something.

Despite the unsettling nature of this feature, I couldn't deny its potential usefulness. In the treacherous world of the Jianghu, where alliances were as fragile as a spider's web, and backstabbing was as common as the morning dew, a tool like this could be invaluable.

*I must use this wisely*, I resolved, storing the information in my mind. The charm from Lady Xiao Yun, now secured in my robe's pocket, reminded me of the intricate web of relationships and agreements that formed the Jianghu.

It was astounding to see how far I had come in just a few weeks.

My Spiritual Herbalism and Nature's Attunement skills had both reached level three after all my classes. Essence Extraction was becoming as natural as breathing, although the ability to extract the essence of metals still eluded me. But I felt as though there was some progress there, as minimal it may be.

Rooted Banyan Stance, now at level two, had become a cornerstone of my physical training. Despite only being a single level, it felt as though my understanding of the technique increased significantly. I could unleash it in quicker intervals, reducing qi usage and lag between offense and defense. Along with it, my Body Refinement had reached level three.

Reading, at level eight, was the most surprising. Comprehension felt easier as long as I took the time to read. Through reading, I expanded my understanding of alchemy, cultivation techniques, and Jianghu lore. At this rate, I'd finish the entire sect's library!

As I scrolled through, a thought struck me. Despite having learned and utilized the Bamboo Reprisal Counter in several spars, it hadn't registered on my interface. This discrepancy puzzled me. Was it an oversight? Or perhaps the Interface only recognized skills when they reached a certain threshold of mastery?

I reflected on the Bamboo Reprisal Counter, recalling the fluidity and precision it required. It was a technique that turned an opponent's strength against them. I had managed to execute it successfully in training, but perhaps the Interface required more consistent application or a deeper understanding of the technique's underlying principles.

I made my way back to the guest quarters to pick up Windy and Tianyi. The two had become quite the celebrities within the sect, especially among the female cultivators. They adored Windy for its unique snow-white scales and beady eyes, though I had to ensure Tianyi kept a close eye on the hatchling to prevent admirers from getting bitten.

I swear I saw Instructor Xia Ji pet Windy during one of my spars, although maybe that was merely a result of Li Na clobbering my skull onto the pavement.

The Verdant Lotus Sect was teeming with life, its forests a natural habitat for Windy to roam and hunt. Since Elder Zhu had given permission, Windy now had full freedom to explore and hunt in the forests. It was fascinating to see how well the hatchling adapted to its surroundings.

I noticed how it had grown significantly in the past weeks, now half the size of my forearm, denser and heavier with each passing day. The moment was fast approaching when Windy would shed its skin for the first time, revealing its gender. The anticipation was exciting, another milestone in our journey together.

I picked up Windy, feeling its weight in my hand. "You're getting heavy, little one," I chuckled as it coiled around my arm with ease. Tianyi fluttered onto my other shoulder, her wings softly brushing against my cheek.

As we reached the edge of the woods, I let Windy down, watching as it slithered into the underbrush, its white scales glinting in the dappled moonlight.

"Be careful, and don't go too far," I called out, knowing Tianyi would keep a watchful eye.

The forest around me was alive with the gentle sounds of nature—the rustling of leaves, the distant hooting of an owl, and the soft rustle of Windy making its way through the underbrush.

My wager with the Silent Moon Sect was in three days.

I couldn't help but reflect on how my thoughts on cultivation had subtly changed ever since I started my training regime here in the Verdant Lotus Sect. The feeling of improving and refining oneself was addicting, and I began to relish it. There was something incredibly satisfying about pushing my limits, feeling my body and mind grow stronger with each passing day.

I walked back to the clearing, where I had set up my training routine for the night. Reaching into my pack, I pulled out a sturdy bag that could be filled with rocks—a makeshift weight to add resistance to my exercises. Courtesy of Li Na's careful instruction, I learned how to make my own bag from canvas and bamboo string. Carefully, I placed the bag on the ground and adjusted the straps, ensuring it was secure.

As I lifted the bag and placed it onto my back, I felt the weight press down on me. But instead of feeling burdened, I felt motivated. Every rep, every push-up was a step toward becoming stronger, toward reaching my full potential.

I got into position for knuckle push-ups, feeling the rough ground beneath my hands. As I began my reps, my thoughts drifted back to the sparring sessions with Li Na and Han Wei. Despite growing stronger, I couldn't derive enjoyment or pleasure from sparring. Fighting hurt, and even when I landed a strike or counter, it didn't fill me with pride.

Deep down, I was thankful I'd never have to wield a blade. I couldn't imagine slicing through someone with a sword, or in someone like Feng Wu's case, a bladed fan. The thought made me nauseous.

"Am I just a coward?" I muttered to myself, pushing through another rep. Despite Li Na and Han Wei's reassurances that I wasn't hurting them, and the dangers of holding back too much during a spar, I couldn't shake off the feeling.

My childhood dreams of beating up young masters seemed so naive now, so far removed from the reality of what fighting truly entailed.

I paused for a moment, catching my breath. The reality was that I much preferred the disciplined process of cultivation and the inner growth that it brought.

As I continued my push-ups, the weight on my back felt lighter, not physically but mentally. I think that acknowledging my reluctance to harm others wasn't a sign of weakness but of empathy. It didn't make me less of a cultivator; it simply meant that my path was different.

The moon hung high in the sky, its light casting long shadows across the clearing. I pushed on, each rep bringing a sense of clarity and purpose. I was not the same person who entered the Verdant Lotus Sect; I was evolving, growing in ways I hadn't imagined.

Continuing my routine, my thoughts drifted to Gentle Wind Village and how my friends would react to my transformation. The children back home would idolize me, and I'd have them call me Supreme Celestial Sovereign of the Eternal Dragon Realm. I imagined the look of surprise on Wang Jun's face when he realized I could now easily outwrestle him. I'd run circles around Elder Ming too. The thought brought a grin to my face.

But more importantly, I wanted to show Elder Ming that I could cultivate on my own without suffering from Qi Deviation. I could almost hear his stern voice cautioning me, yet I knew deep down, he'd be proud. These little thoughts, these snippets of my past, served as fuel, pushing me to strive harder, to become someone they all would be proud of.

I filled the bag with more rocks, adjusting the weight to push my limits further. The added resistance made each rep more challenging, but it also made me stronger. I was not just training my body; I was training my will, my resolve. Another aspect of my training necessary to evolve my Essence Extraction skill.

Once I learned to strengthen my will, Essence Extraction on metal would be as easy as making pork buns!

# CHAPTER THIRTEEN

# Concocting Victory

Kai, we've received the letter from the Silent Moon Sect. They'll be here by tomorrow morning. Are you ready?"

The silence was palpable as Feng Wu delivered the news. Just because I knew the day was coming didn't make it any easier. I took a deep breath and smiled.

"Never better. I'm just hoping I don't bruise their ego too much once I nab the Beast Core from them."

He shook his head. "You ought to watch your words for once in your life . . ."

"Anyway, I need to head to the alchemy pavilion. There's something I need to check on," I said, giving Feng Wu a reassuring pat on the back before setting off.

I clenched and unclenched my fist and sighed, letting go of the tension I was holding in my shoulders. It was time to face the music.

As I meandered through the main halls of the Verdant Lotus Sect, I acknowledged the nods and smiles of various disciples I'd grown familiar with. It's funny how, over time, you start recognizing faces and exchanging silent greetings, a nod here, a smile there.

Reaching the alchemy pavilion, a place I'd come to know well, I entered the room dedicated to student experiments. This room, with its rows of shelves and tables, held alchemical projects in various stages of completion—fermenting, coalescing, distilling.

I walked to the farthest shelf in the back, where my project was stored. There, in a series of carefully labeled vials, was my upgraded version of the Goji Clarity Potion. A culmination of all the lessons and techniques I had absorbed in my classes.

I had added the Mystic Mindroot, an ingredient from Tranquil Breeze Farm. The refining method for it was complex, requiring two full days of preparation.

Under normal circumstances, creating such a potion would be a task for a second-class disciple, someone with the ability to create alchemical array formations to purify its essence. But thanks to my skill, Essence Extraction, I could simulate the effects of an alchemical array and purify it directly. It was an unconventional method, but it worked.

The potion itself was a deep, rich color, almost like liquid ruby. The essence of the goji berries had been enhanced with the properties of the Mystic Mindroot, creating a synergistic effect. The result was a potion that sharpened the mind and harmonized the body's qi flow.

I picked up a vial, holding it to the light. This potion was the result of countless hours of study and could significantly enhance a cultivator's abilities in battle. "I'll call this the Celestial Mind Illuminating Elixir," I said, feeling pride at my naming capabilities.

As I looked at the second set of vials lined up next to my Celestial Mind Illuminating Elixir, I couldn't help but feel a surge of accomplishment. These vials contained my latest creation—an advanced version of the Invigorating Dawn Tonic.

The essence of ginger still formed the base of this new recipe, but I needed something more potent than the Morning Dew Herb to elevate its effects. My breakthrough came during Advanced Herbology, where I learned of a grass with remarkable properties, the Sunfire Blade Grass, an herb that radiated yang qi.

Integrating it into the Invigorating Dawn Tonic transformed it from a mere fatigue reliever to a potion that significantly boosted one's physical capabilities by infusing the body with a strong influx of yang qi. However, this transformation wasn't straightforward. The potent nature of the Sunfire Blade Grass meant it could easily overpower the other ingredients, leading to an unstable concoction.

The inclusion of Moonbeam Petals and Nightshade Flowers, both known for their calming qi properties, created a balance with the intense yang qi of the Sunfire Blade Grass. This was crucial to ensure that its consumption wouldn't overwhelm my system. My qi circulatory system was more . . . *delicate* than other people's, so if I wanted to use it, I'd have to be extra careful.

"And thus, I have created Ambrosia of Radiant Dawn." I cackled maniacally to myself.

It had taken *days* to come up with a plausible recipe. Spending hours in the library, finding potions of similar effect that I could create on my own time, with ingredients priced where they wouldn't leave me in financial ruin . . . It was quite a lot to deal with alongside my already-rigorous training routine.

As I secured the last vial of Ambrosia of Radiant Dawn, a sense of anticipation stirred within me. These two potions—the Celestial Mind Illuminating Elixir and Ambrosia of Radiant Dawn—they were my trump cards for the upcoming duel with the Silent Moon Sect.

By focusing on temporary, potent effects rather than long-term benefits, I granted these concoctions an unprecedented level of flexibility and power. This approach was exactly what I needed for the duel—a situation where each moment could tilt the balance between victory and defeat.

The Silent Moon Sect's open disdain for me, their underestimation of a mere herbalist, was a gap I intended to exploit. With these potions, I would cement myself as a legend by landing a hit—no, by *beating* a third-class disciple of the Silent Moon Sect!

Eager to test the full extent of these potions, I decided to find Feng Wu. He was one of the few I could trust to spar with me at full strength, without holding back. Navigating through the sect's pathways, I kept an eye out for his familiar figure.

As I searched, I approached another disciple, one of the second-class disciples, and asked him if he had seen the man. "Looking for Feng Wu? He's tied up with an elder's tasks right now. Anything I can help with?"

I recognized him. Lan Sheng, one of the regular patrols at the mission chamber, who I knew from my training with Instructor Xia Ji. He was one of the few second-class disciples I have grown acquainted with aside from Feng Wu. "Lan Sheng, I've brewed up a couple of performance-boosting potions. I wanted to test them out in a spar. I was hoping Feng Wu could help me gauge their effectiveness."

Lan Sheng's eyes widened with intrigue. They quickly narrowed, and he let out a curious smile. "Performance-boosting potions, you say? That sounds quite interesting. I might not be Feng Wu, but I can hold my own in a spar. How about I stand in for him?"

"That would be great, Lan Sheng. Thank you."

We made our way to the training grounds, an open space surrounded by fallen autumn leaves. As we prepared, I explained the effects of both potions. Lan Sheng listened intently, nodding in understanding. He was also in my Alchemy Array Crafting class, so he was well versed in the technical jargon I talked about. Li Na and Han Wei weren't too interested when I rambled on for too long.

"I'll start with the Celestial Mind Illuminating Elixir," I said, uncorking the vial. I downed it in one gulp, feeling its effects almost immediately. My mind sharpened, my senses heightened. I could see every detail of Lan Sheng's figure, down to his pores. My eyes strained under the load and narrowed themselves instinctively. This would take some time to get used to.

Next, I took out the Ambrosia of Radiant Dawn. With a deep breath, I drank it, feeling a surge of energy coursing through my veins. The heat went down my esophagus and settled within my stomach, spreading evenly throughout my meridians. I exhaled slightly, half expecting steam to come out.

Lan Sheng observed me closely. "Let's see how they fare in action. I'll give you the first three moves."

The man took on the first stance of the Lotus Palm, although it seemed more rigid than Feng Wu. At this point, I'd analyzed the man within my Memory Palace technique so often I could mimic it with my eyes closed. Feng Wu's posture was more languid, at ease. But that didn't make him better. Lan Sheng and Feng Wu were both in the same generation of disciples, after all. I'd need to hold him in the same regard.

Seeing no choice but to advance, I burst forward on the offensive. I charged toward Lan Sheng, my mind racing ahead of my body.

My first move was a feint—a swift jab at his torso, intended to draw his guard down. Lan Sheng, however, was unfazed. His eyes, sharp and focused, followed my movements with a calm precision. As expected, he easily parried my strike.

"Not bad, Kai, but you'll have to do better than that," Lan Sheng said, his voice calm and collected.

I nodded, acknowledging his skill. The Ambrosia of Radiant Dawn had supercharged my body, infusing me with a strength and agility I had never experienced before. I felt I could take on the world, but Lan Sheng was no ordinary opponent.

I lunged forward again, attempting a sweeping low kick aimed at his ankles. Lan Sheng's reaction was swift. He sidestepped, avoiding my attack with an ease that spoke of years of training and experience. My next move was a combination— quick succession of punches aimed at various points, trying to break through his defense. But Lan Sheng was like a fortress, his blocks and parries a dance of martial prowess.

Then he spoke with a steadiness in his voice. "My turn now, Kai."

Lan Sheng shifted into offense, his palms moving in a blur. The strikes were light but fast, each a test of my reflexes. I dodged and weaved, barely keeping up with his assault. His style was fluid, each movement seamlessly flowing into the next.

Then came the feint—a series of palm strikes that forced me to backpedal, only to realize it was a setup for a leg sweep. My heightened senses caught the shift in his stance, the subtle transfer of weight. I stepped back but still got clipped on one leg, throwing me off balance.

I stumbled, rolling awkwardly to avoid a follow-up strike aimed at my chest. The roll was far from graceful. I managed to get back on my feet, panting slightly from the exertion.

Compared to me, Lan Sheng seemed unruffled. His hair, tied neatly in a bun, didn't have a single strand out of place.

"Would you like to continue, Kai?"

I nodded, trying to slow down my heart rate with deep breaths. "Yes. Please humor this junior. I'd like to see the full extent of my potions."

He chuckled. "Very well, let's see how far you can push yourself."

Lan Sheng's fighting style was a stark contrast to Feng Wu's. While Feng Wu waited for openings and struck with precision, Lan Sheng was a relentless storm of deceptive strikes, making it difficult to predict his next move. He wasn't toying with me; he simply enjoyed pushing me to my limits.

He threw a barrage of strikes, each one casual but packed with intent. It was a dance of feints and real attacks, testing my reaction and adaptability. Despite my enhanced senses and agility from the potions, I struggled to keep up. Lan Sheng outsmarted me, depleting my mental energy rapidly. As the effects of the Celestial Mind Illuminating Elixir waned, my heightened awareness slipped away, and his strikes became harder to anticipate. The physical boost from the Ambrosia of Radiant Dawn wasn't enough.

In desperation, I switched tactics, grounding myself in the Rooted Banyan Stance and channeling qi to harden my muscles. I took his palm thrust head-on, absorbing the impact. Surprised but quick to adjust, he dodged my punch and delivered a kick to my midsection, sending me crashing into a pile of leaves.

The effects of the Ambrosia of Radiant Dawn faded. I groaned in pain, feeling a headache, fatigue, and soreness from the impact. The ground beneath me seemed to spin as I tried to catch my breath.

Lan Sheng offered me a hand, helping me to my feet. "I've seen your spars against the third-class disciples. Those potions of yours truly made a difference in performance."

"Enough to beat Li Na or Han Wei, perhaps?"

"But you gotta remember, these potions are crutches. Don't get too reliant on them. Considering the drawbacks, you may even have to consider whether it's worth fighting with it or not if you expect the match to be a prolonged one."

I didn't particularly appreciate how he deflected my question, but I nodded. He was right, relying on my potions wasn't a long-term solution. But I thought it'd be better than nothing. Perhaps I should leave it as a trump card if the battle becomes a prolonged one.

Lan Sheng continued, sounding like a mentor, "Moreover, your style is too straightforward, Kai. In a real battle, predictability is a weakness. You need to mix things up, and deviate from your normal pattern now and then."

I listened intently, absorbing his advice. Lan Sheng was experienced, and his insights were invaluable.

"Surprise is a weapon in itself. For instance, use your environment to your advantage, or feint with one technique and switch to another unexpectedly. I remember during a spar against Instructor Xia Ji, she'd . . ." He demonstrated a few examples, showing how a simple change in rhythm or an unexpected move could throw off an opponent.

We spent the next few hours discussing various techniques and ideas, with Lan Sheng pointing out nuances and strategies I hadn't considered before. The sun began to set, casting long shadows across the training ground, which was littered with a carpet of fallen leaves.

As we wrapped up, Lan Sheng flashed a mischievous grin. "Now, for helping you with this spar, how about you help me with something in return? Instructor Xia Ji usually has me sweep this training ground. Care to take over for today?"

I chuckled, realizing this was likely his plan all along. "Sure, I owe you one." I grabbed a broom and started sweeping the leaves, which seemed to have fallen in greater numbers than usual. The ground was covered in a thick layer of autumn colors due to the Verdant Lotus Sect's lush surroundings. "Use the surroundings to my advantage, huh?"

My gaze flicked over the training ground, taking in the dense foliage and the abundance of leaves. I swept them away, revealing firmly packed dirt. This environment could be an advantage. It was unconventional, but that was precisely what Lan Sheng had advised—thinking outside the box. I could use the leaves for concealment, create distractions, or even . . .

A plan began to form in my mind, one that could turn the tables in the upcoming duel. The Silent Moon Sect was expecting a straightforward fight, but I would give them something unexpected.

As the moonlight waned overhead, I worked tirelessly to bring my plans to fruition.

# CHAPTER FOURTEEN

# The Silent Moon's Arrival

The early-morning air was cool and crisp, the kind that sent a slight shiver down my spine but somehow felt refreshing at the same time. I stood among the throng of disciples, all of us lined up in a somewhat-formal array as we awaited the arrival of the Silent Moon Sect.

*It's just another day*, I kept thinking, like it was a mantra, but the butterflies in my stomach seemed to disagree. Despite all my mental exercises and preparation, the anxiety was like a stubborn stain, refusing to be scrubbed away.

Elder Zhu stood at the forefront. As the Silent Moon disciples approached, led by Elder Jun, the atmosphere tensed, charged with an unspoken rivalry.

Their words were cordial, laced with the kind of politeness that had more layers than the most intricate pastry. Yet, beneath the surface, there was a subtle verbal spar, a battle of wits and veiled barbs.

Elder Jun's voice was smooth as he said, "Elder Zhu, your hospitality is as renowned as the Verdant Lotus Sect's prowess in alchemy. We are eager to witness the fruits of such *esteemed* teachings."

Elder Zhu replied with a polite smile, but his eyes were sharp. "And we are equally eager to see the talents that the Silent Moon Sect is so proud of. I trust your journey here was comfortable."

It was like watching a dance, each word a step, measured and precise. I scanned the Silent Moon disciples, trying to gauge who my opponent might be. Each carried themselves with a confidence that bordered on arrogance. It was hard to guess who might step into the ring against me.

*Why can't I shake this anxiety?* I thought, chastising myself. *I should be stronger than this, more resolute.* But knowing and feeling were two different things, and as much as I knew I was prepared, my heart still refused to listen.

As we entered the dining hall, a hush fell over the crowd, slicing through my contemplation like a blade. In my lapse of attention, I suddenly found myself face-to-face with Xu Ziqing.

His presence was distinct, his demeanor like an unsheathed sword among the throng of disciples. My previous encounters with him flashed in my mind, a stark reminder of the chasm that once existed between us. And yet, standing here now, that chasm felt even wider. Even after all my training, nothing had changed.

"What do you want?" I asked.

His lips curled into a half smile. "I want to see the Beast Core," he said. "The prize of our sect's wager."

I hesitated for a moment before retrieving the core from my robe. As I handed it to him, I couldn't help but whisper, "Ironically, it seems the Silent Moon Sect will get back what they lost after all. So much for honor."

"Elder Jun's magnanimity is the only thing that stopped us from taking it by force. You should be grateful for his mercy."

Before I could reply, Elder Jun stepped in with a sardonic smile on his crooked face. "Enough, Xu Ziqing. There's no need to show such animosity toward a mere herbalist. It would be quite unfair to disrupt him before such an important trial."

As they turned away, I caught Xu Ziqing's gaze again. Surprisingly, there was no malice, only a complex web of emotions. As if his earlier words were just a facade. I shook my head; this wasn't the time to decipher his actions.

Li Na and Han Wei stood by me, shoulder to shoulder.

"Don't listen to him, Kai. They're just trying to provoke you," Han Wei said, giving me a reassuring pat on the back.

I watched as Xu Ziqing gave the Beast Core to Elder Jun, who examined it with the discerning eye of a seasoned cultivator. The core, a symbol of our wager, gleamed ominously in the morning light. Elder Jun then handed it over to Elder Zhu with a remark that dripped with insinuation. "We trust the honorable Verdant Lotus Sect will judge this contest without bias?"

Elder Zhu simply nodded, accepting the responsibility without a hint of agitation.

As the Silent Moon disciples settled for their meal, I found myself alongside Feng Wu, away from the main gathering. He had heard about my spar with Lan Sheng.

"Sticking to your strengths is important, Kai," Feng Wu said in his usual calm tone. "But knowing when to use those potions is crucial. I trust you understand this?"

I nodded, letting his words sink in. "I do, but I can't shake off this nervousness. It's like a shadow I can't outrun."

Feng Wu offered a reassuring smile. "Fear isn't inherently bad, Kai. Remember: 'A hundred refinings make pure steel.' Each trial you face is a step toward becoming stronger, more resilient."

His words were a balm to my anxious mind. I wished Tianyi and Windy were here with me, their presence always brought a sense of peace. But I knew better than to bring them into the spotlight, especially with the Silent Moon Sect around.

"Kai, remember the spar we had last week?" Li Na began, a small smile playing on her lips. "You managed to counter my Lotus Strike, something I didn't see coming at all. Your growth is amazing. You've come a long way, and you have the skills to prove it."

Her words, direct and sincere, cut through the fog of my anxiety. Li Na wasn't one to give empty praise; her acknowledgment of my progress was a testament to the efforts I'd put into my training.

Before I could fully soak in what Li Na had said, Han Wei chimed in. "If you can keep me on my toes, I'm sure you'll give the Silent Moon Sect more than just a run for their money," he teased.

"Thanks, you two," I managed, feeling the knot of apprehension in my stomach loosen slightly. "I'll make sure not to disappoint."

I glanced over at the Silent Moon disciples, trying to gauge my potential opponent. The order in which they sat was telling—Elder Jun at the head of the table, flanked by Xu Ziqing and a bald, muscular senior disciple whose with a commanding presence. Even with his back turned, I could see the other disciples were wary of him, aside from Xu Ziqing and Elder Jun. The hierarchy was clear, and the third-class disciples adhered to it with almost religious fervor.

It was quite different from what I was used to here in the Verdant Lotus Sect. Although each generation stuck to their respective groups, there was no strict hierarchy like this.

*One of them will be stepping into the ring with me,* I thought. To ease my nerves, I began to pick apart their looks and traits in my mind, a sort of mental game to psych myself up.

*That one with the scar across his cheek, he looks like he's seen a few too many brawls. And the one with the hawk-like eyes, I bet he's quick.* My internal commentary brought a faint smile to my face. It was a silly exercise, but it helped ease the tension of the moment.

My gaze first fell on a tall, lean disciple who appeared focused. *A quick one, probably relies on speed,* I thought, recalling Instructor Xia Ji's advice on countering swift opponents. *Rooted Banyan Stance could offset his agility, keeping me grounded and stable.*

Another caught my attention, this one broader and heavily muscled. He reminded me of Wang Jun if he'd turned to a life of banditry. *Strength-based fighter,* I surmised. *Likely to favor brute force over finesse.* I remembered Lan Sheng's teachings about unpredictability. *I'll need to be agile, strike at the right moment, and avoid direct confrontations of strength.*

Each observation, each mental note, built a strategy in my mind. I felt my confidence slowly returning as I applied the lessons I had learned. *Know your opponent, know yourself,* I thought, recalling Elders Zhu and Ming's teachings.

This mental exercise, categorizing and strategizing, was more than just a distraction from my nerves. I might not be the strongest or the fastest, but I had knowledge, cunning, and the element of surprise on my side.

As the Silent Moon Sect finished their meal, Elder Jun signaled for his disciples to prepare for the duel. "Lead the way," he said, his authority clear. The Silent Moon Sect's organization was indeed militaristic, each member moving with careful discipline.

I followed the procession toward the alchemy pavilion, a place I had become all too familiar with. I noticed it was already half-full. The practical arrangement of the room allowed an unobstructed view for everyone.

Elder Zhu then took center stage, explaining the proceedings of the alchemy duel to the Silent Moon Sect, now seated in the audience. The encirclement was a clean split between green and blue robes.

"To ensure fairness," he began, "we will select the recipe for the contest from this bowl." He gestured to a ceramic bowl containing scrolls of various recipes.

Xu Ziqing voiced a concern that matched the tension in the air. "How can we be assured that the recipe chosen will not be one tailored to the strengths of the Verdant Lotus Sect?"

Elder Zhu's response was calm and measured. "The recipes selected for this bowl are recognized and utilized by any sect with a dedicated alchemy pavilion. They are foundational concoctions that any trained alchemist should be familiar with, regardless of their sect's specific focus."

With the air of clarity restored, Elder Jun was invited to draw a scroll from the bowl. The room held its breath, the rustle of the parchment sounding unnaturally loud in the hushed anticipation. He narrowed his eyes before opening his mouth. "The contest will revolve around the crafting of the Soothing Spirit Pill," he announced, unraveling the scroll to reveal the recipe.

A wave of relief washed over me as I recognized the name. A basic concoction known for its effectiveness in aiding cultivation recovery and mending minor qi disruptions. It was a pill I had practiced with numerous times in my Pill Concoction class. Although I didn't need to use it or make it for myself, largely due to the effects of Tianyi's presence being superior to the pill in every way possible.

Elder Zhu then proceeded to detail the criteria for the bout's judgment. "The outcome of each concoction will be evaluated based on its potency, quality, and purity. These are the pillars upon which the art of alchemy stands, and they shall guide us in determining the victor."

The atmosphere in the pavilion shifted as preparations for the contest began in earnest. The tables were set with an array of alchemy ingredients, each more vibrant and potent than the last, alongside the necessary tools and a basic pill furnace at each station. The seating arrangement for the audience was circular, enveloping the contest area in a ring of eager anticipation. Luxurious seats were designated for the elders, while the rest of them found places among the simpler seating that fanned out from the center.

Elder Zhu's voice cut through the murmurs of the crowd as he called me to step forward. "And who shall represent the Silent Moon Sect in this contest?"

I approached the center, the sect's expectations resting firmly on my shoulders.

Elder Jun stood, commanding the room's attention as he spoke. "In the spirit of fairness, and not to crush a budding flower with a mountain's weight, we shall present our fledgling disciple to partake in both the alchemy and martial bouts. Ping Hai, please come forward."

The name Ping Hai, which sounded gentle and almost poetic, seemed out of place in the militaristic ambiance of the Silent Moon Sect. I glanced toward the disciple I had pegged as the youngest and most nervous among them, half expecting him to be the one called upon. He, however, remained still, his gaze fixated elsewhere, oblivious to Elder Jun's summons.

Confusion knitted my brow as I followed his line of sight, only for my eyes to widen in disbelief when the *real* Ping Hai began to rise from his seat. It wasn't the nervous-looking disciple I had mistaken for Ping Hai but rather the bald, imposing figure who had been sitting across Xu Ziqing in the dining hall.

My jaw nearly hit the floor as Ping Hai stood, his towering form casting a shadow that felt like it extended across the entire pavilion. The ground didn't actually rumble as he walked toward me, but the sheer force of his presence made it feel as though it should. My earlier attempts at boosting my confidence quickly evaporated.

Ping Hai's muscles seemed to bulge against the fabric of his robes, straining the material as if threatening to burst free at any moment. His neck was so thick it looked like it could withstand a direct hit from a battering ram, and his height . . . By the heavens, he was so tall he even dwarfed Wang Jun and Master Qiang from back home, and those two were giants in their own right.

Were those scars along his knuckles? Or was the fear creating hallucinations within my mind?

As Ping Hai approached, he stared me down. My mind raced, trying to reconcile the gentle name of Ping Hai with the mountain of a man who was now approaching. *This is the Silent Moon Sect's idea of grace?!* I swallowed hard, my previous observations of the Silent Moon disciples now seeming trivial and naive in comparison to the reality standing before me.

"Greetings," he rumbled, like a distant thunderstorm, deep and resonant. "I am Ping Hai, a third-class disciple of the Silent Moon Sect. It's an honor to meet you."

"I am Kai Liu. It is an honor . . ." I responded, trying not to look as startled as I felt.

And just like that, I received a notification from the Heavenly Interface that solidified my death sentence.

*Quest: Eclipse the Silent Moon*
*—Triumph over Ping Hai in an Alchemy Duel. (0/1)*
*—Land one strike against Ping Hai in a Martial Contest. (0/1)*

# CHAPTER FIFTEEN

# When Giants Grasp the Delicate

I looked back and forth between Elder Jun and Ping Hai, dismissing the notification from the Heavenly Interface. Was this some sort of sick joke? What was that whole thing he said about not crushing a budding flower with a mountain's weight? This was worse! Elder Jun was trying to crush the flower underfoot and salt the earth so life wouldn't sprout from where it grew!

Elder Zhu coughed into his fist, catching everybody's attention. "Let us begin the alchemy bout. Ping Hai of the Silent Moon Sect and Kai Liu of the Verdant Lotus Sect will have one hour to concoct the Soothing Spirit Pill. All necessary ingredients and tools have been provided at your stations."

My throat constricted as if gripped by an invisible hand, making it hard to swallow. Despite the reassuring glances from Li Na and the others, a shiver traced its way down my spine at the thought of Ping Hai across the arena.

Elder Zhu turned over a small ornate hourglass, its sands beginning to slip through the narrow passage. "The contest begins now."

Taking a deep breath, I tried to channel a sense of calm, to regain the composure I knew was essential for the delicate work of alchemy. The recipe unfurled in my mind. I meticulously checked the ingredients arrayed before me, ensuring everything was in order.

The hustle and bustle of the pavilion faded into the background as I focused. My hands moved with practiced ease, measuring and mixing with the precision of a seasoned alchemist. Yet, despite my concentration, curiosity got the better of me. I couldn't help but steal a glance across the table at Ping Hai.

To my surprise, Ping Hai seemed out of his element. His large and calloused hands fumbled with the delicate alchemy tools, and his brow furrowed as he pored over the recipe. It was an odd sight, the mountain of a man struggling with tasks that required a gentler touch.

His attempts to measure the correct amounts of ingredients were clumsy, and his manipulation of the alchemy tools was awkward at best. I couldn't help but feel a twinge of sympathy for him. Alchemy, after all, was an art that demanded finesse and a delicate touch, qualities that seemed at odds with Ping Hai's formidable physical presence.

From the stands, soft murmurs reached my ears, and I saw a few of Ping Hai's fellow third-class disciples leaning forward, their expressions a mix of concern and encouragement. They began to gesture subtly, offering silent advice and guidance to their struggling comrade. Ping Hai glanced their way, trying to adjust his technique based on their silent cues.

I found myself torn. On one hand, this felt like a breach of the bout's integrity. But on the other, calling it out seemed petty, especially given Ping Hai's clear disadvantage. With a mental shrug, I turned my attention back to my work, pushing aside any thoughts of the fairness of the bout. The familiar motions of grinding, mixing, and heating were soothing, a welcome distraction from the tension of the competition.

As I worked, I couldn't help but steal occasional glances at Ping Hai. Despite the assistance from his peers, his progress was slow, and his movements were uncertain. It was clear that alchemy was not his forte, and I wondered again why the Silent Moon Sect had chosen him for this part of the contest. Was there some deeper strategy at play, or was it simply a matter of pride, a way to demonstrate their confidence in their ability to win in the martial bout, regardless of where it takes place?

My thoughts were interrupted as I carefully added the final ingredient to the mixture. The subtle shift in color and consistency indicated that the reaction was proceeding as expected. I allowed myself a small smile of satisfaction. Despite the distractions, my concoction was coming together nicely.

With precise movements, I transferred the mixture to the pill furnace. The final steps required patience and a steady hand, qualities I had honed over countless hours. As I channeled my qi, I looked to my friends in the stands. Feng Wu smiled approvingly, while Li Na and Han Wei both pumped their fists in quiet encouragement.

My eyes couldn't help but drift toward Xu Ziqing. He seemed almost bored with the proceedings, his eyes closed and arms crossed as if the outcome of this alchemy bout was of no consequence to him.

Turning my gaze to Elder Jun, I found his expression unreadably calm. Despite the clear advantage I held in this alchemy bout, Elder Jun's demeanor betrayed no sign of concern or disappointment. It was as if he had anticipated this outcome, or perhaps the alchemy bout was merely a prelude to a larger scheme I wasn't privy to.

My attention then shifted back to Ping Hai, who was now trying to mix the ingredients together with a spoon that looked comically small in his massive hand.

The sight was almost amusing, and for a brief moment, my anxiety about the upcoming sparring match dissipated, replaced by a flicker of amusement at the incongruous image before me.

However, my momentary distraction proved costly. My concentration faltered, and the cycle of my qi within the pill furnace became erratic, disrupting the delicate balance needed to form the pill. Cursing under my breath, I hastily corrected the flow before it could get worse. *Focus, Kai*, I chided myself. *You can't afford such lapses, especially now.*

With the pill furnace once again under control, I carefully extracted the powdery substance, noting the slight imperfections caused by my earlier distraction. I took a deep breath, channeling my frustration into focus, and began shaping the powder into pills with meticulous care, ensuring each one was as close to perfect as possible under the circumstances.

As the final pill settled onto the tray with a soft clink, my clenched fists relaxed ever so slightly at the sound. The familiar scent of herbs and the faint trace of fire, filled my lungs, grounding me in the moment.

*This is just another challenge. And like the others, I will find a way to overcome it.*

Glancing over at Ping Hai, I saw that he was still struggling with the recipe. No matter how a turtle may twist its body, it couldn't imitate the brilliance of a peacock. His strengths lay in another area.

It made me wonder again about the Silent Moon Sect's strategy. Did they not care about the outcome of the alchemy bout, focusing all their attention on the martial contest instead?

With nothing left to do but wait, I stepped back from my table, watching as Ping Hai continued his painstaking work. Elder Jun remained unfazed, his expression giving nothing away. It was a curious situation, one that left more questions than answers.

The sands in the hourglass dwindled, showing the fleeting time that Ping Hai had to finish his concoction. I watched him awkwardly maneuver around the furnace. His mixture, now ready, was of noticeably poorer quality compared to mine, lacking the refined consistency essential for the perfect Soothing Spirit Pill.

Shaping the powder into pills required a technique that balanced finesse with precision, a skill that seemed at odds with Ping Hai's brute physique. I wondered how he'd go about it.

He scooped a portion of the powder, his hand dwarfing the spoon, and then, with a motion that seemed too crude for the task at hand, he clenched his fist tight.

*Eh?*

The muscles in his forearm bulged, veins popping out like cords under his skin, as he subjected the powder to a pressure I could scarcely imagine.

I stood, mouth agape, as he opened his hand to reveal the result. There, sitting in the center of his palm, was a pill. It was misshapen, far from the perfect sphere expected of a Soothing Spirit Pill, yet its solidity was undeniable. It fell to his tray with a clunk that resonated through the silent pavilion.

A shiver ran down my spine as the implications of Ping Hai's raw strength became painfully clear. The ease with which he had compacted the powder into a solid form was terrifying. If his grip could do that to alchemy ingredients, what would it do to flesh and bone? *My* flesh and bone!

My gaze flickered between the misshapen pill and Ping Hai's impassive face. The casual display of strength was a reminder of the physical disparity between us. A part of me couldn't help but marvel at the sheer physicality he brought to the delicate art of alchemy.

Different people truly had different approaches.

The crowd murmured, a mix of astonishment and disbelief at the unconventional method Ping Hai employed. I could see Elder Jun from the corner of my eye, his expression unchanged, as if this brute-force approach to alchemy was exactly what he had expected from Ping Hai.

I forced myself to look away, to focus on my own set of perfectly shaped pills, trying to anchor myself to the task at hand. Yet the sight of Ping Hai's makeshift alchemy haunted me, a prelude to the daunting physical contest that lay ahead.

"Time's up!"

As Ping Hai finished his last pill, the room fell into a tense silence, all eyes on the two sets of pills before us. The contrast couldn't have been starker—mine shaped with precision, and Ping Hai's forged by sheer force.

Elder Zhu stepped forward to inspect our work, his experienced eyes assessing the quality of our pills. The tension in the room was palpable, the outcome of this bout seemingly clear, yet overshadowed by the impending martial contest.

His examination began with my set of Soothing Spirit Pills, his keen gaze scrutinizing every detail. The moment felt stretched as he picked up one of my pills between his thumb and forefinger.

"Let's review the parameters of this contest," Elder Zhu started, his voice carrying across the silent pavilion. "Potency, quality, and consistency are key." He pressed the pill lightly, and to my dismay, it crumbled slightly under the pressure, revealing some uneven clumping within.

"While the potency of this pill is intact, the inconsistency in its composition could slightly affect its efficacy," Elder Zhu commented, his critique pinpointing the very mistake that had slipped through my focused efforts. A flush of embarrassment warmed my cheeks as I mentally kicked myself for the lapse in attention that had led to this minor flaw.

The room's attention then shifted to Ping Hai's work, the anticipation palpable. Elder Zhu's expression remained neutral as he examined the rough-hewn pills, the result of Ping Hai's unconventional method. The quality, as expected, was far from ideal, the pills lacking the refined texture and uniformity typical of a well-crafted Soothing Spirit Pill.

Elder Zhu's attempt to crumble one of Ping Hai's pills was telling; he had to exert a noticeable amount of force to break it apart, showcasing its dense packing—a direct result of Ping Hai's brute strength. The towering man seemed to shrink slightly under the weight of the elder's unimpressed scrutiny, his head bowing in a display of shame.

With the examination concluded, Elder Zhu faced the audience. "In this alchemy bout, while both contestants showed commendable effort, the victory goes to Kai Liu for a closer adherence to the criteria set forth." He then added, "As the victor, Kai Liu will have the privilege of deciding the location for the upcoming martial bout. Are there any objections?"

Everyone turned to Elder Jun, whose calm demeanor hadn't wavered. He merely nodded, an almost imperceptible smile playing on his lips, as if the unfolding events were aligning perfectly with some unseen plan.

Applause and cheers broke out among the disciples of the Verdant Lotus Sect, their support a balm to my frazzled nerves. Among the Silent Moon Sect's third-class disciples, expressions of disbelief and disappointment were starkly evident. Yet, amid the celebration, a low mutter from Ping Hai reached my ears.

"Honor lost must be reclaimed, no matter the cost. The next match will be my redemption." His forehead veins were pronounced despite him facing away from me, and some of the Silent Moon Sect disciples flinched as he walked in their general direction.

I looked up into the pavilion's ceiling, and a lone tear shed down my cheek.

Was this the will of the heavens? To snuff out the rising star of Kai Liu with the wrath of the mountain known as Ping Hai?

The words, intended or not for my ears, sent a fresh wave of terror through me. The raw power I had witnessed, now paired with his vow of redemption, painted a daunting picture of what awaited me in the sparring ring.

My mind raced with wild thoughts, desperate for any escape from the impending confrontation. *Could I feign illness, perhaps a sudden bout of Qi Deviation?* I mused, only half-serious.

"Kai, as the victor of the bout, where would you like the sparring match to take place?"

I took a deep breath, realizing I couldn't make any more excuses. The training grounds came to the forefront of my thoughts. It was not just a familiar setting; it was a terrain I had analyzed meticulously, especially last night, planning for any possible advantage it might offer against a formidable opponent like Ping Hai.

Straightening my posture, I met his expectant gaze. "I would like the martial bout to take place in the training grounds of the Verdant Lotus Sect." I noticed the third-class disciples exchanging glances. Several of them looked at me with a mix of disdain and arrogance.

Xu Ziqing and Elder Jun, however, remained composed, their faces betraying none of the anxiety that gripped me. Their confidence was unsettling; as if the choice of location was of little consequence to the outcome they anticipated.

But now it was time to reap what I sowed.

*Quest: Eclipse the Silent Moon*
*—Triumph over Ping Hai in an Alchemy Duel. (1/1)*
*—Land one strike against Ping Hai in a Martial Contest. (0/1)*

# CHAPTER SIXTEEN

# Three Steps to Clash

The path to the training grounds felt longer than usual, each step heavy with the weight of the impending duel. The chatter and laughter of the Verdant Lotus Sect disciples, enthused by my victory, did little to lighten the mood.

"Why so glum, Kai? You look like a cow being led to the slaughterhouse," Han Wei teased and nudged me with an elbow that felt more like a jab to my already-fraying nerves.

I shot him a wry look, attempting to muster some semblance of wit under the circumstances. "Oh, I don't know, Han Wei. How would you feel if you were in my shoes, matched up against a walking fortress?"

Lan Sheng chimed in. "It's not entirely impossible to beat him, you know."

That gave me some hope. Although Ping Hai was a monster in my eyes, surely the second-class disciples could see some way to defeat him. Right?

Meanwhile, Feng Wu, steadfast and serene as ever, walked beside us, his calm presence a grounding force amid the rising storm of my anxiety. "Indeed, every opponent has a weakness."

"Sure, he's got the build of a small mountain, but mountains move slowly, right?" Lan Sheng continued, seeming to aim for some casualness but landing squarely in the "not helping" territory. "And yeah, he might have the strength to uproot trees, but who needs to uproot trees in a duel? It's all about speed and wit!"

Feng Wu was the embodiment of calm in the storm of Lan Sheng's encouragement. His serene demeanor a stark contrast to the escalating panic Lan Sheng's words were sowing in my mind.

"And endurance . . . I mean, I've heard the whispers from the other Silent Moon disciples. Apparently he can fight for hours without breaking a sweat, but a duel is short, right? No need for endurance when you're sprinting!" Lan Sheng was blissfully unaware of the images of an unstoppable, tireless juggernaut he was painting in my head.

Just as I was about to be swallowed whole by the horrifying picture he was so cheerfully sketching, Feng Wu's patience had evidently been worn thin. "Lan Sheng, perhaps that's enough 'reassurance' for now." He had an uncharacteristic edge that immediately silenced the disciple.

Then Li Na stepped in like a breath of fresh air. She punched my shoulder, lightly but with enough force to snap me out of my stupor. "Come on, Kai. You've got something Ping Hai will never have." Her conviction was hard to ignore.

"And what's that?" I asked, genuinely curious and clinging to any sliver of hope I could.

Her smile broadened. "Us. He might be a mountain, but even mountains can't stand alone against a storm. And we'll be the gale-force winds at your back."

She eased away at my fears. The realization that I wasn't going into this battle alone—that I had friends who believed in me, ready to support me in any way they could—ignited a spark of courage within me. Now buoyed by Li Na's words, I couldn't help but let out a soft chuckle, the tension in my shoulders easing just slightly. "So, you'll all be in the match with me, fending off Ping Hai?"

Li Na and Han Wei seemed to suddenly find the path beneath our feet fascinating. The silence that followed, punctuated by their lack of eye contact, spoke volumes, but it did little to dampen the confidence Li Na had given me.

"Ah, I see how it is," I said with a feigned sigh, the corners of my mouth twitching upward. "Well, I appreciate the thought anyway." The air around us seemed lighter, the path to the training grounds less daunting than before. "Thank you, really. I'll do my best not to die. That's a promise."

My hand unconsciously drifted to the pouch at my hip, fingers curling around the vials hidden within. "I guess it's a good thing I've got these, then," I murmured, more to myself than to anyone else.

Lan Sheng piped up again. "Just remember, Kai, it's not the size of the cultivator in the fight but the size of the fight in the cultivator. And you've got plenty of fight in you."

As the training grounds came into view, apprehension and determination settled in. I was ready, or as ready as one could be when facing the wall known as Ping Hai. "Let's do this."

As I took in the sight of the training grounds, meticulously swept and prepared by my own hands just the night before, a strange sense of calm began to settle over me. The dirt, solidly packed beneath my feet, offered a familiar resistance. The leaves, which I had cleared away last night, still found their way back onto the grounds. But what my eyes caught were the leaves congregating in small, natural-looking clusters. I noted their locations and committed them to memory. These patches of leaves, seemingly inconsequential to the eyes of the bystanders, would provide the advantage I needed against a foe like Ping Hai.

The gathered disciples from our sect formed a semicircle around the designated area, their faces a mix of excitement and apprehension. Among them, Instructor Xia Ji stood out, her sharp gaze piercing through the crowd to land on me.

Across from me, Ping Hai stood like a statue, his focus and determination palpable even from a distance. In this moment, the jokes and lighthearted banter of my friends seemed like a distant memory. The reality of the challenge before me was crystal clear.

Elder Zhu's voice cut through the tense air as he outlined the terms of our bout. "Kai Liu needs only to land a single hit on Ping Hai to claim victory, while Ping Hai must either force Kai into surrender or achieve a knockout."

"A mere touch won't suffice," Elder Jun interjected sharply. "The blow must be solid, decisive. We trust your judgment to concur with ours on what constitutes a 'solid' hit."

Ping Hai's formidable physique, designed to absorb and shrug off attacks with ease, suddenly seemed like an impenetrable fortress, leaving me with a dwindling list of viable targets.

Inside, my mind raced, frantically devising and discarding plans. The vagueness of what constituted a "solid" blow played tricks on my thoughts, each more elaborate and desperate than the last. My gaze flickered to the patches of leaves once more.

I clenched the vials in my pouch, a tangible reminder of the edge they might provide, yet also a symbol of the dire straits I found myself in.

*Focus, Kai. Treat Ping Hai like a tough alchemy problem, albeit one that could snap my bones if I'm not careful. Every strong ingredient, like Ping Hai, has its counter. It's about using knowledge precisely and finding that balance. Lan Sheng was right, it's all about the right mix: agility, wit, and careful timing.*

In this moment, stripped of all pretense and humor, I stood facing not just Ping Hai but the embodiment of my limits and fears. The path forward was fraught with uncertainty, but retreating was not an option.

"Begin," Elder Zhu resounded, marking the start of the duel.

As Ping Hai stood still, his towering frame a solid mass of muscle and quiet power, he gestured me forward with a slight nod. His deep voice then carried across the training grounds as he said, "I will give you three moves. Make them count." It was clear he saw me as no threat, a mere formality before his inevitable victory.

*Three moves*, I thought. *Let's make them memorable.*

I reached into my pouch for the vials containing my trump card. Without hesitation, I downed them both, the familiar rush of energy and heightened awareness flooding my senses almost instantly. The world around me seemed sharper, every detail magnified, and Ping Hai's imposing stance appeared less like an invincible fortress and more like a puzzle to be solved.

Ping Hai adopted a stance that screamed offense: the Twelve Form Harvest Moon technique. His legs were planted firmly, and his arms raised in a position that promised a devastating counter should I come within his reach. The sight was designed to intimidate, to make one reconsider the folly of engagement.

I took a deep breath, my mind racing through scenarios, discarding one strategy after another as impractical or too risky. *Two moves to create an opening, one to strike*, I reminded myself, the clarity provided by the potions allowing me to focus despite the pounding of my heart. I'd need to conserve my techniques till the very last moment. I couldn't afford to use them so recklessly.

With the potions' power surging through my veins, I darted forward, my feet barely touching the ground. My first move was a straight punch to his head. A firm parry with his forearm stopped it with ease, sending a throbbing sensation throughout my arm.

A swift kick aimed at Ping Hai's solar plexus was a feint. I anticipated his dodge, his towering frame moving with surprising agility.

Spinning on my heel, I transitioned into a roundhouse kick, targeting the same area but from a different angle. My leg cut through the air, but Ping Hai was no novice; he leaned back, evading my strike with minimal effort.

With only a few seconds left before his retaliation, desperation and clarity coalesced within me, guiding my actions. I feigned a stumble from the momentum of my failed kick, an act designed to draw him in, to make him commit to his counter.

"That's three," he intoned. His eyes didn't miss the opening I intentionally left. "Blame yourself for provoking the Silent Moon Sect."

Ping Hai took the bait, moving in with a speed that belied his size, his fist arcing toward me with the force of a battering ram. It was now or never. In a split-second decision, I dropped lower, my body reacting almost on instinct, and threw a punch filled with qi aimed not at Ping Hai but at the space he would occupy should he continue his trajectory. The move was a gamble, a high-stakes bet on my ability to predict his actions and his commitment to the counterattack. His eyes widened in surprise.

Ping Hai had a choice—continue the strike and expose himself to a direct hit or fall back and lose his momentum. In a regular fight, he could've taken the blow with ease and hit me with a counter. But with the match's restrictions in place, it allowed me an opportunity.

In a display of agility and flexibility that contradicted his size, he contorted his body in a bid to avoid my strike, his movements awkward yet effective. The air between us crackled with tension as his counterattack, a straight punch driven by the full weight of his formidable frame, barreled toward me.

The blow was inevitable; even with the potions enhancing my speed and his graceless dodge weakening the power behind the blow, Ping Hai's strike reached my body. I managed to twist myself, turning what would have been a full-on hit into a glancing blow.

Yet, even this reduced impact sent me tumbling backward, the ground rushing up to meet me as I desperately tried to regain my footing.

From where I was lying, I could see Elder Jun with narrowed, calculating eyes. My heart pounded in my chest, not just from the exertion but from the realization of what I had just achieved. I had forced Ping Hai, the Silent Moon's mountain, to retreat.

At that moment, the fear and trepidation that had clouded my mind cleared, replaced by a sharp focus. I knew the odds were still against me, that Ping Hai's next move would be calculated and brutal, but for the first time since the match was announced, I felt a glimmer of hope.

I could do this.

# CHAPTER SEVENTEEN

# When Leaves Fall, the Shadow Rises

Is this the showing a Silent Moon Sect's representative should be proud of?" Elder Jun's voice was icy.

Ping Hai's reaction was telling. A brief flicker of uncertainty appeared, a momentary lapse that revealed a sliver of doubt. It was fleeting, gone almost as soon as it appeared, but it was enough to remind me that beneath the imposing exterior lay a cultivator not unlike myself, susceptible to the same cautions and concerns.

However, as quickly as the moment of vulnerability had appeared, it vanished. Ping Hai now fixed on me with great intensity, seeming to burn with a determination that bordered on ferocity. Elder Jun's words had served their purpose, steeling his resolve for the battle ahead.

I braced myself for Ping Hai's response, knowing that the brief advantage I had gained would only serve to make him more cautious, more deliberate in his approach. Yet, even with this knowledge, the sheer speed of his retaliation caught me off guard.

He blurred, revealing the deceptive agility hidden within his massive frame. The heavens were truly unfair, allowing a man of his stature to move like a mouse. The straight punch he delivered toward my stomach was swift and unyielding. I could only roll off to the side, feeling a gust of wind pass by where I was a split second ago.

The impact of his missed strike sent a shiver down my spine. As I scrambled to my feet, the world around me seemed to slow, the effects of the potions allowing me to perceive each minute detail with crystal clarity.

Unfazed by his missed attack, he adjusted his stance, a subtle shift that warned me of an impending strike.

My entire body was sweating. It hadn't even been a minute yet, but the mental fatigue of knowing one wrong move could spell my doom wore away at me and frayed my nerves.

He delivered his strikes in a simple manner, but because of that, it was hard to counter—specifically, to use the Bamboo Reprisal Counter. But it was getting easier. Maybe it was the elixir, but it felt like I was adjusting to his speed. I glanced over to my right, seeing one of the leaf deposits I committed to memory earlier. If I could just—

*WHOOSH!*

A right hook, faster than anything he'd displayed so far, brushed past my cheek, splitting my skin and drawing blood. If I hadn't turned my head in time, it would've been over.

I stumbled backward, trying to blink the stars out of my eyes and the ringing in my ears.

I'd been a fool.

He was lulling me into a false sense of security, making me adjust to a slower speed than what he was capable of until now. Was this truly someone the same age as Li Na or Han Wei? I didn't feel this sense of suppression even when I fought against Lan Sheng or Feng Wu. I looked over to Ping Hai once again, only to find a cold and determined gaze. His other fist hurtled toward me at an alarming speed. I watched as time slowed to a crawl.

I had to duck. I had to duck! If I took this hit, I'd die!

A scream tore from my throat as every muscle in my body worked to throw myself further into the strike. Ping Hai's fist whiffed my head, and I could feel the barest touch on my hair as I stumbled forward past his guard. I tucked and rolled gracelessly across the grounds.

Before I could regain my bearings, a shadow loomed over me. Ping Hai, his massive frame silhouetted against the sky blotting out the sun, his leg raised high for an axe kick. The fourth stance of the Twelve Form Harvest Moon.

As Ping Hai's shadow loomed over me, his leg raised like a guillotine's blade against the backdrop of a clear sky, a cold shiver ran down my spine. Time seemed to stretch, each second a lifetime, as I lay sprawled beneath him, the hard ground pressing against my back. His towering figure blocked out the sun, casting me into a stark darkness that mirrored my growing despair.

Rooted Banyan Stance? Not in this position. All I could do in this situation was . . .

I crossed my hands above my head and pushed myself forward before the kick could fully be unleashed. As I coalesced qi into my arms, Ping Hai seemed unperturbed, delivering the blow even faster than I'd anticipated. It fell onto my head like the weight of a thousand stones. No matter how much I'd trained up till this point, facing the blow head-on meant there was an inevitable cost to pay.

But by paying that cost . . . I'd opened up the path for survival.

I twisted my core and angled my arms to divert the force into the ground beside me. The first principle of the Bamboo Reprisal Counter: redirecting the flow of an opponent's power and minimizing the damage to oneself. The words came to me unbidden, cutting through the noise of battle.

*Observe the lotus upon the water; it moves with the current yet remains unblemished. So, too, must you flow with the force of your opponent, redirecting their energy while maintaining your core, unshaken.*

Ping Hai's leg came crashing down beside me. Every fiber of my being screamed in protest. Pain radiated from my arms, so intense it bordered on numbness. The odds, ever daunting, now seemed insurmountable. Yet a stubborn flame of defiance within me refused to be extinguished.

My body felt hot. The constant pounding of my heartbeat overwhelmed everything except the man in front of me. A whisper cut through the stimulus. *The path of a leaf adrift on a stream does not resist the current, yet it finds its way.*

Ping Hai, momentarily off-balance from the redirected force of his own attack, regained his composure swiftly. But deep in his eyes, I could see frustration building up. His teeth were clenched, and veins were protruding from his head. His eyes flickered off to the side, back to Elder Jun.

*Emulate this gentleness in your technique, allowing the opponent's force to become the guide to their own defeat.*

In the midst of battle, a strange peace came over me. The noise of the fight turned into a clear rhythm, guiding my responses. Ping Hai's every move became a signal, showing me where to strike or dodge. In this focused calm, my movements were no longer just reactions; they were answers.

The battle's chaos became a dance, and in this dance, I found my moment.

The bamboo, resilient and yielding, bending in the fiercest winds only to rise again, unbroken. And now I could feel those words forming a bridge between my mind and body.

*Your understanding of the dao has deepened.*
*Your Mind has reached Mortal Realm—Rank 4.*

I dashed forward, considering the nearby surroundings without losing focus on Ping Hai's frame. I watched his weight shift and the slightest tensing of his muscles. I needed to think faster. *FASTER!*

Only after this point, this moment of clarity, did I realize that Ping Hai truly wasn't as monstrous as I'd made him out to be. He may have been incredibly strong, and deceptively agile, but he wasn't as fast or dexterous as Li Na or Feng Wu. And they were people whom I sparred with daily. My fear had been clouding my judgment and my reaction all this time.

But now I could fight back.

*A strike at the body, followed by a kick to the head.*

I parried his punch, committing fully to the redirection of its power. It was the only way to defend. My forearms were creaking under the immense weight, but I shifted my body to avoid the incoming kick. Ping Hai stopped his move and readjusted, only taking a second to do so. But that was enough for me.

Seizing the opportunity, I feigned a lunge, drawing his attention—and his guard—to his left. As he adjusted his stance to counter, I pivoted, channeling my qi to my right leg, and unleashed a sweeping kick aimed at the cluster of leaves just between us.

The kick sent a flurry of leaves into the air, compounding the visual chaos of battle. Momentarily taken aback by the unexpected maneuver, Ping Hai faltered, his eyes darting between the airborne leaves in a futile attempt to discern my true location. Now was my chance!

But before I could launch another attack, I saw his hands pierce through the leafy veil, coming together and unleashing a gust of wind that blew away my cover.

"Heeup!"

The gust of wind Ping Hai generated cleared the air, leaving me exposed and momentarily disoriented by the thunderous clap.

As he blew away the leaves in a whirlwind of force and charged forward, unwilling to give me a chance to recover, his forward momentum betrayed him. The ground beneath him, seemingly solid, concealed my last-ditch effort—a small hole hidden beneath the cluster of leaves I had kicked upward in a feint of desperation. The trap I had placed last night. Placed strategically and subtly in areas throughout the training grounds, this wasn't a matter of luck; this opportunity was solely due to preparation.

Ping Hai's foot found the void unexpectedly, his massive frame lurching forward with a suddenness that defied his earlier poise. The surprise in his eyes was a mirror to my own; his for the unforeseen falter, mine for the sliver of opportunity it presented.

Seizing the moment, I surged forward, my body coiled like a spring, my fist aimed upward in an uppercut meant to capitalize on the third-class disciple's compromised stance. The move, fueled by a mix of adrenaline and the last vestiges of hope, was a gamble against the odds.

But even in his moment of imbalance, he was still a force to be reckoned with. His hand, large enough to encase my fist entirely, snapped out with the speed of a striking viper, catching my uppercut in a vise-like grip that halted my momentum cold. The sheer strength in his grasp was a stark reminder of what he did in the alchemy bout, a power that now threatened to snuff out the advantage I had.

"Grrgh!"

The high of my epiphany that I had been riding on for the longest time was broken by the pain in my hand.

"This farce is over," Ping Hai growled, a rumble that seemed to resonate with the very earth beneath us. His other hand reared back, poised to deliver a finishing blow that I knew I could not hope to withstand with the principles of the Bamboo Reprisal Counter alone.

In that moment, suspended between defiance and defeat, the training grounds around us faded into a blur. The cheers and gasps of the spectators and the gentle rustle of the remaining leaves in the breeze—all of it receded into the background, leaving only the impending certainty of Ping Hai's strike.

Yet, even as despair threatened to take hold, a flicker of resolve ignited within me. The countless hours of training, the lessons learned, the challenges faced— all of it culminated in this singular moment of truth.

I shifted my stance at the last possible instant, dropping my center of gravity and anchoring myself into the earth with the Rooted Banyan Stance.

Ping Hai's approaching fist met not the compliance of a defeated foe but the unyielding force of my prepared stance. The collision sent a shockwave through my body and into the ground, a testament to the might behind the blow. Because of my fist stuck in his grip, I couldn't fully complete the technique, weakening the defense and letting a partial amount of damage permeate through my chest. I coughed out blood, feeling the sheer solidity of his strike.

But I was still standing.

The bewildered look that flashed across Ping Hai's face was as satisfying as it was fleeting.

I relinquished my stance, transforming rigidity into fluid motion. Seizing Ping Hai's outstretched arm—the very instrument of his intended victory—I leaned back, my body bending like the bamboo that bends but does not break, guided by Instructor Xia Ji's teachings of the Bamboo Reprisal Counter.

The second principle of the Bamboo Reprisal Counter. To redirect the force of an opponent's blow and to use that diverted power back to the opponent.

With a burst of qi channeled through my core and into my legs, I unleashed a counterstrike, a front kick aimed at Ping Hai's chin. The force of my kick, amplified by the momentum of my fall and the power of my qi, was my final gamble.

In that split second before the collision, I saw it. Ping Hai's attempt to retreat.

It was thwarted by the very trap he had stumbled into moments before. His foot, ensnared in the divot concealed by the leaves, became his undoing.

My front kick connected, the impact reverberating through the air, a testament to the culmination of my journey, the synthesis of countless lessons learned under the tutelage of my mentors and the hardships I had endured.

> *You can now utilize the skill Bamboo Reprisal Counter.*

I let go of his arm and fell to the floor.

The crowd gasped. All I could focus on was the third-class disciple I had put my life on the line to win against. His neck was craned upward, and I could see how stiff his body had gone. For a moment, I thought I knocked him out.

His posture staggered, and for a second it looked like he was about to fall onto one knee.

But his towering form stayed strong, and he brought his head back down as if the strike hadn't even fazed him. In his eyes were shock, fear, and disarray. But he wasn't looking at me; he was looking at someone far into the crowd. I trailed his gaze and saw the frigid expression on Elder Jun and the stupefied expression of Xu Ziqing beside him.

I heard Elder Zhu's voice as my back lay flat on the ground, carrying with it a tinge of disbelief and amazement.

"The bout is decided," Elder Zhu declared with finality. "Kai Liu is the victor."

> *Quest: Eclipse the Silent Moon has been completed.*
> *Due to your status as Interface Manipulator, your rewards*
> *will be adjusted accordingly.*

A cheer erupted from the ranks of the Verdant Lotus Sect, a tidal wave of relief and jubilation that swept through the crowd. My friends—Li Na, Han Wei, Lan Sheng, and Feng Wu—were the first to reach me, their faces alight with excited pride.

"You did it, Kai!" Li Na exclaimed as she knelt beside me. Her hands hovered over me, as though she was unsure of where to touch.

Lan Sheng's laughter rang out, infectious and carefree. "What did I tell you? Size isn't everything!"

Feng Wu's usual calm demeanor was replaced with a rare smile of genuine pride, and he offered his hand, helping me to my feet. "You're the victor. How do you feel?"

As I leaned on my friends for support, my body aching in places I didn't even know could hurt, I couldn't help but let out a pained chuckle. "Victor, huh? Feels more like I've been trampled by a herd of oxen."

Their concern was palpable, their eyes scanning my injuries, but the elation of the moment seemed to overshadow the pain. "You need to get looked at by the healers," Li Na insisted, her brows furrowed in worry.

As we made our way slowly toward the sect's infirmary, the crowd parted for us, their whispers and cheers a swirling mix that filled the air.

"He actually did it . . ."

"Kai beat a disciple of the Silent Moon Sect . . ."

"Is that guy really a third-class disciple?"

Amid the physical pain, my mind was awash with a cascade of reflections. Despite my victory, it rang hollow.

It was a perfect storm of factors leading to an outcome I could hardly believe. The clarity I felt almost otherworldly, as if I had transcended my limitations. Their underestimation of me as an herbalist played to my advantage, allowing me to surprise them with unexpected tactics and potent concoctions. The hole I had dug the night before became a trap Ping Hai couldn't predict. The synergy between the Rooted Banyan Stance and Bamboo Reprisal Counter, combining hard and soft defense to absorb and redirect his attack into a precise counterstrike.

And yet, the kick that I had delivered with every ounce of strength and qi I could muster barely seemed to stun Ping Hai. Maybe it wasn't his strength I should admire, but rather the endurance such a body gave him.

As I watched the third-class disciple in question, his attention wholly consumed by Elder Jun, kowtowing in a display of utter subjugation, a pang of empathy coursed through me. He was not focused on me, the victor of our duel, but rather on the weight of his perceived failure in the eyes of his mentor and sect.

Hadn't I seen a glimpse of their culture with the slightest of interactions? I saw not just a formidable opponent but a fellow cultivator caught in the relentless pursuit of strength and approval within the rigid hierarchy of the Silent Moon Sect. He would likely be facing repercussions for this defeat.

"Guys, could you help me walk over to him?"

Lan Sheng looked surprised. "You truly want to kick him while he's down, eh? Don't worry, Kai. Since this is outside of the match, I can interfere if he tries to—"

Feng Wu drove his elbow into Lan Sheng. The second-class disciple let out a strained noise of pain and immediately went quiet.

"Of course, Kai. Just be mindful—it is best not to provoke them further." Then, to Feng Wu: "That really hurt, you know." But his words fell on deaf ears.

As I limped closer to Ping Hai, he caught my gaze and turned to face me. Behind him were several other Silent Moon Sect disciples. They all looked at me with a myriad of expressions: disdain, anger, suspicion. But there was also something different that had not been there before—caution?

Nevertheless, I took my arms away from Li Na's and Han Wei's supporting shoulders and walked closer. From where I stood, Ping Hai didn't seem so large. I clasped my hands together and folded into a shallow bow. "Thank you for the spar. This junior has learned well."

Ping Hai seemed to hesitate before dipping his head. "I have learned well."

A formality. One that I learned occurred between official matches between cultivators.

This duel was my declaration to the Jianghu—my arrival on a stage I had only dared to dream of.

# CHAPTER EIGHTEEN

# Eclipsing the Ego

Ignoring the throbbing pain that seemed to echo with each heartbeat, I pushed past Ping Hai, my steps deliberate as I approached where Elders Jun and Zhu and Xu Ziqing stood. The air felt heavier here, making my already-labored breathing seem all the more difficult.

I looked over at Xu Ziqing. His stance wavered. It felt good to know that I had broken free of the expectations the Silent Moon Sect had put on me.

Elder Jun's gaze was like a shard of ice, piercing and unwavering, as it fixed upon me. The Heavenly Interface flickered into existence once again, its warning clear.

> *Elder Jun: Essence Awakening Stage Cultivator, Known for*
> *Immense Pride and Ruthlessness.*
> *Suggested Approach: Humility and Diplomacy.*

But the warning was unnecessary; the memories of my past recklessness, the consequences that almost befell the sect and myself, were fresh in my mind. I steadied my voice, cooling the fiery undertone of defiance that had almost become second nature. I recalled the discussions with the Verdant Lotus elders, their warnings echoing throughout my thoughts.

They had been clear; my pursuit of righteousness, however well intentioned, risked not only my safety but that of the entire sect and the innocents of Gentle Wind Village.

"Elder Zhu, may I?" My voice was steady, but inside, a storm of conflict raged. The Beast Core, a symbol of victory and power, lay within Elder Zhu's grasp. Yet, as I reached out, a pang of reluctance seized me.

It symbolized my growth, my commitment to standing up for what I believed was just. After all, we had earned it together, Feng Wu and I, in the heat of battle against the Wind Serpents, side by side with Xu Ziqing and the Silent Moon Sect.

My resistance, born from a sense of righteousness, was reckless. In my fervor to defend what I perceived as fair, I had failed to gauge the depth of the ripples my actions would reach.

Turning to Elder Jun, I mustered all the humility I had learned from the harsh lessons of life. "Elder Jun, I thank you for this opportunity. The duel was a valuable lesson in the depth of cultivation. It has shown me how I've only scratched the surface of its depth."

"Spare us your platitudes. In the Jianghu, a loser is a loser. There's no need to dress it with pretty words."

His remark stung, and I could see Ping Hai flinch from my peripheral. Yet, within me, something stirred—a realization that true strength lay not just in power but in the wisdom to wield it wisely.

"Elder Jun, my victory today does not make me superior to Ping Hai or diminish the Silent Moon Sect's standing. It was the support of the Verdant Lotus Sect and the lessons I've learned that carried me through," I responded, my gaze drifting to where Li Na, Han Wei, and the others stood.

The air felt thick as I bowed respectfully to Elder Jun, an act of submission that went against every fiber of pride in my being. "I apologize for any disrespect my actions may have caused. It was never my intention to sow discord between your sects." I said something similar during my first encounter with them. But here, it was more genuine. I hoped that would come across clearly.

But if it didn't . . .

I carefully took the Beast Core from Elder Zhu, giving him a quiet word of thanks as I stood a little straighter to face Elder Jun. "This core . . . If it can ensure peace and harmony between the Verdant Lotus and Silent Moon Sects, it is worth more than any prize."

Gasps of shock rippled through the crowd. Elder Jun was inscrutable. He considered my words.

Elder Zhu looked at me, a storm of emotions swirling on his face. "Kai, reconsider. This core is your right, won through courage and skill. To relinquish it so easily . . ."

The unsaid implications of my decision hung heavy. The Beast Core, pulsating with energy in his outstretched hand, seemed to beckon, a siren call to the potential it promised.

"Elder Zhu speaks wisely, Kai," Feng Wu said, his voice as calm as the still surface of a lake yet carrying an undercurrent of solemnity. "Consider the path ahead and the challenges it may hold. A Beast Core, especially of one this size, would be a great benefit to your cultivation."

I glanced between the two men, the pillars of wisdom and strength who helped me grow and learn in such a short span of time. Yet, as I gazed at the Beast Core, its luminescent glow reflecting in their expectant eyes, a different kind of resolve settled within me.

"No, Elder Zhu. If my actions have created enmity between the Verdant Lotus and the Silent Moon, then it is my duty to amend them. This core, as precious as it is, holds no value against peace."

If the Beast Core would ensure my village's safety from retaliation, then this was a small price to pay. Sure, it could further my cultivation, but would it be enough to grant me the power to protect the people of the Gentle Wind village from the Silent Moon Sect if they chose revenge against me? Even if the Verdant Lotus Sect stepped in, that only meant my friends—Li Na, Han Wei, Feng Wu— would suffer casualties.

To Sect Leader Shaotian Ye, Elder Jun must've seemed like a frog in a well. But to me, he felt more like a dragon lurking in shallow waters. His presence, though not towering, cast a long shadow, one that could easily envelop those around him in darkness. He was a person who wouldn't hesitate to bring others down with him to the depths if provoked.

And as much as I despised it, I wasn't the dragon-slaying cultivator I had imagined myself to be.

At least, not yet.

Holding the Beast Core out to Elder Jun, I knew the man standing before me was a master at concealing his thoughts, his face a mask that revealed nothing of the storm that might be raging beneath.

Yet, as I extended the core toward him, I saw it—a flicker, a slight twist of his features, so fleeting I almost doubted my own eyes. Elder Jun, the unshakable, had shown a crack in his armor.

Offering the Beast Core, I wasn't just relinquishing a token of power; I was laying down a gauntlet. Would he take the core, reneging on the terms of our wager, and in doing so, admit to a weakness I was certain a man of his stature would never concede? Or would he let it go, acknowledging the gesture for what it was—a plea for peace, for the sake of those who had no part in our conflict?

The silence that stretched between us was deafening. I knew that whatever I was thinking, he had likely considered already. I didn't do this with the hope of winning more but to secure the peace and safety of my sect, my friends, and the innocents of Gentle Wind Village. This was my gambit, my calculated risk to preserve harmony between the Verdant Lotus and the Silent Moon.

I could feel the anticipation from my sect, my friends, and even the Silent Moon disciples bore into us. The weight of the core in my hand felt magnified, a symbol of so much more than the power it contained. It was a test, a question posed to Elder Jun's principles and, by extension, the honor of the Silent Moon Sect itself.

"Do you take us for beggars, boy? The Silent Moon Sect does not renege on its wagers," Elder Jun retorted bitterly. "We accept our loss. This matter is closed."

As he signaled his disciples to prepare for departure, I stayed in place, slowly lowering my hand and letting out a sigh of relief. It was over.

I glanced over at Elder Zhu. It seemed he understood my intentions with my gambit.

The atmosphere around us began to shift. Ping Hai looked at Elder Jun in dismay and then turned back to look at me. He seemed unsure, almost like he wanted to say something, before clenching his fist and following the older man's lead.

My friends rushed me, careful to avoid my injuries.

"Ha . . . I'm exhausted," I murmured, letting my posture sag as I leaned heavily on Han Wei. "But everything turned out better than I imagined."

A shadow loomed over me, and before I could turn my head, I heard Feng Wu's voice speak up.

"Is there something you need, Xu Ziqing?"

I looked up to see the Azure Moon Marauder. Dressed in his cobalt robe, with a dagger-like glint in his eyes, I wondered if he was related to Elder Jun in some way.

"Kai Liu," Xu Ziqing said. "Your gesture today, offering the Beast Core back to Elder Jun was . . . unexpected."

"It was a decision for peace, for the sake of both the sects and those beyond them." Although, I wouldn't tell him that I did it knowing there was a good chance they'd turn down the offer. It was the thought that counted, right?

The man kept his gaze on me, tapping the hilt of his blade. I still felt caution, knowing that among the disciples brought out here today, *he* was the strongest among them. Ping Hai wouldn't stand a chance against the powerful slashes I'd seen that gouged out walls and Wind Serpent scales in Qingmu.

Xu Ziqing's lips twitched into a semblance of a smile, but it lacked any genuine amusement. "Always playing the hero, aren't you? But remember, in the grand scheme of the Jianghu, it's the sect's glory that prevails. Individual sacrifices are but footnotes in our sects' legacies."

Where was he going with this? Was it disdain? Mockery? His acknowledgment of my actions, wrapped in criticism, left me wondering what he was up to.

"Perhaps," I conceded, keeping my tone even, "but I believe it's these 'footnotes' that truly define the character of a sect. Not just its victories but its choices when faced with conflict."

The second-class disciple snorted but narrowed his eyes. "Noble ideals, but idealism doesn't always hold sway in the face of reality."

Before I could respond, Li Na stepped forward. "Senior, your point is made. Perhaps it's best you rejoin your sect now. We've all had a long day."

Feng Wu, silent until now, added with a calm authority that brooked no argument, "It's time to part ways. Let's not sour the peace that's been hard-won today."

Xu Ziqing's gaze lingered on me for a moment longer, the ghost of a challenge flickering in his eyes, before he gave a curt nod and turned to leave, his silhouette soon melding among the Silent Moon Sect disciples.

"We should celebrate tonight, Kai! The dining hall won't know what hit it!" Han Wei exclaimed, his enthusiasm infectious.

I managed a weak smile, feeling the day's events pressing down on me. "I'd like that, but maybe later. I need some time to . . . process everything."

Li Na nodded in understanding. "Take all the time you need. We'll be there when you're ready."

One by one, my friends dispersed, each lost in their own thoughts, leaving me to the silence that I so desperately craved. The training grounds, now empty, felt vast and echoing. It was in this silence that I noticed Instructor Xia Ji approaching. Her gaze fell upon a particular spot on the ground.

"Kai, what happened here?" she inquired lightly.

I followed her gaze to find the divot I had created. A slight flush crept up my cheeks as I remembered Lan Sheng's advice to use my surroundings to my advantage. "It was a . . . precaution, Instructor. A trap, if you will, inspired by Lan Sheng's words. I dug it last night."

"A trap?" she echoed.

I nodded sheepishly. "Yes, I thought it might give me an edge against Ping Hai. I apologize for the dishonorable tactic."

Instructor Xia Ji surveyed the divot, then looked at me with a glint in her eye that I couldn't quite decipher. "And are there more of these 'precautions' around?"

"Um, a few," I admitted, my embarrassment deepening.

"I see. Well, you'll have to repair them before tomorrow afternoon, Kai. We can't have the other disciples falling to the same trick and getting injured, can we?"

"I believe it'd be a nice lesson in vigilance and preparedness, hee hee . . ."

Instructor Xia Ji's stern glare locked me in place. She didn't reply but merely pursed her lips and narrowed her eyes.

"I understand, Instructor. I apologize for the inconvenience," I said. "I'll get it fixed up before your classes. I promise."

With the matter of the divots settled, Instructor Xia Ji turned contemplative. "What's next for you, Kai? After all this excitement, I imagine you have plans."

I paused, the question stirring the whirlpool of thoughts that had been swirling in my mind. "I want to continue my training, Instructor. And there's the Grand Alchemy Gauntlet coming up. I need to prepare, especially now that I have . . . less time."

Instructor Xia Ji nodded, assessing. "You're always welcome at the training sessions, Kai. Though I won't be able to offer personalized instruction anymore. You've outgrown that in many ways."

I felt a pang, a mix of pride and nostalgia for the days when every lesson felt like a new world opening up before me. "I understand, Instructor. And I'm grateful for all the guidance you've given me."

"Then it's settled. Prepare for the Gauntlet, Kai. It's a rare opportunity, and I believe you have the potential to make a significant impact, judging by your results here against the Silent Moon."

Just then, the Heavenly Interface flickered into existence, drawing my gaze with its familiar glow. Amid the day's turmoil, I had almost forgotten about my quest.

> *Reward calculation completed.*
> *Spiritual Herbalism has reached level 2.*
> *You have received a Technique Token.*

*Huh?*

Just under my status menu, I could see another new line of text.

> *Technique Token—1*

What is this?

Like an all-knowing being, the Heavenly Interface responded to my query.

> *Technique Token—When applied, the Technique Token enhances*
> *any chosen skill by elevating it by one level, channeling*
> *the latent potential within the cultivator and refining their mastery*
> *in unprecedented ways. If used on skills that already reached*
> *the maximum level, it will forcefully evolve it to the next stage,*
> *regardless of the prerequisites for evolution being fulfilled.*

I glanced at the text in shock. This reward was incomprehensibly powerful. If I were to use it on something like the Rooted Banyan Stance, once I reached the tenth level, I'd be able to evolve it to the next stage without the prerequisites, wouldn't I?

And what about the Crimson Lotus Purification technique? It didn't have any evolution requirements like my other skills. Wouldn't that mean I could theoretically upgrade the technique into something even better?

"Ha . . . haha! The heavens are truly generous! HAHAH—" I lurched over in pain, clutching my chest. "Oh, laughing too hard is hurting my ribs."

Despite the discomfort, I couldn't hide my excitement. I'd have to think deeply about what I wanted to upgrade with this. More importantly, I'd have to wait.

There was no point upgrading anything right now, when none of my skills had reached the limit. I'd have to weigh the pros and cons.

If I wanted to use it on a skill before the Grand Alchemy Gauntlet, I'd need to work harder than ever! There was no telling how long it'd take to reach the maximum level for each of my skills at this rate.

Left alone in the expanse of the training grounds, the reality of the day's trials began to truly sink in. The adrenaline that had fueled me through the confrontation with Ping Hai, through the strategic give-and-take with Elder Jun, began to ebb, leaving behind a profound sense of weariness.

The setting sun painted the sky in shades of orange and purple, a beautiful backdrop to my tumultuous thoughts. I lay back on the ground, wincing slightly as the aches from the day's exertions made themselves known. I suppose this was a sign I should look further into my healing hydrosol if I wanted to be up and about sooner, along with taking a trip to the sect's infirmary.

As I gazed up at the fading light, my mind wandered to the task at hand—the divots I had strategically placed around the training grounds.

*Great, Kai. Brilliant plan you had there. Now how in the world are you supposed to patch up these holes when you can barely sit up straight?*

"Maybe I can convince Han Wei and the others to help . . ."

The thought of bribing them with alcohol popped up, but I dismissed it as soon as it came. If Feng Wu were to find out . . . I shivered.

With a final glance at the darkening sky, I pushed myself to my feet, my resolve solidifying with each painful step. The Grand Alchemy Gauntlet awaited, and with it, the opportunity to prove my mettle, to forge my path.

And as for the divots? Well, that was a problem for tomorrow's Kai. For now, the promise of rest and a celebratory feast beckoned.

# CHAPTER NINETEEN

# Waning Crescent

The Silent Moon Sect's silent march through Crescent Bay City's evening bustle drew curious glances from civilians, sparking whispered speculation. Civilians paused to observe the procession of dark blue and black robes.

"Isn't that the Silent Moon Sect?" one onlooker murmured.

"Yes, they've come from the direction of the Verdant Lotus Sect," another replied, their voice low and intrigued. "What business might they have had there?"

As the sect members passed, leaving whispered conjectures in their wake, discreet glances were cast toward Ping Hai. His once formidable presence was now seemingly diminished. His bald head and broad shoulders, once a symbol among the third-grade disciples, now seemed more vulnerable than ever.

The looks directed at Ping Hai were mixed—some carried pity, others disdain, and a few held a calculating reassessment of his abilities. The outcome of the bout had shifted perceptions, planting seeds of doubt and speculation.

Yet Xu Ziqing, leading the formation, remained aloof from these undercurrents. His concerns lay not with Ping Hai's loss but with the broader implications. It wasn't just about Ping Hai's defeat; it was Kai Liu's unexpected prowess that challenged their understanding of cultivation.

The second-class disciple found it hard to reconcile the herbalist he had seen in Qingmu with the fledgling cultivator who managed to land a blow against their most talented third-class disciple. Even with his already established vigilance toward the boy, it was simply impossible to predict that level of growth within a month's time.

*Fools*, Xu Ziqing thought, scanning the procession of third-class disciples. Many of them seemed to be revising their assessment of Ping Hai. The tension between them was palpable. *They would've fared the same if not worse than Ping Hai in that battle.*

Approaching the sect's gates, his contemplation deepened. He observed a growing disconnect among the disciples, a worrying sign of eroding unity that threatened the sect's foundational principles.

In the silence of their march, Xu Ziqing's thoughts drifted to the younger third-class disciples he had unofficially mentored. During their skirmishes with the Wind Serpents in Qingmu, he had honed their collective strengths, orchestrating them into formidable formations that played to each disciple's prowess. Back then, a sense of camaraderie had animated their ranks, their shared victories a testament to their unity and mutual respect. But now, as he watched these disciples whom he hadn't worked closely with, that camaraderie was nowhere to be found.

Whispers of division, subtle yet palpable, hinted at factions forming within the third-class disciples—a phenomenon he found both unexpected and disturbing. Among the second-class disciples, such explicit schisms were rare, their competitive spirit never undermining the broader allegiance to the sect.

The disdain that these disciples harbored for Ping Hai in his moment of defeat was a symptom of a deeper malaise. He reflected on the silent whispers and the calculating glances exchanged among the third-class disciples. Their quickness to judge and distance themselves from failure was a concerning trend. The sect seemed to be neglecting the cultivation of bonds that should bind the disciples together, not just as competitors but as members of a singular entity.

This divisive undercurrent, if left unchecked, threatened to undermine the sect's ethos.

He tapped the hilt of his sword, tucked away safely in its sheath. The very thought of the sect's youngest talents splintering into factions worried him.

As they crossed the threshold into the sect's grounds, Xu Ziqing resolved to bring this observation to the attention of the elders. It was his duty as their Senior Brother.

The imposing gates of the Silent Moon Sect closed behind them with a resounding thud, sealing off the outside world and its murmured whispers. Inside these walls, the atmosphere was charged with a different kind of energy—a mix of anticipation and the unyielding weight of tradition.

Xu Ziqing cast a sidelong glance at Ping Hai. The young disciple walked with a subdued air, the defeat evidently weighing heavily on his young shoulders. Yet, beneath the surface, he saw the unquenchable fire that burned within him. At merely fifteen, he had already carved a formidable position for himself within the sect, his talent undeniable and his potential boundless.

Ping Hai's loss, though a setback, was but a ripple in the vast ocean of his journey. The defeat would either temper him into steel or shatter him.

*Knowing him, it will likely be the former.*

The procession halted at the central pavilion, where Elder Jun awaited. The elder's eyes, sharp and discerning, swept over the returning disciples, pausing briefly on Xu Ziqing and Ping Hai.

"Dismissed," Elder Jun declared. The assembled disciples bowed and began to disperse, murmurs of relief and fatigue washing over them as they retreated to their quarters.

"Xu Ziqing, Ping Hai, stay," he commanded, before they could follow suit with the others.

The other disciples cast curious glances their way, the air thick with unspoken questions and conjectures.

Elder Jun turned, leading them away from the pavilion and toward his quarters.

The elder's quarters, nestled in the heart of the sect, were a place few disciples had the privilege to enter. It was a space where the weight of the sect's history and the burden of its future coalesced.

As they entered, the door closing silently behind them, the outside world seemed to fall away.

He took a seat, gesturing for Xu Ziqing and Ping Hai to do the same. The air was heavy with expectation, the silence a canvas for the words yet to be spoken.

"Today's events have implications far beyond the loss of a mere Beast Core. They speak to the very heart of what we stand for as a sect."

Xu Ziqing listened intently, his mind racing to anticipate the elder's thoughts. Ping Hai sat rigid, his gaze fixed on the floor, the weight of his defeat a near-tangible presence in the room.

"Strength, unity, resilience—these are the pillars upon which the Silent Moon Sect stands. Yet, today, we have seen that even the strongest pillars can crack under pressure," Elder Jun continued, his gaze piercing. "Ping Hai, your determination is clear, but I must ask—what fuels it? Is it merely personal ambition, or something more profound?"

Ping Hai's eyes flickered with a hint of surprise, unprepared for the personal nature of the question. He hesitated, then spoke with a sincerity that belied his usual reserve. "My strength is not for myself alone, Elder. It's for those who stand behind me, for my village that looks up to the Silent Moon for hope," he said. He was committed.

Elder Jun nodded, a knowing look in his eyes. "Your village . . . I am aware that you've been sending your sect allowance back to your people. A commendable act indeed." Though approving, Elder Jun had an underlying edge that made the young disciple tense.

Xu Ziqing, watching the conversation envelop, grew wary. There were no rules about what one's allowance from the sect was used for, although it was standard to use it to purchase pills and other resources to further their cultivation. If what the elder said was true, then that meant Ping Hai had come this far without the help of additional pills and resources.

Ping Hai's reaction was immediate; his posture stiffened, and his eyes widened with a blend of fear and surprise. "E-Elder Jun, I . . . I only wished to—" he began, faltering, the smooth facade of the formidable disciple cracking under the weight of his youth and inexperience.

Elder Jun raised a hand, silencing him with a gentle yet firm gesture. "It's a noble act. But remember, your ultimate duty now lies with the Silent Moon Sect. Our path demands sacrifices, and at times, personal attachments must be set aside for the greater cause," he advised, his tone softening, almost coaxing.

Xu Ziqing watched, forgotten in the exchange, with growing unease, noting the subtle shift in Ping Hai's demeanor. The young disciple's initial fear slowly morphed into uncertainty, his eyes flickering between Elder Jun and Xu Ziqing.

"As a gesture of the sect's support for your commendable intentions, I will ensure your allowance for your village is not merely continued but doubled—no, tripled. This, however, will be in line with your dedication and achievements within the sect," Elder Jun proposed, his words carefully chosen, weaving a net of obligation and loyalty around Ping Hai.

Ping Hai swallowed hard, the conflict within him palpable. "I . . . I am grateful, Elder Jun. I will . . . I will work harder for the sect," he stammered, his intonation reflecting gratitude, determination, and an underlying current of fear. The transformation was gradual but evident as if Elder Jun's words were sculpting him, molding his loyalty with a potter's precision.

Elder Jun's eyes glinted with satisfaction at his response, but his voice maintained its firm, encouraging tone. "Excellent, Ping Hai. Remember, the Silent Moon Sect is your new family, your new village. Devote yourself to it fully, and your contributions will not only erase this minor setback but also elevate you and the sect to new heights."

His honeyed words, so sweet and alluring, pulled even at Xu Ziqing's mind. The respected elder's voice was like a calm sea, smooth and inviting, but he could sense the undercurrents swirling beneath. Each word the elder spoke seemed to weave a tighter web around Ping Hai, binding the young disciple's loyalty not just to the sect but to Elder Jun himself.

Ping Hai nodded, a newfound resolve firming his young features. "I will serve the Silent Moon Sect to its fullest, Elder Jun!" he declared, the words carrying a weight that seemed to anchor him firmly to the path laid out by the elder. The third-class disciple fell to one knee and bowed, his eyes burning with a flame that seemed to revitalize his entire being.

"Very well. You are dismissed. We will speak further in the future," Elder Jun said with finality, signaling the end of the conversation.

Ping Hai bowed deeply and exited, leaving Xu Ziqing alone with the older man. His thoughts churned with unease. The young disciple's pledge of loyalty, so fervently offered under Elder Jun's guiding words, sparked a flicker of doubt in his mind. Was Ping Hai's unwavering commitment being anchored to the ideals of the Silent Moon Sect, or was it being subtly redirected toward Elder Jun himself? The distinction was subtle yet critical. He couldn't shake the feeling that there might be more personal motives at play.

*Loyalty should be to the sect first, not to any one individual*, he reminded himself, his wariness of Elder Jun's intentions growing.

The thought unsettled him deeply. The strength of the Silent Moon Sect had always been its unity, a collective force bound by shared ideals and purpose. Yet, if individual loyalties were being siphoned toward singular figures of power, could the sect's cohesion fray, its collective might diluted by divided allegiances?

Xu Ziqing's gaze shifted to Elder Jun, whose silhouette was framed by the dimming light.

The lines between loyalty to the sect and loyalty to its leaders blurred in the twilight, leaving the second-class disciple to wonder at the true nature of the bonds being forged in the quiet confines of these chambers. Elder Jun's words, though cloaked in the language of unity and sect prosperity, seemed to weave a personal bond between the elder and Ping Hai—a bond that might serve to elevate Elder Jun's own standing and agenda.

Once the door had closed behind Ping Hai, Elder Jun turned his penetrating gaze to him. The Azure Moon Marauder swallowed nervously.

"With the right guidance, Ping Hai will move beyond this loss. He has the potential to be instrumental in the sect's future, possibly making up for today's loss of the Beast Core and more."

Xu Ziqing nodded through a flicker of unease. "Ping Hai's loyalty is indeed valuable, Elder. However, the loss of the Wind Serpent Beast Core is a significant setback," he ventured cautiously.

Elder Jun's expression remained impassive, but a small smile played at the corners of his mouth. "The Wind Serpent Beast Core, while valuable, is not the end goal, Xu Ziqing. It is but one of many. What I seek is the accumulation of power for the sect, through whatever means necessary."

His brow furrowed slightly at the elder's words, the implications unsettling. The sect elder leaned forward, his voice dropping to a conspiratorial whisper. "The true strength of the Silent Moon lies not in individual Beast Cores but in our collective power and unity. Securing the third-class disciples' unwavering loyalty today is a gain, not a loss."

He paused, letting his words sink in before continuing. "We stand at the precipice of change, Xu Ziqing. The Silent Moon must evolve, shedding its old skin.

It begins with the hearts of our disciples, yes, but it will not end there. We must be prepared to redefine what it means to belong to the Silent Moon."

The second-class disciple acknowledged it; the sect was undergoing subtle shifts with the succession process for the new sect leader taking place. However, he couldn't help but remark that many of the ripples in the sect were being caused by Elder Jun himself.

The older man rose, his silhouette casting long shadows. "You have a new mission, Xu Ziqing. The auction in Crescent Bay City awaits your presence. Purchase as many Beast Cores as you can. They are but mere keys, opening doors to alliances and powers yet unseen."

As Elder Jun spoke of the upcoming auction and the acquisitions that awaited, Xu Ziqing couldn't help but feel a chill that had nothing to do with the evening air. There was something in the elder's tone, a certain surety, as if the pieces of a grander game were falling into place according to a plan only he could see.

*For the sect or for yourself, Elder?* Xu Ziqing mused silently.

But contrary to his thoughts, he only nodded affirmatively and asked a question, seemingly out of curiosity rather than caution. "May I ask, Elder, why these items? What doors do we aim to unlock?"

Elder Jun's smile widened, cryptic and unsettling. "Every key has its lock, Xu Ziqing. Our chosen gifts will welcome not just a person but a new era for the Silent Moon."

# CHAPTER TWENTY

# Tales and Tonics

Being injured sucked.

In some ways, this was worse than when I got thrashed by the Wind Serpents in Qingmu. At least they had the decency not to fracture my arms.

The infirmary was a world apart from the bustling training grounds and serene gardens of the sect. Its air was thick with the scent of medicinal herbs. It reminded me of home.

But still . . . three days. It had taken me three days to get the approval from the doctor to let me do low-impact activities like turning the pages of books. I had to learn how to hold a book and turn to the next page with my toes!

Whether it was the sheer amount of time I could only read or meditate with, I burned through pages faster than one could say "cultivation breakthrough." Books surrounded my bed. Each volume, with its creased spine and dog-eared pages, kept me busy from the dull, aching pain of my wounds and leveled up my Reading skill. Aside from ruminating about what I should do with the Technique Token I gained from the Interface, there wasn't much else to do.

The doctor, a stern-faced woman by the name of Fei Ni, with hands as gentle as her demeanor was strict, had initially given me a bleak forecast. "A week and a half at the very least," she had said, leaving no room for negotiation. But she hadn't accounted for Tianyi.

Her presence was more than just comforting; it was healing my injuries, stitching together what was broken with a delicacy no human hand could achieve.

Under her watchful care, my left arm had mended with a speed that left the infirmary staff baffled.

"Impossible," Fei Ni had muttered under her breath.

But in the world of cultivators, where the impossible often became possible, Tianyi's healing prowess was a miracle I had come to cherish.

The doctor occasionally requested Tianyi's help, marveling at the potent effects of her skills. Even though the Interface didn't say it outright, I knew she was due for a breakthrough soon. I could feel her abilities strengthening with every passing day.

I reached out to Tianyi with a wave of gratitude, feeling the warm buzz of positive emotions in return through our bond. "This young master pays back grace twofold, and those who treat me unjustly shall see themselves at the unfortunate end of my fist! Thank you for your services, colorful one."

However, my right hand, the one that bore the brunt of Ping Hai's formidable grip, was another story. The fractures were more severe, the damage more profound. It was a constant reminder of the price of my actions, a price I was still paying. The doctor had warned me that this injury would tether me to the infirmary for a longer stretch.

So, I turned to what I could do—read. Each book became a temporary escape, a portal to a realm where my injuries were inconsequential, and my spirit roamed free. Yet, as I read, I couldn't shake off that small twinge of frustration and impatience welling up within me. The Grand Alchemy Gauntlet was fast approaching, and here I was, confined to a bed, my body a patchwork of healing and hurt.

But wallowing in self-pity wasn't my style. I glanced over at my quest, the one I had been focusing on completing since my time away from training, and the screen from the Heavenly Interface flickered to life.

*Quest: Creation of Healing Hydrosol*
*—Study ancient alchemical texts from the Verdant Lotus Sect's library*
*to uncover the secrets of hydrosol creation. (3/3)*
*—Harvest fresh tienchi ginseng, spirit moss, common reed,*
*and hyacinth orchid and deepen your understanding*
*of each ingredient. (3/4)*
*—Extract the pure essence of spirit moss and find its hidden properties. (0/1)*
*—Learn the method to create purified water using alchemy.*

As I poured over the texts, my focus was singular: the creation of the Healing Hydrosol. I had meticulously ticked off almost every requirement of the quest. The tienchi ginseng, common reed, and hyacinth orchid had all been studied extensively.

However, the spirit moss remained the final piece of the puzzle. Despite its unassuming nature and the rather mundane "spirit" in its name, my research revealed its unheralded potential. Rare in our region, used in household remedies, it could treat colds and inflammations with surprising efficacy. Its antibacterial properties made it an excellent material for wound dressings, a natural safeguard against infection.

I already asked Feng Wu about it because I hadn't seen them being cultivated in the sect's greenhouses or gardens. He mentioned that the spirit moss grew farther up north, by a lake just outside of the sect premises.

Lost in thought, I set aside the book I had just finished, its pages filled with the ancient wisdom of alchemists long gone. That's when the familiar glow of the Heavenly Interface caught my eye, a welcome distraction from the frustration of the elusive spirit moss.

A notification floated before me, its message a testament to the countless hours spent with my nose buried in books.

> *Reading has reached level 10.*
> *Your skill has reached the qualifications to evolve to the next stage,*
> *Accelerated Reading.*
> *Accelerated Reading grants you two new abilities.*
> *Enhanced Comprehension—You can understand and assimilate*
> *complex texts and ancient scriptures at an accelerated pace, allowing*
> *for deeper insights and quicker learning.*
> *Increased Reading Speed—Your ability to read and process information*
> *has significantly improved, enabling you to cover vast amounts of text in*
> *a fraction of the usual time without sacrificing retention or understanding.*

I punched the air with a triumphant fist. "At last!"

It took months to get here. The Interface said to read thirty books, but I ended up plowing through way more, trying to grasp the "basic understanding" it wanted. It was a metric that was frustratingly vague.

Tianyi, drawn by my exuberant outburst, fluttered close, her delicate wings casting a subtle glow as she landed on the tip of my nose. The rustle of the curtain announced Fei Ni's arrival, her finger pressed to her lips in a gentle reprimand. "Quiet, please."

"Sorry!" My attention drifted to the stack of books by my bedside, a literary tower that had steadily dwindled to a mere thirteen volumes. Li Na and Han Wei had turned my predicament into a playful wager, continuously updating the stack to challenge my reading limits. Before, the prospect of finishing seemed daunting, but now, with my newfound skill . . .

I grabbed another book and started to read.

The book I had been saving for last was titled *The Ethereal Weave of Qi: Understanding the Intangible.* It was a tome that delved deep into the nuanced theories of qi manipulation and its application in both cultivation and alchemy. To say it was complex would be an understatement. The subject matter was dense, filled with abstract concepts and intricate diagrams that made my head spin after reading the first ten pages.

Yet, as I began to read, something remarkable happened. The words seemed to flow effortlessly, their meanings unraveling before me like a tapestry being woven at the hands of a master weaver.

The Accelerated Reading skill had transformed my reading experience. Complex sentences that would have once required rereading and contemplation now made sense in a single glance. Paragraphs that would have bogged me down with their density were now stepping stones, propelling me forward through the pages with a newfound ease.

Was the skill making me smarter? It certainly felt that way. The implications were profound, extending far beyond just reading faster. This skill had the potential to accelerate my learning in all areas; acquiring new knowledge and skills not just faster but more intuitively.

As I turned the pages, my eyes scanning the text at a pace that would have been unimaginable just days before, I couldn't suppress a grin. The Accelerated Reading skill was a game-changer, a tool that would undoubtedly become one of my most valuable assets on the journey ahead.

*Enlightenment, here I come!*


Li Na and Han Wei burst into the infirmary, their arms laden with yet more stacks of books. Their eyes widened in disbelief as they took in the neatly organized pile of completed reads by my bedside.

"Kai, you didn't . . ." Han Wei began skeptically.

With a smug smile, I leaned back against my pillows. "Every single one," I declared, unable to hide my pride.

Not entirely convinced, Han Wei picked a volume at random from the finished stack and flipped it open. "All right, then. What's the key concept of chapter seven in this one?" he challenged.

I paused for a moment, letting the gears in my mind turn. The Accelerated Reading skill didn't just make the words fly by; it made them stick. "Ah, that chapter delves into the symbiotic relationship between the cultivator's qi and the ambient natural energies. It's about harmonizing the two to enhance cultivation efficiency," I answered confidently, the details coming back to me as if I had just read them.

Li Na's eyebrows shot up, impressed. "Wow, Kai. That's . . . actually correct."

With a resigned chuckle, Han Wei placed the book back on the pile and handed me the new stack, noticeably smaller than the previous ones. "We figured yesterday's was a bit overkill. But, man, carrying these back and forth is becoming a workout in itself."

I accepted the books with a grateful nod, my spirits buoyed by their continued support. "Thanks, you two. I really appreciate it. You know, I was thinking of asking Fei Ni if I could step outside for a bit. Get some fresh air, you know?"

Her concern was immediate. "Are you sure you're up for that? You've been through a lot."

I flexed my left arm, showing its almost complete recovery. "Yeah, I think a little stroll might do me good. Plus, Tianyi's been cooped up here with me. She could use some sunlight."

Together, we approached Fei Ni, who was meticulously organizing her medical instruments. Seeing our approach, she raised an eyebrow in silent inquiry.

Dropping to the floor with all the dramatic flair I could muster, I clasped my hands together. "Oh, great and benevolent healer, might this humble disciple bask in the glory of the sun's rays, if only for a brief moment?"

"Get up, you melodramatic child. You can go outside. But," she added, her tone firming, "if I hear you've overexerted yourself, it's straight back here. Understood?"

"Understood!" I chirped, practically leaping to my feet, excited by the prospect of feeling the sun on my face again.

"So, what's the grand plan? More book hunting?" Han Wei joked mirthfully.

I shook my head, already feeling the gentle warmth of the sun calling to me. "Actually, I'm thinking of taking a little trip just outside the sect. There's some spirit moss I need to track down for the Healing Hydrosol quest."

Li Na's brows furrowed with concern. "That sounds like it could be strenuous. Need a hand or two?"

I appreciated their offer, their readiness to leap into another adventure, no questions asked. But this was something I needed to do on my own. "Thanks, but I'll be fine. I've got Tianyi and Windy for company," I reassured them, smiling at the thought of my two companions. "Don't want to drag you into more of my messes."

After a moment's hesitation, they acquiesced. "All right, but don't do anything too crazy," Han Wei warned, only half joking.

With farewells exchanged, I made my way to the guest quarters, a sense of purpose fueling my steps. I hoped Windy hadn't decided to embark on one of their impromptu hunting expeditions.

Upon entering the guest quarters, a heart-stopping sight greeted me. There, in the dimly lit corner of the room, lay what appeared to be the lifeless form of Windy. My breath hitched, and a cold dread settled in my stomach.

"No, Windy . . . Please, no," I whispered, barely audible, disbelief and despair washing over me. The idea that my adventurous little companion might have met an untimely end was too much to bear.

How could this have happened? I thought it was smart enough to open windows, and I even left one slightly ajar to avoid this exact scenario!

With a trembling hand, I reached out, the finality of the moment weighing heavily upon me. But as my fingers brushed against the supposed remains, a wave of confusion swept through me. The texture was all wrong; it was dry, brittle, and . . . hollow? My heart, which had plummeted to the depths of despair, began a cautious ascent back to hope.

In an instant, the grim atmosphere shattered as realization dawned upon me. It wasn't Windy but its shed skin! Relief flooded through me, so intense it almost bordered on giddiness.

Just then, from the shadowy recesses of the room, a familiar hiss and the gentle rustle of scales approached. Windy, very much alive and sporting a fresh, glossy coat of scales, slithered into view, its tongue flicking out as if amused by my dramatic display.

Cradled gently in its coils was the Wind Serpent Beast Core, its energy pulsating softly.

Relief flooded me, mixed with a burgeoning pride in Windy's growth. "Had me worried there for a second," I chided playfully, picking up the shed skin and examining it. "Looks like you're growing up fast, huh? Soon we'll know if you're a little brother or sister."

Windy's response was a soft hiss, a sign of contentment as it uncoiled and slithered up to my uninjured shoulder. Oof, not a little hatchling anymore, I supposed. No matter! It'd be good to get a bit of physical activity before I fully healed.

With Tianyi fluttering by my side and Windy wrapped securely around my upper body, I stepped back out into the sun, ready to embrace the day's challenges. The quest for the elusive spirit moss awaited, and with my companions at my side, I was ready to depart.

But first, I had to deal with the immediate challenge of navigating the sect's grounds with one good arm and a body still mending. "Let's take it slow, team. We've got moss to find."

# CHAPTER TWENTY-ONE

# Foraging

A h, the fresh scent of adventure! Isn't that right, Tianyi?"

She fluttered up to my nose, signaling her approval. Windy, poking out of my sleeve, flicked out its tongue back and forth before returning back into the darkness of my sleeve.

The weather was getting colder by the day. All the trees turned orange, leaving me with the nice sensation of crackling leaves as I walked the beaten path. I couldn't help but grumble at the uneven terrain. The rocky riverbank, coupled with my arm still snug in its cast, made for a challenging trek.

It wouldn't do to rebreak the careful healing of my arm. Dr. Fei Ni would likely strap me to the bed, and I'd be unable to move a finger at that rate.

Meanwhile, somewhere among this greenery, the elusive spirit moss awaited. Gently, I lowered Windy to the ground. "Seek out our verdant quarry, brave warrior," I encouraged, watching as it slithered away with an eager flick of its tongue.

Tianyi, ever vigilant, hovered nearby, her wings a blur of motion. "We're on the hunt for spirit moss," I explained to her. "Emerald green, with feather-like fronds that sprawl in a spiral pattern. Keep your eyes peeled."

As I began my own search, I muttered to myself about the likely habitats of the moss, based on my extensive yet recently acquired reading. "Near rocks and trees, the texts said. Moist, shaded areas where the sun's touch is gentle, not harsh."

My mind wandered to the role it would play in my hydrosol concoction. As I meandered along the riverbank, my gaze fixed on the nooks and crannies that might harbor the spirit moss, I pondered its peculiar name and scarce references in the sect's archives.

"Not much to go on, really," I mused. "It's more or less a footnote, known more for its luminescent turquoise glow in the evening than any profound medicinal properties." The thought nagged at me as I sifted through the underbrush.

"There's got to be more to it. Perhaps it's like those rare herbs that don't reveal their true potential until put under the alchemist's flame."

Tianyi's sudden, excited fluttering caught my attention. Following her lead, I navigated the uneven terrain with a careful gait, mindful of my still-mending arm. She led me further upstream, where the babbling of the river seemed to sing in harmony with the rustling leaves.

There, nestled between two moss-covered rocks, was Windy, its body coiled with an air of triumph. The surrounding stones were blanketed in a lush layer of moss, its emerald fronds sprawling out in spirals just as the texts had described.

Kneeling beside the serene spectacle, I carefully inspected the moss, confirming its identity against the mental checklist of characteristics I had memorized. The vibrant green hue, the delicate, feather-like texture—it was unmistakably the spirit moss we sought.

I turned to my companions, a wide grin spreading across my face. "May the province sing of this day, when Kai, Tianyi, and Windy conquered the elusive spirit moss!"

Their reactions were as expected—Tianyi buzzed with a joyful hum, while Windy simply flicked its tongue.

The moss felt cool and slightly damp to the touch, its texture both delicate and resilient. I tapped into my Plant Whisperer skill, hoping it might shed some light on the enigmatic spirit moss. "What secrets do you hold?"

The moss remained silent, its secrets locked away beyond my skill's reach. My Plant Whisperer skill, while a boon in the wild, seemed to offer little more than an instinctual understanding of how to interact with plants, a guide to their basic handling and use rather than a key to their deeper mysteries. It was akin to a sixth sense for the green world, an intuitive nudge in the right direction when faced with unfamiliar flora. It was not the all-revealing oracle I might have hoped for in this moment.

With a focused breath, I placed my palm over a small patch of the moss to extract its essence. The moss responded to my touch, a soft, turquoise glow emanating from beneath my hand.

"Now to safely store you away for further study," I muttered, only to realize with a sinking feeling that I forgot a vial.

With my one good arm occupied with maintaining the essence, I awkwardly fumbled through my pouch with my elbow, hoping I had overlooked a spare container. Perhaps I could ask Windy to snake inside my pouch and see.

In my flustered state, I failed to notice a protruding root on the ground. My foot caught on it, and a jolt of panic shot through me. I teetered precariously. Tianyi, sensing my alarm, could only flutter about helplessly. After all, she couldn't steady my fall.

Faced with the choice between preserving the essence and preventing a potentially disastrous fall, I opted for the latter. With a regretful sigh, I tossed the essence orb away and executed a swift handstand, using my good arm to break my fall.

The world turned upside down for a brief moment before I righted myself, standing back up with a flourish that would have made Instructor Xia Ji and Li Na proud.

"Behold the grace of a wounded crane!" I boasted to no one in particular, my heart racing from the close call. If there was one thing that remained from my epic training to defeat the mountain named as Ping Hai, it was that the Bamboo Reprisal Counter helped me become more acrobatic.

> *Bamboo Reprisal Counter (Level 1): This defensive skill draws inspiration from the flexible yet unyielding nature of bamboo.*
> *Absorb the force of incoming attacks, bending without breaking, and then channeling this accumulated energy back toward the assailant.*

It was an odd thing; I'd spent a month learning it and didn't actually register it into the Interface until I used it against Ping Hai. I managed to use it against Han Wei and Li Na in practice, so why didn't I learn it then?

Well, it didn't matter to me much. So long as I learned it eventually. The Interface is vague about many of the things it does. Perhaps one day I'd uncover its secrets.

As I steadied myself after the near miss, a wave of relief washed over me. I looked back to where I had inadvertently thrown the essence orb, half expecting it to have dissipated. Instead, Tianyi was hovering over a small puddle that now glowed with a subtle turquoise light.

Intrigued, I approached and observed the essence interacting with the water. It spread out in a radiant display, reminiscent of ink diffusing in water, creating a mesmerizing pattern that seemed to pulse with life. It continued for a moment longer, before eventually dying down and turning back to a regular puddle.

The sight was not only beautiful but revealing; it dawned on me that the true nature of spirit moss manifested when its essence mingled with water! Of course!

I gathered a handful of the moss, carefully placing it in my pouch for further study. Judging by the lack of activity from the Heavenly Interface, I was only scratching the surface of its hidden qualities. I'd need to go back.

"Tianyi! Windy! We've accomplished our mission. Let's go."

Windy seemed unwilling to return, cozying up near the rocks. It seemed to have found a new favorite spot.

I tried coaxing it with a gentle nudge. "Come on, Windy, adventure's over for today." But it merely flicked its tongue, indifferent to my plea.

Tianyi, with her delicate grace, fluttered over and landed gently on Windy's head. There were no words exchanged, of course, but the subtle shift in Windy's demeanor was unmistakable. With what seemed like a resigned sigh, Windy finally relented, uncoiling itself from its rocky embrace and slithering up to my awaiting hand.

I made a beeline for the alchemy pavilion. The essence's reaction with water had sparked a theory in my mind, one I was eager to test. I remembered reading about the moss's basic properties—its use in dressing wounds due to its antibacterial and anti-inflammatory qualities. My Essence Extraction skill tended to amplify a plant's effects, so it stood to reason that the essence, when combined with water, might create a potent healing solution.

Once in the pavilion, I quickly gathered the necessary materials: a small bowl, purified water, and a sterilized knife. My heart raced with anticipation as I poured the water into the bowl and prepared another sample of spirit moss. With a steady hand, I extracted its essence, watching as the glowing turquoise orb formed above my palm.

Carefully, I dropped the essence into the bowl of water, and the reaction was immediate. The essence dispersed, creating a captivating display reminiscent of the earlier spectacle by the river. This time, however, I was ready to test its effects firsthand.

With a mix of apprehension and excitement, I pressed the knife to my finger, making a small, deliberate cut. A drop of blood welled up, but I didn't give it time to linger. I submerged my finger into the bowl, the cool, essence-infused water enveloping the wound.

The sensation was immediate and unmistakable—a gentle, soothing warmth that seemed to penetrate deep into the cut. I watched, fascinated, as the edges of the wound appeared to draw closer, the skin knitting together with a speed that defied belief.

However, the aura surrounding the water seemed to dissipate, becoming fainter and fainter until the distinct hue was no more.

After a few minutes, I lifted my finger from the water, thinking I might see the cut still there. But no, the skin was healed, leaving only the faintest line to show where the wound had been. Astonishment washed over me. The essence of spirit moss, when merged with water, possessed remarkable healing capabilities, far beyond what I had anticipated.

> *Quest: Creation of Healing Hydrosol has been completed.*
> *Due to your status as Interface Manipulator,*
> *your rewards will be adjusted accordingly.*

Unlike my other quests, the reward came quicker than imagined.

> *Reward calculation completed.*
> *Your reward will put you into a trance-like state. Proceed?*

I'd never encountered such a notification before. As I mentally braced for whatever was to come, a wave of dizziness swept over me, plunging me into darkness.

When my senses returned, I found myself in a nondescript room, devoid of any familiar landmarks. Glancing down, I realized with a start that I had no physical form here.

"What in the . . . ?" I muttered, trying to make sense of the situation. Tianyi and Windy were nowhere to be found.

My hands reached into nothingness where they should have been. The instinctual need to touch, to feel, was met with an eerie absence that sent a shiver through my noncorporeal form. I waved my hands, or at least I thought I did, in front of where my face should have been, but there was nothing—no sensation of air moving, no visual confirmation, just the unsettling void.

"Hello?"

I couldn't feel the sensation of my mouth moving, but the voice clearly echoed.

A robed figure appeared, featureless and enigmatic, moving toward a table laden with the very ingredients I needed for the hydrosol—spirit moss, tienchi ginseng, hyacinth orchid, and common reed. Their movements were precise, almost ritualistic, using tools similar to the ones in the pavilion but intricate designs I couldn't help but notice.

Where had I seen those before?

I watched, fascinated yet bewildered, as the figure demonstrated the creation of the hydrosol. Their method was unfamiliar. It was like watching Elder Zhu at work; I couldn't grasp the full depth of his skills, but I recognized their effectiveness. This figure's handling of the ingredients was beyond my current understanding, yet it resonated with me on an instinctual level; I couldn't miss an iota of what was being demonstrated here.

Their movements were deliberate, almost like they were performing some sacred ritual.

Watching them work was mesmerizing. They didn't just chop the tienchi ginseng; they had a special way of handling it, teasing out its essence without brute force. For the hyacinth orchid . . . Instead of crushing the petals, they gently rubbed them together, preserving their beauty while drawing out the essence. It was nothing like I'd ever seen. The common reed was another surprise. No simple cutting here. They tapped along its length.

Seconds turned into minutes, and minutes turned into hours.

As the demonstration continued, a strange sense of déjà vu hit me. The room's layout, the design of the tools—something about them was eerily familiar. It took me a moment, but then it clicked—the resemblance to the ruins where I first encountered the Heavenly Interface was uncanny.

With each ingredient prepared, the figure began the actual process of creating the hydrosol. They used a distillation setup that was familiar yet foreign, with glassware that seemed to twist and turn in ways that defied my understanding of alchemy.

A small window in the room allowed a sliver of moonlight to filter through, casting a serene glow over the scene.

The figure carefully placed a bowl in the water, ensuring it was in direct view of the moonlight, and slowly poured the essence of the spirit moss into it. The liquid's hue deepened, creating a spectacle of turquoise that was even more intense than what I had observed during my own experiment by the river.

This deliberate action, under the moon's gentle gaze, seemed to amplify the moss's known properties. I realized the significance of this step; the spirit moss was renowned for its ethereal glow in the moonlight, and here, in this trance-induced vision, the figure was harnessing that very trait, enhancing it through the alchemical process.

As the other ingredients were distilled into a hydrosol, dripping steadily into a separate bowl, I watched the entire procedure come together. Each drop seemed to fall with the deliberate slowness of honey sliding down a spoon, pooling into the bowl with a hypnotic regularity that drew me deeper into the vision.

The figure's methodical, precise movements and the careful handling of each element all contributed to the creation of something truly unique—a healing hydrosol imbued with a constant, gentle glow.

What struck me was the permanence of this glow. Even as the figure moved the finished product away from the moonlight, the hydrosol continued to emit a subtle, turquoise light. It was a revelation; the temporary, natural luminescence of the spirit moss had been transformed into a permanent feature of the hydrosol through this intricate and deliberate method.

I committed every single detail to memory. I'd have to analyze every single move, every touch. It went beyond the basic alchemical processes I was familiar with, hinting at a level of mastery that I had yet to fully comprehend.

Although I knew the figure wouldn't hear me, seeing as it hadn't reacted to my presence as it darted around the room throughout the entire process, I thanked it. "Uh, thank you! I learned very well from this experience!" After all, a man who doesn't show grace is no more than a beast!

To my disbelief, the figure paused in its meticulous work and turned toward where I perceived myself to stand. Despite lacking any discernible facial features or a clear form, the gesture was unmistakably directed at me—a wave that acknowledged my presence in this ethereal space.

With a start, I found myself back in the present, the sensation of my physical form returning in a rush of sensory overload.

Tianyi and Windy seemed to be doing their thing, unaware of the mental journey I'd just been on. I checked outside—still midafternoon. That whole vision felt like hours, but here, only minutes had passed.

"Time's weird," I muttered to myself. There was a lot to unpack from what I'd just seen. That detailed process of making the hydrosol wasn't something I could just wing later. I needed to get this right, especially with how the spirit moss essence worked in the moonlight.

# CHAPTER TWENTY-TWO

# Under the Glow of Turquoise Light

Please, pay me no mind," Elder Zhu said mischievously. "I'm merely here as an assistant."

I offered a sheepish grin, the weight of my cast-laden arm multiplying at this moment. "Thank you, Elder. I just hope my current predicament doesn't hinder the process too much."

The array of ingredients before me was meticulously arranged, illuminated by the brilliant moonlight that now bathed the pavilion just after midnight. I mentally rehearsed the procedure once more, ensuring the alchemical apparatus and tools were primed for the task.

Recalling the unique preparation methods from my vision, I felt a twinge of apprehension. The precise handling required was daunting, especially with my injured hand cocooned in plaster.

Gaining access to the pavilion outside regular hours required an instructor's consent. The heavens smiled upon me when I encountered Elder Zhu securing the premises for the night.

Sensing my hesitation, he offered a reassuring smile. "It is my duty as an instructor to help you overcome them. How may I assist you in this endeavor?"

"If you could help me stir this into the moonlight water, Elder, I'd be much obliged. The essence . . . it's delicate, and I fear my current clumsiness might not do it justice."

As Elder Zhu followed, I set my focus on preparing the ingredients.

Doubt nibbled at the edges of my focus as I worked. Had I captured every nuance of the recipe? The vision had been replayed countless times within the confines of my Memory Palace, each review a desperate attempt to understand the reasoning behind the figure's every move. Though the insights gleaned were sparse, they lent a certain sureness to my hands.

*Ancestors, guide me! Let this work!*

With each ingredient prepared like how the figure did in my trance and placed in the alchemical still, I activated the flame under the equipment with a pulse of qi. Soon, the hydrosol would be ready. I turned to Elder Zhu. The memory of rejecting his offer to become his apprentice still stabbed away at me. To think he'd be so willing to help despite all that . . .

"Elder, your help tonight, it means more than I can say."

He chuckled softly, his focus unwavering from the bowl before him. Even something as simple as stirring looked like a work of art. "It's my honor to assist in bringing your vision to life."

*One day, maybe . . . No.*

*I* will *reach that realm. That level of expertise. I will reach it, without a doubt. Like the figure from my trance, like Elder Zhu, I'll be able to create the finest of pills and potions with a wave of my hand!*

"Is this satisfactory, Kai?"

He showed me the bowl. The bowl Elder Zhu held out to me shimmered with a captivating turquoise glow.

"It's perfect, Elder. Thank you."

With a nod of acknowledgment, Elder Zhu placed the bowl carefully on the workbench, his eyes reflecting the mixture's gentle luminescence. I turned my attention to the alchemical still, where the hydrosol had been quietly accumulating, drop by drop, a clear liquid that held the promise of healing.

"Elder Zhu, might I impose upon your kindness once more?" I asked, gesturing toward the still. "The hydrosol needs to be introduced to the spirit moss–moonlight water mix slowly, in a steady stream, just as the figure in my vision demonstrated."

Without a word, Elder Zhu assisted, his hands steady as he manipulated the apparatus to allow the hydrosol to flow into the glowing bowl. The mixture's reaction was immediate; the glow intensified, casting an ethereal light that seemed to fill the pavilion. But as quickly as it flared, the glow simmered down to a persistent, gentle radiance.

Elder Zhu, his curiosity piqued, leaned in closer. "Is the concoction complete, then?"

"Not quite. What makes this hydrosol special isn't just its healing properties but its enduring glow. The spirit moss's effect typically fades swiftly, but this . . . this recipe ensures the glow remains, preserving its properties."

To test its efficacy, I gingerly removed the cast from my fractured hand, the plaster coming away with a soft crunch. The moonlight cast stark shadows over the healed yet still tender skin. I hesitated for only a moment before submerging my hand in the glowing mixture.

The sensation was unlike anything I'd experienced—a gentle, tingling warmth that seeped deep into my skin, soothing the lingering ache in my bones. Elder Zhu watched, his expression thoughtful.

Minutes stretched on, the pavilion wrapped in a tranquil silence broken only by the soft murmur of the night. When I finally withdrew my hand, the anticipation was palpable. Flexing my fingers, I braced for the familiar stab of pain—but it never came. The discomfort had been significantly alleviated.

"Remarkable," he murmured, his gaze shifting between my hand and the still-glowing mixture.

I couldn't help but smile. I tried to show a dignified side of me, but all I could muster was a bare whisper. "It worked, Elder. The recipe is complete."

Elder Zhu leaned in, observing the persistent glow of the mixture. "This is most intriguing, Kai. The properties of this hydrosol . . . they remind me of a concoction I once read about in the ancient archives. There might be a historical precedent for your discovery."

"That's . . . quite an honor, Elder. To think my experimentation might align with the works of the great alchemists of old."

Perhaps that was intentional on the Heavenly Interface's part. Who knows how long it had existed, in those ruins waiting to be activated? Essence Extraction was an ability only known to Master Li Tao, the previous head of the alchemy pavilion. But now it was alive in me.

Maybe even the Rooted Banyan Stance and Crimson Lotus Purification Method were skills or techniques that had been lost to time, revived by the Heavenly Interface.

Or maybe it's still out there somewhere, the closely guarded secret of a sect. I suppose they wouldn't take too kindly to a civilian possessing their techniques. Then they'd probably send assassins after me or make me pay for learning such a thing . . .

The thought of several Ping Hai-sized assassins aiming for my life terrified me. I didn't want to think about it. Let's hope nobody else knew my techniques.

Elder Zhu placed a reassuring hand on my shoulder, his smile warm in the moonlit pavilion. "It's more than an honor, Kai. Your dedication enabled you to recreate and enhance a possibly forgotten alchemical recipe. That is no small feat."

I felt embarrassment flooding my cheeks. This praise was too much! "Elder Zhu, this accomplishment . . . it isn't mine alone. Without your invaluable assistance tonight, I wouldn't have come this far. I believe the credit should be shared with the sect. I'd like to offer the recipe to our archives and assist in any way I can with producing more of the spirit moss essence."

The head of the alchemy pavilion regarded me for a long moment. "Your generosity is commendable, but you must remember that you are the creator of this hydrosol. It's a significant contribution to the art of alchemy, and you shouldn't part with your achievements so lightly."

I glanced at Windy and Tianyi, who, despite their inability to speak, seemed to be hanging on to every word of our conversation.

"I understand, Elder, but my aim has always been to aid those around me. This hydrosol . . . I was inspired to create it partly because I saw how it could benefit disciples like Feng Wu. They push themselves to the limit with conditioning drills, and if this concoction can help them heal faster without relying solely on healing pills, then I believe it's worth sharing."

Elder Zhu's gaze softened, the moonlight highlighting the thoughtful creases on his brow. "Your heart is in the right place, Kai. To repay grace and contribute to the betterment of our community is a noble path. If you insist on this course, then I will support you."

The encouragement in his words bolstered my resolve. "Thank you, Elder Zhu. I will. And I'll make sure that whatever I create in the future, it will serve not just the Verdant Lotus Sect but the wider cultivation world."

As the conversation drew to a close, the mixture before us continued to glow with a steady turquoise light, a symbol of the night's success.

"Now, I'll have to get going. Let's ensure everything is stored properly before we close the pavilion for the night."

As I packed away the equipment and stored the hydrosol in a small container, my thoughts lingered on the nameless figure that had helped me bring this recipe to life.

*Thank you, Heavenly Interface!*

A grin tugged at the corners of my mouth. The completion of the hydrosol was only the beginning. With the formula perfected and its effects verified, the second phase of my plan could now commence. But before embarking on this new journey, there was one more step to complete—the formal closure of my chapter in the infirmary.

Despite her disbelief, Dr. Fei Ni scolded me for the recklessness of testing an unproven concoction on myself and for prematurely removing the plaster. Yet she couldn't argue with the results. After insisting I stay the night for observation, she grudgingly admitted by morning that my recovery was indeed remarkable, and I was free to go. However, she wasn't about to let me off easy.

"Before you leave, Kai, ensure all these books your friends have piled up here are returned to the library," she instructed.

I glanced at the two towering stacks of books on the bedside table. "Dr. Fei Ni, you do realize you're tasking someone who's just recovered from arm injuries with quite a tall task, don't you?"

Her response was an unamused raised eyebrow. "If you're well enough to concoct alchemical miracles, I'm sure a few books won't pose much of a challenge. Unless, of course, you're not as healed as you claim, in which case . . ." Her voice trailed off, but the message was clear.

With a resigned sigh and a smile, I carefully balanced the stacks of books in my arms, making sure not to strain my recently healed hand. Windy peeked out from my sleeve, their tongue flicking in what I interpreted as a silent chuckle at my predicament. Tianyi, fluttering above, seemed to share in Windy's amusement, her light dance casting playful shadows on the walls.

The stacks of books swayed precariously, a balancing act that required all my focus. Windy and Tianyi, sensing the importance of the task at hand, flanked me on either side, as if they were ready to catch them in case they fell.

As I approached the library, the sight of the third-class disciple tasked with its upkeep brought a new wave of apprehension. I've heard from Li Na and Han Wei about him cussing them out for the sheer amount of books they borrowed and returned during my stint in the infirmary. He stared at me from afar. It seemed he wasn't very happy to see me.

"Hail, esteemed keeper of tomes!" I announced with a grandiose wave. "Behold, I return with the sacred scrolls borrowed during my convalescence!"

The disciple, barely looking up from his ledger, replied dryly, "Just put them on the desk, please."

If there's one thing the third-class disciples don't have, it's poetic wisdom. There must be something in between those formative years between a third- and second-class disciple that make them sound so wise.

Other than Lan Sheng. But he seems like the exception to the rule.

I couldn't help but feel a sense of excitement bubbling within me. If my sense of time was right, Advanced Herbology and Pill Concoction classes would be today. I was eager to dive back into the rhythms of sect life.

The familiarity of the classrooms, the scent of herbs, and the subtle energies of concoction processes welcomed me back like an old friend. Instructor Xiao-Hu, strict as ever, acknowledged my presence. My enthusiasm was palpable, fueling my participation and experimentation with a vigor that felt like making up for lost time.

But it was the training grounds that called to me as the day progressed. It was the testing grounds for my new concoction!

"Instructor, if it wouldn't be too much of a bother, may I participate in the drills? I've been eager to get back into the swing of things," I ventured, cautiously optimistic.

She cast a discerning glance my way, likely weighing my request against her knowledge of my recent injuries. After a moment's contemplation, she nodded, the gesture firm yet not without a hint of warning. "All right. But I expect you to know your limits."

"Understood, Instructor. I'll be careful," I assured her.

I started with my fists, striking the rugged surface of the pole with controlled precision. Each impact sent a jarring vibration up my arm. I cloaked any hint of agony, the maroon fabric of my robes serving as an unwitting ally in concealing the reddening of my skin.

The air, once a benign presence, now felt like a swarm of needles against my sensitized skin, each breath a reminder of the price of progress. But I endured. I had to see it through.

As the session drew to a close, my body ached with a hundred silent protests, I made my way back to the guest quarters.

The door to my quarters creaked open, a welcome sight after the grueling session. The pain was a sharp, constant reminder of the day's exertions, yet it was accompanied by a sense of accomplishment. The physical toll was tangible, but so was the potential for recovery, thanks to the hydrosol waiting within.

Tianyi and Windy greeted me as I entered, their presence a comforting balm to the day's hardships. Tianyi, ever perceptive, fluttered closer, her glow intensifying as if ready to weave her healing magic around me. But today, her usual intervention wasn't part of the plan.

"Not today, Tianyi," I said gently, preempting her well-intentioned care. "I've got a different kind of healing in mind." Her glow dimmed slightly in understanding, though she remained close, a silent sentinel.

Windy seemed to sense the gravity of the moment, its usual playful antics subdued. It watched, curious yet respectful, as I set about the next phase of my recovery.

With deliberate movements, I retrieved the healing hydrosol and a roll of gauze from my bag. Carefully, I began to wrap my hands, ensuring every inch of skin was covered, a protective barrier between the rawness of my wounds and the outside world. The gauze was snug but not constricting, a cocoon that promised relief and regeneration.

Once secured, I hesitated for a moment, steeling myself for the next step. Then, with a deep breath, I dipped my wrapped hands into the jar of hydrosol, immersing them fully. The liquid was cool, a stark contrast to the lingering heat of my exertions.

I held them there, counting the seconds, allowing the hydrosol to seep through the gauze and interact with my skin. The sensation was immediate and profound—a cooling relief that seemed to penetrate to the very core of my injuries. It knit together flesh and spirit in a silent, harmonious dance.

Next came my shins. I soaked additional gauze in the hydrosol before carefully applying it to the tender areas, the fabric clinging to my skin, imbued with the promise of relief.

I allowed myself a moment of respite, sinking onto the bed with a sigh. The pain hadn't vanished, but its edges had softened, blurred by the hydrosol's potent effects. It was a gamble, this unconventional approach to recovery, but it was one I felt compelled to take.

The hydrosol had already proven its worth, but its true potential was yet to be fully realized. If today's experiment bore fruit, it could mark the beginning of a new era for conditioning, not just for me but for the entire sect.

For now, though, rest was paramount. The healing process, both physical and spiritual, required time and patience. I contemplated for a moment whether I should use my Memory Palace technique to review and go over what I had learned, but I thought my mind craved some actual rest for once in my life.

Tomorrow would come soon enough, but for now the world could wait.

# CHAPTER TWENTY-THREE

# Beneath Windy Skies, Resolve Takes Flight

I perched silently, my gaze fixed on Kai. He stood alone outside his resting area, his fist repeatedly colliding with the sturdy bark of a tree as the moonlight waned overhead.

His hand, swathed in a white material, bore the marks of his exertion; once pristine, it was now stained with toil and blood.

To an untrained eye, it might seem a dance of folly, a deliberate pursuit of pain. The tree, an unwitting participant in his ritual, stood resolute, its bark etched with the story of his determination. But I knew there was a purpose to it. There always was.

The sun rose and fell multiple times since he embarked on this journey. Every night after he finished, he held the "staff" made by his fellow comrade from home while in a meditative position.

I could tell it was important, so I refrained from bothering him. I had more of that so-called lychee wine to dine on while he worked diligently.

Of course, I secretly healed him during his sleep, but he would never know that.

I watched, a silent guardian, as the skin around Kai's fists transformed. Where once there was softness, now lay a landscape rugged and unyielding, akin to the very tree he challenged with his might. The texture, rough and calloused, was a testament to his discipline, a contrast to the delicate touch he possessed when tending to plants of our garden.

His strikes, initially marred by winces of pain and stifled groans, eventually turned into a silent storm of speed and precision. This transformation was not lost on me. In Kai's silent perseverance, I found a lesson etched deep within the heart of pain and endurance.

Just when I'd thought I had the human figured out, he continued to show me more and more.

The sight stirred something within me, a whisper of discontent at my own limitations. Fragile, ephemeral, my existence was a stark contrast to Kai's burgeoning fortitude. Bound by my form, I lamented the fragility of my being, the delicate wings that carried me, beautiful yet so easily marred.

If only I had appendages like his, perhaps I could've been an even greater help in the battle against those scaly serpents. Those of Windy's ilk. Remembering Kai's form, between the border of life and death, shook me to my very core.

Had it not been for the powerful immortals supporting us, would we have survived? It was only through luck that I managed to land a blow against one of those monstrous wind-whipping serpents. Had my wings met with their hardened scales, I didn't think there was any room for doubt about what would've happened.

Never. I'd never let myself be so useless ever again.

With a heart buoyed by newfound determination, I channeled qi into the gossamer threads of my wings, feeling the familiar surge of energy coursing through me, lending strength and sharpness to my delicate form. I focused on an orange leaf, gently descending in the breeze. With a burst of speed, I blurred from sight, slicing through the air. The leaf, bisected by my passage, fluttered to the ground.

Emboldened, I faced a tree. My wings, humming with qi, struck its surface. A faint mark appeared, a small start. The shockwave reminded me of the tree's unyielding nature and my own fragility.

But I did not falter. Drawing from the determination Kai had unknowingly given me, I pressed on. Strike after strike, I honed my technique, each attempt a step on the path Kai had laid before me.

From my secluded perch, my attention momentarily drifted from his relentless training to a familiar presence overhead.

Windy, our serpentine companion, was nestled comfortably on a branch, its white scales with a subtle blue hue shimmering softly in the moonlight that filtered through the leaves. I couldn't help but notice the slight bulge in its stomach, a telltale sign of a recent hunt. It filled me with a sense of relief and pride to see the hatchling thriving, growing stronger and more formidable with each passing day.

Despite the initial trepidation I felt toward Windy, stemming from the harrowing memories of the battle against its kind, my heart had since warmed to the little hatchling.

I saw in Windy not just a kin's shadow but a sibling, a companion in our journey with Kai. The thought of Windy in our garden deterring pests brought joy to my heart. Although Windy didn't see Kai as a friend like I did, I knew their bond would deepen over time.

Windy's curious gaze alternated between Kai and me, intrigued by our training. With tentative determination, it tried to replicate our actions, striking a tree with its tail. The attempt was clumsy, a departure from its hunting instincts. Moved by Windy's effort, I flew over discreetly to offer guidance without distracting Kai.

I demonstrated the way I channeled qi into my wings, hoping to convey the concept of focusing energy into a precise point. The energy coursed through the intricate design along my wings. It was a complex lesson, one I anticipated would take time for Windy to grasp fully.

The hatchling tilted its head. I knew it held considerable power under those shimmering scales, but to use it was an entirely different matter. But I knew they could do it.

It took a near-death experience against one of my most feared foes to learn how to infuse qi into my wings in the same way Kai and other immortals did. It wasn't something that could be done easily.

True training required time, patience, and often a touch of desperation. I watched Windy, expecting it to struggle, to falter, and to learn from the arduous process just as I had. A lesson in humility, perhaps, a spark to ignite the latent potential I knew slumbered within its serpentine form. Till then, I would—

*CRUNCH!*

The sound of wood being splintered alerted me, pulling my attention back with swiftness. Mid-flight, I pivoted, my gaze scanning the surroundings for the source of the disturbance.

And there was Windy, its presence unmistakable against the backdrop of the forest's deep greens and browns. The hatchling's tail, once a mere extension of its curious, playful self, now stood raised like a banner of triumph, emanating a soft, ethereal blue glow. The unmistakable aura of qi.

But it was the mark on the tree bark that truly caught my attention—a clear, undeniable gouge made by Windy's tail. Not just a scratch, but a mark of significant depth.

For a moment, I hovered in stunned silence, my mind grappling with the reality before me. The hatchling had achieved what I had deemed a distant goal in mere moments.

The realization brought with it a cascade of emotions—pride for the undeniable progress Windy had made; wonder at the ease with which it had adapted a technique so foreign to its natural instincts; and, lurking beneath the surface, something else. It was . . . unpleasant.

The hatchling's gaze met mine, a silent question in its eyes. Was it seeking approval, or perhaps validation of its achievement? In response, I allowed my own light to brighten, a silent nod of recognition and encouragement.

*Yes, Windy, you've done well.*

I fluttered away as a sense of unease lingered. It was an unfamiliar sensation, gnawing at the edges of my consciousness, demanding attention. I flew just at the edge of the forest's perimeter and away from Kai's or Windy's sight.

The whispering leaves seemed to echo the tumult within me. I sought solitude, a quiet corner of the forest where I could unravel the knot of emotions that had ensnared me.

Alone, with only the gentle rustle of the forest for company, I allowed the feelings to surface, to take shape in the clarity of my thoughts. The memory of Kai's voice came unbidden, a conversation from days past when he spoke of his own struggles, of the daunting task of catching up to the immortals who walked the halls of the Verdant Lotus Sect.

*Ah, Li Na and Han Wei are too strong! I'm so—*

Jealous. Yes, that was the word, foreign and yet so fitting. It described the turmoil within me. It was jealousy that had tainted the pride I felt for Windy's success, jealousy that whispered of my own limitations in comparison.

In the quiet of the forest, I contemplated my path.

Windy, with its innate hunter's prowess, had adapted and overcome, finding strength in its nature. Kai, ever determined, pushed past the pain and limitations, seeking growth through perseverance. Day by day, he grew more unfathomable. Stronger, faster, smarter . . . No matter what, he always found some way to improve.

And me? Where did my path lead?

I couldn't shake the feeling, the unsettling realization that my role might always be that of support, watching from the sidelines as Kai and Windy took center stage in the battles that lay ahead. If one day, there came a time when I could no longer protect the garden . . . The thought was a thorn in my side, a constant reminder of what I perceived to be my own inadequacies.

Jealousy, though a bitter companion, also held a mirror to my desires, to the aspirations that soared as high as my flights. I knew my healing powers were potent, invaluable even, yet the idea of being relegated to the background, to merely watch as others fought and struggled, was disheartening.

I gazed down at my delicate form, at the wings that had carried me through countless trials yet seemed so fragile in the grand scheme of things. A single misstep, a moment of inattention, could spell my demise. The thought was a reminder of the limitations I had been born with.

*CRACK!*

As I grappled with the storm of thoughts swirling within me, my contemplation was abruptly shattered by a roar that echoed through the forest. My gaze snapped toward the source, finding Kai standing before a tree, its trunk bearing the testament of his relentless assault. His fists, wrapped in tattered gauze, dripped with crimson. His face was dripping with sweat, marred with dirt and exhaustion. But his smile was as bright as the stars in the sky.

With a flourish that belied his evident pain, Kai threw back his head and pointed at the damaged tree, proclaiming with exaggerated grandeur, "You have met your match this day! By the unwavering might of my fists and the indomitable spirit of my will, I have bested thee in honorable combat!"

He struck an odd pose, with one foot off the ground and both his hands raised up to the sky. "Let it be known across the realm that not even the trees can withstand my resolve!"

Yet no sooner had the words left his mouth than a grimace of pain contorted his features, a stark reminder of the physical toll his victory had exacted. "Ah, but let it also be recorded that the path to glory is fraught with trials most—ouch!—arduous. I should call it a day," he added, wincing as he gingerly inspected his battered hands.

Despite the gravity of my earlier reflections, I couldn't help but be drawn into the moment. It was moments like these, where the weight of our journey seemed to lift ever so slightly.

As I watched him laugh off the pain with a bravado that was quintessentially Kai, I felt a renewed sense of purpose stir within me.

His words echoed in my mind once more, a beacon in the darkness of my doubts. He spoke of defying the heavens, of challenging the natural order to carve out one's own path. It was a sentiment that resonated with me now more than ever.

I didn't want to be just a delicate butterfly, admired for my beauty but underestimated for my strength. I wanted more. I wanted to defy the constraints of my form, to push beyond the boundaries that nature had set for me.

With renewed determination, I channeled my qi to its utmost limits, feeling the energy surge through my veins with an intensity I had never dared to reach before. My wings, a blur of motion, became honed edges of pure force, more refined and sharper than they had ever been.

I turned my attention to the base of a nearby tree trunk, a silent witness to my inner turmoil. With a burst of speed and precision, I struck, my wings cutting through the air with a force that belied my delicate appearance.

A gouge, as deep as my own wingspan, marred the tree's surface, a physical manifestation of my resolve.

In that moment, I solidified my determination to overcome my body's limitations, to rise above the preconceptions of what I was capable of. I would not be confined by my form, nor would I settle for a role that did not satisfy the fire that burned within me.

I was Tianyi. I would forge my own path, one that would see me stand shoulder to shoulder with Kai and Windy, not as a mere support but as a force to be reckoned with.

---

*Your dao is slowly forming.*

The world seemed to acknowledge my resolve, the rustling leaves and whispering winds a chorus of encouragement. I knew the journey ahead would be fraught with challenges, but I also knew that I was no longer the same creature that had once doubted her place in this world.

The Interface brought itself back to my attention once more.

*Quest: Wings of Resolve*
*—Infuse qi into your wings for one hour.*
*—Slice through a stalk of bamboo.*

With a heart full of purpose and wings ready to defy the heavens, I soared into the sky, embracing the unknown with a spirit that refused to be caged. The path ahead was mine to shape, and I would do so with every beat of my wings, every drop of my qi.

And so, I flew on, toward a future where I was more than just a delicate butterfly, toward a destiny that I would carve out with my own two wings.

# CHAPTER TWENTY-FOUR

# Steel Will, Iron Fists

I stood outside my quarters under the fading moonlight, my fists repeatedly meeting the rough bark of a chosen tree. The notification came, and with it, immense satisfaction.

> *Your Body has reached Mortal Realm—Rank 4.*

Recovering from my injuries was a turning point. Despite exhaustion and bone-deep fatigue, I persisted, bathing my wounds in hydrosol nightly and feeling my resilience grow.

Embracing the brutal regimen of body tempering, I saw untapped potential in physical conditioning, crucial for martial and alchemy greatness. I quickly absorbed knowledge from ancient manuals, which emphasized that our bodies adapt under duress. With my hydrosol, I accelerated this process, compressing months of progress into days.

The initial days were a blur of pain, testing my endurance even in my dreams. But as I persevered, the pain subsided, and my mind acclimated, allowing me to channel my full potential into each strike. My brain recognized my body's capacity to withstand force, narrowing the gap in physical strength with Li Na.

This cycle of pain and recovery propelled me forward. Within two weeks, I ascended two levels in the Mortal Realm, my body catching up to my mind and qi.

Consistency in training clashed with my limited resources, but I refused to relent. I knew that if conditioning was comfortable or easy, it wasn't hard enough.

I sighed, my fist resting against the tree's battered bark. "Tianyi! Windy! Let's go!"

The hatchling slithered down obediently as Tianyi glided over to perch on my shoulder. Their recent behavior intrigued me. Were they copying me? I had noticed gouges and cuts on the trees and branches around the guest quarters. Unless some errant beast was responsible, only two culprits could have made those markings.

I was so proud! The two would be the first students of the Kai Liu School of Martial Arts!

Returning to the quarters, I shed my sweat-stained robes and settled down with the iron staff for a session of essence extraction practice. This was crucial in understanding how to apply my Essence Extraction skill beyond the realm of flora.

*Place your hand upon a piece of metal and attempt to sense its core. Do not extract. Instead, attune yourself. Feel its solidity, its weight, and its resistance.*

Master Li Tao's journal had been my guide, emphasizing the need for a fortified will through meditation and visualization. The adversity from training sharpened my will, preparing me to break through the metaphorical wall and building a mental resilience I didn't have before.

Bit by bit, day by day, I could feel the metal finally yielding to my demands, though I never got close enough to extract it. But today was different. Having reached the fourth rank of the Mortal Realm, I had the fortitude to withstand it.

It was daunting, like trying to bend a river's flow with sheer willpower. A migraine burgeoned within my skull, but pain had become the forge for my resolve. The staff remained obstinate, but even the strongest boulders are eroded by drops of water. Slowly, the resistance began to wane. My will, a constant pressure against the metal's essence, started to make inroads. It was like chiseling away at an immense wall, each effort making the slightest mark.

The migraine intensified. The battle raged within me, a tempest of will against the metal's stubbornness.

With a final, concerted effort, I pushed through the remaining resistance. The metal essence yielded, bending to my will. Slowly, a silvery-gray essence poured from where my hand met the staff. It felt like pulling a string at the base of my palm, trying to uproot a tree with the force of my arm.

The veins along my hand bulged in exertion. *Almost. THERE!*

*Anomaly detected: Skill evolution beyond system parameters.*

"H—" I coughed and saw droplets of blood splatter onto the pristine wood. I steadied myself before I could fall, dropping the staff to the floor. I glanced down at my hand, admiring the pearlescent ball of energy circulating within my hand casting a dim white light over the room.

I had done it.

> *Achievement unlocked.*
> *Due to your status as Interface Manipulator, your rewards*
> *will be adjusted accordingly.*
> *New perk: Dao Pioneer*
> *Dao Pioneer—Evolving an Interface-given ability or skill without the support*
> *of the Heavenly Interface. Actively innovating and adapting, this perk grants*
> *a unique status that softens the rigid thresholds that usually constrain skill*
> *acquisition and evolution, allowing for more fluid and spontaneous development*
> *of one's skills and cultivation techniques.*

"Crap, my nose is bleeding," I murmured, looking for a vial. I grabbed one of the smooth glass bottles nearby and carefully placed the extracted metal essence inside before ripping out gauze and plugging it into my nostrils.

I looked at the new Perk. So now, along with Interface Manipulator, I had two perks. Judging by its description, having it meant I'd have an even easier time evolving skills like I did with Essence Extraction! I mentally commanded the skill description for Essence Extraction to come up so I could see if anything had changed.

> *Essence Extraction—You can extract the spiritual essence*
> *of plants and metals for the creation of pills and elixirs.*

My thoughts lingered on the application of metal essences in alchemy, traditionally used to imbue pills and elixirs with unique attributes. Holding Wang Jun's staff, I felt its weight and texture. It seemed lighter, and upon closer inspection, I noticed it had become hollow and lost its original sheen. *Oops.*

My heart sank at the thought of Wang Jun's disappointment. He had crafted this staff with skill and care, and now I had rendered it useless. The extraction process had altered its physical state. Perhaps I should've practiced on a mineral or ore first.

I needed to address the immediate consequence of my actions. Holding the altered staff, I contemplated my next steps.

*What now?*

With a technique token and several skills to focus on, the options felt overwhelming. Should I dive deeper into essence extraction and figure out how to extract from Beast Cores? Or maybe focus on my Accelerated Reading skill? What about the Memory Palace technique? I hadn't even figured out the full potential of the Spiritual Plant Cultivation technique, as I didn't know how to introduce new properties into plants.

"Tianyi, Windy, what do you think?"

Of course, they couldn't provide the solutions I sought, but just voicing my thoughts helped clear my mind.

I decided then to consult my friends and teachers tomorrow.

With a newfound sense of direction, I felt my anxiety recede. My path forward wasn't about choosing the perfect skill or technique at this moment. It was about continuing to grow, learn, and, most importantly, embrace the journey with the people who made it meaningful.

"I'll see what they have to say tomorrow. It's getting late."

One step at a time.

"You know I'm—we aren't really good at all that alchemy, herbalism mumbo jumbo," said Han Wei.

I couldn't suppress an eye roll, earning a giggle from Li Na. "I know you aren't, but I need some advice here. I've got too many paths to choose from, and it's just too much sometimes."

Li Na, always the more considerate one, said, "Being overwhelmed is a sign of your talent, Kai. You've got potential in so many areas, it's impressive."

"Yeah, I get that, but it's like standing at a crossroads with too many directions. Should I play to my strengths or patch up my weaknesses? Any wisdom would be great right now," I said, reaching for another serving of tofu.

Han Wei, munching thoughtfully, finally offered, "Maybe you need a balance. Play to your strengths but don't ignore your weaknesses. It's like training—balance is key."

Li Na nodded in agreement, adding, "And don't rush. You've got time to explore each path and see which one feels right. Trust your instincts."

They both made sense. *Balance and patience, huh?* As I pondered over my crispy tofu, their advice echoed in my mind. Maybe I was trying too hard to find a clear answer when I should be letting the journey guide me.

Grateful for their insights, I thanked Li Na and Han Wei before clearing my dishes. Their advice lingered in my mind as I made my way to Instructor Xiao-Hu's office. I had rarely sought him out personally. But he was probably one of the best people I could go to aside from Elder Zhu. Perhaps he could give me some clarity on my situation, to just tell it to me without sugarcoating his words.

"Kai Liu, this is unusual. What brings you here outside of regular class hours?" he inquired, a hint of curiosity beneath its usual severity.

"Instructor, I've been facing some challenges in prioritizing my learning paths and development. I've got options, maybe too many, and it's a bit overwhelming."

He listened intently. When I finished explaining, he leaned back, steepling his fingers in contemplation. "While your skill in herbalism and your unique ability in Essence Extraction are commendable, have you considered whether you could surpass Elder Zhu or myself in concocting a superior pill or elixir?"

The question caught me off guard. "Well, no," I admitted, feeling somewhat deflated. "I mean, your experience and mastery in alchemy are beyond what I've managed to achieve so far."

He nodded. "Experience and skill, honed over years of dedicated practice, give us an advantage. Our knowledge in alchemy allows us to craft concoctions with precision and efficacy that stand the test of time. While you have a remarkable talent, Kai, it is the depth of understanding and the mastery of fundamentals that truly empower an alchemist."

This resonated deeply with me, grounding my swirling thoughts. I bowed, grateful. "Thank you, Instructor Xiao-Hu. I appreciate everything you and the sect have done for me all this time."

Instructor Xiao-Hu merely nodded again, his stern facade softening slightly. "It is my duty to guide the next generation. You possess a level of insight and maturity rare for your age. Continue on this path, and you will undoubtedly achieve great things in your journey."

Our little chat had hit home. No heaven-defying shortcuts in this game; it was all about grinding through the alchemy textbooks and getting my hands dirty, literally. And that was just the way I liked it. It was how I had done things my whole life.

On the stroll back, the crisp autumn air felt like a slap of cold water, sobering and strangely refreshing. My brain had been doing gymnastics over every possible path, but now I had more confidence in what I needed to do.

A grin cracked my face as I realized I'd been like a cultivator at a rare herb auction with only one bid to place. It was time to quit circling the auction block and claim my prize—spiritually speaking, that was.

Day and night passed again and again. Before I knew it, the time for the Gauntlet had arrived.

# CHAPTER TWENTY-FIVE

# In the City

It was getting cold now. The air had a biting chill to it, and I let out cold puffs of mist with every breath. I wouldn't be surprised if it began snowing anytime soon.

Crescent Bay City was as busy as ever. It seemed as though everybody was outside despite the cold weather.

"I'll just bring the horses over to a stable," Feng Wu said. He was wearing a padded cloth cloak with a green hue that represented the Verdant Lotus Sect. "Do you feel ready?"

I snorted. "Does a tiger become anxious before a hunt?"

He shook his head with a small laugh, pulling gently at the harness to guide the steeds past the bustling alleys. "I don't know where you learned all these quotes with that busy schedule of yours . . ."

"A lot of reading, my friend. A lot of reading."

Accelerated Reading helped me compress my time studying to a fraction of what it used to be, so I spent what little free time reading other novels that the sect library had to offer.

But despite my joke, I did feel apprehensive. The Grand Alchemy Gauntlet was here. It was where the fruits of my labors would be put on display. In front of an audience, likely numbering in the hundreds or thousands . . .

"It looks like it's quite busy. While I go to the stable, would you mind grabbing a seat at one of the restaurants?"

"Sure, does the Spirited Noodle sound good?"

"All right, I'll see you there."

I diverted from Feng Wu in search of the restaurant, the first one I'd ever come to when I'd arrived here at the capital city. It felt like a lifetime ago, but in reality it had only been a few months. Although I had no doubt it'd be a volatile atmosphere, the noodles were just too good to pass up. I'd consider it a treat for how hard I trained.

"Come to think of it, you ran out of lychee wine, didn't you?"

I raised the cage in my hand, where Tianyi rested peacefully. It was a simple contraption I had custom-made just for her, so I could bring her around in a discrete manner without having her fly about. Of course, if she really wanted to, she could slip through the space between the metal, it wasn't meant to keep her trapped. The only reason she stayed inside was because I asked her politely.

An outpouring of desire flooded our connection at the word "wine." The rate at which she consumed alcohol was concerning. It was dozens of times her body weight and was supposed to last at least a few months. Where was she putting all this?

"Hiss . . ."

I snuck a peek in my other sleeve. In all his glory, Windy was wrapped carefully around my entire arm. Finding out his gender was quite a surprise. Judging by how pretty Windy had been, I was fully convinced they'd be a girl.

He was getting really heavy nowadays. I suppose it was motivation to keep getting stronger.

Eventually, it'd be impossible. Windy would become the size of his parents, enough to swallow a cow whole. He wouldn't be wrapped around my limb, I'd be wrapped around *him* instead.

For now, I'd enjoy the sensation of carrying him. It was bittersweet, seeing your children grow up so quickly. Soon they'd be in their rebellious phase, and maybe even leave the house to start their own life! The thought brought a tear to my eye.

I sighed, continuing through the bustling crowds. Spirited Noodle was just up ahead. From the looks of it, it was quite busy.

Securing a table was my mission, and as I stepped into the restaurant, the savory aroma of broth and spices hit me. A server approached, a teen with black hair and tired eyes. I raised my fingers to indicate I wanted a seat for two.

He nodded, surveying the restaurant. "It'll be ten more minutes before you can be seated. Will that be all right?"

"Yes, I'm fine with that."

They guided me over to a waiting area, already packed with people. Some were martial artists, by the looks of it. They held themselves in a distinct manner and wore beige-and-gray attire emblazoned with their emblem on the back.

*Narrow Stone Peak, eh?*

I faintly recalled the sect. They weren't situated near Crescent Bay City, if the textbook I read was accurate. They were nowhere near as famous as the Silent Moon or Verdant Lotus, either.

*They seem strong, though,* I thought, seeing the subtle outlines of muscle along their robes. Judging by their lack of weapons, I concluded they were fist fighters.

All the seats were taken, so I stood at the furthest point while I waited patiently. It didn't matter too much, as this would give time for Feng Wu to finish putting the horses away.

Resting my shoulder along the wall, I thought back on what I needed to do. Buying souvenirs for everyone back home was paramount. *What's something I could get here that wasn't available back home?*

New books for Elder Ming were a given. He's probably reread every text in the village, front and back. Maybe some more of Liang Feng's works?

Perhaps some alcohol for Master Qiang, a calligraphy set for Wang Jun, and some new ceramics for Lan-Yin! I'd look at what the Azure Silk Trading Company had to offer. Since I got a discount with them, that was where I would start my search.

I couldn't wait to see their reaction, both to my growth and Windy.

"Please follow me to your seat." My thoughts were interrupted by the server, and I got up to oblige.

A loud voice cut through the din of the restaurant. "Hey, why's he getting a table before us? We've been waiting longer!" The burly man from Narrow Stone Peak, flanked by four others, stood up.

*Great.* Just what I needed.

I turned, facing the group. My initial urge was to retort, to stand my ground, but the looming Gauntlet whispered caution in my mind, so instead, in an attempt to defuse the situation before it escalated, I asked the server, "Is there a way to accommodate them first?"

The server, a young man with an apologetic look, glanced between me and the imposing group from Narrow Stone Peak. "I'm sorry, but we only had a small table for two. A group of five would have to wait for a larger space," he explained steadily despite the tension. Although he maintained a strong front, I could see a bead of sweat running down his forehead.

I faced the men and tried to keep the peace. "Looks like you'll have to wait your turn," I said, hoping reason would prevail.

But reason, it seemed, was not a guest at their table today. The largest of the lot, a burly man with a sneer, stepped closer, his eyes narrowing. "We're the Five Fists of Narrow Stone Peak," he growled, attempting to tower over me. "We don't wait."

Weren't they completely fine waiting just before all this? Why did they take it as an issue once I came up? I felt a surge of defiance but quelled it, mindful of the bigger picture. However, when he reached out, likely to shove or intimidate, I reacted instinctively. My hand shot out, gripping his wrist. He attempted to shake free, and I let go only after a moment.

That was close. He almost touched the spot where Windy was hiding.

Their annoyance turned to anger, and they started to posture, the lead thug flexing his free hand. "You think you're tough, huh? Let's see if your pet is as tough as you," he sneered, eyeing Tianyi's cage with what looked like malicious intent. My jaw clenched in anger.

But before I could act, something sinister poured into my mind. I glanced down at the butterfly in the cage and saw a subtle blue glow encapsulating her wings. I realized the malevolent emotions were coming from our telepathic link.

*Killing intent. Rage.*

My heart raced, panic edging in as I envisioned the chaos if Tianyi or Windy were provoked. The Narrow Stone Peak disciples were strong, sure, but I've seen Tianyi gouge out a Wind Serpent's eye. Windy's tail twitched ominously beneath my sleeve. I couldn't handle the aftermath of this! I'd be held responsible for murder at this point! The thought of being thrown into a prison pervaded my vision.

Just as the situation teetered on the brink of violence, a cold, authoritative voice sliced through the tension. "Is there a problem here?"

They turned around to glare behind them, but then recognition flickered in their eyes as they took in the green coat he wore and the small insignia emblazoned on it. The Five Fists hesitated, their bravado crumbling under Feng Wu's icy stare.

Feng Wu approached steadily, freezing them in place.

"No problem, just a misunderstanding," the leader mumbled, motioning his group to back down.

"Truly?" Feng Wu kept a small smile on his face, albeit a frosty one that didn't quite reach his eyes. "That's good. Because had the situation been what it looked like, I'd have to arrange a visit to the Narrow Stone Peak and ask just why their disciples are harassing the Verdant Lotus Sect's *guest*."

The leader paled, muttering something incomprehensible before leaving the noodle shop in a hurry.

I exhaled slowly, feeling Windy relax and Tianyi's killing intent subside.

The server, visibly relieved, hurried to lead us to our table, offering thanks with a bow. As we settled into our seats, I couldn't help but feel a twinge of gratitude for the second-class disciple's timely intervention.

Once we had our menus, and had Tianyi settled on the table, I looked at him and grinned. "This young master thanks thee, O Mighty Protector of the Verdant Lotus Sect, for thy timely intervention and saving us from the unruly hands of the Narrow Stone Peak."

He chuckled, shaking his head. "Those Narrow Stone guys are known troublemakers. They wouldn't dare cross the Verdant Lotus Sect, though."

Those guys were cowards. Five Fist? More like Five Flee! They scampered faster than a rabbit with its tail on fire.

Feng Wu leaned back, a mischievous glint in his eye. "You know, if you were a disciple of the Verdant Lotus, these 'trials' might be less frequent."

I raised an eyebrow, feigning contemplation. "And get tethered to the sect for the rest of my days? No thanks," I replied with a lighthearted tone, signaling my contentment with the path I walked, even if it meant dealing with the occasional sect bully.

He just smiled, as if acknowledging my choice but also leaving the door open, should I ever reconsider.

The Spirited Noodle lived up to its reputation once again. Each slurp of the rich, steaming broth and the perfectly cooked noodles reminded me why this place was worth the trouble. Beside me, Feng Wu seemed to relish his meal with equal enthusiasm, the earlier altercation forgotten amid the culinary delights.

Between mouthfuls, I couldn't help but notice the tense atmosphere around us. At least seven different altercations flared up and died down in the time it took to finish our meal. It was like watching a drama unfold in real time, each act more absurd than the last.

I leaned back, patting my stomach, and remarked, "They should really consider hiring some guards or something. It's like a free-for-all in here."

Feng Wu chuckled, nodding in agreement. "It's Crescent Bay City. What do you expect? But you're right. A little order wouldn't hurt, especially with the Grand Alchemy Gauntlet drawing in crowds from all over."

As we finished our meal, the chaos of the restaurant seemed a world away from the calm at our little table. The server, now looking less harried, came over to clear our dishes, casting a wary eye around the room as if expecting another brawl to break out.

Feng Wu threw a silver coin onto the table for the bill, standing up and stretching. "Ready to brave the cold again?"

I nodded, feeling the warmth of the meal combat the chill in my bones. "Let's go. I've got souvenirs to buy, and it looks like I'll need to add some peace and quiet to that list."

The noise of Spirited Noodle faded behind us. The air was crisp, and I could see my breath fogging in the night. Feng Wu led me toward the heart of the city where the Grand Alchemy Gauntlet was to take place. As we approached, he pointed out the massive, ornate structure that towered over the surrounding buildings.

"Over there—that's the venue for the Gauntlet."

The Marble Jade Arena.

As we approached the massive circular structure of the venue, Feng Wu began to casually fill me in, his eyes scanning it nonchalantly. "This place, it's like the heart of Crescent Bay City, especially when it comes to big events."

A colossal line snaked around the venue, composed of individuals from all walks of life. Among them, a dark-haired man, his build and attire screaming "blacksmith," was visibly vibrating with excitement.

"WOOOO!" he shouted. Many people lined up glared at the man, covering their ears.

Curious, I turned to Feng Wu. "What's all this about?"

"That"—he gestured to the winding queue—"is the line for preliminary registration. It's been open for a couple of days now."

*What?!* That was the line for registering? I thought it was for tickets to watch it!

I stared, dumbfounded at the length of the line. "Are we supposed to wait in that?" The thought of standing for hours in the cold was less than appealing.

Feng Wu simply smiled and continued walking, bypassing the line entirely. "Not us," he replied.

Puzzled, I followed him to a side entrance of the venue, where a much shorter line awaited, manned by yellow-robed officials who looked more discerning and, frankly, more intimidating than those managing the main queue.

"These are the sponsored participants' registration," Feng Wu explained as we joined this second line, receiving curious and somewhat-evaluating glances from the others.

Inside, the venue was even more impressive, with high ceilings and walls adorned with intricate murals, some of fights, some of alchemy. The air buzzed with anticipation and the murmur of conversations filled the space.

"The Marble Jade Arena's been around for ages. Built by the ancestors of the city, it's seen more battles and contests than the old library has books. And let me tell you, it's not just about fighting; it's where the mind meets might. Alchemy, strategy, you name it, it's all been tested here."

I looked over at the line, and what I assumed was my competition. I recognized a few of their attires and insignias from my studies. Mystic River Pavilion, Rainy Dew Sect, Golden Summit Foundation . . . These were all storied names, and they talked to each other with familiarity. But one particular person was missing. A certain girl with white hair and blue eyes.

"No sign of that girl from the Lian clan?" Feng Wu asked.

"No . . ." Narrowing my eyes, I glanced over at him. "How'd you know I was looking for her?"

"You talk about her often enough, like a love-drunk teen."

I felt my face heat up at the accusation, quickly shaking my head. "It's not like that. I just— I want to make sure she sees that I'm not the amateur she thinks I am."

"Oh, sure. Just a friendly competition, right?"

I sighed, rolling my eyes. "Yes, exactly. Just a competition. Nothing more."

Feng Wu chuckled, patting my shoulder. "Don't worry, Kai. Your secret's safe with me. But seriously, it's good to have a goal. Keeps you sharp."

He'd been hanging out with Lan Sheng too much.

The thought of facing her again, proving my growth—it wasn't just about pride; it was about showing the fruits of my hard work.

As we reached the registration desk, Feng Wu leaned in, lowering his voice. "Just remember, it's not just her you have to impress. There are eyes and ears everywhere here. Make them all remember the name Kai Liu."

I straightened up, a determined spark lighting up within me. He was right. I'd be the one to win it all.

# CHAPTER TWENTY-SIX

# A Whiff of Competition

Ugh, what is that odor?" A wrinkled nose greeted me, followed by a purple sleeve pressed against it. A man looked at me with scrunched eyes, but his every movement was graceful and refined.

My own sense of smell was assaulted by a potent, almost-invasive fragrance reminiscent of jasmine incense, strong and heady, filling the air around us.

As he approached me, I inwardly sighed. What was with all these people picking a fight with me? I didn't think I looked or smelled *that* different from everyone here. I snuck a glance at the crowd.

I turned to ignore him. It wasn't worth getting riled up over a small comment. I'd heard worse from the villagers back home, and that was when they were being nice.

"Hey! I'm talking to you!" The man tapped my shoulder.

Feng Wu gave me a look of commiseration.

I turned to the man again. We were the same height, so I stared him square in the face. "Can I help you, sir?"

He tilted his head upward. "Yes, by accepting this!" His sleeves unfolded suddenly, and I tensed. Was he really going to attack me over smelling bad?!

But contrary to my expectations, he took out a small, narrow-necked vial of brown liquid and handed it to me. Cautiously, I sniffed it. The aroma was rich and creamy, infused with sweet, earthy notes that immediately soothed my senses.

"That's quite pleasant," Feng Wu remarked.

"Sandalwood," the man stated. He offered the vial to us as a remedy. "It should help with that unpleasant smell around you."

A discreet sniff revealed only the fading scent of my bath soap. Had I unknowingly committed some social offense?

"Ah, I forgot to introduce myself. I am Bai Hua, of the Summer Sun Cosmetics," he said with a flourish and a slight smirk.

*. . . Who?*

I snuck a glance at the second-class disciple beside me. His face had shifted upon hearing the name.

"Summer Sun Cosmetics? You're the heir of the Hua family?"

"The one and only."

Feng Wu dipped his head in acknowledgment, a quick greeting. Out of politeness, I mimicked the gesture, despite my unfamiliarity with his fame. Applying the sandalwood essence to my neck and wrists, I noted Bai Hua's approving glance and the deep breath he took, his satisfaction evident in the relaxed exhale.

"That's better, but still . . . there's something peculiar," he murmured, almost to himself. "You're of the Verdant Lotus Sect, correct? Is this disciple the representative?"

"Not a disciple, but he is our representative this time around."

I stepped forward to introduce myself. "Kai Liu. A pleasure to meet you. Are you here to register as well?"

He nodded, lips curving into another smile. "Yes, I'm participating this year. It's my debut. I plan to merge the worlds of aromatherapy and alchemy to create a new era where Summer Sun Cosmetics reigns at the top!"

Feng Wu raised a brow. "This is news. To think the heir would be participating in the Gauntlet."

"Our company has been on the cusp of revolutionary breakthroughs recently, all under my direction and blessed by my father's wisdom. I assure you, our triumph in the Grand Alchemy Gauntlet is not just anticipated—it's destined." He leaned closer to me, inhaling deeply before nodding with certainty. "You've been training hard, haven't you? I can tell by the lingering scent of sweat. It's quite . . . distinct."

I felt a shiver run down my spine. Embarrassed yet intrigued, I watched as he produced another vial, this one filled with a clear liquid.

"You must be experiencing some fatigue. Here, try this," he said, uncapping it and waving it under my nose.

The sharp scent of menthol and eucalyptus hit me instantly, clearing my sinuses and sending a wave of energy through my body. "Oh, wow!" A minty aftertaste pervaded my nose and mouth. My airways felt like they had widened as breathing became easier.

"Aromatherapy isn't just about pleasant scents; it's about practical effects. I aim to prove that in the Gauntlet and elevate the stature of Summer Sun Cosmetics." Bai Hua's eyes gleamed. "Such a shame, though. The Verdant Lotus Sect might just have to accept second place this year."

My senses were heightened. The initial wave of sandalwood's creamy warmth had been comforting, familiar, yet something else teased the edges of my perception. I closed my eyes for a moment, allowing the aroma to envelop me.

In my shop, surrounded by rows of dried herbs, flowers, and roots, I spent countless hours blending, testing, and perfecting scents and remedies. Sandalwood was unmistakable, with its rich, woody base a canvas on which other scents played their parts. But this was different—there was a warmth here, a spicy undercurrent, one that reminded me of Elder Ming's home.

I opened my eyes to see Bai Hua, who seemed to be watching me with curiosity and something of a challenge. Had he expected me to notice? "Is that a hint of cinnamon I detect in your perfume?" I asked.

His surprise was genuine. "Impressive. You're right; there's a subtle note of cinnamon to add warmth. Not many can pick that up on the first try."

I shrugged, a small grin playing on my lips. "I run my own herbalism shop. I'm quite familiar with these scents."

Bai Hua's interest was piqued. "Oh, is that so? And have I heard of this shop of yours?"

I hesitated before answering, "Perhaps not the shop but one of my products. Have you come across the Invigorating Dawn Tonic?"

"I can't say I have."

*Well, that's embarrassing.*

Bai Hua chuckled. "I jest, Kai Liu. Who isn't aware of the Invigorating Dawn Tonic? To think the inventor would be participating in this year's Gauntlet—many new faces coming out of the woodwork."

"Glad to hear it made an impression. As for how I created it, well, let's just say you might get a glimpse of my methods during the Gauntlet."

"I'm eager to see your skills firsthand."

The line shortened then, signaling it was my turn to register.

Bai Hua's gaze shifted slightly, a playful smirk forming on his face. "Be careful, Kai Liu. Carrying a snake around one's arm is a risky affair, especially in a crowd like this. I had thought it was your sweat that was particularly repugnant, but . . ."

I stiffened and glanced down at Windy, who was still safely concealed.

Bai Hua laughed softly. "Don't worry. Your secret's safe with me. But I must say, you do keep fascinating company."

"Thanks for the warning. I'll see you in the Gauntlet." I nodded respectfully, my mind buzzing.

Feng Wu and I then made our move forward to register with the tired-looking official before us. Once out of earshot from Bai Hua, I remarked to Feng Wu, "That's the competition, huh? He's quite a character."

"It's my first time meeting him. Although I've heard the heir of the Hua family was quite eccentric."

"Name?" the official asked.

"Kai Liu, representing the Verdant Lotus Sect," I responded as Feng Wu nodded in affirmation beside me.

The official glanced up, a flicker of recognition crossing his features. "Ah, the Verdant Lotus Sect. Very well." He scribbled something on a parchment, then handed me a small, ornately designed token. "This is your entry token. Keep it safe; you'll need it to access the competition grounds tomorrow."

Feng Wu added, "We're also here to check in to the lodgings provided for the sponsored participants."

"Of course," the official replied, unfurling a map and pointing toward a square on the map, not too far from what I presumed was the venue. "Your accommodations are in the Jade Harmony Inn. Show your token at the desk. They will take care of you."

We thanked him and made our way to the inn. A blast of icy wind whipped past as we stepped outside, making my teeth chatter. The sun dipped below the rooftops, yet the queue for registration had seemingly doubled in length, now snaking down the street.

"Is the Summer Sun Cosmetics really that famous?" I asked Feng Wu.

"Of course. They're extremely popular with nobles and officials. Their focus has always been on external beauty, of course. Perfumes, lotions, hair treatments—anything to enhance one's physical appearance. This foray into alchemy, particularly the Gauntlet, is quite unorthodox for them. Perhaps their ambition has shifted . . ."

"Confident, that guy. Maybe they have a secret weapon hidden up their perfumed sleeve."

"Indeed. Although he's stranger than most, his development of Summer Sun Cosmetics' aromatherapy lineup has only bolstered their position in the industry. It wouldn't be a stretch to say they're the best in that regard."

"A whole new path in alchemy," I mused, the wheels turning in my mind. "Makes you realize how much there is to learn, right? Maybe after the Gauntlet, I could explore it."

The Jade Harmony Inn was as luxurious as its name suggested, with sweeping eaves and delicate carvings decorating its jade-colored walls.

"Not too shabby for a night's rest before the preliminaries," commented Feng Wu.

I could only nod, awestruck by the opulence. "This is incredible. I've never stayed anywhere like this."

"Enjoy it, Kai. Tomorrow's a big day. I'll see you in the morning; I have some errands to run before the event starts."

Once alone, I checked in at the front desk and headed to my room, which was as lavish as the rest of the inn, with plush furnishings and a view overlooking the city. I let Tianyi and Windy out, watching them explore the spacious room with curiosity. The butterfly fluttered out of her cage, inspecting every corner and edge. Windy slid past my arm and onto the floor. I rolled my shoulders in relief. Holding him for that long was tiring! I sat down on the bed, almost sinking into the sin-fully soft mattress. What was this made of? Clouds?

I forced my mind to rest, quieting any intrusive thoughts, focusing on the sensation of my body sinking into the luxurious bed. Yet a familiar tightness settled in my chest.

I'd come so far, spent countless hours at home and in the Verdant Lotus Sect, grinding herbs, mixing concoctions, experimenting endlessly. The Invigorating Dawn Tonic, along with my other inventions, had gained recognition and even earned me a small fortune. But here, with the Gauntlet looming, the familiar ache of doubt returned. Was I truly prepared to stand among so many skilled alchemists?

A wave of tiredness washed over me as I thought back to my encounters that day. Each person in that line had carried an air of certainty, an unshakable confidence in their skills. It was almost unnerving. Were they all master alchemists? Had they spent their lives immersed in this world while I focused on running my shop and surviving day to day?

I shook my head, trying to banish the negativity. It wouldn't do to get worked up now. The Gauntlet was my chance, not just to prove myself but to take my alchemy to new heights. Even meeting Bai Hua, the eccentric heir with his exotic perfumes and thinly veiled challenges, had ignited a spark of excitement. The potential of aromatherapy was an avenue I hadn't even considered.

"I should get some rest. I'll need to wake up early tomorrow. Right, Tianyi?"

The Azure Moonlight Flutter perched herself on my nose, sending waves of encouragement and positivity through our bond. Maybe it was just me, but I swear these emotions were on the cusp of forming words. Was our bond getting stronger?

I flopped back onto the cloud-like mattress, sighing deeply. The scent of some exotic flower, probably infused in the absurdly expensive sheets, filled my nose. "This is how one lives in the big city, huh, Windy?" I mumbled, stroking his scales absentmindedly. "Maybe a little rest would be good."

As I started to succumb to my need for rest, a nagging voice lurked within the confines of my mind. *Nap? Are you kidding me, Kai? This is the Grand Alchemy Gauntlet, not a picnic! The others are probably hunched over ancient tomes right now, deciphering alchemical secrets your simple village brain can't even comprehend!*

Defeated, I screamed into my pillow. Then I got up and glared at the wall, cursing my anxiety. Before I knew it, I was cross-legged on the floor, eyes closed, entering the familiar mental landscape.

"Maybe just a quick peek inside my Memory Palace. Just to double-check a few formulas . . ."

The scent of roasted nuts and steaming pastries drifted from street vendors' stalls, teasing my empty stomach as Feng Wu and I walked toward the venue.

Dawn had barely broken, the sky a canvas of soft pinks and oranges. I shivered, tightening my cotton-padded coat around me.

"Sleep well?" Feng Wu asked, a knowing smile playing on his lips.

I mumbled something between a grunt and a sigh. ". . . Something like that." The night had been a blur of frenzied memorization within my Memory Palace, followed by fitful tossing and turning whenever I'd managed to slip out of my mental abode.

Thankfully, the Jade Harmony Inn had lived up to its name, serving a breakfast fit for royalty. The warm porridge filled my stomach, and the strong tea was a jolt to my senses.

When we approached the familiar building where the Gauntlet was held, the long line from yesterday was gone. Instead, a sense of tense anticipation hung in the air. Participants stood in small clusters, eyes darting nervously toward the entrance.

Feng Wu gestured to a side entrance, where a stern-looking official stood guard. It seemed sponsored participants received preferential treatment, even up to the preliminaries!

As we neared, the official scrutinized my token and the list in his other hand. "Kai Liu?" A curt nod was his only acknowledgment before he stepped aside. "Right through there. The preliminaries are about to begin."

My heart thudded against my ribs as I walked through the entrance.

Feng Wu followed, placing a hand on my shoulder. "Good luck, Kai. Show them what you've got."

My pulse quickened. Unlike the vast room from yesterday, the floor here was meticulously organized. The space had been divided into three distinct sections, and within each, row upon row of simple booths curved around like a giant amphitheater. Clearly, this was designed to accommodate hundreds of participants.

Each booth was remarkably minimal: a small table, a cushioned stool, an ink pot, an ink brush, and a stack of what seemed like thick, high-quality paper.

"Follow me," a voice said. I turned to see a middle-aged woman in a crisp uniform gesturing toward me.

Here were young men and women dressed in the finest silks. There were stern-faced alchemists with weathered hands, likely journeymen hoping for a breakthrough. I even spotted a group of elderly scholars, their beards flecked with gray, who whispered among themselves with an air of quiet confidence. I suppose the Grand Alchemy Gauntlet allowed it; the only limiting factor for applicants was the level their cultivation was at.

"Your booth is this way," the woman said, finally stopping at the edge of one of the concentric rows. "Please, do not touch anything until the start of the preliminaries is officially announced." She nodded respectfully before moving on to guide the next person.

I sat on the stool and took a deep breath. So, this was it. I was just one face in a sea of alchemists, all hoping to prove their worth. I scanned the vast arena. The silence that had initially greeted us was slowly being replaced by murmurs and nervous chatter.

A glance around revealed a diverse cast of competitors. Young competitors fidgeted with the ink brushes we weren't supposed to touch, their silks rustling with every movement. Weathered alchemists examined the paper and ink pots with stoic expressions.

A sudden movement caught my eye. Bai Hua, his colorful attire a beacon among the sea of neutral tones, sauntered into my section, a playful glint in his eyes. He couldn't see me, but inwardly I smiled upon seeing the familiar face from yesterday.

Before I could try to get his attention, a hush fell over the room. The murmurs ceased, replaced by a tense anticipation. All eyes turned toward the center of the arena, where a raised platform stood, empty.

A spotlight flared to life, illuminating a figure who strode onto the stage with an air of quiet authority. He was a man of average height, his face etched with the lines of experience. Dressed in ornately embroidered robes of midnight blue, he held the crowd's attention effortlessly.

"Welcome, honored participants," he boomed in a voice surprisingly rich for such a lean figure. "I am Ma Hualong, the coordinator of the Grand Alchemy Gauntlet's preliminary rounds. Today, you each have the opportunity to prove your mettle, to demonstrate your alchemical prowess and secure your place in the prestigious competition proper."

A ripple of excitement ran through the crowd.

Ma Hualong raised a hand, silencing the murmurs. "However," he continued, "the first challenge will not be what you expect." He paused, letting that sink in. "Today, we test your knowledge, not your practical skills. The written portion of the preliminaries will now commence."

# CHAPTER TWENTY-SEVEN

# Preliminaries

From where I could see, a symbol manifested on the epicenter of each station: a jagged rock in my station, a twisty stalk to the far right, and a paw print to my left.

"There are three sections. Minerals, herbs, and animal components. Each section will have a hundred ingredients assigned to them." With a flick of his fingers and an alchemical flash, Ma Hualong conjured a whirlwind of levitating plates.

I could see the colorful contents that sparkled on each plate. My heart flipped. *Amethyst? Beetle wings? A clump of . . . tree bark?*

An hourglass on the podium lit up like a beacon, sand shimmering as it began its descent.

"You have one incense stick's worth of time to identify as many ingredients in your assigned section as possible. You must be precise, as alchemy is a precise endeavor. After the hourglass runs dry, the plates will rotate. Only the top hundred scores will make it to the first round. Good luck, contestants!"

And with that, dozens of plates gathered in a neat circular formation right above the jagged rock symbol before settling in a paced orbit.

The noise of hundreds of pages being turned occurred simultaneously throughout the Marble Jade Arena. I could hear curses and mutters from the people closest to me, despite their faces being obscured by the walls of the booth.

Time to work.

Eyes flitting from plate to plate—what was that spiky black crystal? That fist-sized stone was cinnabar that was easy enough. But the golden liquid . . . Mercury? It looked too thick.

As the minutes passed, my brush moved faster and faster. Mostly standard ingredients, true, but a few were slipping through my grasp. That bluish-green rock—nothing in my recipe knowledge matched it. Jade, maybe, but the color was too vibrant, the luster too . . . off.

*Jade? Wait a minute.*

My mind raced through the Memory Palace, searching for an image, a snippet of a forgotten conversation. Then it hit me, a bolt from the blue. *That's not an ingredient at all! That's Qinglian Jadeite!*

"I should've known . . ." I muttered to myself, filling in the page before I forgot what it was.

The memory unfolded—Elder Zhu lecturing about the Jade Alchemic Flame, the sect's prized treasure. This was the base material used to create it, the same prize the Silent Moon Sect had demanded! A rush of excitement washed over the panic. So, it wasn't just identifying recipe ingredients. It was recognizing any material with alchemical potential, even those used indirectly!

This realization was a game-changer. My eyes swept across the plates with new-found purpose. Not just the potions but the tools, the processes . . . What else was here that wasn't in a standard alchemist's tool kit?

*There! Not some obscure ore but a simple clay bowl. Yet the texture . . .* A touch of glimmer I'd seen only once, helping Elder Ming prepare a heat-resistant crucible back as a child. This wasn't ordinary clay but a blend infused with refractory minerals. My brush scratched along the page: *Refractory Clay Mix.*

And that strange vial? A simple jar of oil—except it had the subtle sheen of firefly luminescence. Not some potion base but the fuel for alchemical lamps! The ones with that barely there flickering light that wouldn't disturb sensitive reactions. My hand wrote swiftly: *Firefly Lamp Oil.*

A sense of power filled me. This wasn't a test of rote memorization. It was a challenge to see beyond the obvious, to understand the wider world of alchemical practice. It was the difference between a recipe-follower and a true alchemist. This, I could do!

"Time's up!" Ma Hualong declared, his voice reverberating throughout the venue. "You have another incense stick's worth of time to identify the ingredients in your new section!"

Seventy, maybe eighty identifications. Not bad, considering I had been completely lost with the last thirty or so. Still, a gnawing frustration bubbled in my gut. Those last unknown minerals troubled me.

The world blurred as the plates whirred. One moment they were filled with gleaming stones and curious vials, the next a kaleidoscope of greens, browns, and vibrant reds filled my vision. Herbs and plants!

This was my territory—years spent scouring the forests, compounded by my experience at the Verdant Lotus Sect, I had complete confidence here.

There was no time to waste. I dipped my brush before the plates even settled, my mind already racing. Moonlit Grace Lily, Breezesong Fruit, the rarest ingredients in the entire province!

My hand flew across the page, barely keeping pace with the frantic recognition flooding my mind. Skyreach Flower, Nightshade, Dragon's Breath Pepper, Mystic Mindroot . . . each name a familiar friend from countless concoctions. Only one remained unidentified as the sand in the hourglass dwindled to its final grains. A spindly, crimson flower with an unsettlingly pulsating core.

"The plates will now rotate once more!"

They whirred into place, and my eyes widened. A flash of gray—Wind Serpent scales!

Beside the scales, a mound of shimmering white fur—Snow Hare, no doubt. But that curled iridescent horn . . . ? Likely an antelope variant from the far north with medicinal properties. My mind searched the depths of my Memory Palace, grasping for a name. It came to me like a spark: Frostbreath Antelope Horn.

The plates were a whirlwind of claws, feathers, and glistening vials of unidentified fluids. It was overwhelming. But I pushed on.

With each name, I recalled fragments of animal lore, their habitats, their uses. My brush raced against the draining hourglass, leaving smudges of ink as I tried to match my memories to the bizarre specimens before me. Some of these weren't even from our province!

Despite my efforts, I couldn't name them all. I was sure I did worse here compared to any of the other sections; maybe only half of which I identified correctly.

"And that concludes it! Don't move from your seats, officials will be picking up your papers, ensure it is labeled properly with the number on your entry token and your name. If you don't adhere to these instructions, your papers will be thrown out and you'll be automatically disqualified!"

I swallowed, double-checking and turning over every page to do so. The venue was silent, save for the turning of pages. Slowly but surely, officials came by and collected my work.

With a relieved sigh, I leaned back in my chair. It was done. Regardless of the outcome, I'd given it my all. A quick mental calculation reassured me—I was confident at least two hundred of my identifications were correct. Even with the lackluster animal component round, that should place me comfortably within the top hundred.

The tension bled from my shoulders as I watched other contestants anxiously awaiting the collection of their papers. Sighs, groans, and even a few muffled sobs echoed through the booths. The Grand Alchemy Gauntlet, it seemed, wasn't for the faint of heart.

"I NEARLY FAILED!" a man shouted from the animal component section to be immediately shushed by the official picking up his paper. Wasn't that the blacksmith I saw waiting outside in the line? They actually let him participate?

My gaze snagged on a familiar figure in the swirling crowd. A burst of vibrant silks and perfume marked Bai Hua's presence. Curiosity piqued, I made my way toward him, weaving through the dispersing competitors.

"Bai Hua," I called out, a hint of a smile playing on my lips.

He turned, offering me one of his theatrical flourishes. "Ah, Kai Liu! And here I thought fate had separated us after our delightful encounter yesterday."

I chuckled. "The Gauntlet is unpredictable, I suppose. So, how did the preliminaries go for you?"

"Splendidly! My nose never betrays me, you see."

I blinked, puzzled. There was no way he could've used it here. "Your nose? I don't quite follow."

He grinned at me. "Why, each ingredient has its distinct scent, Kai Liu! Even when its appearance confounds, the aroma always reveals the truth. Years of experience have made me quite the expert on olfactory identification."

My mouth opened to ask how he could have smelled the ingredients from such a distance, but then it clicked. Bai Hua had been assigned one of the closer booths, right near the center of the arena where the ingredients rotated. That gave him a distinct advantage, one I hadn't even considered.

Before I could dwell on the unfairness of it, he continued, "However, even without my gifted nose, I am well versed in the properties of countless ingredients. My family's business extends far beyond the world of perfumes. We dabble in a wide range of industries, all of which intersect with alchemy in some way or another."

"Well," I said, extending my hand, "I'm eager to see how you fare in the next stage. Until then, I bid you farewell."

"The feeling is mutual, Kai Liu. If you ever find yourself nearby, do visit our shop."

Releasing his hand, I turned to spot a familiar figure weaving through the crowd. "Feng Wu!" I called out, a wave of relief washing over me.

As my friend approached, a sense of accomplishment settled upon me. The odds might be stacked against me, a village herbalist facing off against renowned alchemists from across the empire. But I knew genius and hard work would triumph over them all!

We were nearing the exit when a booming voice echoed across the arena. It was Ma Hualong, still standing upon his elevated platform.

"Contestants! The results of your preliminary examinations will be announced here tonight," he declared excitedly. "It would be wise for all of you to return and discover whether you have the honor of proceeding to the competition proper."

There were hundreds of people here. Each one had submitted a small stack of papers just like me. Getting us all sorted out; how would that be possible?

My heart skipped a beat. Tonight. The waiting wouldn't be long, but the uncertainty was suddenly unbearable.

"Well, it seems our evening plans have just been determined for us," Feng Wu said. "So, what now, Kowtow Kai? Ready to explore the delights of Crescent Bay City?"

I playfully nudged him. "Hold on there, who appointed you my tour guide? This young master requires the finest of jade beauties to escort him!"

He winked. "Well, you wouldn't want to get lost in this labyrinth of alchemical shops and bustling markets, would you? Unless you'd like me to procure a certain white-haired cultivator to be your guide."

"Lead the way," I declared, a smile tugging at the corners of my lips. "Let's see what Crescent Bay City has to offer."

Our first stop was a bookshop. Perhaps something that would satisfy both my and Elder Ming's desire to read and be entertained? I wouldn't accept anything other than the finest, after all.

The sheer scale of Crescent Bay City continued to amaze me. Vendors hawked their wares—glistening gemstones, exotic spices, and contraptions that defied an easy description.

"Feng Wu," I said, trying hard to be heard over the din, "do they have any bookstores in the city? I'm interested in acquiring more of Liang Feng's works."

He looked puzzled. "Bookstores? Certainly. But Liang Feng? I don't know about that specific author." He shrugged. "Perhaps he is a regional author from your area?"

My disappointment was clear. So, my favorite writer wasn't a renowned author. Maybe I could still find his works somewhere . . .

As we turned down a narrower street, a sign caught my eye—*The Scroll and Tome*, it proclaimed in elegant calligraphy. "Feng Wu, wait! Let's check this place out first. Maybe they have what I'm looking for."

He hesitated. "Kai, about that—it's mostly . . . Well . . ." He trailed off.

I tilted my head, utterly confused. It was rare to see the usually eloquent man at a loss for words.

"Mostly what? That's nonsense! I can see all the books in there! There'll be something in there."

Before he could answer, my curiosity propelled me into the store. Immediately, the change in atmosphere became apparent. The air hummed with an almost tangible feminine energy, and the scent of floral perfumes, much like the one Bai Hua wore, hung heavy in the air.

And the clientele were almost exclusively women, their gazes flitting over the vibrant covers of the books that lined the shelves.

My eyes landed on a particularly flamboyant title, *The Dragon Tamer and His Feisty Concubine*.

". . . Huh."

Below was another—*The CEO of the Immortal Sect Falls for Me!*

Such unique titles . . . I don't think I'd seen anything quite like them.

Something in my brain was warning me, screaming at me that something was off. But the titles . . . They were so grand, so full of promise and intrigue. Perhaps, just perhaps, there was more to them than met the eye. "One peek wouldn't hurt . . ." I muttered, reaching out to a book whose title practically screamed adventure: *The Peasant Who Stole the Demonic Senior Disciple's Heart.*

A romance! No wonder there were so many women. I suppose it didn't hurt to broaden my horizons!

As I flipped open the book, realization struck me like a lightning bolt. It wasn't just an adventure.

It wasn't just a romance.

It was a romance . . . between two men.

A flicker of curiosity pierced through my frantic attempts to compose myself. Surely this . . . this wasn't just some tale of forbidden passion? No, it must be a heroic tale of adventure! With shaking hands, I turned the pages, my eyes skimming a few paragraphs.

*Kai Luo, the humble tea seller, shivered as rain lashed his meager stall. The mountain pass was deserted, the usual flow of travelers halted by the torrential downpour. A bolt of lightning rent the sky, illuminating a figure standing amid the storm.*

My heart skipped a beat. This sounded more promising already! It was an adventure!

*The stranger's robes, a vibrant crimson against the backdrop of the tempest, bespoke membership in the illustrious Crimson Lotus Sect. His eyes, pools of molten rubies, held an unreadable intensity. A sword of exquisite craftsmanship gleamed at his hip, promising prowess in the martial arts.*

Interesting. So, this was a cultivator, a member of a renowned sect meeting a humble villager? Why did it sound so familiar?

I dared a glance upward, to the chapter title.

*Chapter 1: The Crimson Demon and His Captivating Tea Merchant*

My jaw hung open in astonishment. *Captivating? Oh my.* This was *definitely* not Elder Ming's sort of reading material. He would undergo Qi Deviation on the spot if I bought this for him!

*"I seek shelter," the cultivator's voice boomed, deep and resonant like distant thunder. "What price for your tea?"*

*Kai Luo, though intimidated, found his voice. "For a cultivator of your stature, this humble one offers his finest brew as a gift."*

*The man paused, a flicker of surprise crossing his handsome features. "A gift? You understand the implications, mortal?"*

*"Of course, my lord. But kindness knows no cultivation level. A simple cup of tea is the least I can offer to one who braves the storm."*

*The demon lord's gaze softened, the barest hint of a smile tugging at his lips. "Very well. Your courage intrigues me, tea merchant. I shall accept your offering."*

*And so, the demon lord's bloodred lips neared closer and closer, until*

I slammed the book shut and whirled around, scanning the room frantically for an escape route. I ran past an elderly woman adorned in jewels. Her expression was unreadable. I left the store as fast as my legs could take me.

Unable to look Feng Wu in the eyes, I could only make out the faint tremors wracking his body, as well as the sound of snickering.

"Ahem, I was just . . . I think I must be feeling ill, Feng Wu," I stammered, my voice reaching a fever pitch. "The forbidden scriptures. They've given me some sort of . . . heart demon? Qi Deviation?"

Feng Wu didn't even try to hide his laughter.

# CHAPTER TWENTY-EIGHT

# Underdogs and Unexpected Results

You've been awfully quiet ever since we left the Scroll and Tome. Perhaps you found . . . enlightenment?"

My face flushed hotter than a blacksmith's forge. "Don't be ridiculous! I was merely contemplating the profound impact certain literary works can have on the unsuspecting reader."

"The profound impact of . . . *forbidden knowledge*?" Feng Wu finished, a teasing glint in his eye. "Perhaps you've stumbled upon an awakening, my friend?"

"An awakening?" I nearly choked on the words. "More like a descent into madness! Those scandalous texts could give a cultivator Qi Deviation just by gazing upon the first page!"

A burst of laughter escaped Feng Wu's lips. "Here I thought you were an adventurous spirit, eager to explore the unknown, and yet a few simple books send you into a panic."

"Simple is an understatement," I grumbled, crossing my arms defensively. "Those were weapons of mass distraction, designed to corrupt the minds of the innocent!"

Feng Wu leaned closer, a mischievous twinkle in his eyes. "It truly is a corrupting influence. I'll make sure to keep watch on you, before you get into the idea of making aphrodisiacs and other sinister potions of that natu—"

"I swear, you're courting death," I warned, though I couldn't suppress a reluctant smile. "Trying to induce a heart demon in a fellow cultivator at such a critical moment—you have no shame!"

Feng Wu's teasing may have been relentless, but his lightheartedness was a welcome distraction. The results of the preliminaries would be announced soon, and my fate in the Grand Alchemy Gauntlet hung in the balance.

As we neared the venue, the energy shifted. The playful atmosphere dissipated, replaced by a palpable tension that hung in the air like a storm cloud. Hundreds of contestants milled about outside the arena, their faces etched with a mixture of anticipation and dread.

"LET'S DO THIS!" A booming voice cut through the nervous chatter. The blacksmith from the preliminaries, with his broad shoulders and a grin that seemed permanently etched onto his features.

He stood out like a crane among chickens. It made me truly curious, what was someone like him doing here?

I couldn't help but notice the subtle disdain from some of the other competitors. Perhaps they saw him as a brute, an outsider crashing their world of meticulous concoctions and complex theory.

"Excuse me," I said, stepping forward, "but I don't believe we've properly met. You're . . . ?"

"The name's Tao Ren! And who might you be?"

"Kai Liu," I replied, clasping my hands together for an introductory bow. "I must admit, I wasn't expecting to see a blacksmith competing in the Grand Alchemy Gauntlet."

Tao Ren's wide grin faltered for a moment, surprised. "Blacksmith? How did you figure that out?"

I gestured toward him, taking in the worn leather apron tied around his waist, the heavy hammer strapped to his side, and the impressive musculature that spoke of years spent wielding heavy tools. "Reminds me a bit of a friend back home who's a blacksmith himself. You both have a certain, well, blacksmithy vibe."

A grin split across Tao Ren's face. "A blacksmithy vibe, you say? I like the sound of that! You've earned a spot as my honorary observer for the competition. Prepare to witness greatness!"

"Greatness, huh? But why are you here at the Grand Alchemy Gauntlet?"

Tao Ren's grin widened. "My old man thinks this competition might finally get me to take alchemy seriously and inherit his shop. He sent me here to compete. Truth be told, the only fire I care about is the one in my forge."

"So, you're not here for alchemy?"

He chuckled, a hearty, full-bodied sound. "It's a strategic investment. I'm opening a blacksmithing business soon. What better way to drum up clientele than by showing I'm not just a hammer-swinger but a man of refined skill, capable of wielding both fire and potion at the biggest event in Crescent Bay City?"

He thumped his chest proudly. "Imagine the whispers! 'Tao Ren, the alchemist-blacksmith! His blades are sharper than his mind, and his elixirs are unrivaled.' Marketing genius, right?"

I blinked, struggling to process his logic. "But wouldn't it be more effective to focus on your blacksmithing skills if that's your true passion?"

Tao Ren's grin wavered briefly, then he laughed and clapped me on the shoulder. "Details, details, my friend! Who says a blacksmith can't master both?

Just wait and see. The Grand Alchemy Gauntlet is about to witness the rise of a legend!"

Just as I opened my mouth to reply, a wave of anticipation rippled through the crowd. A hush fell over the gathered contestants as a figure emerged from the grand entrance of the Marble Jade Arena.

Ma Hualong carried a scroll so long it nearly reached the ground. With a flourish that belied his age, he unfurled the parchment, his voice resonating across the vast space.

"Contestants of the Grand Alchemy Gauntlet! The moment has come to reveal those who shall advance! Gather close and listen intently. Please head inside once your name is called. Further instructions await you."

My heart pounded like a war drum. This was it. After months of preparation, studying ancient texts, and battling burnout, I would finally know my fate. Would I make the cut? Was I destined to be one of the hundred, or would my journey end here, outside the Marble Jade Arena, a mere footnote?

"At last place we have Tao Ren, of the . . . Jade Flame Foundry?"

Ma Hualong leaned in closer, squinting his eyes in disbelief as he reread the paper.

"YEAH!"

My left eardrum nearly burst from his shout of glee. He turned to me again with a large grin, showing his molars. "I'll see you at the top, Kai Liu!"

I watched as the cheery blacksmith was pointed toward the area we were supposed to go, eliciting several whispers from contestants trailing behind him.

"Did you hear that? One hundredth place? Surely a mistake . . ."

". . . A blacksmith? How undignified. Perhaps he got lucky during the identification section."

"Such uncouth individuals have no business in a competition as esteemed as this . . ."

I grew angry, not for myself but for Tao Ren. He might have been loud and confident, but he wasn't as ignorant as these snobbish alchemists assumed. He had heard them, I was sure. They were idiots who didn't know a thing about him.

A snide voice cut through my thoughts. "Well, well. It seems even the preliminaries fail to truly separate the wheat from the chaff. We'll see how long that buffoon lasts in the actual competition."

The speaker, a young man with robes embroidered with intricate cloud patterns signifying his prestige, barely spared me a glance as he passed.

With a sigh, I tucked away my doubts and anger. It wasn't my place to fight his battles. Tao Ren seemed blissfully unaware of the insults, or perhaps he chose to ignore them. It was his journey, and I trusted he had the strength to see it through, regardless of the scorn from those who only valued pedigree and tradition.

Ma Hualong continued announcing names, most of which I didn't recognize. The snobby man, Jian Duan, made it to sixtieth place. He seemed assured by his results, smirking as the crowd parted for him. I saw people already leaving, muttering and bemoaning their chances.

"At twentieth, Bai Hua of Summer Sun Cosmetics!"

I scanned the crowd and spotted Bai Hua's flamboyant robes near the front. I grinned, pleased he made it. But the absence of my own name put a knot in my stomach.

"I know what you're thinking, Kai," Feng Wu said without looking at me. "Effort does not betray the dedicated. I've seen your work. You'll make it through the preliminaries, no doubt."

His words eased my shoulders, a testament to our friendship and his knowing the right words even when I said nothing.

"At twelfth, Kai Liu of the Verdant Lotus Sect!"

And just like that, all my fears and anxieties washed away.

With a grin spreading across my face, I realized that despite my internal turmoil, there was an undeniable thrill simmering just beneath the surface. I'd always been the underdog. Now it was time to prove I had teeth.

As I slowly pushed my way through the crowd, countless eyes settled on me—some with curiosity, many with disdain, others with a dismissive indifference that stung even more.

*Let them look. Let them underestimate me.* It would only make my eventual triumph all the sweeter.

I approached Ma Hualong and the band of officials beside him. He gave me a curt nod and an appraising eye, before motioning toward a scholarly-looking official with a small bag.

They unveiled another token, with the number twelve emblazoned on it. "Please head inside the waiting area for further instruction."

I said my thanks and moved forward, taking one last look back. Hundreds of contestants remained. To think less than a dozen had a higher score than I did.

The more incredible part was how I doubted my genius. I should've known. I was the chosen one!

I moved deeper into the Marble Jade Arena. The open space had been completely transformed. Now a simple seating area had been set up against one wall, facing what appeared to be a large, raised platform.

Scanning the other competitors, I spotted a familiar face. Bai Hua, in his flamboyant robes, was engaged in animated conversation with Tao Ren. The blacksmith's boisterous laughter echoed through the space.

A flicker of warmth spread through me. These two, so different, had both defied expectations to reach this stage. Perhaps the Gauntlet was about more than pedigree and tradition after all.

"Well, well, well. If it isn't the perfumer extraordinaire and the blacksmith," I remarked.

Bai Hua turned toward me, his smile dazzling. "Kai Liu! I trust the preliminaries treated you well? Your placement is most impressive . . . for an herbalist, of course."

Tao Ren let out a booming laugh. "Don't listen to him, Kai. This pretty boy might know his perfumes, but he hasn't got an ounce of alchemical sense in his head! You're the real threat here."

"Oh, hush now," Bai Hua retorted, swatting Tao Ren's arm playfully. "Don't fill his head with nonsense. Clearly, I'll be the one to win this contest." He raised his robe to cover his face.

I held up my hands in mock surrender. "Gentlemen, gentlemen, please! I'm but a humble village apothecary. You both outshine me by leagues." My grin broadened. "Even if I scored higher than the both of you."

As our bickering continued, I noticed Jian Duan's scornful gaze on us, not too far from where we were seated. Perhaps it was foolish, perhaps it was reckless, but a stubborn defiance surged within me. My fingers twitched. For a fleeting moment, a different face superimposed itself over Jian Duan's—the visage of Elder Jun. The all-too-recent memory of that chilling brush with true power sent a shiver down my spine. The stakes had been so much higher back then, not just for my own life but the safety of my village and sect friends hanging in the balance.

Yet another part of me, a bolder voice fueled by resentment, refused to yield. If I were afraid of risk, I never would've left the confines of Gentle Wind Village. And after everything I'd faced with the Silent Moon Sect, his posturing felt almost petty. Jian Duan might throw obstacles in my path, but I doubted he had the inclination to truly destroy me.

A mischievous smirk tugged at my lips. "After all," I continued, my voice carrying across the space, "perhaps those concerned with separating wheat from chaff should first ensure they can tell the difference themselves."

# CHAPTER TWENTY-NINE

# The Nail That Sticks Out

Jian Duan's eyes narrowed his eyes at me, a flicker of rage as he realized the meaning behind my words.

Hadn't I endured enough veiled insults, enough dismissive glances? These arrogant alchemists, they saw us as an insignificant speck, a bit of chaff to be swept aside without a thought.

He took a deliberate step forward, the cloud patterns on his robes swirling as if stirred by a sudden gust of wind. "You dare mock me, village boy? Do you know who I am? The prestige of my clan?"

"Oh?" I feigned innocence, tilting my head in mock curiosity. "Do enlighten me. Does your esteemed clan specialize in growing chaff?"

The insult elicited a few laughs, and a low murmur of whispers rippled through the crowd.

Jian Duan's face flushed an ugly shade of crimson. "How dare you!" he snarled, his voice rising in anger. "You—you insignificant worm! Don't think your petty tricks will save you. I'll see you fail in the first round, and then you'll learn the price of disrespect!"

"Perhaps," I continued, edged with steel, "you should be more concerned with passing the competition. After all, empty threats won't enhance your skill."

His nostrils flared, and the muscles in his jaw twitched. For a long moment, he simply stared at me, a silent battle of wills unfolding in the space between us. "You'll regret this, peasant." Then, abruptly, he turned on his heel, the swirl of his robes a final display of disdain.

I watched him go, my hands clenched into fists at my sides. Jian Duan's smoldering glare left a prickling sensation on the back of my neck. Had I gotten too cocky? Provoking someone of his caliber could backfire spectacularly.

"Don't let him get to you," Bai Hua said, his voice low. "There are always those who measure worth by lineage and not by skill."

People like him had connections that could make my path impossibly difficult. But as I fixed my gaze on his arrogant sneer, a different kind of fear gnawed at me—the fear of living a life forever on the sidelines, forever underestimated.

"Easy for you to say," I muttered, still tense. "You come from a renowned family, even if they aren't cultivators. They won't trash you like they do me and Tao Ren."

"They were insulting me? When did that ever happen?"

Despite my lingering annoyance, I couldn't help but smile. The blacksmith's obliviousness was something to behold.

As the remaining competitors trickled in, my gaze swept across the room, analyzing each face. Most I didn't recognize, but over half had been present at the sponsored registry, their robes and demeanors marking them as elite. A pang of insecurity wormed its way into my chest. To think that even with my Memory Palace technique, my Accelerated Reading, and a mind-numbing amount of work, over ten people boasted a score higher than me.

The air crackled with anticipation as a new figure appeared in the entrance. A cascade of white hair shimmered under the arena lights, followed by eyes the color of winter ice. It was her, the girl from the Lian clan, representing the Whispering Winds Sect.

Even among this group of the best, she held an undeniable presence, her ethereal beauty adding to her mystique. The way others bowed in acknowledgment as she passed, her regal nod in return, it all screamed of her being far more important than I initially thought.

Then, with a confident strut, she walked straight toward me, Bai Hua, and Tao Ren.

Jian Duan seemed busy tidying himself, rearranging the bun on his head and fixing the wrinkles on his robes. As soon as she neared him, he spoke. "This young master greets—"

She continued forward, not sparing a glance his way. Stopping directly in front of our small circle, her icy blue gaze landed on me. "So, it seems you've managed to scrape through." There was no warmth in her voice, only a cold assessment.

"Indeed, and may I have the honor of knowing your name? As fellow competitors, I believe that courtesy is due."

A chilling smile stretched across her lips, a predator sizing up its prey. "Jingyu Lian."

A flicker of surprise coursed through me as I noticed the number two emblazoned on the token in her hand. With her imperious attitude and that declaration back when I first encountered her—*this Gauntlet is no playground for amateurs*—I'd assumed she would easily snag the top score.

A wry smile tugged at the corner of my lips. I couldn't resist a small jab. "Quite the surprise, wouldn't you say, Lady Lian? Your words about amateurs ring a bit hollow when you couldn't secure the first-place spot."

Her answering snort was as cold as her gaze. "I hardly expected someone to surpass me. Though I suppose it makes for a more interesting challenge."

Before I could fire back a retort, my gaze flickered over her shoulder, seeing the final entrant who passed the preliminaries.

And there, framed by the entrance to the waiting room, stood a decidedly unassuming figure. He seemed to be in his midthirties, with a lackadaisical manner and unkempt appearance. His plain brown robes were wrinkled, his hair in disarray, and there was a smudge of what looked like ink across his cheek.

A collective murmur of surprise rippled through the crowd. No one seemed to know his name, and I couldn't recall him being present during the registry. Was he one of the unsponsored competitors?

The newcomer blinked at the sudden attention, a look of mild confusion crossing his face. It seemed he hadn't even realized he'd caused such a stir.

My own shock mirrored that of the room. The person who secured the top score . . . was so ordinary-looking.

"Move along now," Ma Hualong chided from behind the man standing by the entrance. He inclined his head and moved to the nearest vacant seat not too far from where I was sitting. He joined the others in stepping past the contestants, striding toward the raised platform. "You stand before us, talented flames, flickering with the potential to become great alchemists." He swept his gaze across the room, lingering on a few faces, including Jingyu Lian's. "As you may know, the Grand Alchemy Gauntlet is not a competition confined by age but by cultivation level. Think of it as a way to ensure fairness. Most alchemists at the first stage of Qi Initiation haven't yet grasped the complexities needed to truly manipulate the alchemical process."

It made perfect sense. Elder Zhu had once told a similar story about how he found his calling for alchemy later in life. This Gauntlet wasn't just about raw talent, but about the dedication and refinement it takes to become a master alchemist.

"It ensures what truly matters rises to the surface," Ma Hualong continued. "The strength of your spirit, the keenness of your mind. This allows those who find their passion later in life to compete on equal footing. That is how I began my alchemical journey and achieved victory here in the Grand Alchemy Gauntlet many years ago. With that said, please line up. We will be testing your cultivation rank to ensure you're below the threshold."

We all shuffled quietly into a line. The test didn't take very long, evidenced by how quickly the contestants moved up. Once it was my turn, they grabbed a golden slip, a talisman of some sort, and placed it on my head. It glowed for a split second before going inert.

The official removed it from my forehead and nodded. "Next!"

The test went by without any issue, so it meant everybody here was basically the same cultivation rank. From the snobby Jian Duan to Jingyu Lian, it would be a level playing field.

Ma Hualong stood up once more, coughing to gather everyone's attention. "The best alchemists, the ones whose names echo through history," he said with conviction, "are lifelong learners. Their pursuit of knowledge is unbound by age or early achievements. The flames of their curiosity burn eternally."

His words struck a chord within me. Unlike martial arts, alchemy offered a more forgiving path. Dedication and a thirst for knowledge could bridge the gap between age and experience. A talented cultivator might reach Qi Initiation at fifteen, while another might find their alchemical calling in their thirties. Yet, in this Gauntlet, both could compete on an even playing field.

Martial arts, however, were different. Instructor Xia Ji had drilled this into me. The years between ten and thirty were a cultivator's golden age, when their bodies were most receptive to foundational techniques. It was a period of explosive growth, where raw talent and rigorous training laid the groundwork for martial prowess. Missing those critical years could leave an insurmountable gap.

The way Li Na and Han Wei moved was fundamentally different from someone like me, who had started less than a year ago. But I didn't despair. Life taught me that hard work can bridge the chasms talent and experience create.

Bit by bit, day by day, I would inch closer to their level. If it took me twice as long to master a new form, I would spend twice the time. I might not have a strong affinity for martial arts, but I'd overcome challenges before through sheer grit and determination. I had earned my place here, and I would prove myself worthy, regardless of my age or late start.

Ma Hualong continued his speech, bringing me back to the present. "So with that, I hope that all of you, regardless of status, age, or background will push the limits of skill and knowledge. Let your spirits blaze with the fire of creation! Now, for the first round . . ." He paused, suspense building.

*Come on! Get on with it!*

"Your knowledge was tested in the preliminaries," he boomed through the hall. "Your application and theory will be put to the test. Seek the ingredients around you to forge your path to the flag hidden in the abyss."

The cryptic clue had an immediate effect. A chorus of whispers erupted as alchemists strained to decipher its meaning. What abyss? What ingredients? My mind raced, trying to make sense of it. *Forge your path . . .* Could it be a metaphor for creating an elixir?

"Quiet!" Ma Hualong commanded. "There are no set ingredients, nor is there a single solution." A gleam appeared in his eye, a touch of sly amusement playing on his lips. "The abyss, however, is quite literal." He swept off with a final nod, leaving the room buzzing with energy.

I glanced to the unassuming man who had caused such a stir. The top scorer. Seeing him now, in the context of Ma Hualong's speech, I felt he was a testament to the power of perseverance.

A sudden urge to talk to him warred with the nerves coiling in my gut. What if he thought I was presumptuous? Yet a curiosity about his journey burned within me. I glanced over at Bai Hua and Tao Ren.

"I think I'll introduce myself to . . ." I gestured toward the man, the one who reminded me that life wasn't about starting strong but about finishing strong. "Be back in a bit."

As I approached him, he offered a surprised smile. "Can I help you with something?"

"I wanted to introduce myself." I extended a hand in a shallow bow. "Kai Liu, Verdant Lotus Sect. Congratulations on your results in the preliminaries."

His smile widened, a warmth entering his eyes. "Thank you. Zhi Ruo, from the Million Book Pavilion. It all feels a bit surreal, to be honest."

My eyebrows shot up. The Million Book Pavilion? That was the largest library in Crescent Bay City. "So, it's safe to assume you weren't always an alchemist?"

Zhi Ruo chuckled. "Not exactly. I dabbled a bit, but . . ." There was a touch of self-deprecation in his voice. "Well, recent events changed that. I figured I'd enter the Gauntlet, see how far my newfound abilities could take me."

*Intriguing.* First a perfumer, then a blacksmith, and now a librarian. I supposed I shouldn't have been so apprehensive of my background as an herbalist. My inner scholar itched to know more, but I zeroed in on his score first. "Speaking of knowledge, any idea what your score was in the preliminaries?"

He shrugged, an air of nonchalance about him that seemed at odds with someone who'd topped the charts. "Perfect, they said. Though I suppose that shouldn't be too surprising, considering my background. But I know knowledge is only half the battle; it's learning how to use it that's most important."

*Perfect?* My competitive spirit awakened. But there was something I just couldn't put my finger on . . . I shook my head and decided to ask him my most burning question. "Say, do you recall that strange flower in the herb section? Spindly, red, pulsating slightly?" It was the only one in the herb category that stumped me. But if he scored a perfect, then that means he correctly identified it.

Zhi Ruo's smile faltered, replaced by something akin to . . . apprehension? "Ah, yes. That . . . that would be a Bloodsoul Bloom," he said slowly. "Commonly known as the flesh flower. It was a tricky one, and I merely ventured out an educated guess based on its described appearance, so I'd understand why you didn't know."

The name sent a chill through me, evoking something far more sinister than any mere plant. "Flesh flower?" I repeated, a sense of foreboding growing in the pit of my stomach.

"They're supposed to be extinct. Or at least, that's what the records in the Pavilion claimed."

"Extinct? Do you know why?"

"Because they're relics of a far darker era," Zhi Ruo explained, his eyes shadowed. "They don't grow like normal herbs. They . . . subsist off blood. A constant fresh supply. In centuries past, traces of them were found in the territory of demonic cultivators, those who practiced forbidden methods to increase their power. Horrific things." He shuddered.

Terrifying and, more so, impossible to identify. Demonic cultivators were a thing of the past, and haven't been a problem here for centuries. Records of them were sparse, even among the Verdant Lotus Sect's records. I wonder if they put that in the preliminaries as a way to throw people off.

I lingered for a moment, absorbing Zhi Ruo's insights, then shifted the topic. "What are your thoughts about the first round? Ma Hualong's words about forging our path in the abyss were rather cryptic."

He pondered, his gaze turning inward. "The abyss, to me, signifies the unknown depths of alchemy, where theory meets practice in unexpected ways. I anticipate challenges that will test application rather than recitation."

Intrigued by his perspective, I probed further. "How'll you be preparing?"

With a decisive nod, he responded, "I'll be at the Pavilion, studying. Despite the preliminary success, I can't afford complacency. The true test is yet to come, and I must be ready."

His dedication sparked a realization in me. Being twelfth was an achievement, but it shouldn't have been the pinnacle of my aspirations. Inspired, I made an impulsive request. "Would you mind if I joined you at the Million Book Pavilion for study?"

# CHAPTER THIRTY

# First Round Blues

You look like you've seen better days," Bai Hua remarked.

I scoffed at him. I certainly have. But who could blame me? The Million Books Pavilion was *huge*! There was no doubt in my mind that the building lived up to its epithet.

Despite being competitors, Zhi Ruo eagerly shared his knowledge, confident that revealing his treasure trove posed no threat.

I spent the night in the city's largest library, reading and learning with Zhi Ruo. I explored aspects of alchemy I hadn't seen in the Verdant Lotus Sect's archives.

I rubbed the back of my neck where a crick had formed from hours spent hunched over books. "I've certainly had more restful nights, but the wealth of knowledge in there is a treasure worth every second of lost sleep."

"Speaking of treasures, your Spirit Beasts, that serpent and butterfly . . . they're quite extraordinary. Do you possess some unique beast-taming skill? Perhaps a fruit borne from the Heavenly Interface?"

I shook my head, smiling at the thought of my companions. I trusted them to Feng Wu's care for the night, though I worried about Windy's voracious appetite. "Nothing of the sort. Our bond isn't from skills or techniques. They recognize my aura and potential and chose to stay with me, not because of any control I exert over them."

"Intriguing. Such relationships are rare. They speak of a deeper connection, perhaps aligned with your destiny or fate. I had thought it was something from the Heavenly Interface, much like my own abilities."

That was fair. Even for me, the Heavenly Interface was responsible for most of my growth. It gave me skills that accelerated my growth, like Accelerated Reading, and ones that fit the direction I wanted to pursue, like the Crimson Lotus Purification Technique. I perked up at that last part of his sentence.

"Yours is from the Heavenly Interface?"

Bai Hua's expression turned solemn. "I believe so, at least a good part of it. Without its aid, I doubt I would have ventured into this competition. It's helped me realize and harness my potential in ways I never imagined."

"How so?"

Bai Hua smirked before covering his face with his sleeve in a conspiring manner. "You'll see in the first round, ho ho ho!"

As we walked together toward the Marble Jade Arena, I thought back on how many of the competitors benefited from the Heavenly Interface. Likely all of them, but I doubt they experienced it in the same way I did. I wonder what triggering factor there was in place that gave people more from the Interface. I mean, I didn't see Lan-Yin—despite her hard work at the tea shop, gain any skills like mine. Was it due to one's ambition? Some underlying ancestry? Did it pick at random?

If it was at random, it meant a variety of people would benefit from the Interface. Even shady figures like Elder Jun or Xu Ziqing or annoying ones like Jian Duan.

The Interface was a fickle thing indeed.

As we neared the Marble Jade Arena, the sheer scale of the crowd outside the main entrance was staggering. People from all walks of life, from the curious townsfolk to the wealthy nobles, thronged the area, all clamoring for a glimpse of the first round's commencement. But with so many people, there was bound to be conflict.

"Look at this mess!" a portly woman in a thick cerulean robe complained, shivering slightly. "We've been here for hours and haven't budged an inch!"

"Patience, Madam Li," came a nervous voice from behind her. "The Grand Alchemy Gauntlet only happens every five years. It's bound to draw a crowd."

"Patience be hanged!" A burly man with a thick, braided beard slammed his meaty fist into his palm. "I could have concocted three batches of my Ironscale Tincture in the time we've been standing here!"

Just then, a young man shoved his way in front of the burly man. "Coming through, coming through! Make way for the illustrious Howling Crane Sect!"

The burly man's eyes narrowed. "Howling Crane Sect? More like a flock of twittering sparrows, if you ask me. What's the point of you nitwits coming to watch the Gauntlet? You wouldn't know true alchemy if it bit you in the—"

"ENOUGH!" a voice boomed, silencing the line. An imposing woman with a fierce expression and yellow robes adorned with the telltale symbol of an official. "Do you fools have no respect for decorum? This is a competition, not a marketplace squabble!"

She glared at the young man who cut in line. "And you, boy! The line starts back there. Unless your Howling Crane Sect teaches nothing but barnyard manners, you'll rejoin like everyone else."

"But—but I am Wu Long, most esteemed disciple of Master Wei! Surely you wouldn't dare—"

The woman snorted. "Wu Long? Cutting in line and spouting nonsense. Your mother must be truly desperate to have saddled a disrespectful brat like you with such a dignified name!"

"You—you take that back, you old shrew!" He lunged at the woman, his fists clenched.

The conflict continued to escalate and remained audible despite us walking farther away.

Bai Hua commented, "It seems the Gauntlet has garnered more attention than usual this year . . ."

I nodded, taking in the spectacle. "More like a grand festival. But we should head to the competitors' entrance."

Turning away from the teeming masses, we made our way to a less conspicuous entrance marked for participants. The contrast was stark, with only a handful of individuals presenting their tokens to the guards and slipping through the doors.

After showing our tokens, we entered a spacious antechamber, distinct from the main arena yet buzzing with its own undercurrent of energy. It was the same place where the sponsored participants registered.

Here, the air was thick with the concentrated tension of the contestants.

Through the walls, the muffled roar of the crowd from the arena reached us, a constant reminder of the grand stage upon which we were about to perform. It felt like standing at the edge of a vast, unseen ocean, its waves crashing just beyond sight.

"Nervous?" Bai Hua asked.

"Of course not! I'm as cool as a cucumber, in fact."

"HEY! YOU TWO!" Tao Ren waved at us, beckoning us to the pillar he was standing by. "You both ready?"

"As I can be," I said, rubbing my eyes. Perhaps I should've drunk some of the Ambrosia of Radiant Dawn to get me nice and energized. Although perhaps I shouldn't be so reliant on potions to keep me up, I'd be finding the consequences if I drank it too often.

I scanned over the rest of the contestants. I saw Jingyu Lian leaning across a pillar at the farthest corner of the room by herself. It seemed she was the frigid-beauty type. She had her eyes closed and arms crossed.

Zhi Ruo was absent, although I do remember him still being awake and waving me farewell when I left early in the morning to return to the Jade Harmony Inn. Perhaps he overslept. That'd be quite unfortunate.

"Zhi Ruo isn't here yet?" I asked Tao Ren.

"Maybe he decided to meditate or do some last-minute prep," Bai Hua suggested.

I chuckled despite my worry. Just then, a commotion at the entrance drew our attention. A figure, disheveled and panting, burst into the antechamber. It was Zhi Ruo, hair a mess, his eyes bloodshot.

He gasped, clutching his side. "I . . . overslept. Ran all the way from the Pavilion . . ."

Murmurs spread throughout the contestants, who shook their heads.

Jingyu Lian cracked one eye open to gauge Zhi Ruo, though she closed it as soon as her gaze met mine.

"We were getting worried," I said, trying to hide my grin. "Looks like someone was reading a bit too late."

The librarian groaned, running a hand through his unruly hair. "I completely lost track of time." He shook his head sheepishly. "But no excuses! I'm here now, ready to compete."

Tao Ren thumped him on the back, nearly sending the man tumbling over. "Welcome to the Gauntlet, sleepyhead. Just make sure you and Kai don't doze off when the round starts!"

The tension in the room began to spike as an official walked onto a small platform at the front of the antechamber. With a booming voice, he announced, "Honored competitors, the first round is about to commence! Please form a line! Single file, please!"

"Seeking ingredients . . . Forging a path . . . Do you have any memories of the past Gauntlet? What they did?" I asked.

"Not me, but my father says it changes each time. Keeps things interesting, I suppose. Last Gauntlet, they had a round where the contestants were poisoned and had to find the ingredients for an antidote within the arena before succumbing to it."

"WHAT?!" I shouted incredulously.

"Well, the poison was pretty weak. It just kept them in a state of paralysis. They wouldn't want to kill the contestants."

"Oh." I sighed in relief. I wasn't enthused about putting my life on the line for the contest, regardless of how much I wanted to win. "Okay, that's less terrifying. Still, makes me wonder, maybe this round is like an obstacle course. A hidden flag, somewhere tricky to reach? Like in the dark, if the abyss is anything to go by . . ."

"That's a good guess, but I—"

As we followed the line, the antechamber gave way to the vastness of the Marble Jade Arena, which had undergone a dramatic transformation. A sandy expanse stretched before us, bordered by a serene beach on our side and crystal-clear water on the other, mimicking a natural coastal landscape. Scattered across the sand were simplified alchemical stations, each isolated yet part of a larger, intricate setup. It felt like I entered a different dimension, one where the province was still in the midst of summer rather than the approaching winter.

The area was positively teeming with ingredients that all seemed to share common properties . . . They related to the sea.

*Ingredients, flags, an abyss . . .*

And just like that, everything clicked.

The previously empty stands now buzzed with life, filled with thousands of spectators. Their collective voices merged into a thunderous roar, echoing the pounding waves of the artificial ocean, their excitement palpable and contagious. The atmosphere was electric, charged with anticipation for the spectacle about to unfold.

"Let's welcome the contestants," Ma Hualong shouted from his place in the stands, "with a big round of applause!"

The crowd erupted as we stepped onto the field, the air thick with anticipation and the salty tang of the simulated sea breeze.

"Today will be a challenge that will not only test our competitors' alchemical prowess but also their ingenuity and resolve." He continued, outlining the specifics of the challenge. "Before you lies a body of water, deep and daunting. Below its surface, flags are placed at various depths, each representing the continuation of your journey in this gauntlet. Your task is to concoct an alchemical solution that enables you to reach these depths and retrieve a flag."

The rules were straightforward but daunting and only confirmed what I had thought.

We were to use the ingredients available in our surroundings to create an alchemical product that aids in underwater travel and deep diving. Each contestant had to secure their own flag to advance by diving into the water, and they couldn't take a person's flag after they had gotten out. Only twenty of the hundred participants would move to the next round, based on the order of flag retrieval.

Ma Hualong added a crucial detail: "To ensure fairness and safety, several invigilators will monitor the competition. Any attempt at sabotage or obstruction among contestants will result in immediate disqualification. Remember, this is a test of individual merit and creativity."

"A worthy challenge! Wouldn't you say, friends?!" Tao Ren boasted.

Some looked excited, others apprehensive. The depth of the water and the need for a creative alchemical approach to navigate it added layers of complexity to the task. But me—I was already planning ahead my moves.

I scanned the area, my mind racing. They'd given us the obvious ingredients for Breath Gel—Tidecaller Vine, Horsetail Pine—but there clearly weren't enough for everyone. Which meant the organizers were forcing us to think beyond the standard recipe. There had to be more, less common ingredients hidden within the environment they created here.

A thrill of excitement coursed through me. This was the kind of challenge that separated rote memorization from true alchemy, where ingenuity and adaptation were key! A fitting challenge for the alchemy god Kai Liu!

While I strategized, a wave of chatter rippled through the crowd above.

"Did you hear that? Underwater potions! This is going to be fascinating!"

"Hah! Those pampered young alchemists won't last a minute!" a geezer with sun-leathered skin scoffed. "How many of those upstarts can even swim?"

The crowd's energy was contagious. I spotted flashes of silver as bets were exchanged, adding more tension to the atmosphere.

As I turned back, Bai Hua and Tao Ren mirrored the crowd's excitement but with a focused intensity. Zhi Ruo scratched his head, muttering frantically to himself. "Water . . . need something . . . pressure . . ."

"Well, Kai," Bai Hua said thoughtfully, "it seems our theories weren't entirely off the mark. We'll indeed be looking for the flag in a tricky place! And now, to add a twist to our tale, the top ten from the preliminaries will receive a head start!" He gestured grandly toward the side of the arena. "Those in the top ten, step forward!"

The crowd cheered as Zhi Ruo and Jingyu Lian, along with eight others, moved toward the front. The librarian, slightly disheveled from his earlier rush, adjusted his stance as his eyes darted nervously across the selection of resources.

"Contestants will have five minutes to gather their ingredients before the rest of you may begin," Ma Hualong declared. "Your time starts . . . now!"

# CHAPTER THIRTY-ONE

# Beneath the Surface

The top ten moved swiftly, splitting into two groups: those focused on the Tidecaller Vine and those, like Zhi Ruo and Jingyu Lian, starting on the Horsetail Pine. A smart initial strategy to create the standard Breath Gel recipe. Jingyu Lian was a blur, swift and precise, while Zhi Ruo struggled to keep up, his movements clumsy. By the time he'd finally sawed off one branch, she'd moved on to the vines, her icy efficiency drawing murmurs from the onlookers.

Meanwhile, I cursed under my breath. The early birds had snatched up a hefty chunk of the obvious ingredients.

The less-common Gill Pill was my only shot now, and that meant getting Bubblebloom Algae, which meant a dip in the water.

"Should've worn something more . . . sensible," I muttered, the silk of my robes feeling suddenly extravagant. I'd have to make this count.

"The rest of you, BEGIN!" Ma Hualong boomed.

I dashed forward and made it to where the Sea Lantern fruit was growing before anybody else did.

Sea Lantern fruits usually had enough to make one pill, so getting two on the off chance I messed up the recipe should be good. The Sea Lanterns required nothing more than a quick pluck—and I was already on the move again, heading for the water's edge. As I jogged, I noticed Jian Duan cornering one of the frantic contestants. His hand rested on the smaller alchemist's shoulder, and Jian Duan spoke, low and insistent.

". . . heard your family runs a small apothecary, down in the market . . . The Misty Sky Sect always repays favors tenfold . . . Think of it as an investment for the future."

The other alchemist shifted nervously, glancing around as if searching for an escape route. My own stomach twisted. Was he coercing ingredients? Bullying someone into helping him? It felt wrong, a violation of the spirit of the competition, but . . .

I scanned the arena. The invigilators hadn't reacted. Technically, there was no rule against sharing resources. I forced myself to look away; I couldn't lose focus on him.

The water's edge shimmered before me, the sand giving way to the crystal-clear depths. My heart pounded in anticipation. I scanned the surface, spotting the delicate blue globes of Bubblebloom Algae swaying gently with the current just below. A rush of relief washed over me—at least that part of the plan was still on track.

But something else caught my eye. The underwater landscape wasn't barren, as I'd initially expected. Iridescent clams nestled in the sand, their shells slightly ajar. Strands of gleaming seaweed wove through the water like liquid emerald.

This place was filled with more ingredients than there were on the floor. So this was how they were going to get the other contestants the ingredients they needed!

First things first: securing that Sea Lantern and algae for the Gill Pills. I couldn't afford to lose sight of my main objective. I waded into the water, inwardly lamenting the fact I was getting my silk robe wet, and grabbed the algae growing just under the surface. Not giving us baskets was smart, because it prevented the competitors from collecting too many ingredients at once. That didn't make it any less inconvenient, however, I thought as I held two Sea Lantern fruits in my hands.

Reaching a station, I scrabbled for the familiar shape of a furnace, a mortar and pestle. The basics were present, alongside a collection of commonplace ingredients—a smart setup, forcing us to consider what was readily available as well as the treasures found underwater.

My gaze swept across the arena. Already, the top ten were well into their Breath Gel creation. Jingyu Lian had a small flame flickering beneath her furnace, while others had focused on the grinding process first.

Zhi Ruo, still damp from his sprint to the Horsetail Pines, was farther behind. By the look of his meager ingredients pile, I suspected he'd run into trouble with acquiring enough to create a proper Breath Gel. I frowned. He had the knowledge but perhaps lacked the physical ability to keep pace in this round. A pity.

Bai Hua was as enigmatic as ever. He seemed to be gathering a bit of everything, his movements almost leisurely. Was he already planning beyond Breath Gel? Had he noticed the underwater possibilities as I had?

"Focus, Kai!" I gave myself a light slap on the cheek to get my head in the game.

The sun was high, its light scattering dazzling reflections across the surface of the artificial lagoon. I spread out my collected ingredients before me—Sea

Lantern fruits, Bubblebloom Algae, and a handful of supplemental materials from the station.

First, I crushed the algae using the mortar and pestle, the delicate strands releasing a burst of oxygen-rich bubbles as they were ground into a fine, glowing paste. This was the core that would allow one's lungs to extract oxygen directly from the water.

"COME TO THE JADE FOUNDRY FOR ALL YOUR SMITHING AND ALCHEMY NEEDS!" Tao Ren shouted from afar. I glanced over, seeing him point and wave at the crowd with several ingredients in his arms. What a character. To think he registered just to spread the word of his forge . . .

Shaking my head, I sliced the Sea Lantern fruit in half, insides shimmering with a bioluminescent gel. It would act as a catalyst in the reaction, enhancing the body's ability to absorb the dissolved oxygen. The slicing had to be precise; too thin and the gel would dry out, too thick and it wouldn't mix properly with the algae paste.

With a steady hand, I mixed the algae paste and the Sea Lantern gel together, the mixture emitting a faint, ethereal glow. The combination needed to be homogenous.

Once mixed, I carefully transferred the concoction into the pill furnace. The contents of the furnace needed constant, even motion to ensure the energy flowed evenly through the mixture, aiding in the transformation from raw ingredients to a finished, potent pill. This was where the real skill in alchemy came into play—maintaining a balance of physical effort, spiritual energy, and mental focus.

As I stirred, I could feel the resistance from the mixture begin to lessen. The glow from the mixture began to stabilize, shifting from a bright, erratic flash to a steady, pulsating light.

"Almost there," I muttered to myself, beads of sweat forming on my brow.

Just as I began focusing on the careful temperature adjustments required for the final stages, a jarring splash ripped my attention away. A wave of water cascaded over me, the sudden chill raising goose bumps on my skin.

"Whoops! Clumsy me!" Jian Duan said.

I sputtered, momentarily blinded, my precious concoction splattered with cold droplets. Fury bubbled in my chest. I wanted to wipe that grin off his face.

"You did that on purpose!" My accusation rang across the sandy beach.

Jian Duan merely shrugged, the picture of nonchalance. "An accident, I assure you," he said, but the gleam in his eyes told a different story.

"An accident?! You were an accident, you son of a—!"

Before I could argue further, an invigilator stood between us. "While a bit . . . unfortunate, it appears to have been an unintended mishap. However, any further attempts at deliberate disruption, Competitor Duan, will result in immediate disqualification."

Jian Duan bowed slightly. "Of course, Invigilator. My sincerest apologies."

Seething, I returned to my furnace. Despite the setback, my mixture seemed salvageable. I blocked most of the water with my back, now my entire body was dripping wet again. I took a deep breath to regain my composure. Sabotage or not, I wouldn't be derailed.

My focus narrowed on the task at hand. The aroma of the mixture intensified, turning from a fresh, oceanic scent into something sharper, almost metallic. This was the crucial moment.

With a practiced flick of my wrist, I extinguished the qi, plunging the furnace into darkness. The glow from the mixture pulsed faintly, the rhythm slowing, stabilizing. My shoulders slumped slightly in relief. It seemed I'd salvaged it. A small victory.

I took out the contents, a light blue clump of powder that I'd need to arrange into proper pill form. I pinched a sample, felt it on my fingertip, and noticed that the texture was lacking. That singular moment of distraction had netted me a worse result than I would've otherwise had. If I had to guess, this batch of Gill Pills could get me underwater for only ten to fifteen minutes.

From afar, I could see Zhi Ruo in a panic. He seemed lost. Looking at my spare Sea Lantern fruit, I decided my next course of action. "Zhi Ruo, catch!" I called out, tossing one of the Sea Lantern fruits to him. He fumbled slightly but managed to catch it. "You know the recipe for the Gill Pill, right? Use it."

"Th-thank you! How can I repay you for this?"

"Don't worry about it," I replied, brushing off his concern with a wave of my hand. "Just grant me free access to all those secret tomes in the Million Books Pavilion, and we'll call it even."

His laugh was shaky but genuine. "It's a deal, Kai. You have no idea how much this means to me."

"Just make it worth your while, and mine. Get to work. The clock's ticking!"

"Thanks, Kai. And listen"—he lowered his voice, glancing toward the shimmering expanse of water—"breathing underwater isn't the only thing you should be worried about."

I paused in the midst of organizing my workstation, raising an eyebrow. "What do you mean?"

He gestured subtly toward the artificial lagoon. "It's darker than it looks. The farther down you go, the murkier it gets. If you can't see, finding those flags is going to be more than a little difficult."

I cursed under my breath. Of course, visibility! In my focus on breathing underwater, I had completely overlooked the simple fact that I needed to see what I was doing.

He nodded, then turned back to his station, leaving me to ponder this new challenge. Visibility. I needed something that could illuminate the dark waters.

My eyes scanned the available ingredients, none of which were particularly known for their luminescent properties.

Then it hit me—the Essence Extraction technique. My essences always glowed, so if I just got one into a vial, I could just use it as a lamp of some sort. Any ingredient would do, honestly.

As I said that, I saw Jingyu Lian approach the water's edge with her completed Breath Gel concoction. In her hands, she held the container of her Breath Gel. With a fluid motion, she poured its contents into the water. The gel spread quickly, forming a thin, shimmering layer on the liquid's surface.

She took a moment to survey her work, ensuring coverage, then, with a grace that spoke of her confidence and skill, she dipped herself headfirst. As she submerged, the gel adhered to her skin seamlessly, forming a semipermeable membrane that clung to her like a second skin.

From the sidelines, I watched in awe and a bit of envy. The membrane was a brilliant application of alchemy—allowing oxygen to pass through while filtering out the water and maintaining a stable internal pressure. Jingyu Lian had managed to create enough gel to cover her entire body. It indicated that her measurements and technique were flawless, with absolutely no wastage of ingredients.

The realization struck me hard. If she could maximize her resources to that extent, I needed to up my game, especially now that I was aware of the visibility issue in the water.

With this new problem to solve, I turned back to my own station. Pulling out a small vial, I selected a few strands of the luminous algae I had set aside earlier. Though not as naturally bright as the Sea Lantern fruit, when concentrated, they could emit a sufficient glow.

Utilizing the Essence Extraction technique, I carefully drew out the luminescent essence of the algae. As the extraction proceeded, the essence began to glow brightly within the vial, its light piercing the surroundings of my workstation.

The algae's essence filled a portion of the vial, casting shadows as it intensified in brightness. Satisfied with the potency, I sealed the vial, now a makeshift lamp that would illuminate the murky depths below.

Securing the vial to my belt, I prepared myself for the dive. With the Gill Pills and my new source of light, I felt ready to face whatever lay hidden in the depths of the lagoon. The other contestants had already begun to dive in, spurred on by Jingyu Lian. There was no time to waste!

Popping the pill in my mouth, I dove in without hesitation.

The water closed over me, a sudden chill that sent a shiver down my spine. For a terrifying moment, panic flared—a primal, instinctive fear. Then the Gill Pill kicked in. My lungs expanded in a gasp that turned into a breath underwater.

I felt relief, mingled with a jolt of awe. It worked! I could breathe here. I kicked my legs, propelling myself deeper, the glimmering vial at my waist cutting a path through the increasingly murky water.

The bottom of the lagoon wasn't visible, the depths shrouded in an unsettling gloom. How had they constructed this overnight?

The light from my vial, though strong, only illuminated a few chi around me. My heart pounded against my ribs. It was unsettling, being under the sea.

. . . No way they put anything underwater, right? Nothing that would eat an unsuspecting contestant?

I scanned the area, my eyes adjusting to the dimness. *There!* A glimmer in the distance. Was that a flag?

# CHAPTER THIRTY-TWO

# Underwater Gauntlet

Through the murky water and sediment, the silhouette became clearer. In fact, it was moving too—

"Wargh!" I screamed, warbled from the water. I veered off to the side as Jingyu Lian passed by me, nearly butting heads, her eyes wide with focus and a flag gripped tightly in her hand. She didn't glance my way as she swam frantically toward the surface. The sight was almost comical if not for the urgency driving her.

As she darted away, I noticed her Breath Gel disintegrating, peeling off like old paint. Breath Gel, when prepared correctly, should last at least half an hour under these conditions. Yet hers was failing after merely five minutes. What caused such rapid degradation?

I continued my descent. The water grew colder and dimmer, then I felt the unsettling brush of Slickweed Kelp against my legs. A vast field of it lay at the lagoon's bottom, swaying gently in the currents. Why was there so much here?

Slickweed Kelp was a common component in several alchemical recipes, especially solvents. That was it—solvents! The kelp's ability to dissolve certain compounds included the alchemical gel used in Breath Gel. She must have swam through a patch of it, causing her gel to break down prematurely.

I suppose it was a way to trick those who thought they had it easy using the Breath Gel; my Gill Pill was focused on internal effects, and dispelling that was beyond the effect of any regular plant, unless I ate it.

Internally, I was keeping track of how long I had. The fact I had a light source and didn't have to worry about the Slickweed Kelp made it less stressful for me.

*There!*

As I drew closer, the shape became distinct—a flag, anchored in a crevice, untouched by the kelp. Excitement surged through me. I reached out, fingers closing around the fabric. I had found one!

Clutching the flag, I surveyed my surroundings. My artificial breath came in steady rhythms, and the glow from my vial cast an eerie light on the seafloor. An idea began to form . . .

I collected several pieces of Slickweed Kelp and carefully extracted its essence, creating a green ball of light, enough to form a fist-sized glob. Swimming closer to the surface, where light permeated the floor, I took my second Gill Pill for additional time.

Looking upward, I calculated Jian Duan's likely position . . .

His gaudy robes were hard to miss, even underwater. The Breath Gel covered him, although it was misshapen and uneven in certain places, showing just how inferior he was to Jingyu Lian.

I swam to where he was descending, staying out of sight as I released the Slickweed Kelp extract into the water, turning it into a thin stream of glowing green energy. It was hard to predict where the essence would go, but with enough extract, I spread it over a wide area.

The cold seeped into my bones. Despite the pill's effects, it couldn't protect me from the deep water's chill, and I began to feel lightheaded.

As Jian Duan descended, he went straight to the glowing green essence, likely thinking it marked a flag. Almost immediately, his Breath Gel began sloughing off. Though I couldn't hear it, I saw him thrashing in panic as his protective gel crumbled, leaving him vulnerable to the water and pressure.

*Ha ha ha!* Seeing it was so cathartic. Karma was catching up to him. That's what he gets for messing with this invincible young master! A frog in a well, challenging a phoenix like yours truly!

Still clutching my hard-won flag and fueled by a surge of wicked delight, I kicked toward the surface. I gasped, air flooding my grateful lungs. The cool breeze was a shock after the icy depths. I blinked against the blinding light within the arena and the salty water. For a moment, the only sound was the frantic beating of my heart and my ragged breaths.

Then the cheers of the crowd hit me like a wave. I glanced around, and my heart swelled. I closed my eyes, focusing my hearing to make out what the crowd was saying.

"Move aside, runt! Can't you see the Ice Queen has emerged? Such perfection!"

"Out of the way, out of the way!" a high-pitched voice shrieked. "Some of us want a proper look at Master Bai! Did you see his muscles? Like carved jade!"

I snapped my eyes open. What was going on up there?

Why was I being discarded like some unwanted ingredient? My gaze followed the crowd and settled on Bai Hua, who was coming out of the water with a flag in hand. His skin glistened and, oddly enough, seemed to repel the remaining water droplets rolling across his form. It looked like the Breath Gel but much thinner.

"Tsk. Show-off," I grumbled, crossing my arms. The spectacle unfolding in front of me was infuriatingly absurd. Had the crowd completely forgotten about the actual competition? Weren't they here for alchemy, not some kind of physique showcase?

"You there! Competitor! Out of the way!" a portly woman screeched, brandishing a fan menacingly. "Don't obscure the view!"

Was this what fame felt like? To be acknowledged, then instantly forgotten, swept aside by a fickle crowd chasing after the next shiny thing?

I sulked and trudged forward, but as I glanced back, I saw Jian Duan floundering as the remnants of his Breath Gel dissolved completely.

I made eye contact with Bai Hua.

He smiled at me and waved. "Looks like we're both making it to the next round."

"Yeah, but how'd you get a flag so quickly? You didn't even have the full ingredients needed for Breath Gel."

He retrieved a narrow-necked vial, one that was similar to the sample he gave me from before. Grabbing my hand, he applied it, and I felt the substance quickly spread along my arm. I touched it, noting how slippery it was, like handling mucus.

"I made a degraded version, one that enhances the gel aspect using the Tidecaller Vine's sap. Not only does it help with surface resistance to help me swim faster"—he touched his face—"it makes your skin supple and smooth."

As expected of the Summer Sun Cosmetics heir.

Only about fifty people remained on land, still creating their concoctions. We both walked past the remaining contestants, many of whom stared at the flags in our hands with visible jealousy. Some hastened their efforts, feeling the pressure.

"Dammit all!"

Jian Duan clambered onto the shore, coughing and sputtering, a picture of disheveled desperation. His eyes, red-rimmed and wild, flickered between the dwindling crowd and those of us who had successfully obtained flags. When they finally landed on me, they narrowed, his lips twisting into a snarl.

*Ha ha ha! Revenge is a dish best served cold, after all!*

"You!" he sputtered, pointing an accusing finger. "You . . . This was some kind of trick, wasn't it?"

"Me? I would never do such a thing. It goes against my principles as an alchemist," I said. "It's quite unfortunate that your concoction failed, but there's plenty of time to try again. Or perhaps beg for ingredients . . ."

If looks could kill, I'd be a messy pile of ashes by now.

Bai Hua and I made our way to the invigilators' table to hand over our flags. The official behind the table nodded at us, marking something on a large, leather-bound ledger.

"Congratulations, Kai Liu, Bai Hua," Ma Hualong said, his voice neutral.

We nodded and stepped back, watching as the official raised his voice to make the announcement. "Attention, competitors! Fifteen flags remain!"

The crowd stirred, some with renewed hope, others with despair. It was a reminder—only the quickest, the cleverest, or the luckiest would advance.

We walked to a makeshift lounge where those who secured their flags could wait out the rest of the round. Jingyu Lian was already there, now changed into dry clothes.

She barely acknowledged us as we entered. I simply closed my eyes and turned away. All I had to do here was prove her wrong, and by making the first round, I already had.

Several others were there too—two other competitors who had managed to secure their flags early. They were engaged in quiet conversation, their expressions a mix of relief and anticipation.

As I settled into a seat, my clothes still damp and clinging uncomfortably to my skin, a couple of officials approached us.

"Gentlemen, if you'd like, we can take your clothes for drying," one offered, gesturing to a secluded area set up with privacy screens and a variety of alchemical heaters.

"Thank you," I said, standing. The prospect of warm, dry clothes was too good to pass up. Bai Hua and I followed them, passing our soggy garments to be treated.

While waiting for our clothes, Bai Hua leaned against a partition, his gaze thoughtful. "This round is more intense than I expected," he mused.

"What do you think about Tao Ren's chances?" I asked him.

Tao Ren had marketed himself as a simple blacksmith, but his earlier enthusiasm and the way he'd handled himself suggested there might be more to him.

Bai Hua's eyes flicked toward the man.

"From the brief moments I observed, Tao Ren is much more capable than he lets on. His approach to alchemy stems more from practicality than theoretical knowledge."

At that moment, the officials returned with our dried clothes. I quickly changed back into my now warm and comfortable attire, feeling a renewed sense of vigor.

As we settled back to observe the ongoing competition, my thoughts drifted to the remaining contestants below. I watched as each one scrambled to secure one of the dwindling number of flags.

Even though I harbored a strong dislike for Jian Duan, I couldn't help but grudgingly respect his ability to work under pressure. He was already back in the water, his movements calculated and desperate as he tried to concoct another batch of Breath Gel.

Just then, a commotion snapped me out of my thoughts. Emerging from the water with a triumphant splash, Tao Ren surfaced, a flag in one hand, and a clam clamped firmly in his mouth. The crowd erupted into cheers and laughter as he waved his flag, his other hand making a grand gesture toward the Jade Flame Foundry banner draped nearby.

I even heard a few swoons from the women admiring his musculature.

*I have muscles too . . . They're just hidden under my robes . . .*

"Only at Jade Flame Foundry! We're taking commissions after the Gauntlet! For all your alchemy and smithing needs!" he shouted after spitting out the clam.

I watched as he walked over to where Bai Hua and I were sitting, a wide grin splitting his face.

"Did you just . . . swim with a clam in your mouth?" I asked, incredulous as he plopped down beside us, still dripping. "And how did you sneak a banner into the arena?"

Tao Ren chuckled, holding up the clam for us to see. "Ah, this little beauty? Pearl Diver clams—they're nifty little buggers. Used it as a makeshift air reservoir. Works well when you combine it with some of the Breath Coral. Not the most orthodox method, but hey, it worked!"

I didn't even ponder the idea of using the clams as an ingredient. As I took the clam from his hand, I noticed how it had a natural contour on the shell that could fit around a human's lips.

"These guys have siphon-like appendages on the inside. If you just fiddle with it, it can take you from the bottom of the water and back."

Bai Hua made a face. "Breathing through *that* doesn't seem pleasant at all."

I raised an eyebrow, impressed despite myself. "And the Breath Coral? Did you use it to enhance the clam's properties?"

"Sorta just mashed them together in my palm with some Tidecaller sap. It wasn't precise, but it formed a sort of pulpy mix that seemed to do the trick. Once you slather it on the clam, it'll make these large air bubbles you can breathe from."

He understood how things reacted and worked together not through studied knowledge but through a hands-on, trial-and-error approach. That was something I couldn't do.

"I learned a lot of this stuff when I was a kid. Old man used to try and teach me the finer points of alchemy, but I only stuck with what I thought was useful. Turns out, it really came in handy today."

Laughing, I shook my head. "Well, it certainly paid off. You've got a knack for making the most out of unusual situations."

The competition was winding down, with only a few flags left. The intensity of the remaining contestants was palpable; each one desperate not to be left behind. Jian Duan rose from the depths with an ugly expression on his face, trudging over to hand his flag in to Ma Hualong.

"Two flags remain!"

Each competitor here brought something unique to the table, showcasing the wide array of approaches and innovations that alchemy could foster. From Jingyu

Lian's precise technique to Tao Ren's resourceful pragmatism, and even Jian Duan's fierce determination under pressure—each had proven themselves a formidable opponent. Yet as I peered over the water's edge, my focus settled on Zhi Ruo.

As the top contender from the preliminaries, I had expected more from him. But he seemed to lack the practical skills to effectively apply his vast knowledge. Many of the older contestants also struggled with this challenge, either unable to keep up with the physical demands of the task or the pace required to swim deep underwater, even with alchemical aids. Was it unfair? Perhaps. But as I scanned the crowd, noting the flurry of bets and the spectators' animated discussions, I realized that the Grand Alchemy Gauntlet was as much a spectacle as it was a test of alchemy skills.

*Come on, Zhi Ruo! Don't let it end here . . . !*

Another person rose from the water. I recognized the brown-haired woman because she looked like Lan-Yin, one of the top-ten contestants. It seemed everybody who got first dibs for the Breath Gel made it through without any issues.

"One flag remaining!"

The crowd's interest was reaching its crescendo. Many hurled curses at the remaining competitors, either for losing the crowd their bets or for giving up. The body language was visible from here; shoulders sagged, eyes facing downward . . . Many of the participants had given up already.

My gaze was locked on the water's surface, each ripple a tease, a hint of movement from below.

"First place was just lucky," scoffed Jian Duan, his voice loud enough to carry over the murmurs of the crowd. "Preliminaries mean nothing in the real challenge!"

I clenched my fists, feeling the tension knot further in my chest.

Every second stretched longer, the weight of the final flag heavy in the air. Parents shuffled, children stood on tiptoes, all eyes fixed on the shimmering blue that had become the arena for this spectacle.

"Useless! He's too slow," someone else shouted, a sneer in his tone. "I wasted my silver."

I scanned the water's edge, the cool breeze off the lake doing nothing to soothe the heat of my frustration. How can they judge so harshly from the comfort of their seats? Making the Breath Gel or Gill Pill was immensely difficult given the circumsta—

A splash.

Then another splash—louder, closer.

He emerged.

# CHAPTER THIRTY-THREE

# First Round Conclusions

Zhi Ruo's head broke the surface, water sluicing off his face, his hair plastered to his skull. And there, in his right hand, clutched with a grip that spoke of no intention to let go, was the final flag.

A cheer erupted from some, a stunned silence from others. Jian Duan was momentarily speechless, sneer wiped clean.

The librarian's eyes met mine across the distance, a flash of triumphant relief visible even from afar. He'd done it.

"UWOHHH! WHAT A MAN!" Tao Ren shouted, looping his arms around my and Bai Hua's neck while jumping like a maniac.

"Get off me! Can't! Breathe!" the perfumer wheezed, trying to escape the chokehold. I struggled similarly as well. What on earth was Tao Ren made of?!

All the contestants' shoulders seemed to droop even further, looking at Zhi Ruo as he walked past them all with a multitude of emotions: anger, jealousy, resignation . . . Eighty people had been eliminated just like that.

Ma Hualong shouted at the top of his lungs as the contest came to a close. "THE FIRST ROUND IS OVER!" His voice boomed through speakers enchanted for clarity, reverberating across the arena.

The crowd erupted. Zhi Ruo, drenched and panting, stood beneath the arena wall, the flag still clutched white-knuckled in his fist. As Ma Hualong's announcement registered, a grin split his face, wider and more genuine than I'd ever seen.

We watched as Ma Hualong stepped onto a raised platform. His gaze swept the arena, and the crowd quieted, a ripple of anticipation washing over the spectators.

"Competitors, congratulations on reaching this stage," he began, his voice carrying an undercurrent of authority. "Those who have failed, learn from this setback. There is no shame in defeat, only in not learning from it."

A few of the unsuccessful contestants looked up, their faces tight, but most kept their heads bowed. Ma Hualong nodded solemnly, then raised a hand.

"However, the ones who made it deserve a reward, not just for their skill but for their perseverance and clever use of their knowledge under pressure," Ma Hualong continued, his voice swelling with pride. "Each of you will be granted a unique opportunity—unrestricted access to choose any ingredient from the Alchemist Association's vault."

I could only imagine what sort of treasures were available in their vaults.

"And let me remind you," he added, his voice dropping to ensure everyone leaned in, "the further you advance in the rounds, the more treasures you will be allowed to claim. The ultimate reward awaits the winner, an honor that will define your career as an alchemist. Please, visit the Alchemist Association's building tomorrow at any time you wish to collect your reward. The next round is in two days, giving you all some time to prepare and relax."

As the group left the artificial lagoon, the cheers of the crowd began to fade into a dull roar, then silenced. The thrill of the crowd was replaced by a quiet anticipation as we walked back through the corridors leading to the competitors' area.

I felt a mix of exhilaration and tension. The chance to access the vault was a game-changer. I needed to play my cards right. What was the best thing to grab from the vault?

As we reached the area where competitors could relax and gather their belongings, I bid farewell to Bai Hua, Tao Ren, and Zhi Ruo. The librarian, still damp from his time in the water, clasped my hand with a grateful look. "Kai, I can't thank you enough. If it wasn't for you, I wouldn't have made it past the first round."

I shook my head, dismissing his thanks with a light smile. "You owe me nothing, Zhi Ruo. Just make sure you choose wisely at the vault tomorrow."

As I turned to leave, someone blocked my path.

Jingyu Lian. Her white hair was stark against the deep blue of her eyes, which scrutinized me intently. "That Gill Pill of yours was quite shoddy. The texture was inconsistent, and your timing and heat control were mediocre. Even from a distance, it was clear your recipe wasn't up to par."

*This rude girl!* Did she neglect the fact that Jian Duan spilled water on me in the middle of my work?

Her words stung, more because they were true than anything else. My first instinct was anger, but I caught it, turning the edge of my response into something smoother, more pointed. "Watching me that closely, huh? Must be because you know I'm a threat."

"Don't flatter yourself too much. The next round will show just how wide the gap is between us."

"Clearly it can't be that wide, since your Breath Gel was breaking down so quickly under the water!"

She stomped toward me, affronted. "That's because of the Slickweed Kelp, you dolt! Not because of a mistake on my part!"

I rolled my eyes and spoke in a mocking falsetto. *"You'll regret underestimating the Jianghu! Look at me, I'm the infallible Jingyu Lian! I'd never make a mistake!"*

My impression of her words from our first meeting rang true, and she flushed red. "You're insufferable!"

I grinned, enjoying her frustration a little too much. "Takes one to know one," I retorted. "Seems like an oversight for someone of your supposed caliber."

Her eyes narrowed. "I don't need to explain myself to the likes of you." She spun on her heel, but not before taunting, "Just know this, Kai Liu. The next round is where the real competition begins. Don't get too comfortable."

I waved her off. There were more important things to worry about other than some snobby aristocrat. How was I going to find Feng Wu?

"...And he accused me of sabotaging him! Can you believe it?" I said, mid-chew.

"Well, did you?" Feng Wu asked.

"That's neither here nor there."

His eyebrows arched ever so slightly—a clear sign he was gearing up for one of his wisdom drops. "Like throwing a stone in your own road, it might trip up your enemy. But it's you who'll have to walk that path again."

I pushed the food around my plate. He was right. In my eagerness to get back at Jian Duan, I had nearly compromised my own standing in the competition. Still, the satisfaction of seeing him flounder had been too sweet to resist at the moment.

"Is Jian Duan from a powerful clan?" I asked, pouring him some more tea.

"They're more wealthy than powerful," he responded, picking at a piece of tofu with his chopsticks. "But wealth often equates to power in its own right. And regardless of their actual strength, it's unwise to provoke them so needlessly."

The restaurant buzzed around us, the clatter of dishes and murmur of conversations. Wealthy not powerful—yet wealth could muster resources, sway opinions, perhaps even influence judges. I mean, he convinced a few participants to part with some of their ingredients during the first round.

I thought about the various competitors, the alliances forming, the quiet exchanges of favors and promises. This competition was as much about navigating these treacherous social undercurrents as it was about alchemical prowess.

"So, they could make things difficult for me?" I asked, trying to gauge just how much I should worry.

"Possibly," Feng Wu replied, his tone noncommittal but his eyes sharp. "It's always prudent to choose your battles wisely, especially when the stakes are as high as they are now."

I nodded, a plan beginning to form. Avoiding direct confrontations with Jian Duan might be wise, but that didn't mean I couldn't prepare for any indirect challenges he might throw my way. If the Duan family's influence was as extensive as their wealth suggested, I needed to be ready for anything.

The meal continued, the flavors of the dishes somewhat muted by the heavier thoughts about the Gauntlet.

"Thanks, Feng Wu. For the advice, and for . . . well, keeping me grounded."

"Just remember, Kai, the smartest warrior is one who knows when to sheathe his sword. The vault visit tomorrow could be a game-changer for you. Focus on that."

As we left the bustling ambiance of the restaurant, the cool evening breeze felt refreshing after the intense discussions. We made our way through the lantern-lit streets toward the Jade Harmony Inn. The inn, with the soft, melodious sounds of a qin playing somewhere in the background, felt like stepping back into a world of tranquility away from the competitive fervor of the day.

Upon entering my room, the first sight to greet me was Tianyi, fluttering around the space with an almost ethereal grace. Close by, Windy lay coiled on a silk cushion, his eyes bright and attentive as he sensed my presence.

"It feels like a lifetime since I last saw you two!"

I pulled out a small bottle of fruit wine from my bag, the one I'd saved just for her, and poured a little into a shallow dish. Tianyi fluttered down, her proboscis delicately sipping the sweet liquid.

For Windy, I fetched some fresh meat from a pouch, laying it out on a small plate. He uncoiled slowly, slithering over with evident enthusiasm.

"They've missed you," Feng Wu observed, settling into a chair by the window.

I nodded, sitting down across from him, the warmth from Tianyi's gentle weight on my hand spreading through me. "I missed them too. It's strange how a couple of days felt like months."

As the Spirit Beasts settled, I turned the conversation back to the upcoming challenge. "So, about the vault, any thoughts on what I should be looking for? There are bound to be hundreds of rare ingredients and items, but I need something . . . impactful."

Feng Wu stroked his chin, pondering. "It's a rare opportunity indeed. They have many items that can boost your cultivation, if that's what you so please."

"I suppose you wouldn't know what they'd have in their vaults, would you?"

"No, but the association would surely provide a list. Instead of thinking a specific item, maybe look into what you want from the vault instead."

"You're right. Maybe instead of looking for a powerful consumable that might give me a temporary edge, perhaps I should look for something sustainable—something that I can grow."

"That's certainly a good idea, Kai. Finding a rare herb or a plant that you can cultivate would be a gift that keeps on giving. You could use it repeatedly, not just in this once but beyond, enhancing your abilities and concoctions over time."

I leaned back in my chair, my mind racing with possibilities. "That makes sense. A plant, maybe . . . something that can adapt to my garden's conditions. Something resilient yet potent."

Another addition to my garden back home, alongside the Moonlit Grace Lily!

"I've seen your garden, Kai. You have a knack for making even the most stubborn plants thrive. Whatever you choose, I'm confident it will flourish under your care."

As we discussed the potential candidates, the excitement of what lay ahead filled the room. Each plant had its merits, but finding one that aligned with my goals as a cultivator and an alchemist was the real challenge.

# CHAPTER THIRTY-FOUR

# The Alchemy Association's Vault

I made my way to the Alchemy Association's towering building. It dwarfed nearby structures with its imposing height and grand design. It was probably one of the tallest buildings here in Crescent Bay City.

From my time with Feng Wu and the teachings at the Verdant Lotus Sect, I knew the Alchemy Association's role well. It was the foremost organization in setting the standards for alchemy across the region, where one's skills could be honed, tested, and certified. Elder Zhu mentioned that one of their elders had taken a position here, which helped bring the Verdant Lotus Sect closer to the Alchemy Association, and that I'd likely see her during my time in the Gauntlet.

I approached the reception, where a clerk looked up at me with a practiced smile. "Good morning. I'm here to collect a reward from the vault," I announced, flashing my entry token.

"Ah, yes, from the tournament . . . Kai Liu, correct? Congratulations. Please follow me."

She led me through a series of secured doors. We descended a wide staircase that spiraled into the lower levels of the building, where the air grew cooler and the buzz of the lobby faded into a hushed silence.

Finally, we arrived at a heavy, ornate door. Standing before it was an elderly man, his back straight, eyes sharp—a vault-keeper. He held a talisman in one hand, which shimmered faintly with intricate glyphs. "Here to access the vault?" he asked, his voice carrying an undercurrent of curiosity as he sized me up.

"Yes, sir. I'm Kai, one of the twenty qualifiers," I replied, extending the token I had been given as proof.

The vault-keeper nodded. He stepped forward, placing the talisman against the vault door. A series of clicks echoed throughout the hall. He pushed open the heavy door with a grunt, revealing rows upon rows of shelves laden with alchemical treasures. "Here, we keep rare but nonessential goods—the kind that can significantly aid an alchemist but are not pivotal to the major operations of the Association." The vault was a meticulously organized labyrinth, each category neatly labeled and sectioned. "You may ask about anything you find. I can provide information on them."

Intrigued by his offer, I decided to dive straight into my primary interest. "Can you show me to the herbs and plants section? I'm particularly interested in those."

"Ah, an herbalist, then!" he exclaimed, chuckling softly as if pleased by my choice. He led me past several aisles to a section filled with a diverse array of botanicals.

As we walked, I glanced over the myriad of ingredients, rare ingredients, including those that didn't belong to this province, littered the area. My Plant Whisperer skill felt like needles along my skin, telling me that everything here held untold potential. But among them, I was drawn to a peculiar sight: a see-through container carrying golden seeds that shimmered with a subtle, enticing luster.

"What are these?"

"Ah, those are Golden Bamboo seeds. Not very creatively named but quite rare. They come from a distant province and were once abundant here in the Tranquil Breeze Province. Sadly, they haven't grown here for centuries. The innate qi in the environment has diminished, and with it, their ability to thrive."

"What were they used for?" I inquired, considering the possibilities of such a plant.

"Golden Bamboo was primarily used in body refinement pills," he explained quietly, as if sharing a secret. "It helps cleanse one's body of impurities and strengthens resistance to diseases and has a myriad of other beneficial effects not dissimilar to ginseng. Quite a valuable ingredient for any cultivator looking to fortify their physique."

"And there's no record of how to cultivate it anymore?"

"The methods were lost indeed."

While others might dismiss the Golden Bamboo as a relic of the past, lost to the annals of time, I sensed it—the potential, just waiting for its time to bloom. Was it the work of my skill? It felt like I just *knew* the Golden Bamboo was something special.

Both my pride as an herbalist and the desire to strengthen myself as a cultivator united. I want to revive the Golden Bamboo. But I couldn't do this blindly. "Can you tell me more about the Golden Bamboo? Anything at all?" If I understood what the plant once thrived on, perhaps I could replicate the conditions here.

"It was brought here from a different region, although the specifics of which were unfortunately lost. The last known sect to have grown this Golden Bamboo died out centuries ago, and our attempts at reviving the species have failed time and again."

I sighed. It was worth a shot. Hearing that, I couldn't help but feel discouraged. So many alchemists have attempted to . . . Who could say that I was any better than them?

"Tell me," I said, focusing my gaze on the vault-keeper, "do you think there's any chance, even a small one, that I could revive this plant?"

"Young man, the word 'impossible' is a dangerous one to an alchemist's vocabulary. Reviving the Golden Bamboo . . . difficult, yes. But with dedication and perhaps a hint of good fortune, who knows what you might accomplish?"

That was all I needed.

*Quest: Seeds of a Lost Era*
*—Revive the Golden Bamboo.*

"You got *seeds*?!" Bai Hua exclaimed. "Of all the treasures available in the Alchemy Association's vault, you got those?"

I looked at him, affronted. "How can you judge me? You took a Beauty Preservation pill! Pot calling the kettle black!"

"Well, it can't be worse than Tao Ren's . . ."

I turned to the blacksmith in question. He gave me a wide grin before pulling out a large black rock from his pocket.

". . . Coal?"

"NO!" Tao Ren shouted, slamming his fist with the coal clenched in his hand and rattling the dining table. "It's an Ember Stone! Feel it!"

I placed a finger on it, feeling warm to the touch. No, it was actually really hot! Like a boiling cup of water! How was Tao Ren just holding on to it like that?

Tao Ren chuckled at my confused expression. "It's used as a material to light up flames, part of the nine hundred Human Flames. This Ember Stone is rare and valuable because it can raise its heat to incredibly high temperatures, perfect for both alchemy and smithing. It's like having a furnace in your pocket!"

Intrigued, I nodded, understanding the potential of such an item in his crafts. Of the nine hundred and ninety-nine flames under heaven, there was no doubt that it was a valuable piece of treasure. "So, it's similar to the Qinglian Jadeite, then. Both are used to induce specific effects with their flames."

"Bah! You maniacs and your flames! All that matters is that of all the items in the Alchemy Association's vault, you chose that! When there's a myriad of ingredients to choose from!"

"You have eyes but fail to see Mt. Tai! The nine hundred and ninety-nine flames under heaven are far more valuable than a mere pill that keeps you less wrinkled! For ex—"

He waved us off. "I know what the flames are! I'm saying it doesn't make sense to get them when there's so much more useful things to get!"

Tao Ren only shook his head. "Don't worry, Kai! Bai won't understand; only true men of academia could understand the value of this," he said, tossing the rock up in the air.

"How rude! I'll have you know I aced my imperial examination! With flying colors!"

The restaurant we'd chosen for the evening was a bustling hub in the heart of the city, known for its fiery cuisine. The interior was a vibrant mix of red and gold, with lanterns casting a warm, inviting glow over the intricately carved wooden panels. Every table was occupied, the air filled with lively conversations and the clattering of chopsticks against porcelain. Our own lively exchange seemed to blend seamlessly into the restaurant's spirited atmosphere.

Some of the patrons seemed to recognize us from the contest but didn't say much apart from that.

The dishes arrived in quick succession. The first was a platter of bite-sized pieces of chicken buried under a mountain of dried red chilies and peppercorns. The intense heat was a shock to the system, but in the most delightful way, making my lips tingle and our taste buds dance.

Then came the water-boiled fish, a dish deceptive in name but ferocious in flavor. The tender slices of fish were submerged in a fiery broth, enriched with more peppercorns and vibrant green herbs that did little to temper the dish's aggressive spiciness.

*How could I return back home with meals like this in the city?! I should hire a chef from this restaurant to work at the Soaring Swallow Tea House!*

"Is there a reason why Zhi Ruo didn't come for dinner?"

"Busy. It's his loss! More food for the three of us."

Our dinner went by smoothly as we talked among each other, sharing stories and bantering. If there was one thing I wasn't expecting, it was that I'd have the opportunity to make some friends in the Gauntlet. I expected a more cutthroat opposition, willing to sabotage each other to get the upper hand in the competition.

"Tao Ren, I have to ask. Why'd you choose to pursue smithing?"

He looked up from his bowl of food and answered with a smile, "Because it's cooler!"

I sighed. Perhaps expecting a more sophisticated answer from him was too much.

"I'm joking, I'm joking!" Tao Ren said, slapping me on the back. If he had slapped me any harder, I'd have to trigger Rooted Banyan Stance to avoid injury!

His smile became softer, and he continued, "My old man always pestered me to take over the family business, inherit his techniques, yadda, yadda, yadda. That was until the day the Heavenly Interface manifested for everyone. It changed everything. Gave me quests for smithing, aligning with what I truly wanted to pursue. It was like the universe telling me, 'Go for it, lad!' So, I did."

I found myself nodding along, understanding the profound impact such an event could have on a person's life. "And alchemy?"

"Alchemy . . . Well, that's more for my dad's sake. He's a lifelong alchemist, after all. I couldn't just abandon that part of my heritage. So, I do both—smithing as my passion, alchemy to keep the family legacy going."

Bai Hua laughed lightly. "Sounds like a heavy burden to carry, my friend."

"Not really," Tao Ren countered with a grin. "It's like being handed two swords. One I wield for my dreams, the other for my duties. Not everyone gets to play with one, let alone two."

His analogy made me chuckle. It reminded me of my own dual pursuits of martial arts and alchemy. "I can relate to that. I train in martial arts and study alchemy. Each discipline supports and enhances the other."

Bai Hua raised an eyebrow, a bit surprised. "Martial arts, too? You truly are a man of many talents, Kai."

"It's all about balance," I replied, smiling at the notion. "Pursuing both paths keeps me grounded. Each discipline teaches me something valuable about the other."

The conversation lightened as we continued to enjoy our meal. The aroma of fragrant spices filled the air, mingling with the sounds of laughter and the occasional cough from an underestimated chili.

As the evening wore on, our conversation drifted to the upcoming round of the Gauntlet.

"Tomorrow's going to be intense," I mused, picking up my cup. "But whatever happens, here's to making it a memorable one!"

"Cheers to that!" Tao Ren and Bai Hua responded in unison, clinking their cups against mine.

The perfumer ended up footing the bill this time around. I was thankful, considering how much Tao Ren ate. I clasped my hands and bowed to the heir of Summer Sun Cosmetics. Tao Ren followed suit, letting out a small satisfied burp before bowing.

"This young master gratefully acknowledges the boundless generosity of Young Master Hua. May your cauldron always bubble and your elixirs never sour!" I said.

"Senior is too kind!" Tao Ren replied.

Bai Hua took it in stride, inclining his head in acknowledgment. "Think nothing of it. Enjoy this meal. Mark my words, friends, for tomorrow, you shall taste the bitter defeat against me in the Gauntlet!"

We all laughed, the mood airy and teasing, though a spark of competitive fire lit up all of our eyes. The challenges of tomorrow loomed over us, yet here we were, reveling in the camaraderie that only such trials could forge.

"As generous as you are, Bai, don't think we'll go easy on you just because you've paid for our meal," I said, raising an eyebrow playfully.

"And don't expect me to share my Ember Stone!" Tao Ren added, wagging a finger at him.

Bai Hua grinned, waving us off with a dismissive hand. "Ah, but generosity is my weapon! I lull my rivals into complacency with kindness before I strike on the battlefield!"

As the night drew to a close, the cool night air felt like a balm, and the city lights flickered like distant stars—witnesses to our vows of facing whatever challenge lay in the Gauntlet.

# CHAPTER THIRTY-FIVE

# Into the Second Round

I yawned, stretching my arms as I strode toward the Marble Jade Arena. After staying out with Bai Hua and Tao Ren, I felt the pleasant fatigue of a night well spent.

"My arm is killing me . . ." I muttered to myself.

I considered learning acupuncture, recalling Elder Zhu's lessons on its dual nature—harming and healing. The seamless blend of martial arts and medicine never ceased to amaze me.

The winding hallways eventually led me to the reception, where an official led me to the contestant's lounge. They opened the door, revealing tables laden with delectable treats and drinks stretched as far as the eye could see, the aroma of roasted meats and spiced fruits teasing my senses. This was a banquet hall straight out of an indulgent emperor's dream.

My stomach rumbled in protest, reminding me of the simple fare I've been eating at the Verdant Lotus Sect for the past few months.

The other contestants were already mingling. A few were focused on the food, sampling delicacies with practiced refinement, while others perched on velvet armchairs, gossiping in hushed tones. My fingers twitched, hesitation holding me back.

*No, Kai. Stay focused. Remember, this is a battleground, not a buffet.* I couldn't afford to look like some country bumpkin drooling over fancy pastries when everyone else was strategizing.

Suddenly, the air filled with boisterous shouts, and I spotted the unmistakable figure of Tao Ren bounding across the room. His hands were laden with food.

"Kai!" he yelled, echoing through the luxurious chamber. "You gotta try this!" With remarkable speed, he reached my side, shoving a steaming dumpling under my nose. "It's so juicy! And the filling, so savory . . ."

He was a force of nature, a whirlwind of unabashed enthusiasm, and my carefully constructed facade of cool composure began to crumble. "Okay, okay, give me a second," I managed, my voice betraying the slightest hint of desperation as I snatched a bun from his overflowing tray.

Seeing him gorge himself without a care in the world was admirable. The disgusted looks from the contestants was as good as invisible to him.

Bai Hua and Zhi Ruo came over, carrying much more modest plates.

"You're here! What was so important you had to ditch us, eh?" I asked the librarian, who scratched at his head slightly.

"Well, my family wanted to celebrate making the first round. I couldn't leave my wife and son alone to eat with you all, so I apologize for that."

My jaw hung open slightly. "You have kids?! And a wife?!"

Because of his demeanor, I had completely forgotten that Zhi Ruo was a full-grown man. It shouldn't have been surprising for him to have children, but for some reason, his lackadaisical mannerisms and occupation as a librarian made me subconsciously disregard that possibility.

As the four of us chatted, I couldn't help but scan the rest of the room. The other contestants were watching us with varying degrees of curiosity and disdain.

Suddenly, the room fell silent. I turned to see Jian Duan striding in, his gaze cold. My eyes met his, and a sneer crossed his face.

Then another figure entered the room, drawing all eyes to her. Jingyu Lian moved with the grace of a wintry wind, her pale features a mask of perfect calm. With her arrival, the full complement of contestants was gathered.

Almost immediately after, Ma Hualong came in, carrying something in his hands. "Welcome, competitors," he began, his voice carrying an undercurrent of authority. "This luxurious spread has been provided as a respite before the real challenge begins. Before the next round, I'd like to explain what is to be expected."

He drew our attention to the item in his hand, clothed in a purple silk. Ma Hualong swept the cloth away with a flourish, revealing a chunk of some gleaming golden mineral. It sparkled deceptively in the soft light of the lounge.

"Competitors, today's challenge centers around this," he declared, amused. "Pyrite."

Several contestants leaned forward, their eyes widening. Others scoffed, their expressions dripping with disdain.

"Pyrite?" Jian Duan questioned, his face twisting in confusion. "Isn't that . . . useless?"

"You're not entirely wrong," Ma Hualong admitted, a slight smile on his lips. "Pyrite, often referred to as fool's gold, lacks the beneficial properties of its more illustrious cousin. It deteriorates over time and is brittle and unusable for practical purposes. Historically, many were deceived by its golden luster, mistaking it for something far more valuable."

The challenge was taking shape, and it was already clear this wouldn't be a straightforward test of alchemical skill.

"However, alchemy is, in essence, about transformation. Your task is to create something from this unpromising material. It can be anything—a potion, an elixir, a powder, an ointment—should you deem it possible."

The room erupted in whispers. Some faces paled while others flushed with a determined glint. I felt a sudden, familiar thrill shoot through me. Challenges like these were where I thrived.

"A panel of esteemed judges will evaluate your creations," Ma Hualong pressed on. "We will consider three main factors: quality, ingenuity, and how effectively you incorporate the pyrite."

I caught Bai Hua's eye, his brow furrowed in concentration, already deep in thought. Jingyu Lian, with her usual icy composure, remained outwardly unmoved, although I noticed her fingers drumming lightly against her thigh.

Jian Duan, however, was smirking openly. "So," he drawled, his voice loud enough for all to hear, "it seems this round is tailor-made for the peasants among us. They likely have plenty of experience working with useless things, wouldn't you agree?"

Some of the other contestants snickered, and I clenched my fists.

Ma Hualong raised his hand, restoring order. "The purpose of this round is to challenge preconceived notions and push boundaries," he stated firmly. "Remember, the most unexpected avenues often lead to the greatest discoveries." To the rest of us, he said, "You have one hour to strategize before the competition officially begins." His eyes swept across the eager yet nervous faces. "During which, you'll be provided with a list of ingredients and their quantities that will be readily available for your use. Choose wisely, competitors, for your success will depend heavily on your decisions."

As servants began distributing scrolls, the room became a whirlwind of activity. Some competitors huddled in intense discussion, pouring over the lists, while others retreated into secluded corners, their focus intense. The luxurious lounge had transformed into a battlefield of ideas, buzzing with nervous energy and determined focus.

A grin escaped my lips as Ma Hualong finished his explanation. Pyrite useless? Hardly. Maybe to someone who only saw shiny objects as valuable, but pyrite held a potential many overlooked. I discarded ideas before they fully formed. A potion of strength? Too obvious. An elixir of what, exactly? The key was in understanding pyrite's true nature, not the fool's-gold image it projected.

The days I spent hunched over ancient texts in the Verdant Lotus library paid off. Pyrite, that deceptive golden imposter, had a hidden secret—it could be refined into sulfur. Sulfur, a pungent yellow element, might not look impressive, but in the right hands, it became a powerful alchemical tool. With sulfur, you could create explosives. Not exactly the peaceful elixirs most alchemists strived for but undeniably useful. More importantly, sulfur was a key ingredient in a whole host of potent concoctions—smoke bombs for distraction, sulfuric acid for etching and purification, etc.

The possibilities unfurled before me. But this was a competition, not a time for brute force. A weaponized concoction might win points for ingenuity, but subtlety and control were valued even higher. Besides, causing explosions in an enclosed space wasn't exactly a recipe for success (or my continued existence).

My gaze darted toward the approaching servant, a scroll clutched in his hand. The list of available ingredients would be the final piece of the puzzle. Before I could reach out and grab for it, Ma Hualong spoke once again.

"Before you review your ingredient options, there is one additional benefit for those who excelled in the previous round. The top five performers may request one additional ingredient for this round, within reason, of course. Ask for it now or at any point during the brainstorm session."

An extra ingredient could be the key to unleashing pyrite's full potential.

"The top performers are," he announced, "in no particular order: Tian Zhu, Fang Xiang, Bai Hua, Jingyu Lian, and Kai Liu!"

Bai Hua, ever cool and collected, simply nodded in acknowledgment. Jingyu Lian seemed more interested in overlooking the available ingredients on her scroll.

Then Ma Hualong's next words turned my focus inward.

"Remember competitors, this round is about embracing the unexpected," he explained with gravity. "Do not let preconceptions or the opinions of others limit your imagination. You have one hour. Use it wisely."

Looking over the scroll, I could see a distinct lack of qi plants here. If we were allowed any ingredient, that widened my options even further. But I had to narrow them down. Out of all of them, what was the best item I could use pyrite in? A kaleidoscope of potential ingredients swirled before my eyes. They were the standard alchemist's tool kit. But I needed something special, something to elevate my creation beyond a mere potion or powder.

Elixir. That seemed the most appropriate form. Elixirs were potent, precise liquids, their magic coursing through the bloodstream, capable of both subtle and profound effects. I was also specialized in them, even over pills, because of my history as an herbalist. But what elixir?

I regarded the opulent decorations adorning the lounge, looking just past Jian Duan, who appeared ready to rip his hair out in frustration. Then my eyes snagged on a golden tapestry depicting a majestic dragon wreathed in flames.

And just like that, inspiration struck.

A memory surfaced of a warm summer night back in Gentle Wind Village. Wang Jun, at the beginning of his apprenticeship, fumbling with the forge. The coals refused to catch, and his frustration grew. I'd offered a suggestion, a trick my father used when kindling a fire.

"Grind some pyrite into the coal dust," I'd told him. "It'll burn hotter."

Out of desperation, he had obeyed. The ensuing flare-up had been more than he'd bargained for, momentarily setting his eyebrows alight and sending him running for a bucket of water. But it had done the trick, the forge finally roaring to life. The memory faded, but the lesson lingered.

The plan was taking shape.

"I have my additional ingredient request."

# CHAPTER THIRTY-SIX

# Fool's Gold, Wise Decisions

As the final moments of preparation ticked away, the air in the contestants' lounge thickened with anticipation. I clutched my scroll tightly, the additional ingredient I had chosen resting heavily in my mind—a bold selection, perhaps, but one that felt right.

"Interesting choice. Seeking to balance the uselessness of pyrite with another useless substance? It seems your affinity for fool's gold extends to your ingredients as well."

I almost rolled my eyes at Jian Duan. So annoying and persistent. He was like a flea. Yes, a flea on a mangy dog—perfect. Imagining the puffy aristocrat as a flea soothed me, cooling me down before I responded. "A plan is only as good as its execution. You should focus more on that, especially since you seemed to be floundering during the brainstorming."

His face tightened, the smirk faltering just a bit as if my words had hit closer to home than he cared to admit.

Before he could retort, an official called out, "All contestants, please proceed to the arena. We will be beginning shortly."

Jian Duan shot me a final glare before turning sharply on his heel and striding away. I watched him go, feeling a surge of determination. This was no time for distractions. Today, my focus was on the challenge at hand, not the petty squabbles of a rival.

The stands were filled not just with excited spectators but with many who I recognized as eliminated from the preliminaries and the first round. It seemed that the technical complexity of this round had drawn a crowd more appreciative of the intellectual rigor involved in our craft.

As they should! Unlike those uncouth folk who were here to ogle Bai Hua and Jingyu Lian. *Hmph!*

Twenty alchemical stations were arrayed in an outward-facing circle, with a rectangular judges' table at the center. Several distinguished figures sat at the table, their presence commanding attention. Ma Hualong stood before them, outlining the rules of the Gauntlet with authoritative ease.

"Allow me to introduce our esteemed judges from the Alchemy Association," Ma Hualong announced. "Please welcome Elder Mingmei!"

An older woman in verdant robes stood before us, her gaze piercing and analytical, her gray hair meticulously coiffed into a bun. Her reputation preceded her; she was a figure I recognized immediately. Elder Zhu had often spoken of her with fondness.

She was his mentor, a titan in the field of alchemy who had left the sect to devote herself entirely to the craft, propelling the Alchemy Association's Pavilion of Arts to new heights without ever seeking the spotlight for herself.

Determined, I steeled myself to meet her stringent standards, knowing well that no personal connections would sway her judgment in this competition.

Ma Hualong introduced the next judge. "And finally, please give a warm welcome to Elder Wei Lian!"

A distinguished man with snow-white hair and piercing blue eyes stood up, acknowledging the crowd with a graceful nod. His features were quite striking. It's almost like . . .

I glanced at Jingyu Lian, noticing an unmistakable tension in her posture. Her eyes, usually so composed, flicked toward Elder Wei Lian with an unreadable expression.

This was crazy! Blatant favoritism! How could a judge be directly related to a contestant? However, no one seemed to mind or comment, so I just kept my thoughts to myself.

Grumbling along the way, I found my designated station containing all the requested materials I planned on working with for this round. And along with it, my requested ingredient, as a reward for being the top five of the first round.

The Sunfire Blade Grass.

The core of my most recent invention, the Ambrosia of Radiant Dawn. It was going to be the key that unlocks the pyrite's full potential.

Whether it was intentional or by chance, Jian Duan's station was as far as possible from mine. Perhaps to prevent any further sabotage attempts. Zhi Ruo and Tao Ren were adjacent to me, each absorbed in their preparations.

"Place your bets! The round will begin shortly!"

As the officials made their final checks, I closed my eyes for a moment to center myself. The task was clear, the objective set. All that remained was to execute my plan with precision.

I had many people's expectations riding on me! As well as the prizes, the fame and acclaim! I had to prove myself here, or I'd never be able to live it down.

The sound of Ma Hualong's voice rang out. "Let the second challenge commence! You have two hours!"

As I prepared, I selected the dandelion root and milk thistle first for their renowned purification properties. Each root was firm and earthy, promising potent effects. I laid out a small amount of cinnabar next, crucial for stabilization. This delicate balance was key—too little could yield a volatile mixture, and too much would suppress the desired effects.

Across the way, Tao Ren's workstation was a spectacle of its own. He had the pill furnace fired up, and the flames beneath it danced with an almost sentient vigor, reacting to his precise manipulations.

Turning back to my task, I took the dried reishi mushroom, known for its properties as an adaptogen. It was essential for tempering the yang element in the elixir, allowing whoever consumed it to adapt gradually to the increased body temperature it would provoke. With practiced movements, I ground the mushroom to a fine powder using mortar and pestle, its earthy aroma rising subtly into the air. Followed by ginseng, Moonbeam Petals, and Nightshade Flowers.

With all the ingredients ready, I began the actual concoction. Pouring distilled water into the pill furnace, I infused it with my qi, gradually increasing the heat until the water bubbled fiercely, ready to receive the essence of the ingredients.

Next came the most critical part of the process—extracting the essence from the pyrite. Placing my hand on the metallic stone, I focused deeply, feeling for the core of the pyrite. With a practiced push and pull of my internal energy, I coaxed the essence out, drawing it into my palm. Tiny beads of sweat pricked along my brow.

All the late nights, the hours of training, studying, and preparing . . . It came to fruition right here.

Ma Hualong's voice broke through the murmurs of the crowd, tinged with surprise. "What we are witnessing is essence extraction, a formidable technique that once belonged to Master Li Tao of the Verdant Lotus Sect. Remarkably, it has been revived by contestant Kai Liu."

*Ha! That's right! Praise me more!*

Steadily, I mixed the extracted essence into the boiling water, watching as the liquid took on a new character, a soft golden hue emerging.

For the essence to combine properly into the water, I'd have to keep this up for some time. Just a steady flow of qi to keep the flame at the same temperature, along with precise stirring. Easy enough to do without thinking.

As I worked, I swept my eyes over the competition. It was hard to turn and see the others working at the opposite side of the arena with how the stations were positioned. Which meant I couldn't see competitors like Bai Hua and Jian Duan, but I could see Jingyu Lian working diligently on hers by turning my head to the right.

A subtle hum cut through the chatter of the crowd. Her station glowed brightly, catching the crowd's attention. Sigils and runes ran along her table, glowing blue. I recognized them, but didn't quite understand. They were from my most difficult class, Alchemy Array Crafting, a concept I couldn't grasp with my current skills.

"Jingyu Lian is utilizing intermediate array formations with ease! It's remarkable to see such a technique being applied effectively, especially given that array formations of this complexity are usually reserved for more advanced alchemists with higher cultivation levels," Ma Hualong added. "It's no wonder she's the favorite to win the Gauntlet!"

Her hands moved in a blur, meticulously tracing symbols on the table, her brow furrowed with concentration. Sweat beaded on her forehead, her expression intense. It was unlike anything I'd seen before.

Glancing toward the judges' table, I caught Elder Wei Lian watching Jingyu intently, a small smirk playing on his lips as he observed her work. His apparent pride in her performance was clear. Perhaps that was why Jingyu Lian seemed so harried.

Shaking off the distracting thoughts, I refocused on my own task. I wouldn't be so discouraged! I have weapons of my own, to bring me to the top!

The crowd's gasps had faded into a background hum, their attention now divided among the various alchemists' techniques being displayed.

"Contestants! You have thirty minutes left!"

I moved, made aware of the looming deadline. I added the ingredients carefully, favoring precision over speed. From Tao Ren's direction, I could hear flames rising and light from my peripheral, raising the temperature to an uncomfortable degree and shouting expletives. But I refused to take my eyes off my work. I was almost there!

Tweaking the recipe had some risks, but it was necessary to accommodate the two-hour time limit we had to make our concoctions. This meant my concoction wouldn't be as strong as the Ambrosia of Radiant Dawn, but I took that into consideration when thinking up what to make for the second round.

Jian Duan was right in a way. Mixing together metal and wood-element ingredients was a fool's errand. But pyrite had a special quality; its ability to ignite. This dual-element alignment of metal and fire gave it a unique edge. Because fire and wood elements are compatible, the combination not only reduced the risk of failure but also enhanced the yang properties of my elixir.

Contrary to Ma Hualong's words in the contestant's lounge, pyrite was far from useless. That was something many of the alchemists gathered here understood, and I was certain it would bring about Jian Duan's downfall. To call any ingredient without worth showed just how shallow his skills and understanding were of the alchemical arts.

The concoction laid before me, boiling softly in the pill furnace, still in liquid form. A metallic tang cut through the earthy aroma of my elixir, like the smell of blood amid a blooming field.

In the final minutes, I meticulously bottled the completed elixir. Everything was within expectation. I revised and devised my recipe many times in my head, although the time limitation certainly made it so I couldn't fully realize the concoction's potential.

"TIME'S UP! CONTESTANTS, PREPARE TO PRESENT YOUR PRODUCTS TO THE JUDGES!"

Ma Hualong stood at the center of the arena, his voice commanding the attention of every onlooker as he reached into a large, ornate basket. "The order of presentation will be determined at random," he announced, his hand swirling around before pulling out a small, engraved ball.

"First up, Tian Zhu!" he declared, holding the ball high for all to see.

Tian Zhu, one of the top five, stepped forward confidently. His demeanor was stern, almost unreadable, as he approached the judges' table. I watched intently, curious to see what innovative use of pyrite he had concocted. "Esteemed judges, I have synthesized a pyrite crystal that not only collects but also stores solar energy." He held up a small, brilliantly gleaming crystal, and the crowd murmured in appreciation and surprise. "This crystal," he continued, "functions similarly to a lantern, providing sustainable light. Furthermore, in situations requiring a tactical advantage, it can be used as a blinding light when shattered or thrown."

The judges leaned forward, their interest visibly piqued. Elder Mingmei, her eyes sharp, asked, "How did you manage to stabilize the crystal's structure to store such energy without degradation?"

Elder Wei Lian, his expression contemplative, chimed in. "And the safety measures? Such a device, if misused, could pose significant risks."

They peppered him with questions about his product. He answered smoothly, explaining the nitty gritty details of his crystal lantern.

His answers seemed to satisfy the judges, who nodded appreciatively. I couldn't help but admire his ingenuity. Integrating alchemy with practical applications always required a deep understanding of both the materials and the desired outcomes.

As Tian Zhu concluded his presentation and stepped back, the tension in my shoulders grew. I glanced at my own product, hoping it would be enough.

I wished they would let me present as soon as possible! The wait was unbearable!

A tense hush fell over the arena as a wide, ear-to-ear grin spread across Tao Ren's face when Ma Hualong called his name. He bounced out of his station, practically radiating excitement, a stark contrast to the composed Tian Zhu. His enthusiasm was contagious, a ripple of amused whispers running through the crowd.

"My turn!" he announced, practically vibrating with energy as he approached the judges' table with a clothed item.

# CHAPTER THIRTY-SEVEN

# Metals and Mettle

What on earth was he up to? It was clear none of the judges had any idea how to prepare for Tao Ren's presentation, as they exchanged puzzled looks. He always had a flair for the dramatic, but this seemed especially extravagant.

Without a word of explanation, Tao Ren unwrapped the clothed item with a flourish, revealing a gleaming blade.

The judges blinked in unison, their expressions a mix of utter bewilderment.

Finally, Elder Wei Lian broke the absurdity of the moment. "Young man," he said, a touch of incredulity in his voice, "I trust this isn't meant to be a threat? This is, after all, an alchemy competition."

Tao Ren's grin widened. "Not a threat, Elder, a marvel!" he declared, thrusting the blade forward. "Crafted from that useless lump of pyrite, transformed into a weapon fit for a warrior—all without ever stepping foot near a forge!"

This time, the silence was replaced by a wave of shocked murmurs rippling through the crowd. I stared, my jaw threatening to hit the floor. Sure, I'd expected something flashy from Tao Ren, but this was . . . unprecedented. How the hell had he forged a blade?

"Impossible!" Ma Hualong exclaimed, voicing the skepticism echoing through the room. "There are no forges in the arena."

"Who needs a forge when you've got a pill furnace?" Tao Ren countered, puffing out his chest with pride. "First, I extracted the trace amounts of iron from the pyrite. Then, by manipulating the sulfur content, I refined it into workable steel! Some shaping, a bit of tempering, and voilà! Tao Ren's Jade Foundry is always open for business!" He concluded with a dramatic bow, clearly enjoying the audience's stunned reactions.

Despite the absurdity, a flicker of doubt crept into my mind. It was true, the volatile sulfur content in pyrite was well known. And with the right technique, perhaps some of that sulfur could be coaxed out, leaving behind a crude, low-quality form of iron. Difficult, but possible. But shaping, tempering . . . how? It defied everything I knew about forging metal . . .

My thoughts were interrupted by the judges' hushed deliberation. Elder Mingmei's sharp gaze swept across the blade, while Elder Wei Lian whispered something that made Ma Hualong's brows furrow.

Finally, Elder Mingmei spoke, her voice as crisp as ever. "Young Tao Ren," she said, "while your resourcefulness is noteworthy, this is, undeniably, an unorthodox approach. Alchemy and smithing, while sharing some roots, are distinct disciplines."

"But, Elder," he argued, "isn't the transformation of raw materials into something useful the very essence of both? All I did was apply alchemical principles to a different craft! My forge is simply an extension of my alchemy!"

I had to hand it to him. His logic was twisted, but not entirely without merit. The judges exchanged another round of glances, and I found myself holding my breath.

"May I examine this 'marvel' more closely?" Elder Mingmei requested.

He beamed, practically shoving the blade into her hand.

Elder Wei Lian adjusted his posture, leaning forward with curiosity. All eyes were glued to the interaction.

She didn't inspect the blade visually for long. Instead, she closed her eyes, running her fingers across the metal. Perhaps she was inspecting its inner workings.

A low hum resonated from the blade as she examined it.

"Hmm. Certainly an unorthodox approach, as I mentioned. Extracting usable iron from pyrite is a feat in itself. Your resourcefulness deserves recognition."

Tao Ren puffed out his chest, a triumphant grin threatening to split his face in two.

"However," she continued, her voice turning firm, "refining iron from pyrite carries a crucial drawback. The high sulfur content, while potentially manageable during extraction, leaves the final product riddled with impurities." She raised the blade a fraction, her gaze meeting Tao Ren's directly. "An alchemist's skill lies not just in transformation," she stated, gaining power with each word, "but in understanding the inherent properties of materials and mitigating their weaknesses." With shocking speed and power for her age, Elder Mingmei slammed the blade flat against the judges' table. A sickening crack echoed through the arena as the blade snapped cleanly in two.

A gasp rippled through the crowd. Tao Ren's eyes widened in disbelief as he stared at the fractured metal in the judge's hand. The weight of her words settled heavily. Yes, Tao Ren had extracted iron from pyrite, but the resulting metal was brittle and weak—unsuitable for even basic tasks, let alone a warrior's weapon.

Her critique was harsh but fair. The ingenuity of the concept couldn't mask its fundamental flaws. I glanced at Tao Ren, expecting anger or dejection. Instead, he let out a hearty laugh, a touch sheepish but genuinely amused.

"You make a very valid point," he boomed, completely unfazed. "Looks like my forge still has a lot to learn about managing those pesky impurities! But hey, that's what comes with pushing the boundaries, right? Come visit the Jade Foundry sometime, we'll get you a blade worthy of a true elder!" He winked, somehow managing to spin the situation into a shameless promotion of his business.

The crowd, initially stunned, erupted in a mixture of cheers and groans. Elder Mingmei remained impassive, simply placing the broken blade on the table with a faint sigh.

Ma Hualong cleared his throat, attempting to restore order. "Next up," he announced, "Zhi Ruo!"

The librarian, ever the picture of quiet diligence, stepped forward. Unlike the first round, he seemed more composed and confident. I could see his eyes sweep over to a particular spot in the crowd. I followed his gaze, and spotted in the crowd, a brown-haired woman carrying a child, wearing a soft smile and pointing at Zhi Ruo.

He bowed respectfully to the judges before reaching into a small pouch at his waist. He drew out a length of white silk, carefully unfurling it to reveal two small, glistening pills. "Esteemed judges, I present to you a Purification Pill. This elixir, crafted using a combination of pyrite, knotweed root, jade blossom, and water deer antlers, is designed to cleanse the body of impurities and toxins." He gestured toward the pills. "I have created a pair, one for presentation and the other for immediate testing."

A younger judge, his face marked with scholarly curiosity, reached forward and examined the pills with keen eyes. He leaned in, taking a long sniff. His brow furrowed for a moment before a smile broke out across his face. "Remarkable! The aroma is clean and balanced, with no hint of impurities. If I may?" He looked toward Elder Mingmei and Elder Wei Lian, who nodded their assent.

He popped it into his mouth. A hush fell over the arena as everyone waited, anticipation thick in the air. The judge chewed thoughtfully for a moment, his eyes widening in surprise. "This is impressive!" he exclaimed, filled with genuine awe. "The potency . . . it rivals that of the standard purification pill recipe! You said you made it using only those ingredients?!"

The librarian nodded, serene. "Yes, each ingredient has been carefully chosen not only for its individual properties but for the synergistic effects they can create together, particularly with the unique qualities of pyrite."

The judge, intrigued, prodded further. "Could you elaborate on the reaction between the components? How do they interact to amplify the purification properties of the pyrite?"

Elder Wei Lian, his interest clearly piqued, leaned forward to ask. "And how does this interaction manifest in the efficacy of the pill?"

Zhi Ruo droned on for several minutes. Even though I'd consider myself well versed in alchemy, the terms he was throwing around started to make my eyes glaze over. From the corner of my eye, I could see Tao Ren's eyes closed, and a line of drool slowly hanging down his face.

". . . Your understanding of the materials is commendable, young man. The intricacy of its creation might be beyond the reach of an average alchemist. This requires not only in-depth knowledge but also precise timing and handling of the ingredients. It's quite sophisticated."

The younger judge continued from where Elder Wei Lian left off. "However, the final product, while effective, lacks refinement in texture and consistency. This indicates a gap in your practical skills, which are as crucial as theoretical knowledge in alchemy."

His thoughts were punctuated by a finger breaking the pill down into a powder, showing the uneven clumps in the pill. It was a minor mistake, but one that shows how the purification pill he created could've been even better.

Zhi Ruo bowed slightly, accepting the feedback with grace. "I appreciate your insights, Elders. I strive to bridge that gap and refine my techniques further."

I watched him return to his station, his stride confident yet contemplative. It was clear now why Zhi Ruo had placed first in the preliminaries. His vast knowledge and ability to integrate complex concepts were impressive, though his practical skills needed honing.

The rest of the contestants presented one by one. Most were variations on familiar themes—enhanced strength potions, accelerated healing balms, and the like. Though competently made, they lacked the spark of innovation or the bold application of theory that could stir the judges from their growing ennui.

Polite applause followed each presentation, but the murmurs of the crowd were tepid, the energy in the arena dipping with every passing moment.

Then Jian Duan's name was called. The man himself stepped forward with a swagger, his robe gleaming almost as brightly as his confident smile. He held a single, small pill between his fingers, presenting it with a flourish that seemed to promise wonders.

"Ladies and gentlemen, what I present to you today is not just a pill, but a lifeline," Jian Duan began, his voice smooth and assured. "This is a Qi Replenishment Pill, crafted to not only restore a cultivator's energy reserves swiftly but to enhance their qi flow, making each use an opportunity to refine and strengthen one's core."

Interest piqued, the audience leaned closer, the previous presentations forgotten in the wake of Jian Duan's bold claims. Even the judges seemed to perk up, their expressions sharpening as they considered the potential impact of such a creation.

Elder Mingmei, always direct, wasted no time. "An impressive claim. However, the core of this challenge was to incorporate pyrite into your creation effectively. How have you achieved this, given pyrite's known properties?"

"Thank you, Elder Mingmei. I used the pyrite not directly in the pill's formation but as a catalyst during the synthesis process. The pyrite was ground into a fine powder and used in the initial concoction phase to enhance the absorption of the high-class ingredients, magnifying their effects."

Elder Wei Lian chimed in, his tone more skeptical. "While innovative, using pyrite merely as a catalytic agent does not truly integrate it into the product. You've used it to bolster the process but not as a fundamental component. This approach seems to sidestep the challenge rather than meeting it head-on."

His composure faltered. "With respect, Elder Wei, the properties of pyrite are limited. It lacks the inherent benefits of gold or other rare metals. I have simply used it as a catalyst to enhance the pill's overall effect."

"The pyrite seems to be an afterthought, a mere addition rather than a transformative element. Did you consider the potential side effects of combining pyrite with synergistic ingredients like Zhi Ruo's? Or the possibility of refining it into something else, like Tao Ren, something that truly showcases the versatility of this mineral?"

As Jian Duan stumbled through his response, I couldn't help but feel a pang of sympathy for him. He was clearly a skilled alchemist, but his arrogance and reliance on high-quality ingredients had blinded him to the true potential of the challenge.

Ma Hualong, his expression carefully neutral, nodded toward the judges. "Thank you, Jian Duan. We will take your creation into consideration."

He bowed stiffly and returned to his station, his face flushed with a mixture of frustration and embarrassment.

"And now," he announced, pulling out another engraved ball, "let's see who's next . . ."

The anticipation was a physical weight in my chest. I was ready, my mind racing through every detail of my presentation. My eyes followed Ma Hualong's movements closely, every second stretching out interminably as he read the name inscribed on the small sphere.

"Next up, we have Kai Liu!"

# CHAPTER THIRTY-EIGHT

# The Ambrosia of Radiant Dawn

Clearing my throat slightly, I carefully placed the elixir on the display table before the judges. Their expressions remained inscrutable as I adjusted the sleeves of my robe.

"Esteemed judges," I started, my voice steadier than I felt, making a conscious effort to speak clearly and project confidence despite the sea of faces around us. "The elixir I present today harnesses the combined powers of Sunfire Blade Grass and essence of pyrite, intricately balanced with other select ingredients to enhance both body and spirit."

Elder Wei Lian picked up the elixir, allowing the light to catch its subtle glow.

I paused, ensuring I had their full attention, then continued, "It begins with dandelion root and milk thistle for purification, forming the foundation by cleansing the body from within. Next, a carefully measured dose of cinnabar ensures the elixir's stability. The core transformative power lies in the reishi mushroom, moderating the yang energy from the Sunfire Blade Grass to increase resilience and vitality. I added ginseng for endurance, Moonbeam Petals to balance the mind, and Nightshade Flowers to deepen the cleansing process. This blend temporarily revitalizes physical abilities and purifies, using pyrite's essence to bind and amplify each ingredient, achieving harmonious, stable revitalization without harm to the user."

Despite the nervous energy coursing through me, my voice held a note of pride as I finished. It was a shame Zhi Ruo presented first, considering how our concoctions both had purification properties. I just hoped I could bridge the gap in the quality of my work, as well as the effects of my essence extraction!

I watched their faces, searching for any sign of approval or criticism.

Elder Wei Lian leaned forward, his piercing blue eyes fixed on me. "Kai Liu, was it?" His voice was smooth, his tone measured. "A most intriguing concoction. But tell me, where did you acquire the knowledge to perform essence extraction?"

"I learned it after the Heavenly Interface evolved my herbalism skill," I answered honestly.

A flicker of interest crossed Wei Lian's face, and he began to speak again, "That's fascinating. Now, are you—"

But before he could finish his question, Elder Mingmei interrupted. "Wei Lian, let us focus on the young man's creation, shall we? We are here to judge the product at hand, not his personal history."

There was a subtle undercurrent in her tone, a protective edge that I hadn't noticed before. Wei Lian, though slightly taken aback, offered a polite smile. "Of course, Elder Mingmei. Forgive my curiosity."

"May I?" the younger judge interjected, gesturing toward the elixir. His eagerness was palpable, a stark contrast to the usual reserved demeanor of the panel. With my nod, he lifted the small bottle, uncorking it to allow the delicate, complex aroma to waft through the air.

*That's right! Be wowed! Be amazed!*

Carefully, he poured a small measure into a glass, swirling it gently before bringing it to his lips. The arena fell silent, every spectator and contestant watching as he took a cautious sip, then another, more confident one.

After swallowing, the judge paused, contemplating. Slowly, his eyes widened, not with alarm but with a clear, unmistakable spark of excitement. "Remarkable," he murmured, more to himself than to the audience, then louder for everyone to hear, "I can feel a gentle heat spreading through my body, not burning but invigorating. My fatigue seems to be washing away with each breath I take."

Turning to face the audience, and particularly the judges, his enthusiasm was evident. "As someone in the peak of the Qi Initiation stage, I can attest to the potency of this concoction. It's a refined burst of energy, one that could be invaluable for cultivators, especially during prolonged engagements or recovery periods."

Encouraged by his reaction, I added, "The reishi mushroom plays a crucial role in that. It helps the elixir acclimate to different constitutions, making it safe for a wide range of users, not just cultivators. This adaptability ensures that the elixir provides benefits without overwhelming the user, no matter their level of resilience.

"I was inspired by the commercial success of my earlier potion, the Invigorating Dawn Tonic," I continued, aiming to connect this new creation with something familiar to the alchemical community. Some among the crowd murmured, recognizing the name. "This elixir, which I've named the Ambrosia of Radiant Dawn, builds on that foundation but introduces a deeper, more nuanced approach to bodily enhancement and purification."

Elder Mingmei nodded thoughtfully. "It's clear you've put considerable thought and skill into this, Kai Liu. The ability to harness such potent effects while maintaining balance is no small feat."

The other judges gave similar praise, filling me with a deep sense of pride and relief.

"However," she continued, "while the theoretical underpinnings of your elixir are sound, and your execution is commendable for one so young, there are certain . . . oversights." She kept her gaze on me. "The addition of Nightshade, while intended to counter the yang energy of the pyrite, introduces an element of instability. Combined with the potent effects of the Sunfire Blade Grass, the elixir's overall consistency and longevity are compromised."

A knot of disappointment tightened in my stomach. My gaze flickered toward the shimmering potion on the table. It *had* been a gamble, although I focused more on how to make the potion effective rather than its long-term storage capabilities.

"Furthermore," Elder Mingmei pressed, "a pill form would have been a more stable and easily distributable medium for this concoction. The addition of a binding agent, such as powdered moonpetal, would have also mitigated the potential for qi fluctuations."

She continued her precise dissection of my work, laying bare the flaws I'd desperately hoped to conceal or wouldn't be noticed so easily.

"Thank you for your valuable feedback, Elder Mingmei," I said, bowing my head respectfully. "I acknowledge the shortcomings of my elixir. This competition has taught me much, and I will strive to learn from my mistakes and refine my craft further."

"That is the mark of a true alchemist," she said, softening slightly. "Remember, even the greatest masters began as novices. It is through acknowledging our flaws that we pave the path toward true mastery."

I bowed again, accepting her critique with gratitude. Even in criticism, there was valuable knowledge to be gleaned.

My eyes sought out Jian Duan's, and I couldn't help but smirk as I caught a glimpse of his clenched fists, his head lowered in frustration. He'd expected me to crumble, to fail, but it turned out to be his fate rather than mine.

Each challenge, each critique, was a chance to learn, to adapt, to evolve.

My entry was impressive enough to make it to the next round, that I was sure, but I needed to know how it stacked up against Jingyu Lian. To see just how high the wall I needed to climb was.

As the judges discussed among themselves, Ma Hualong began to reach for another sphere to select a contestant. Only two remained.

"Bai Hua!"

I watched with interest as Bai Hua stepped forward, a confident smile on his face and a beautifully crafted incense holder in his hands.

"Esteemed judges," Bai Hua began, his voice smooth and captivating, "today, I present to you an incense that harnesses the purification properties of refined sulfur extracted from pyrite. This incense, when burned, not only cleanses the air of impurities but also revitalizes the spirit and enhances mental clarity."

"WHAT?!" a judge asked, his eyes alight with fear. Tao Ren seemed to snap out of his stupor and draped his apron across his mouth.

Wait, *sulfur*? He was going to light sulfur on fire?

He placed the incense holder on the display table with a flourish, and as he prepared to light it, a ripple of realization swept through the audience and the judges. Several judges instinctively covered their mouths, and I felt a jolt of panic. Cleanse the air of impurities?! He was going to fill the area with them and suffocate everyone in it!

With a dramatic flourish, Bai Hua lit the incense. A delicate plume of smoke began to rise, swirling in intricate patterns. With a subtle gesture, Bai Hua seemed to control the rate at which the incense burned, guiding the smoke to roam across the stadium.

The aromatic cloud drifted gently toward the audience, reaching as far as my station. As I inhaled the scent, a profound sense of calm and tranquility washed over me, the stress of the competition momentarily fading away. But the tension remained thick in the air as the judges looked ready to bolt.

Bai Hua raised his hands in a placating gesture, a charming smile gracing his lips. "Please, do not be alarmed, esteemed judges. Allow me to explain. While sulfur can indeed be hazardous, I have tempered its properties using Celestial Ice Crystals. These crystals not only neutralize any potential danger but enhance its purifying effects."

The judge who had feared for his life drooped his shoulders and glared at Bai Hua, still keeping his nose closed. "You should've started with that earlier!"

I blinked, realization dawning. So that's what he chose as his additional ingredient—the Celestial Ice Crystals. Ingenious and incredibly risky, but clearly, it paid off.

The younger judge, still holding the incense holder, took a cautious sniff. "The aroma is balanced and pleasant, and I can already feel a clarity in my thoughts," he said, his voice carrying a hint of respect. "This incense could be invaluable in meditation and focus, especially for cultivators."

Bai Hua continued with a flourish, "The lavender soothes the mind, promoting relaxation and reducing stress. White sage purifies the environment, removing negative energies and fostering a sense of calm."

"Ingenious," Elder Wei Lian remarked. "But I am curious about potential side effects. Sulfur, if not properly controlled, can be quite harsh on the senses."

Bai Hua nodded, his eyes twinkling with a hint of mischief. "An astute observation, Elder Wei. However, the Celestial Ice Crystals temper the sulfur's harshness while ensuring its potency. In fact . . ."

With a graceful gesture, he adjusted the incense holder, hastening the burn. The previously light, tangy scent transformed into something crisper, cooler, revitalizing. A sudden surge of energy coursed through me, as if a veil had been lifted from my mind.

Elder Mingmei's eyebrows rose, a flicker of surprise crossing her stoic features. "Two distinct stages?" she murmured. "This is a complex and impressive creation, Bai Hua."

"Truly remarkable. But tell me," Elder Wei Lian began, "why choose such a difficult path? One wrong move and the sulfur could have overwhelmed the other ingredients."

Bai Hua's smile faded, replaced by a look of sincere passion. "As an alchemist, I am drawn to the unexplored, the unconventional. I believe true innovation lies in pushing boundaries, and in finding harmony where others see only chaos. I could have crafted a simple elixir or pill, this is a testament to my unique approach, my passion for aromatherapy, and my belief in the transformative power of scent. As the heir of Summer Sun Cosmetics, I cannot make such boring products!"

The judges exchanged glances, a silent conversation passing between them. It was clear that Bai Hua's passion and ambition had struck a chord. His pride and ambition shone through every word and gesture, making me realize that perhaps I shouldn't be looking at only Jingyu Lian as the wall to climb in this Gauntlet. He was a formidable contender in his own right.

As she was called up, I tensed, my focus shifting to her. This was the moment I had been waiting for, the true test of my abilities. The white-haired alchemist stepped forward with calm confidence, her every move precise and deliberate.

I couldn't help but feel a mixture of anticipation and anxiety. What would she present? How would it compare to Bai Hua's incense and my own elixir? My mind raced with possibilities as she began her presentation.

# CHAPTER THIRTY-NINE

# Exploding Pill

She was poised, her blue eyes taking a distinct, determined look with her brows furrowed. "Esteemed judges, today, I present to you an exploding pill. When infused with qi, it can be set to explode and cause significant damage, even to peak Qi Initiation stage cultivators." She held up a small, seemingly unremarkable pill, letting the light catch its surface. "The process begins with refining pyrite into sulfur," she continued. "I then used this sulfur in an array to ensure the pill is stable and safe to handle. The core of the pill's explosive power comes from a thunderstone, which generates a powerful electrical explosion."

My breath caught. An explosive pill? Using a thunderstone? I searched my memory for any mention of the ingredient. Found on mountain peaks where thunderstorms frequent, they contained and absorb the energy from lightning strikes, usually detonating once broken.

The risk of creating such a volatile concoction was immense. One wrong move and the consequences could be catastrophic. Perhaps she was sweating earlier not because of how difficult it was to create the array, but the potential consequences of failure.

"To demonstrate its effectiveness, I will infuse it with my qi and show its controlled detonation."

Even Elder Mingmei, who was usually so composed, seemed impressed. Elder Wei Lian, however, maintained a neutral expression, his gaze steady and unreadable.

She placed the pill on a small platform and infused it with qi. I watched, holding my breath. A faint glow emanated from the pill as she stepped back and counted down from five. At one, the pill detonated in a burst of light and energy, sending a gust of wind through the arena. Dust flew, and the air filled with the pungent smell of ozone. All that remained was a slight indentation, scorched earth, and scattered rocks.

Significant damage? Feng Wu was at the fourth stage of the Qi Initiation stage, and I was pretty sure he'd be injured if he took that head-on!

Gasps echoed around me, and I couldn't help but feel a mix of awe and admiration. The sheer skill and control required to create and handle such a dangerous concoction at our level . . .

"I used an array to allow the user to control the detonation time. By infusing their qi, they can set the pill to explode between one to five seconds, allowing for greater strategic use in combat."

Elder Mingmei was the first to speak. "Your workmanship is impressive. Utilizing arrays in this manner is usually reserved for more advanced alchemists."

Wei Lian's expression remained unreadable, and I expected him to sing her praises, given their familial connection. Instead, his voice cut through the arena with an edge of criticism. "Jingyu Lian, while it is impressive to use such complex techniques at your age, the quality of your array is shoddy. The consequences of making it poorly cannot be ignored."

I blinked in disbelief. He continued to drone on, picking apart the pill with what seemed to be valid points but overall felt nitpicky and almost spiteful.

"The array's stability is questionable. The containment of the sulfur and thunderstone components is rudimentary. Have you considered the risks of handling such volatile ingredients with such an elementary array?"

The other judges exchanged uncomfortable glances but didn't contest his points. Elder Mingmei eventually spoke up, her voice firm. "Wei Lian, your critique is too harsh and overly meticulous. Jingyu Lian's work here is commendable, especially for someone of her experience."

Jingyu Lian's face was a mask of conflict, her emotions tightly controlled. But her fist was balled up into a fist, trembling slightly.

Elder Wei Lian's expression hardened further. "The most critical flaw, however, is that if a higher-tier cultivator were to send out their qi outwardly, the array could destabilize and explode preemptively." He demonstrated by tossing another pill into the air and releasing a pulse of qi. A subtle blue hue radiated from the man.

Wasn't that qi projection? Something limited to those in the Essence Awakening stage!

As his energy passed through the pill, it began to glow, filling the air with the scent of ozone once again. It exploded midair, sending a shock wave through the arena. I could see Jingyu Lian's struggle to keep her composure. Her eyes were tightly shut, and her shoulders sagged in front of the judges.

Elder Wei Lian's voice was stern and cold. "Presenting something so dangerous is irresponsible. You must think about the potential dangers that come with creating such a concoction."

Jingyu Lian bowed her head slightly. "Thank you, judges. I will take this into consideration."

She walked back to her station, her posture rigid, and the atmosphere in the arena grew tense. I couldn't believe what I had just witnessed.

He had torn her pill apart with merciless precision.

Ma Hualong coughed into his palm, announcing the end of the round. "Competitors, please return to the lounge and await the results. The judges will discuss among themselves, ranking based on criteria, and tally the points together at the end."

We all filed back into the lounge, where the tables were once again laden with food and drink. Before I could join my friends, I noticed Jian Duan approaching Jingyu Lian.

"That was really unjust, the way Elder Wei Lian criticized you," Jian Duan said, attempting to sound sympathetic. "As the young master of the Duan clan, there's no—"

Jingyu Lian shot him a frosty glare. "I'm not in the mood to talk. Be quiet," she warned. "Or else I'll make you."

Clearly taken aback by her curt response, he slunk away.

I turned my attention back to my friends, who were gathering near one of the tables.

Bai Hua grinned as I approached. "Quite the show out there, huh?"

Tao Ren joined us, his usual exuberance on full display. "Did you see that knife? Pure genius. A shame the judges didn't see it that way. But I think they'll use this time to realize its brilliance!"

"Genius, sure," Bai Hua said, trying to keep a straight face.

We both laughed, and despite being the butt end of the joke, Tao Ren couldn't help but chuckle.

Zhi Ruo joined our little group, a quiet smile on his face. "The atmosphere among you is quite easy, considering how the other competitors seem nervous."

I nodded, realizing just how odd it was. Perhaps it was that freedom, the lack of expectations in comparison to them, but I was confident in the results. My eyes drifted to Jian Duan, who was brooding in a corner.

"This round might end with all of us, except maybe Tao Ren, qualifying for the next round," I mused, earning a playful punch from the blacksmith.

*Ow. That really hurt.*

"Hey! Don't count me out just yet," he retorted, grinning. "The story of Tao Ren's Jade Foundry doesn't end here! BELIEVE IT!"

Everyone's product was ingenious. Even though I joked with Tao Ren, being able to create a blade from the pyrite chunk we were given was nothing short of incredible. Bai Hua's two-stage incense showcased the potential of a neglected art in alchemy. And Zhi Ruo's . . .

Turning to the librarian, I asked, "How did you create your purification pill? Do you have an eidetic memory or something? It's hard to take into consideration every single reaction, property, and alignment of the ingredients. And don't say that you're just well learned. Even those judges were stumped by the sheer detail."

Zhi Ruo's expression grew thoughtful. "I have a skill called the Memory Palace technique," he explained. "It allows me to store and recall vast amounts of information with perfect clarity. It's something I learned recently, after the Heavenly Interface came into play."

I blinked in surprise. "You have the Memory Palace technique too?"

His eyes widened, clearly baffled. "Too? You have the Memory Palace as well?"

I nodded. "Yes, I learned it quite early on after completing a quest. It was to refine my mind, you see."

The older man shook his head in amazement. "That's incredible. I thought my Memory Palace technique was impressive, but essence extraction . . . Is that why you have that skill? The one where you extract the ingredient's essences that Ma Hualong mentioned?"

"Yeah, I do. It's completely changed the way I approached alchemy. I credit that to my expertise in herbalism." Our conversation sparked a realization. I turned to the other two, curious about their experiences. "Bai Hua, Tao Ren, have you experienced anything similar with the Heavenly Interface?"

Bai Hua nodded enthusiastically. "Most of my techniques come from the Heavenly Interface. All my aromatherapy techniques . . . they came with a quest, much like you said."

"And your sense of smell?"

He waved his hand. "No, no, I had that since I was born."

"And you? Surely you received something as well,"

Tao Ren grinned, eager to chip in. "Absolutely. The Heavenly Interface gave me several quests to increase my proficiency in smithing, which eventually gave me a technique to control flames just like my old man. He couldn't believe I learned it at my age. That's how I managed to create the blade with the pill furnace."

As he spoke, a realization dawned on me. All of us—Bai Hua, Zhi Ruo, Tao Ren, and myself—were here thanks to the Heavenly Interface granting us unique skills. I glanced around the room at Jian Duan and the other competitors. None of them seemed to have received such skills; their concoctions adhered strictly to the standard alchemy principles taught just like those in the Verdant Lotus Sect.

Why didn't the Interface grant them any special skills or abilities? Thinking back to the day it appeared, I remembered the message.

---

*WE ILLUMINATE THE PATH TO ASCENSION.*
*A NEW ERA.*
*HIDDEN PATHS AWAIT.*

These cryptic words turned out to be true, illuminating hidden paths for those who dared to tread them.

Someone like Jian Duan wouldn't be interested in cultivating knowledge in aromatherapy or learning how to control flames in the same way we did. The Interface always responded to one's desires, and it was no wonder they didn't have as impressive a showing. This might also explain how Jingyu Lian was capable of utilizing arrays despite it being near impossible at our current cultivation stage.

The Heavenly Interface was more than just a tool; it was a gateway to lost techniques and abilities, ones that many sects and cultivators hoarded, hiding their secrets from the rest of the world. It granted us skills and knowledge that we might never have discovered on our own.

"Do any of you know anything about the Interface Mani-"

A loud gong resonated through the lounge, signaling that it was time to return to the arena. We filed back in, the atmosphere thick with anticipation and anxiety. I kept my thoughts to myself, deciding to explore them at a later date. Ma Hualong stood at the center once again, ready to announce the results.

Ma Hualong's voice echoed through the arena, signaling the announcement of the results.

"Ladies and gentlemen, the judges have reached a decision," he began. "The top ten contestants who will move on to the next round are . . ."

Ma Hualong started listing the names, beginning with those who placed lower in the top ten. My anxiety spiked with each name that wasn't mine, but I reminded myself to stay confident. The fact that I hadn't heard my name yet meant I likely placed higher.

"And in fourth place, with his ingenious dual-stage incense, Bai Hua of Summer Sun Cosmetics."

Bai Hua stepped forward, his smile confident.

"In third place, with his thoughtful Purification Pill, Zhi Ruo of the Million Book Pavilion."

His face lit up with a quiet pride as he stepped forward.

"In second place, showing incredible creativity and a high degree of theoretical knowledge, but hampered by the design flaw and volatility of her Exploding Pill, Jingyu Lian of the Whispering Wind Sect."

She stepped forward, her expression composed but her clenched jaw and stiff movements betrayed her frustration. Her blue eyes flicked briefly toward Elder Wei Lian before she bowed to the judges and took her place among the qualifiers.

"And finally, in first place, with the best overall product due to its effectiveness, versatility, and clever usage of Sunfire Blade Grass and pyrite essence, Kai Liu of the Verdant Lotus Sect!"

# CHAPTER FORTY

# Pyrite's Promise

*I won?*

*First place?*

It felt like the entire arena had their gaze on me. Heart hammering in my ribcage, I did my best to look confident and reassured. I couldn't lose face in front of all these people.

It didn't work.

"HELL YEAH!" I pumped my fist, raising it in the air. The anxiety that had gripped me moments before melted away, replaced by an intoxicating sense of triumph. This feeling, this rush—it was addictive.

I caught sight of Jian Duan, his face twisted in disbelief and anger. His fists were clenched, and his eyes burned with frustration. Before I could even think of what to say, he stormed toward the judges. "On what basis was I eliminated?" he demanded with barely restrained fury. "I demand that the results be checked by an unbiased party!"

The crowd became dead silent, and I felt goosebumps as all the judges glared at him, including Ma Hualong.

Elder Mingmei stepped forward, her gaze icy. Despite being a head shorter, her presence commanded respect. "Are you insinuating that we were biased in our judgment, Jian Duan?"

He faltered for a moment, but he seemed to make his mind up and double down. "I am merely stating that my Qi Replenishment Pill was of high quality. It deserves to be reconsidered."

"All ten of the chosen contestants boasted high-quality alchemical products that adhered to the Gauntlet's restrictions. Your Qi Replenishment Pill, however, barely utilized pyrite. It was an afterthought, not a core component."

Elder Wei Lian stepped forward, his voice cold and precise. "Furthermore, your pill was not up to par with those among the top ten. It lacked the innovative use of pyrite that we sought in this challenge."

Jian Duan's face reddened, but he refused to back down. "This doesn't mean I am less of an alchemist than they are. Pyrite is a useless ingredient. One that only lowly blacksmiths"—he pointed a derisive finger at Tao Ren—"would use in their career."

Was he angered about being eliminated? Or because he got eliminated in the same round as Tao Ren?

Even among the eliminated contestants, some nodded their heads, although they didn't verbalize their agreement. The judges looked among each other and all sighed.

Elder Wei Lian picked up a chunk of unused pyrite from Jian Duan's station and held it up. "Pyrite is only useless in the eyes of useless alchemists," he stated coldly.

With a speed belying his age, he traced symbols onto the surface of the table. Alchemical arrays, just like Jingyu Lian's . . . but they were far more complex.

As the symbols glowed brighter, the chunk of pyrite in Elder Wei Lian's hand began to change. Before our eyes, it started to crystallize, the transformation almost mesmerizing.

I could feel my heart pounding, my breath caught in my throat. Was this the pinnacle of alchemical mastery?

Elder Wei Lian continued without touching the pyrite, his arrays doing all the work. When the transformation was complete, he held up a perfectly crystallized piece of pyrite, its facets catching the light in a dazzling display.

"Observe," he said. "On top of its properties shown so far, pyrite also boasts protective properties, ones that can be drawn out in several ways. The way I showed you is just one of them." He then crushed the crystal in his hand, and it disintegrated into a fine powder. With a smooth motion, he let the powder fall onto his skin, where it seemed to dissolve and form a thin, shimmering layer. The layer moved and swirled like oil on water, a mesmerizing sight.

"This powder, when applied to the skin, creates a protective barrier. It can deflect attacks from cultivators." To demonstrate, he struck his arm with a qi-infused finger. The shimmering layer glowed and absorbed the impact, dispersing the energy harmlessly. "The perceived uselessness of an ingredient lies not in the material itself but in the eyes of the alchemist who uses it. An alchemist's true power is in their ability to see potential where others see none."

Jian Duan's face drained of color. He opened his mouth to speak, but no words came out. Thoroughly cowed, he lowered his head, unable to meet anyone's eyes.

As I watched Elder Wei Lian's demonstration, a realization dawned on me. Despite my victory, there was still so much to learn about alchemy. To them, we must've looked like bumbling, clumsy fools. I had only begun to scratch the surface.

"That's right!" a faint voice from the stands shouted out.

I looked over to see someone shoving their way out of the stands and into the arena. The height from the stands and where we competed was not insignificant, as an older gentleman fell out. Landing on one knee, the old man grunted in pain. "Dammit all, my body doesn't work like it used to . . ." he muttered, dusting his robes off nonchalantly, as though he hadn't trespassed onto the premises.

Ma Hualong's stern voice cut through the murmurs of the crowd. "Sir, this area is restricted. You are trespassing—"

But as he took a closer look at the intruder, his eyes widened in recognition. "Master Ren?"

The name didn't ring a bell for me, but the judges reacted instantly. They hurried forward, their previously stern faces now filled with respect. Even Elder Mingmei and Elder Wei Lian, venerable elders themselves, seemed to hold this man in high regard.

"Master Ren, it's an honor," Elder Mingmei said, bowing slightly.

"Indeed, welcome," Elder Wei Lian added. "We weren't expecting your presence, we would've had an open place for you on the panels otherwise."

He greeted them all with grace, a warm smile spreading across his weathered face. "Thank you, esteemed judges. I was merely here as an observer."

Who was he? Master Ren? If they called him that, then was he on the same level as Master Li Tao, who boasted the Essence Extraction skill? How come I had never heard of him?

I glanced over at the others. Many of them had the same reaction I did. Tao Ren, however, shifted uncomfortably, rubbing his eyes in disbelief. Something about this old man unsettled him far more than the rest of us.

Master Ren turned to the audience, building upon Elder Wei Lian's point. "Transforming ingredients is a fundamental skill in alchemy. It's about seeing potential where others see only limitations."

"But there's a limit." He narrowed his eyes, turning on his heel and beelining for a certain blacksmith.

"Dad?" the blacksmith squeaked, his voice barely a whisper compared to his usual bellow.

"Don't you 'dad' me, you overgrown lump of charcoal!" Master Ren roared, his voice echoing through the arena. "I send you here to prove your worth as an alchemist, not to turn this prestigious competition into a . . . a blacksmithing demonstration!"

The revelation hit me like a bolt of lightning. Master Ren was Tao Ren's father. The whispers in the crowd grew louder as the realization spread.

"But, Dad," he protested, "who says a great alchemist can't be a great blacksmith? The principles are practically the same—harnessing the essence of materials, transforming them with skill and intent! It's just a different kind of furnace!"

Master Ren's left eye twitched. "Oh, is it now?" He said, standing chest to chest with his son. It was comical, considering how different their physiques were. "The only reason you even know how to extract iron from pyrite is because you were too lazy to gather the proper ores for your failed attempts at making swords. And the tempering technique? *My* flame tempering technique, no less! Used to forge a blade? If I were dead, I'd be rolling in my grave right now! All the knowledge I taught you, put to waste!"

"But . . . Dad, we're not just your dusty old alchemy shop anymore, you know? We're the future of alchemically enhanced blacksmithing!"

Master Ren sagged his shoulders and sighed. With a beaming smile to the judges, he spoke. "I apologize for the interruption. I'll just be taking this fool with me for a much needed conversation."

He gripped the blacksmith's ear, pulling him down with not so considerable strength. It was comical; a short, frail-looking elder pulling along a blacksmith with a robust physique as though he were a petulant child. Master Ren's dramatic exit with Tao Ren in tow left the audience buzzing with murmurs and speculations. Ma Hualong quickly stepped forward, taking control of the situation with his authoritative presence.

"This round is officially over," he proclaimed. "Contestants, the next round will commence in two days. During this time, you will have the opportunity to gather another item from the vault."

I nodded. This was perfect. I'd have to think more about what reward I'd like to receive.

Ma Hualong continued, dropping a tantalizing hint about the next round. "The next round will be straightforward. It is a test of your ability to understand the history of alchemy. We have tested your theoretical knowledge, practical skills, and innovative approaches. Now we will see how well you understand the roots of our craft."

As we dispersed, I found myself walking alongside Bai Hua and Zhi Ruo toward the lounge. We congratulated each other, feeling a mixture of pride and relief. However, our thoughts soon turned to Tao Ren.

"I feel bad for Tao Ren. He really gave it his all."

"Yeah," Zhi Ruo agreed, his expression thoughtful. "But he has a lot to learn about focus and context. Crafting a knife in an alchemy competition . . . Well, it shows his creativity, if nothing else."

We shared a quiet laugh at his situation. To think the "old geezer" he kept talking about was a renowned alchemist . . . One that even the elders treated with respect. As we talked, I noticed Jingyu Lian making a swift exit from the arena. She didn't even glance at Elder Wei Lian, her movements stiff and deliberate.

My smile faded. I knew that between our products, hers could've just as easily been first place. And I was sure Elder Wei Lian had something to do with it. The man in question was talking animatedly with the other judges. A powerful senior alchemist from the Lian clan, boasting ties with the strongest sect in the region along with the Alchemy Association. He clearly seemed interested in my Essence extraction skill, but—

"Kai? You there? Hello?" Bai Hua said in a singsong voice, waving his hand by my face. "We're going to eat. Are you coming?"

"Ah," I scratched my head. "I'm feeling a bit tired after today. Maybe another time."

"Suit yourself. Come on, Zhi Ruo. Let's go!"

The two quickly made their way out of the arena, and I stood quietly there in the empty lounge. I didn't know what was going on in the background, and I had no real desire to find out. Her business was hers, after all.

"Eyes on the prize, Kai," I muttered to myself like a mantra. "Eyes on the prize."

Regardless the idea that I won solely due to Elder Wei Lian's machinations left a bitter taste in my mouth. I wanted to win against Jingyu Lian at her best, to face her fairly.

If I didn't win on my own terms, could I really call it a victory?

As I stepped out of the arena, lost in thought, a familiar voice called out to me. "Kai! Congratulations on your victory!"

It was Feng Wu, his face beaming with pride. He clapped me on the shoulder, his grip firm and reassuring. "I knew you had it in you. First place! That's no small feat. From Kowtow Kai to this . . . It's really been a marvel to see you grow."

I managed a smile, but it felt strained. I couldn't even point out his use of my demeaning nickname. "Thanks, Feng Wu. It's just . . . I can't help but feel like something's off."

Feng Wu's brow furrowed. "What do you mean?"

I hesitated, unsure if I should voice my concerns. But Feng Wu was my friend and mentor. If anyone could offer insight, it was him. "It's about Elder Wei Lian and Jingyu Lian. Did you see how harsh he was on her? It seemed personal. And then there's the fact that he seemed so interested in my Essence Extraction skill. What if . . . what if he deliberately pushed Jingyu Lian down to ensure my victory? What agenda does he have?"

Feng Wu was silent for a moment, considering my words. "It's a possibility," he admitted. "But Kai, even if that were the case, it doesn't diminish your achievement. Your elixir was exceptional. Even if Elder Wei Lian had ulterior motives, he's just one judge. The others recognized your skill too. Don't let this overshadow your success."

I sighed, running a hand through my hair. "I know. But it doesn't feel right. I want to win on my own merits, not because someone else was unfairly judged."

I couldn't let suspicions and what-ifs distract me from what lay ahead. The Gauntlet was far from over, and I needed to stay focused.

"You're right," I said, my resolve strengthening. "I can't change what happened. All I can do is keep pushing forward, keep improving."

Feng Wu nodded, his smile widening. "That's the spirit. Now, about that reward from the vault. Any ideas?"

I felt a grin tugging at my lips. "A few. But I need to think it over."

As we walked away from the arena, my mind was already racing with possibilities. The vault was a treasure trove of alchemical resources. With the right choice, I could solidify my position, far after the competition is over.

But more than that, I was determined to prove myself, to show that my victory was earned through skill and knowledge, not favoritism or politics. The next round, with its focus on alchemical history, was the perfect opportunity.

I would show the judges, the audience, and most importantly, myself, that I was a true alchemist, worthy of the title.

The Gauntlet had challenged me in ways I never expected, pushing me to my limits and beyond. But with each obstacle, each trial, I felt myself growing, evolving. And I knew, deep in my bones, that this was just the beginning.

The Interface sparked to life with two distinct notifications.

> *Your understanding of the dao has deepened.*
> *Your Mind has reached Mortal Realm—Rank 5.*

> *Quest: Mind Refinement (Breakthrough)*
> *—Revise one hundred alchemical recipes and improve*
> *upon the processes within your Memory Palace. (0/100)*

The world of alchemy was about to see what I was truly made of.

# CHAPTER FORTY-ONE

# Moonlit Shadows

I sat cross-legged in the confines of my room at the Jade Harmony Inn.

Tianyi fluttered around excitedly, as though she knew I was celebrating a victory. Or maybe she was excited to drink. That silly little drunkard.

Windy coiled comfortably on the floor, his eyes glinting with curiosity.

"It's good to celebrate your victories," Feng Wu said.

I felt bad and apologized for keeping him here when he could be training or cultivating. Being my escort must've been exhausting. But all he responded with was a shake of his head, saying it was merely his duty.

I couldn't help but grin. Having the one who brought me to the Verdant Lotus Sect witness this was the best I could ask for.

"Yeah, it still feels a bit surreal." I had prepared for this moment, gathering a few items to celebrate properly.

Reaching into a small satchel, I pulled out a delicate porcelain cup and poured a generous amount of green plum wine for myself. The sweet, slightly tangy aroma filled the room, mixing with the scent of incense. Next, I poured a small amount into another cup for Tianyi, careful not to spill a drop. Her proboscis extended eagerly as she settled down to drink.

I handed Feng Wu a steaming cup of green tea. He accepted it with a nod of gratitude, the steam curling up around his face.

To complete our little celebration, I placed a small bundle of freshly caught rodents—courtesy of a local child I'd paid handsomely—near Windy. His eyes lit up, and he slithered over to inspect his feast.

With our drinks ready, I raised my cup.

Feng Wu lifted his tea with a serene smile. "To your hard work paying off, Kai."

Tianyi flitted to the edge of her cup, her wings brushing against the rim as she dipped her proboscis into the wine.

I considered clinking cups with Windy, but the idea of a dead rodent touching my cup made me reconsider. Instead, I reached out and gently petted him on the head. "And to you, Windy. Thanks for sticking with me."

The serpent turned, its blue eyes lingering on my figure for a second longer than usual. He quickly turned his attention back to his meal, his slender body coiling around the first rodent.

A notification quickly appeared before my eyes.

*You have deepened your bond with the Spirit Beast Windy.*

*Name: Windy*
*Race: Wind Serpent (Aberrant)*
*Affinity: Wood and Metal*
*Cultivation Rank: Qi Initiation Stage—Rank 1*
*Special Abilities:*
*Tail Whip: Delivers a swift and powerful tail strike infused with Qi.*
*Paralyzing Venom: Injects venom that temporarily paralyzes the target.*
*Moonlight Empowerment: Gains increased power*
*and vitality under the moonlight.*
*Bond Level: 1 (Acquaintance)—Windy is familiar with*
*you but does not yet possess a deep connection.*

Oho! This was a first! Did this mean he now considered me a friend? What did he think I was prior? Emergency food?

Another thing to celebrate, I supposed!

The night was ours, a brief respite before the challenges resumed.

In this moment of calm, surrounded by friends and familiars, I felt ready for whatever lay ahead.

After a while, I felt the need to clear my head and stretch my legs. "I think I'll go for a walk," I announced, setting my empty cup down.

Feng Wu looked up. "Do you want me to come with you?"

I shook my head, smiling. "No, it's all right. I think I'll bring Tianyi and Windy. They can be my bodyguards for the evening." I said it lightly, but I could tell he understood my need for some alone time.

"Very well," he said, nodding. "Just be careful, and don't wander too far. The city can be a maze if you're not familiar with it."

"I will," I assured him. "Besides, I know you could use some time to relax and cultivate in peace."

"Thank you, Kai. Enjoy your walk."

With Tianyi perched on my shoulder and Windy coiled around my arm, I left the inn and stepped out into the cool night air. Crescent Bay City was a wonder, its labyrinthine alleys connecting residences to markets, temples, and other areas with an elegant, seamless flow. For someone like me, who had spent most of my life in a village, it was a marvel.

Perhaps I'd find some additional trinkets to buy along the way. I had a village's worth of people to grab souvenirs for.

Tianyi fluttered around me, her wings creating a soft, rhythmic sound, while Windy slithered gracefully along my arm, his eyes alert and watchful.

After a while, I noticed the alleys becoming narrower and the sounds of the city fading. I realized I had wandered into a part of the city I hadn't explored before. Just as I decided to turn back, I found myself in a dead-end alleyway.

"Well, this isn't ideal," I muttered to myself, turning to retrace my steps.

Before I could move, a figure stepped into the alley, blocking my way. Jian Duan. His eyes were bloodshot, and the smell of alcohol wafted from him. He wasn't alone; a few other men, who looked just as rough and intoxicated, stood behind him wearing beige and gray attire. They looked familiar. Where had I seen them before?

"You!" Jian Duan spat, his voice slurred with anger and drink. "You're the reason I lost!"

I took a deep breath, trying to keep calm. "Jian Duan, you're drunk. Let's not do anything rash. We can settle this without escalating."

He sneered, his eyes narrowing. "Settle this? You think you're better than me because you won? I'll show you."

The men pushed past, showing varying signs of inebriation. All of them were burly men reminiscent of Ping Hai. That's when I realized who they were.

". . . Narrow Stone Peak? Weren't there supposed to be five of you?"

The cultivators seemed to sag their shoulders upon mentioning that.

"Gu Bei . . . He's passed out right now."

Their leader, the burliest one among them, elbowed the one who responded to me. "Don't answer him!"

He turned to me with a cocky grin on his face, cracking his knuckles. "You're going to pay for making us lose face at Spirited Noodle, alchemist. Thanks to you, we became laughingstocks!"

I didn't even do anything! What was he talking about? How did they even know Jian Duan?

Backing away, I kept a close eye on Tianyi and Windy. I tried to send the butterfly waves of relaxation and calm, but it was rather hard to accomplish with five people cutting off my only path to escape. I grasped Windy's head, preventing him from poking out with a firm hand.

I couldn't risk escalating it beyond this point or risk my companions getting hurt. I searched my mind for possible options.

"Do you really want to provoke the Verdant Lotus Sect by attacking me? Is that something your sect can handle?!" I bellowed out loud. Hopefully it was loud enough to attract attention, that of guards or civilians.

Contrary to my expectations, the Narrow Stone Peak disciples exchanged glances, then pointed at Jian Duan with a unified nod.

"The young master of the Jian family will pull strings to make sure we don't face any repercussions!" one of them declared, puffing out his chest. "The Jian family is far stronger than the Verdant Lotus Sect!"

I froze at this claim, knowing for a fact that they weren't. The Jian family was wealthy and powerful, yes, but not even a fraction as strong as the Verdant Lotus Sect, which was a prestigious sect that had been around for over a century. I looked at Jian Duan, who seemed to be avoiding eye contact with me. It clicked—he had likely lied to these gullible meatheads, making himself seem more important than he was.

Taking a deep breath, I decided on a new approach. "Tianyi, Windy," I whispered softly, "stay out of this. Find a chance to escape and call for Feng Wu if things get out of hand."

Windy tightened his coils around my arm, clearly unhappy with my instructions. But I needed them safe. I couldn't bear the thought of them getting hurt because of me.

The leader of the group stepped forward, cracking his knuckles menacingly. "You're going to regret crossing us."

With no other choice, I struck preemptively. I lunged forward, aiming a swift kick right at the leader's groin. He doubled over with a groan, collapsing to the ground.

Enraged by their comrade's pain, they surged forward, fists and feet flying.

Slow.

I dodged one punch and parried another, keeping my back close to the wall. Even though I was cornering myself, it was better than having to worry about another person attacking me from behind. Tianyi darted out of the alleyway in a burst of qi, and Windy quickly slithered out of my sleeve and onto the floor with a hiss.

"Wh-what the hell?!"

I took advantage of their surprise and landed a backfist at another disciple's jaw. Instead of falling over, the man grabbed my arm and prevented me from moving any further.

"Come on! While I have him in my—AGH!"

Windy's serpentine body coiled around the man's leg, and I heard something pop as he glowed blue and continued to tighten his grip around the disciple's leg. That rebellious little snake! He wasn't listening to my instructions!

Before I could wrestle my arm out and continue the battle, a voice cut through the din of battle.

"What's going on here?" a chilly voice echoed through the alley, freezing everyone in their tracks. A voice I hadn't hoped to hear.

We all turned to see Xu Ziqing standing at the entrance of the alley, his expression as cold as ice.

"What are you doing causing a ruckus in the Silent Moon's territory?"

Jian Duan sneered, trying to maintain his bravado. "We're just taking out the trash. I hope the Azure Moon Marauder won't mind us cleaning up a bit."

Xu Ziqing's eyes narrowed. "I do mind. You and your lackeys should leave now or else be forced to."

Clearly emboldened by the alcohol and his newfound allies, he barked out a laugh. "Why would you, a member of the Silent Moon Sect, help him? Verdant Lotus and Silent Moon are rivals. Shouldn't you be enjoying this?"

The older man's expression darkened. In a blink of an eye, his sword was drawn, and a thin line of blood appeared on Jian Duan's cheek. The threat hung in the air, palpable and undeniable.

"*Leave.* Or the next cut won't be so gentle."

The Narrow Stone Peak disciples paled, their drunken bravado evaporating in the face of Xu Ziqing's deadly seriousness. They backed away, helping their leader to his feet. With Jian Duan clutching his cheek, they beat a hasty retreat, disappearing into the night.

Windy uncoiled himself and slithered back to me, while Tianyi fluttered back to my shoulder, her wings stilling as she settled. I hastily picked up the snake, cradling him protectively.

Xu Ziqing had seen Windy, and now I had no idea what he would do with that information.

The second-class disciple sheathed his sword and approached me, his gaze sharp and assessing. Our eyes met, and I couldn't read his expression.

"Well, well, well," Xu Ziqing drawled, his voice dripping with disdain. "Look what we have here—the pathetic little alchemist who can't even protect himself."

I felt the sting of embarrassment and humiliation rise within me, but I kept my composure. "Why did you save me?"

A sardonic smile twisted Xu Ziqing's lips. "Do you think I care about your well-being? Don't flatter yourself. If those fools had injured a Grand Alchemy Gauntlet contestant while on Silent Moon territory, it would have reflected poorly on us. Besides," he paused, his eyes gleaming with a strange light, "consider this repayment for your interference in Qingmu."

I stared at him, a mix of confusion and gratitude swirling within me. Could it be that Xu Ziqing wasn't as heartless as he appeared? Before I could dwell on this thought, he spoke again, his voice as cold as ice.

"A Wind Serpent . . ." he said, his gaze fixated on Windy. "Where did you find this creature?"

"None of your business," I retorted, holding Windy tighter. His blue eyes shimmered and his body glowed a faint blue as if sensing my unease.

"Feisty, aren't we? A pity that your spirit is stronger than your cultivation. If you remain as weak as you are, it's only a matter of time before this Wind Serpent, and that butterfly, are taken away from you."

My blood ran cold. He was right. As much as I hated to admit it, my current strength wasn't enough to protect my familiars. But the thought of losing them filled me with a rage I had never known before.

"What are you doing here, Xu Ziqing?" I asked, my voice hardening. "Why are you lurking in the shadows like a common thief?"

He chuckled, a low, throaty sound that sent chills down my spine. "I'm merely running errands for Elder Jun. You'll see for yourself soon enough."

His words hung in the air, heavy with unspoken menace. I watched as he turned and disappeared into the darkness, leaving me alone with my thoughts and fears.

As I stood there in the empty alleyway, the weight of Xu Ziqing's words pressed down on me. He was right. I was weak.

I should've known. I just decided to ignore the signs; and now I owe a debt to Xu Ziqing. Who knows what he'll do with it?

I made my way back to Jade Harmony Inn as fast as I possibly could. Every shadow in the dark felt like a potential enemy, just waiting for me to drop my guard.

Finally reaching the inn, I burst through the door of our room, startling Feng Wu.

"Kai, what happened?" Hh asked, his voice filled with concern.

I took a deep breath, trying to steady myself. "I . . . I got into some trouble. Jian Duan and a few of his lackeys ambushed me. You remember those guys from Spirited Noodle? The bald guys? They said they were out for revenge because I won the Gauntlet round or something, drunk off their minds . . . I managed to fight them off, but then Xu Ziqing showed up. He saved me, sort of. But now I owe him."

The words flowed out of me like a waterfall, trying to get every detail I could.

Feng Wu's expression hardened. "Elder Zhu needs to be informed. We won't take this lightly."

I nodded, feeling a wave of guilt wash over me. "I'm sorry, Feng Wu. I should've known better. I put myself in danger and now I've dragged the sect into it."

He shook his head, placing a reassuring hand on my shoulder. "You can't blame yourself, Kai. Your entry into the Jianghu was recent. You're still learning. But from now on, you need to be more cautious. Avoid leaving the inn unless you're in a group or it's broad daylight. It's much harder to be attacked under those conditions. I should've known better as well, letting you out on your own."

Despite his reassurance, I couldn't shake the feeling of stupidity that lingered.

"But why was Xu Ziqing there? Didn't you mention the Silent Moon Sect has been laying low since the duel against Ping Hai?"

"That's another concern," Feng Wu admitted. "The Silent Moon Sect's reappearance could mean they're planning something. We'll need to keep our eyes open."

I cursed myself again. "I should have known. I was so stupid to wander off alone."

"What matters is that you learn from this." he said, his expression softening slightly. "Get some rest. I'll keep an eye out tonight."

As I lay down, the events of the night replayed in my mind.

The image of Tianyi being crushed underfoot by the Narrow Stone Peak disciples and Windy being taken away haunted my vision. My hands trembled, and I curled up in my bed trying to erase that thought.

I wouldn't let that happen again.

I dove into my Memory Palace, replaying the events again and again until I fell asleep.

# CHAPTER FORTY-TWO

# Guowei Wang

The streets of Crescent Bay City were already bustling with activity, merchants setting up their stalls and vendors calling out their wares. I walked briskly, my mind focused on the task at hand. I knew exactly what I wanted to get.

Approaching the Alchemy Association's towering building, I felt a feeling of readiness. The sun was just beginning to rise, casting long shadows from the spire.

Taking my entry token, the clerk quickly guided me downstairs to where the vault was.

The vault-keeper was dressed in robes of sky blue, their dignified appearance lending an air of authority to the room. His eyes, though clouded with age, sparkled with a sharp intelligence.

I greeted him respectfully, bowing slightly. "Good morning, sir."

He inclined his head in response. "Ah . . . Kai Liu, correct? It's good to see you again. Have you had any success in reviving the Golden Bamboo yet?"

"Uh, not yet, sir. It's only been a few days since we last spoke. These things take time."

I supposed it was quite telling if he expected me to revive a nigh-extinct species in just three days. I always gave off that genius vibe, after all.

He chuckled, the sound warm and genuine. "Of course, of course. Forgive an old man his impatience. My memory isn't what it used to be, especially when I spend most of my days down here. Time tends to blur."

*Oh.* He was just senile.

I nodded, wondering who this man truly was. His demeanor and knowledge suggested someone of great importance, yet his humility was striking. Before I could ponder further, he gestured toward the vault.

"Now, then, where would you like to start?"

"I think I'd like to look around first, if that's all right," I said. "I'd like to consider all the options before making a decision."

The vault-keeper smiled, a hint of pride in his expression. "Very well. Follow me."

As we walked through the vault, he provided information about every item we passed. The depth of his knowledge was astounding. Each artifact had a story, each ingredient a history. The vault was filled with treasures, some I had only read about in ancient texts.

"This here is the Cinnabar Rock Crystal," he said, pointing to a crystalline object encased in glass. "When processed carefully, it can help you cultivate yang-based martial arts.

"And this," he continued, moving to a shelf lined with small vials, "is the Deep Sea Kelp Heart. It has been dehydrated for preservation and concentration of its properties, used mainly in products to raise resistance against cold and yin energies."

I listened, fascinated, as he described each item. It didn't feel like knowledge from a book, but one gained from firsthand experience. Something about the way he talked, and explained each item, it was as though he had personal history with them.

"Who are you?" I finally asked, unable to contain my curiosity any longer. "You know so much about all of these obscure ingredients, and extensively at that. It's incredible."

"My name is Guowei Wang. I . . . I am merely a custodian of these treasures, ensuring they are preserved and protected for future generations."

"Thank you, Guowei Wang. Your guidance has been invaluable. I've made my decision. I'd like to select the Breezesong Fruit."

He nodded approvingly. "A wise choice. Although the vault contains many treasures that are never seen in the public light, it doesn't necessarily mean they are better. The Breezesong Fruit is still an incredible ingredient. I hope it serves you well."

I bowed deeply. "Thank you, Master Guowei. Your guidance has been invaluable. Perhaps I could visit you again sometime to hear more of your stories?"

The vault-keeper's cloudy eyes looked at me in surprise. For a moment, he looked down before bursting out in laughter.

"Ah, it's been a long time since anyone's shown interest in an old man's tales. I'd be delighted, young man. Visit whenever you please," Guowei Wang said with a gracious smile.

He grabbed a slip of paper from his desk and began scrawling symbols on it. They were old and archaic, nothing that I had seen before.

"Show this to the clerk outside," he explained. "It will allow you to meet me."

"Thank you, sir," I said, accepting the paper with a deep bow. "Regarding the fruit, I'd like to have it delivered to the Verdant Lotus Sect. It's difficult to keep it safe at this point in time."

My mind wandered to Jian Duan and his goons.

The vault-keeper nodded in understanding. "Very well. It will be sent out shortly."

As I made my way out, lost in thought, a boisterous voice jolted me back to reality, my heart leaping in my chest.

"KAI! OVER HERE!"

I turned to see Tao Ren, looking slightly worse for wear but decidedly more refined in a distinguished robe. His short, unruly hair had been slicked back, transforming his appearance from the crazed smith I knew to a dignified noble. It was the first time I'd seen him since his father had dragged him out of the arena.

"Tao Ren? What happened to you?"

He sagged his shoulders, glancing around as if worried someone might overhear. "That geezer of mine's wants me to meet some of his buddies from the association, make connections and all that."

The blacksmith jabbed his thumb to where the clerk was, and I could see his father talking.

I couldn't resist a teasing jab. "Tch. I can't believe you were hiding such a thing from your friends. You were secretly a noble! Just like those snobbish contestants looking down on us." I wiped a fake tear from my eye with my sleeve. To think that Bai Hua and Tao Ren came from such outstanding backgrounds.

What's next, Zhi Ruo being the long-lost descendant of the Imperial Emperor?

He rolled his eyes and slung his arm around my neck as we walked together. "Come on, don't be like that! I knew my geezer was an alchemist too, but not at that scale. He never said he was a big shot with the Alchemy Association."

I looked at him incredulously. Was he really that obtuse, having never picked up on such a detail? "So, you're still going to meet with them?"

"Of course! I may have been eliminated from the Gauntlet, but if I get buddy-buddy with some of these powerful people, won't it make starting my own smithing business a breeze? Acquiring a permit to set up shop here's the next step, after all!"

Tao Ren was still the same; that sheer determination would get him somewhere in life, without a doubt.

"Hey, how about after this, we go grab a meal together? This meeting shouldn't take too long."

I hesitated for a moment, remembering Feng Wu's words. But it was still daytime, and as long as I was accompanied by others and stayed in crowded areas, it should be fine. "Sure, where do you think would be good?"

"The Cloudrift Pavilion was good according to Bai Hua. Ever heard of it?"

I nodded, recalling my previous visit with Feng Wu. "I have. I'll go if it's on your tab, young Master Tao Ren."

He waved me off. "Of course, of course! Anything for my juniors," he said with a cheeky grin. To be fair, this dignified look suited him. With his towering physique, I noticed many women around us glancing at him with flushed faces. How ironic, to think that the one Jian Duan despised as a peasant would be related to someone so important.

"I'll go grab a seat then, I know how busy it gets. Don't take too long, okay?"

Our plans confirmed, I looked over to the Cloudrift Pavilion, visible from where we stood. It was situated in a prime location, one of the most popular spots in the city. With its proximity to the Whispering Wind Sect, I was confident there'd be no place to stage an ambush like in the alleys.

I just have to be careful.

With that mantra repeating in my head, I began my trek toward the restaurant.

Walking into Cloudrift Pavilion, I was met with an airy, elegant interior that instantly put me at ease. The restaurant was designed with a wind theme, giving it an open, breezy feel. The walls were adorned with delicate paintings of clouds and gusts of wind. The dining area was spacious, with tables arranged to provide a scenic view of the city from all angles. Open windows allowed natural light to flood in and offer breathtaking views of the city.

A waiter approached me with a polite smile. "Good evening, sir. How many will be dining with us tonight?"

"Just two. I'm expecting someone shortly," I replied.

"Of course. Do you have a seating preference? We have several tables available, and there are even more options upstairs if you prefer."

I glanced around the room, my eyes drawn to a corner table situated at the edge of the dining area. It offered an unobstructed view of the city, with the lights twinkling like stars below.

"I'll take that table in the corner,"

"Excellent choice," the waiter said, leading me to the table. "Please, have a seat. Here is the menu. Can I get you something to drink while you decide on your order?"

"I'll have a cup of green tea, please," I said, needing something to calm my nerves after the tumultuous day.

As I waited, I opened the menu and began to peruse the offerings. My mind, however, kept drifting back to the events of the day and the possibilities ahead. The Breezesong Fruit, Jian Duan, and tomorrow's round . . . It was a lot to digest.

The waiter set the steaming cup before me with a practiced grace. "Here you go, sir. Have you decided on your order, or do you need a few more minutes?"

I smiled, shaking my head. "I need a few more minutes, thank you."

I sipped the tea, feeling the warmth spread through me. It was soothing, a momentary respite from the whirlwind of my thoughts. The gentle hum of conversations all around helped me to relax, if only slightly. The view from my table was mesmerizing. Crescent Bay City stretched out below, the buildings illuminated by the soft glow of lanterns.

But through the din of idle chatter, I heard a voice, faint but familiar. "Father, I—"

I froze, my ears straining. Jingyu Lian's voice. Glancing up, I realized the source was from the floor above. My heart raced as I strained to catch more of the conversation.

# CHAPTER FORTY-THREE

# Nuts About Secrets

B e quiet and let me keep speaking," another voice chided. It was strong and authoritative.

The voices faded into a quiet, unintelligible whisper. My curiosity was piqued, I needed to hear more. Half tempted to crawl up the railing and strain my ears, I considered my options. Moving my table upstairs was out of the question.

Desperately, I glanced at the menu, searching for inspiration. My eyes landed on the Gingko Nut Stir Fry Vegetables dish. An idea sparked, and I waved the waiter over.

"Excuse me," I said, trying to keep my voice steady. "Could I order this? But could you serve the gingko nuts separately and as quickly as possible?"

The waiter looked slightly puzzled but nodded. "Of course, sir. I'll have that prepared right away."

As he walked away, I tapped my fingers on the table, my mind racing. The gingko nuts, known for their properties to enhance cognitive functions and senses, were my best bet. If I could enhance my hearing, I might catch more of the conversation upstairs.

Minutes felt like hours as I waited for the dish to arrive. The voices above remained low, frustratingly just out of reach. I sipped my tea, trying to maintain my composure, but the urgency gnawed at me.

Finally, the waiter returned with a small bowl of gingko nuts, fragrant as cow manure. "Here you are, sir," he said, placing them before me.

*Eugh!* That smell was potent!

I double-checked the nuts and how thoroughly cooked they were. Translucent bright green and tender to the touch, they were cooked perfectly. That would help degrade the toxin that caused vomiting. Hopefully this gamble pays off.

Taking the bowl and discretely hiding it under the tablecloth, I began extracting their essences, hoping that glow wouldn't be too powerful.

I quickly slipped the essences into my green tea, watching as the liquid took on a dull glow and emitted a potent smell, multiplying the intensity of the gingko nut's odor. Almost immediately, the people around me began to wrinkle their noses and mutter complaints about the garbage-like scent wafting through the air. Ignoring the commotion, I swiftly drank the tea, the strange odor persisting.

Despite the horrendous violation the gingko nuts brought upon my nose, the taste was quite pleasant.

Setting the now dull and stale-looking gingko nuts back on the table, I closed my eyes, feeling the immediate effects. My senses sharpened to an uncomfortable extent—smells, sounds, and sights all intensified. Even the lingering scent of gingko nuts came back in full force. I had to focus, tuning out the overwhelming sensory input to concentrate on the voices above.

With my enhanced hearing, I could catch every word, even their hushed tones.

"We can't afford to take chances," her father continued. "Taking risks is a luxury we cannot afford. Your victory must be assured, even if it requires certain . . . adjustments. The upcoming round will test your ability to decipher a partially-given recipe. We have put measures in place to ensure your success. You will follow them. Is that clear?"

My heart raced as I leaned in closer, straining to hear every word. Deciphering a recipe? Her father knew what was happening in the next round?

"Father, *please*," she pressed on, her voice still in a low whisper. "Elder Wei Lian can't—"

"My brother can and *will*," her father interrupted. Even though I was an entire floor down, I could feel chills going down my spine. Jingyu Lian quieted down immediately. "Do you realize how long he's been waiting for this? This extends beyond your personal honor; it encompasses my standing within the sect. Your defeat would bolster his son's claim to lead the alchemy pavilion, an outcome disastrous for our clan. Can you shoulder this responsibility?"

The last words leaving his mouth felt like a punch to the gut.

She didn't respond. Only silence remained, before her father continued, albeit softer this time.

". . . Although the specific recipe isn't chosen until the round begins, my informant's made sure that the *interior* of the envelope in your station will contain all the information you need to pass the round at first place. Make sure to revise before then."

Jingyu Lian's reluctance was palpable in her silence. I could almost imagine her conflicted gaze.

"Little Jing," her father said affectionately, "this is all to secure your future. If it weren't for Wei Lian's interference, you would have won the Gauntlet cleanly, and I would have allowed you to go unimpeded. But we must adapt to the situation. You understand, don't you?"

There was a heavy pause before she finally spoke in the slightest whisper that even I could barely hear with my enhanced senses.

"Yes, Father. I understand."

"Our clan's legacy rests upon your shoulders, Jingyu. This is not merely about winning a competition, but about upholding our family's honor and maintaining our position. You have the talent, but you must also wield the wisdom to navigate these trials if you want to be the next head. Do not let sentiment cloud your judgment."

Her father's chair scraped against the floor as he stood up, the sound echoing in the now silent space. His footsteps were deliberate and measured as he walked away, leaving Jingyu Lian alone. The quiet that followed was profound, filled only with the subtle rustle of fabric and the occasional clink of cutlery from the other diners.

My back was covered in sweat, from both intense focus and the weight of this situation.

My mind swirled. The depth of the competition's intrigue was far beyond what I had imagined. Not only was there personal pride at stake, but the very fabric of sect politics and family honor was intertwined in this Gauntlet.

What should I do with this information? If I revealed it, it could ruin Jingyu Lian's reputation and her father's standing. But if I kept it to myself, it would mean allowing this deceit to potentially mar the competition. The fairness and integrity of the Gauntlet were at risk.

She was an arrogant, entitled princess who thought the world belonged to her. But . . . I couldn't call her a bad person. But even she didn't want to do this. It was all because of stupid sect politics and geezers interfering, putting their noses where they didn't belong. It had parallels to the situation between me, Ping Hai, and Elder Jun.

I supposed it was true; one could know a person's face but not their heart.

"Dammit . . ." I whispered, rubbing my forehead for the ensuing headache.

I glanced over to the entrance of the restaurant, spotting Tao Ren. As he glanced around looking for me, I already knew what he was going to do.

With my sharp reflexes, I bolted out of my table and sprinted toward him. The noise caught his attention, and he stared right at me with a big grin on his face. I could see the slightest intake of breath as he prepared to shout.

"K— Urgh!"

But before he could say my name and reveal my presence to the unaware Lian family on the second floor, I slapped a hand across his mouth and placed a finger to my lips.

"Please, please! Just be quiet. Let's bring you to the table," I muttered, looking around and apologizing to the nearby tables for the commotion.

I grabbed the muscled man and practically dragged him to the corner where our table was. Looking around, I swiveled his seat to face the open window and moved myself across from him.

"Sorry, Tao Ren. Just be quiet for a little bit and don't move. Just stay in place."

Despite my instructions, he glanced from left to right, obviously confused. "Kai, what is going on?"

"I'll tell you in a bit. Just—just be quiet, okay?"

I hid my face as best I could, taking advantage of Tao Ren's large frame. I watched as Jingyu Lian's father came down the stairs. It was the first time I had ever seen him.

Her father had a dignified aura, one that didn't command much attention. His robes were nice, but not to the level of opulence I expected from a clan leader, especially considering how extravagantly Jian Duan was dressed. He was probably trying to be inconspicuous. His face was stern, lined with the weight of responsibilities and perhaps the toll of endless scheming.

As he reached the bottom of the stairs, he paused for a moment. My heart skipped a beat, hoping he didn't sense my gaze. But then he snapped his head in my direction, and I hurriedly looked down, pretending to focus on the menu and praying he didn't notice me.

"I'd like to place my order," Tao Ren called to the waiter, breaking the tension. He ordered his dish, chatting casually while I kept my head low, feigning interest in the menu.

A few tense seconds passed, and then I saw Jingyu Lian's father glide toward the door. His steps echoed in my heightened senses until he finally exited. I breathed a sigh of relief, my muscles relaxing as the tension ebbed away.

The blacksmith leaned in, curiosity written all over his face. "All right, spill it! What's with all the cloak-and-dagger stuff?"

I didn't even know where to begin. Or rather, should I have even begun?

He tilted his head to the side. His slicked-back hair was already beginning to fall back into its natural, tousled mess. He reminded me of a large, friendly buffalo. I thought Tao Ren could be trusted with this information.

My mouth moved, as quiet as humanly possible, explaining the situation to him. His eyes widened in shock as he glanced to the ceiling as though expecting to see Jingyu Lian peering down on us from above.

"I know that you're usually quite . . ." I fumbled around for the proper word to call him. "Lively, but please, for my sake and yours, keep this between us."

"You know me, Kai. I won't tell a soul. Blacksmith's honor. But this is your problem more than it is mine. What are you going to do about it?"

I was thankful he minded his voice, lowering it to a quiet whisper. "That's my problem. I don't know what to do. Clearly there's more to this than what we've seen. I don't want to ruin her here. But if it puts the integrity of the Gauntlet at risk . . ."

Tao Ren waggled his eyebrows. "You don't want to rat out the girl you've been fancying; I understand. I don't know what I'd do in your situation; maybe I'd tell my old man. He could do something about it."

I clenched my fist, fighting the strong urge to sock him in the face. But as he said the last part, something in my mind clicked.

". . . Tao Ren, is your father still around? Perhaps there is a way we can go about this."

# CHAPTER FORTY-FOUR

# The Weight of History (and Pestles)

Kai!"

A wave of exotic fragrance washed over me, snapping me out of my reverie. I looked over to see Bai Hua. "What happened to your hair?"

The perfumer's usual style was to wear it half-up and half-down, but he now let it flow down his shoulders. His hair shimmered like spun silk, cascading smoothly and catching the light in an almost-mesmerizing way.

"Do you like it?" Bai Hua asked with a grin, running a hand through his glossy locks.

"Can I touch it?"

He leaned forward, offering a lock of his hair. I reached out, gently running my fingers through it. It was unbelievably soft, like touching a cloud made of the finest threads.

"This feels amazing," I marveled. "What did you use?"

Bai Hua's grin widened, his eyes twinkling with amusement. "Bee propolis, also known as Bee's Glue, to be specific. It's from a rare, extinct species I managed to wrangle from the Alchemy Association's vault. But pure propolis has a rather pungent aroma, if you will."

"Pungent?" I echoed.

"Precisely," he chuckled. "That's why I added a touch of my own creation—a special blend of floral essences and musk to enhance its conditioning properties and mask the less-desirable aspects of the propolis."

I sighed, shaking my head playfully. "Here we go again with the vanity," I teased, a small smile tugging at my lips despite myself.

He lightened the mood a bit, pushing aside the pre-competition nerves gnawing at me.

But my relief was short-lived. A quick scan of the room confirmed my suspicion—Jingyu Lian was absent. Where could she be?

His laughter filled the air, oblivious to my internal turmoil. "And here we go with the denial about your appearance. Remember that 'special' aroma you sported when we first met?"

I clutched myself, embarrassed. "Only you could detect that with your freakish sense of smell! And for the record, that was Windy, not me! I assure you, I usually smell perfectly pleasant."

This was going to be an ongoing thing, wasn't it? First it was Ma Xi sniffing me at the Tranquil Breeze Farm, now this! Gardeners, after all, were practically one with nature, right? Why shouldn't I smell like it—a delightful mix of fresh earth and blooming flowers?

"Maybe so, maybe not. But a little effort in self-care never hurt anyone, Kai. A touch of perfume, some well-chosen garments—it all contributes to a good first impression."

I rolled my eyes. This was a familiar back-and-forth we'd developed over time. We continued our banter for a few minutes, the air thick with the playful energy of our sparring. Zhi Ruo sat nearby, engrossed in a book, his studious demeanor a contrast to our lively exchange.

"Now, don't get me wrong, the vanity part is true, but there's a purpose behind the madness. It's not just about my glorious locks, you see." A glint of genuine passion ignited in his eyes. "I'm planning to use this to convince my father to invest in bee farms. He has no idea about the potential of bees beyond honey production."

With the way he talked, I sometimes forgot Bai Hua was the heir to a large and famous business, one that made more money in a day than I had in my entire lifetime. But that's what I liked about him; he was down to earth and never treated others lower due to their status. Why couldn't all young masters be like him?

He pressed another narrow-necked vial to my face, covering his nose and mouth with his sleeve. "Do something about that odor, will you? I can *still* smell that repugnant snake musk! Do you have it draped over your shoulders when you sleep?"

Well, maybe not exactly like him.

At that moment, Jingyu Lian entered the room. Her presence demanded attention, everyone's eye turning to see the favorite to win the Gauntlet.

I had always grouped her with the other aristocrat and clan-affiliated contestants, but the longer I observed her, the more I noticed she didn't play nice with them either. When Jian Duan attempted to curry favor with her, she shot it down every single time. Her self-assured presence coupled with her striking looks made her into a one-woman show.

But now her body language screamed anxiety and fatigue. Her usually sharp eyes had bags underneath, and her expression was dark and gloomy. She leaned against the wall near the door, closing her eyes as if trying to find a moment of peace amid the chaos.

"You're staring," Bai Hua teased, nudging me with his elbow. "In most cultures, that's taken as a sign of romantic interest."

I pushed him lightly. "It's not like that. She just looks . . . different."

"Uh-huh, sure. Just remember, if you start composing poetry for her, make sure to send me a copy."

He was lucky that this young master was so magnanimous! A lesser person would've face-slapped him back into the cycle of reincarnation. But I, Kai Liu, would spare this puny perfumer's life. Just this once!

I was about to strike back with a retort when Ma Hualong entered the room. The conversations died down as all eyes turned to him.

He stared at us for a second, one that seemed to last for hours. Then he spoke.

"Every ingredient, every technique, every symbol . . . They all hold a story." Ma Hualong paused, allowing for the words to sink in. Then: "This round, you will be presented with a partially translated recipe. It is a relic from a bygone era, and it is your task to create the original product based on what you have."

I bit my lip. Jingyu Lian's father was right, and it only confirmed the fact he truly had an insider within the Gauntlet. Her eyes were closed, and her brows furrowed upon hearing the information. As though she hoped it would be wrong.

Many of the contestants seemed nervous at the idea of deciphering a recipe. In a way, wasn't it harder than creating your own? My mind whirled with possible ways they could misdirect the contestants; a single step missed or one differing ingredient could give you a poison or an antidote. That was how volatile most recipes were.

"The recipe will be made available on your stations," Ma Hualong continued. "And as a reward for their high performance in the previous round, the top-three contestants of the previous round will have the chance to ask me a question regarding the recipe. However, I can only answer with a yes or no."

My heart raced. Being one of the top three performers meant I had an immense opportunity. A single question, if used wisely, could make the difference between success and failure.

Ma Hualong then concluded, "At the end of this round, the original recipe will be revealed. The five contestants who produce the closest product and recipe will advance to the finals, where the champion of this year's Gauntlet will be decided."

The gravity of his words filled the room with a palpable tension. This was it— the moment we had all been working toward. Despite the burdens I carried, the excitement of seeing my goal so close was electrifying.

The door to the arena opened, and we filed out in a line. I could see Zhi Ruo ahead of me, deep in thought and muttering to himself.

As we were led from the lounge to the arena, my thoughts were a whirlwind. But amid these thoughts, something else caught my attention. In the middle of the arena, Ma Hualong was introducing an unexpected late addition to the panel of judges.

"The Alchemy Association is pleased to welcome a distinguished alumni member as a judge for this crucial round," Ma Hualong announced, his voice carrying over the hushed crowd. "Master Lei Ren!"

I pumped my fist quietly, realizing my ploy had worked. Tao Ren's father would act as a judge. Not only to counteract Elder Wei Lian's bias against Jingyu Lian, but also as an impartial party through and through. This was the break I needed. With him, I wouldn't have to worry so much about the clan conflicts among the Jian family!

The arena was a hive of activity. Spectators filled the stands, their murmurs and whispers creating a low hum that underscored the tension in the air. The ten remaining contestants took their places at their respective stations, each one equipped with the tools and ingredients we would need.

The stations were arranged in a circle, each facing inward. The only items on the stations at the moment were a brush and paper, waiting for us to begin. Ma Hualong continued his explanation as envelopes were distributed to each contestant.

"You are not to open the envelopes until I say so," he instructed. "You will be given thirty minutes to analyze the recipe inside and create a list of ingredients and tools you require. Once your lists are approved, you will have one hour to create the product. Remember, the top three performers from the previous round can ask me one question each, which I will answer with a simple yes or no."

"Do any of you have questions?" Ma Hualong asked, his gaze sweeping over us. Silence filled the arena, the tension almost suffocating.

Before we began, I took a longer glance at Jingyu Lian. Her body language was tense, her eyes dark and sunken. She gazed at the envelope with an expression that spoke volumes. She seemed to know what was inside, or perhaps feared it.

I couldn't help but wonder about the insider her father mentioned. How had they managed to ensure she had the answers without being detected? The number of perceptive cultivators and alchemists present made it seem impossible to cheat.

He swept a hand over the stations where envelopes awaited. "Inside, you'll find a fragmented recipe, a relic from a dark time. Centuries ago, demonic cultivators unleashed a plague carried by violet rain. The Amethyst Plague, they called it. By targeting the meridians, it turned skin a sickly purple, brought high fevers, hemorrhaging, dysentery, and inevitably, an agonizing death. No one was spared, neither cultivator nor commoner."

Ma Hualong's delivery was on point. He must've been a storyteller, or some sort of government official in a past life. Considering how articulate he is, no wonder they have him as the main announcer and coordinator. He had the entire crowd hanging on his every word.

"The greatest alchemists of that era joined forces," the man continued, his voice filled with respect. "They toiled day and night to create a remedy, a way to counteract the rain's poison. This recipe you hold? It's a piece of that legacy. A testament to what alchemy can achieve in the face of despair. The basis of most antidotes were formed by this recipe.

"It saved lives. Lives that would shape the future of alchemy itself. Among them a young boy named Zhang Wei. The very same Zhang Wei who, years later, would go on to found the Alchemy Association we know today." He gestured to the waiting envelopes. "This round is about more than just creating a product. It's about honoring the past, about understanding the very foundation of our art. Analyze the recipe, create your ingredient list, and remember—the weight of history rests on your mortar and pestle."

A reverent hush fell over the crowd. Lei Ren seemed to nod in approval at his speech, like a particularly proud father. Now that I thought of it, hadn't he mentioned that Ma Hualong was his student once upon a time? How *old* was Tao Ren's father?

Ma Hualong's voice cut through my thoughts. "You may now open your envelopes."

This was it—the challenge that would determine my place in the finals.

# CHAPTER FORTY-FIVE

# A Recipe in Pieces

And you want me to help with this? Why?"

I had swallowed, the dryness in my throat making the words stick. Lei Ren, dwarfed by the high-backed chair in his opulent Jade Harmony suite, was a mountain in repose. His reaction to the whispered conspiracy, however, was not the eruption I feared. He hadn't seemed surprised when I spilled the situation to him.

"Because of your influence," I pressed on, my hands clenching and unclenching in my lap. "I've seen how the other judges defer to you. Elder Wei Lian's bias . . . With you there, it'd be harder for him to sway the results."

Lei Ren had stroked his beard, snowy white against the silver of his robes. "Hm. If my fool of a son hadn't washed out, I'd have to refuse on principle. Judging kin . . . messy business." His sharp eyes flicked to Tao Ren, who beamed back unashamedly.

"What of the girl, then?" Lei Ren continued, his voice a low rasp. "Jingyu Lian. You heard her father gift-wrapping her the answers. Why not expose her now, be done with it?"

My gaze met his, Jingyu Lian's conflicted voice echoing in my memory. "I want to give her a chance. To prove her own skill, not her father's underhandedness. But if she uses the envelope, then yes, exposure is the only fair outcome."

"To clarify, Kai here fancies the girl," Tao Ren had piped up then, leaning forward with a shit-eating grin. "Doesn't want to see her disqualified without goo—mmmph!"

I clamped a hand over his mouth, my cheeks burning. "Apologies, Master Lei Ren."

He merely waved a dismissive hand. "Puppy love," he grunted, not unkindly. "But not my concern. My concern is, what do I get out of this?"

"Dad, come on! He's my friend!" Tao Ren protested, wriggling out from under my hand.

"Hush, boy," his father chided. "Friendship is fine, but business is business."

Of course. Dealing with the Azure Silk Trading Company, the Silent Moon, and even the Verdant Lotus Sect . . . everything in the Jianghu was about give and take. What could I, an alchemist with only potential to his name, have offered a man like Lei Ren? My thoughts churned for a moment.

"I understand, Master Lei Ren. This is a favor, and favors must be repaid. Right now, I may not have much to offer. But that's only now."

Letting my words sink in, I continued and met his gaze head-on. "I am the holder of the Essence Extraction skill. With the path I walk, I will have the means to repay any debt I incur. Tenfold, if that's what it takes."

Lei Ren's eyebrows had risen, a glint of amusement in his eyes. "Bold words, young man. But are you sure you want to owe a debt to someone like me? I have a reputation for . . . extracting my due."

I hadn't flinched. "From what I've seen of your son," I replied, a hint of a smile playing on my lips, "I believe you to be a man of honor, Master Lei Ren. And a man of honor keeps his word, just as I intend to keep mine."

For a long moment, he was silent. Then, a deep chuckle rumbled from his chest, shaking his whole body. "Audacity," he said, a smile finally cracking his stern facade. "I like it. Very well, Kai Liu. I will help you. But remember"—his voice turned serious—"you owe me. And debts must be paid."

Relief had flooded through me, but I knew this was only the beginning.

Now the conversation echoed in my mind as I divided my attention between the fragmented recipe in my hand and Master Lei Ren, seated among the other judges. He was an unmovable presence, a silent sentinel watching over Jingyu Lian as she delicately broke the seal on the envelope. Would he catch the slightest tremor in her hand, the flicker of her eyes as she glimpsed the forbidden knowledge within?

Her face was pale, the porcelain skin stretched taut over high cheekbones. With trembling fingers, she unfolded the paper inside the envelope, her eyes scanning the contents for a heart-stopping moment.

What was she thinking? Would she succumb to temptation, betraying her own pride and skill for a hollow victory?

I left it in her hands. I had done what I could.

Jingyu Lian regarded Elder Wei Lian, who sat in the center of the arena, a smug smirk twisting his lips. A muscle twitched in her jaw, and something sparked within her eyes.

Then, with a deep breath, she opened the envelope, letting all the scattered pieces of the recipe fall before crushing the envelope with one hand and tossing it away.

Ma Hualong's voice cut through my thoughts. "Kai Liu, it would be wise to focus on the recipe in front of you rather than the other contestants."

I flushed with embarrassment, realizing I had been caught staring. "Sorry," I mumbled, quickly turning my attention back to my station. But I couldn't help but smile, seeing that happen. I'd be facing Jingyu Lian at her best, and that was how I wanted it to be.

I took a deep breath, trying to clear my mind and focus. The doubts and worries about her faded, replaced by the anticipation of the task ahead. I could do this. I had to.

With a steady hand, I opened the envelope and pulled out the paper inside. It was torn to pieces, much like Jingyu Lian's and the other contestants'. I'd need to put them together and get an understanding of how much of the recipe is missing.

The recipe pieces were torn into similarly-sized squares, each one a fragment of the whole. It was like putting together a puzzle. I took a moment to steady my breathing, then got to work. My hands moved swiftly, my focus narrowing to the task before me. Within seconds, I had pieced the fragments together.

The title of the recipe, Violet Bloom Antidote, stood out clearly. But as I scanned the rest of the page, my heart sank. Most of the ingredients were missing, and bits and pieces of the steps were too fragmented to make out clearly. This would be a challenge.

I muttered the title under my breath, trying to commit it to memory. Violet Bloom Antidote. With so many pieces missing, I'd need to rely on my intuition and knowledge.

Ma Hualong's voice resonated in the arena. "Remember, the top three performers from the previous round can ask me one question each, which I will answer with a simple yes or no."

This was my chance. I needed to use my question wisely.

The fragments of the recipe were scattered across my station, each one a clue to the final product. I picked up the brush and started to write down what I knew so far, a way of visualizing what I'd need.

The known ingredients so far was wolfsbane and Bloodthorn Seeds. The former was a potent poison, but when processed, it turned into a medicine that could combat fevers. The latter ingredient, however, was troubling since the only recipe I knew it was used for was the forbidden Blood-Bursting Pill, which was as dangerous as it sounded.

I wanted to rip my hair out in frustration. This was harder than I thought it'd be!

Filled with broken sentences cleverly taking out the names of the ingredients, they still read out words that would glean some clues onto what the other ingredients potentially were.

"... until it is charred. So there's two ingredients, both of which need to be charred."

Charred ingredients often meant activated charcoal. I recalled Ma Hualong mentioning this antidote providing a foundation build upon for alchemy. Activated charcoal was a key component, preventing poison from being absorbed from the stomach into the body, used in most antidotes today. Now I had to figure out which herbs were used in the process to make this activated charcoal.

I needed to focus. I closed my eyes and entered my Memory Palace, where I stored all the herbal knowledge I had accumulated over the years. Ma Hualong had mentioned the symptoms of the Amethyst Plague: purple skin, high fevers, hemorrhaging, and dysentery. I mentally sifted through the myriad of herbs I had archived, searching for ones that could counteract these symptoms.

Rare ingredients were unlikely since the antidote had to be distributed widely. It had to be something common, accessible to all. I homed in on two candidates that fit the bill: lotus rhizomes and skullcaps. Both were known for their detoxifying properties and were common enough to be used in an antidote distributed throughout the province.

With my choices made, I opened my eyes, exiting my Memory Palace. I didn't have time to hesitate. My instincts and experience as an herbalist would have to guide me.

I picked up my brush and wrote down the ingredients.

My eyes flitted over to the rest of the competition. Bai Hua seemed completely at ease, humming to himself as he looked over the recipe with a critiquing eye. I was surprised; of all the contestants, I thought he'd be struggling the most.

But never mind that! I needed to focus. If those two were combined to make activated charcoal, then that left only two ingredients to figure out.

My eyes caught a crucial fragment in the steps that mentioned slicing. This had to be important. The only herb that I could think of was ginseng.

As Elder Zhu said, when in doubt, use ginseng. It *was* a pretty versatile herb, after all.

Raising my hand, I caught Ma Hualong's attention. As soon as he walked up to my station, I asked, "Master Ma, is one of the ingredients ginseng?" Tension gnawed at me.

He didn't answer for a brief moment, his brow furrowing slightly. "No," he finally replied.

Confusion overtook me. *No? But ... Elder Zhu's advice ... The slicing ... It all pointed to ginseng!* Had I been too hasty? A cold dread trickled down my spine. What if I was wrong about everything? I squeezed my eyes shut, trying to banish the wave of self-doubt. There had to be another herb, another answer.

My mind raced, sifting through my knowledge of herbs. Honeysuckle? No, that was more for tonics. Moonlit Grace Lily? Too rare and difficult to obtain for a widespread antidote. Frustration gnawed at me. The clock was ticking, and I was running out of time.

Then it hit me—dandelion root. Of course! While not as potent as ginseng, it was known to enhance the detoxifying properties of other herbs, making it a valuable addition to any antidote. Plus, it was incredibly common, growing practically everywhere, and the root needed to be carefully sliced to prepare it properly. It fit perfectly within the context of the recipe.

A small smile tugged at my lips. Of course. Sometimes, the simplest solutions were the most effective. The Violet Bloom Antidote wasn't meant to be a luxurious concoction for the elite; it was a remedy for the masses, and dandelion root was the perfect embodiment of that principle.

As I scanned the remaining fragments of the recipe, I noticed that the final steps were blocked out, preventing me from determining whether the antidote was intended to be a pill or an elixir. Given the historical context, I recalled that elixirs were more common before the convenience of pills became widespread. Elixirs were particularly favored for their ease of consumption, especially by the elderly and young children. If this targeted people in varying stages of the Amethyst Plague, then they'd have to consider the mode of delivery for those who were too weak to chew.

With that in mind, I decided to list the final ingredient as distilled water. It made sense—water was essential in the preparation of an elixir, providing a medium for dissolving and mixing the ingredients thoroughly.

I picked up my brush again and wrote down *distilled water* as the final ingredient. The list was now complete:

*Wolfsbane, Bloodthorn Seeds, lotus rhizomes, skullcaps, dandelion root, and distilled water.*

Why did I feel like I was missing something? Ma Hualong's pause when he answered my question. It felt like there was a "but" that he'd wanted to say but couldn't.

The ingredients seemed to cover all the symptoms and stages of the Amethyst Plague. The combination of immediate symptom relief, toxin absorption, and blood cleansing made this a comprehensive antidote. Even the Bloodthorn seeds made sense, capable of breaking down blood alongside the poison which reached the bloodstream. It was designed to combat the plague at every level, from the initial infection to the severe, life-threatening stages.

But Ma Hualong's hesitation still nagged at me. Had I overlooked something crucial?

I glanced at the other contestants. I know they already used their questions as well. Zhi Ruo was furiously scribbling notes, his face a mask of concentration. Jingyu Lian was calm, her eyes focused on her recipe with a determination that matched my own.

There was no time to second-guess myself. I had to trust in my knowledge and my instincts. The pieces of the recipe were coming together, and now it was time to put them to the test.

Ma Hualong's voice rang out again, breaking through my thoughts. "Stop! The preparation time has finished. Invigilators will be coming over to note down the ingredients you need. Specify what ingredients you require, and prepare your stations for the next stage of this round!"

I cracked my knuckles and sighed.

This was the final stretch. I couldn't lose focus here!

# CHAPTER FORTY-SIX

# The Color of Mastery

As the invigilators filed into the arena, their arms laden with trays of ingredients, a hush fell over the crowd. My heart pounded in my chest as I scanned the approaching figures, eager to see the components I'd requested.

Each invigilator stopped at a contestant's station, carefully placing down the requested ingredients. My eyes landed on an invigilator who was struggling with an unusually large tray. It was piled high with an assortment of ingredients—many of which didn't make sense for this specific antidote. Herbs and roots either too exotic or unrelated to the symptoms we were combating. My brows furrowed in confusion and curiosity.

There was only one person in this competition I knew who would request such an eclectic mix, and I wasn't surprised when the invigilator stopped in front of Bai Hua's station, gently setting down the cumbersome tray.

While the rest of us were focused on the straightforward path, he was off exploring uncharted territory. Though, I'm not sure how well it'd be rewarded this round.

My own ingredients had arrived, neatly arranged in front of me. Wolfsbane, Bloodthorn Seeds, dandelion root, lotus rhizomes, skullcaps, and distilled water. I took a deep breath, my mind sharpening with determination. There was no room for error; I had to follow the recipe as closely as possible while improvising where necessary.

"I should start with this . . ."

The clock was ticking, and I knew that every second counted. I began with the charring process, carefully controlling the heat to ensure the lotus rhizomes and skullcaps reached the perfect consistency for activated charcoal.

As the herbs charred, I moved to the next step, soaking the wolfsbane in water. The pill furnace roared to life, boiling the wolfsbane as I taste-tested it to ensure the toxins were fully neutralized. The bitterness gradually faded, a sign that the poison was being effectively removed. Although this round was difficult, It still dealt with herbs. I was in my element.

The steady rhythm of my tasks was almost hypnotic, each step flowing seamlessly into the next. I couldn't afford to rush. Each step had to be executed with care and accuracy. The wolfsbane was finally ready, and I carefully drained it, setting it aside.

The next would be the most challenging yet: the Bloodthorn Seeds. They were volatile, their properties teetering on the edge of medicine and poison. But then again, so were most of the ingredients here.

I was unfamiliar with them. What did I need Bloodthorn Seeds for when I was only dealing with common, everyday ailments as the village herbalist?

Processing them correctly was critical; one misstep could turn the antidote into a lethal concoction. The recipe didn't specify how to prepare them, only mentioning their incorporation into the final product. But that was no problem. I stretched my arms and wrist, loosening myself up before taking on the task.

With a swift movement, I grabbed the quartz mortar and pestle and began crushing them. It would neutralize some of its effects. The seeds broke down into a fine powder under the steady pressure.

I let the crushed seeds soak in distilled water, carefully monitoring the process to ensure they dissolved properly. While the seeds soaked, I turned my attention back to the steaming process for the charcoal. It was time to turn up the heat on the stove, allowing the steam to dehydrate them back into a fine powder and completing the process.

As the steam rose and the herbs dried, I could feel the intensity of the competition around me. The charcoal was ready, a deep, dark hue that promised potency. I set it aside, making sure it was finely ground and ready for the next step.

Next, I began combining the prepared ingredients.

I added the charred lotus rhizomes and skullcaps to the pill furnace, integrating them slowly to avoid clumping. The mixture took on a rich, inky shade, the colors blending perfectly as planned. The activated charcoal combined with the Bloodthorn Seeds created a strong base, capable of absorbing toxins and purifying the blood.

All around me, the other contestants were reaching a critical stage in their recipes. Everyone seemed to have similar ingredients, except for Bai Hua, who was doing something entirely different. But I couldn't afford to be distracted. I refocused on the task at hand, knowing that the final steps required my utmost attention.

The wolfsbane, now free of toxins, was ready to be incorporated. I added it to the mixture in the pill furnace, carefully blending it with the other ingredients.

The dandelion root followed, sliced thin and precise, adding its immune-boosting properties to the antidote. The distilled water came last, binding the ingredients into a smooth, consistent elixir.

With the final ingredients added, I watched the mixture closely. The color deepened, a rich, dark hue that signified the potency of the antidote.

Now I just had to wait.

After several minutes, I opened the pill furnace to reveal the steaming liquid within.

I peered into the pill furnace. The mixture had a deep, dark hue, but something felt off. I referenced the recipe and the step I was supposed to be on, where it described the mixture taking on a deep, murky violet color. Instead, what I had was a darker brown with a purple tone. I stirred the mixture, ensuring there were no clumps that hadn't integrated fully with the elixir, but there was none.

Panic welled up in my chest. I must have messed up one of the ingredients, but I didn't have time to pinpoint the exact mistake.

"Thirty minutes left!"

It was too late to change anything.

I forced myself to stay calm, convincing myself that the recipe might still work. Even if I wasn't perfectly accurate, it was enough on its own. I couldn't add any more ingredients. I just had to forge through and make sure I was perfect everywhere else.

I took a deep breath, focusing on the next crucial step: the filtration process. I placed a coarse filter over the container, ready to strain out the larger particles. Carefully, I poured the mixture through, watching as it flowed steadily, leaving behind the unwanted debris. The liquid that emerged was clearer but still far from perfect.

Next, I grabbed a piece of fine cloth, folding it over several times to create a dense filter for the finer particulates. The process was painstakingly slow, but essential for the purity of the antidote.

I couldn't help but think how much easier this would be with Essence Extraction. When collecting the essence of an ingredient, it didn't come with impurities. But that was off-limits here. Accuracy and adherence to traditional methods were the rules of this round. No shortcuts, no advanced techniques. Just skill and precision.

With the final minutes ticking away, I carefully poured the finished elixir into a small vial, sealing it tightly. I examined my finished product: a clear liquid, free of impurities but dark blue rather than the intended violet.

It was done.

"Contestants, step forward and place your antidotes, as well as your recipe, on the table."

We obeyed, and everyone placed their products on the table. Seven of them were pills, and three were in vials. As we proceeded to stand in a line, the judges came forward to analyze our works with a critical eye.

Lei Ren, Wei Lian, and Elder Mingmei walked around the table, reading out the interpreted recipes and picking up the individual products and discussing among themselves. But soon, all the judges started converging on one side of the table.

"Bai Hua, this recipe of yours is quite . . . different. May I ask about your thought process?" Elder Wei Lian said, analyzing the vial in his hand.

The perfumer stepped forward with a flourish, bowing his head in respect. "I confess, I am not a scholar of ancient recipes. The past, while fascinating, holds little interest for me. I prefer to forge my own path, to explore the uncharted territories of alchemy. Which is why I took some . . . liberties when interpreting the recipe."

Elder Mingmei's eyes narrowed, her voice sharp and unyielding. "You are quite arrogant in thinking you can do better than the ancient recipe when you have so much to learn. Alchemy is not merely about creativity; it is about understanding and respecting the wisdom of those who came before us."

Undeterred by the stern rebuke, he met her gaze with calm defiance. "Elder Mingmei, I mean no disrespect to the ancients. I respect your adherence to tradition, but must we be forever bound by the past? Tradition is the foundation, but innovation is the fragrance that captivates the senses. Don't you agree?"

The crowd murmured in response, and a mix of curiosity and skepticism rippled through the audience.

Bai Hua continued to speak, explaining his chosen ingredients to the judges. Blooming Wisteria, Good Morning Roses . . . all nontraditional ingredients. But it was ingenious in its own way.

His voice filled with conviction. "By utilizing the properties of Blooming Wisteria and Good Morning Roses, I created a diffusion method that allows the antidote's effects to spread over a wide area. This makes it much more practical for treating large groups of people quickly, especially in an outbreak scenario where time is of the essence."

Despite this sounding good in practice, Lei Ren was not easily swayed. "While the method of application is innovative," he said, his tone measured, "the antidote itself is lacking when it comes to dealing with the effects of the Amethyst Plague. While useful in other contexts, Blooming Wisteria and Good Morning Roses lack the potency needed to combat the Amethyst Plague."

His words were indifferent and unfeeling, and Bai Hua looked down in embarrassment.

"You may disregard the knowledge and history of alchemy," he continued, his gaze firm on Bai Hua, "but it is not a playground for whimsical experimentation.

It is a discipline rooted in centuries of knowledge and tradition. While innovation is important, it must not come at the expense of foundational principles."

The judges all nodded in response.

Bai Hua's confident facade faltered for a moment, humbled by Lei Ren's critique. "I understand, Master Lei Ren," he said, bowing his head.

He slipped back into line, and the other judges began to take notice of the product beside Bai Hua's. Mine.

"Kai Liu, could you explain your reason as to why you used distilled water in your recipe?"

I took a deep breath, trying to calm my nerves. "Yes, Elder Wei Lian," I began. "I used distilled water because, historically, elixirs were more commonly used than pill forms. An elixir is easier to consume, especially for the elderly, babies, and those too weak to chew a pill. It ensures that the antidote can be administered quickly and effectively to those who need it the most."

The judges nodded approvingly, their expressions thoughtful. I felt a small surge of confidence, but it was short-lived.

Lei Ren's voice cut through the silence. "Kai Liu, your reasoning for using an elixir is sound. However, I must ask about the elixir's color. The name 'Violet Bloom Antidote' implies a specific coloration, yet your elixir is dark blue. Why is that?"

I swallowed hard, trying to formulate my response carefully. "I believe it is likely due to an incorrect ingredient choice," I admitted. "I followed the recipe as best as I could interpret it, but I must have chosen a substitute that affected the final color."

"Can you pinpoint where in the recipe you went wrong?"

I shook my head slowly, feeling the weight of my own uncertainty. "No, Master Lei Ren. I cannot say for certain where I made the mistake."

There was a moment of silence, the air thick with anticipation. Lei Ren's eyes bore into mine, searching for any hint of understanding. Finally, he spoke again, his tone both instructive and challenging.

"Kai Liu, alchemy is as much about precision as it is about intuition. Your work shows promise, but there is a crucial lesson here. The Bloodthorn Seeds, while essential, are highly volatile. Their correct preparation is critical. Their properties, while breaking down the toxin in the bloodstream, also risk leaving the patient severely weakened due to blood loss. Your antidote is effective in curing the Amethyst Plague, but it lacks an element to support blood regeneration after the seeds have run their course."

The realization hit me like a bolt of lightning. Of course! How could I have forgotten that?

"But the rest of the work shows promise," Elder Wei Lian interjected smoothly. "The rest of the ingredients were sound, made with care and precision. Your elixir, though not perfect, demonstrates a strong affinity toward herbs and an understanding of their properties. Your decision to use an elixir form is commendable and shows your consideration for those who might have difficulty consuming a pill."

The compliments felt hollow, knowing that I had missed a crucial aspect of the antidote. I glanced at Elder Wei Lian, aware that his praise might have ulterior motives, possibly using me to undermine Jingyu Lian. This awareness dulled the satisfaction of his words, but I accepted them with a polite bow.

"Thank you, Elder Wei Lian," I said, keeping my tone respectful.

I stepped back as the rest of the products were judged. None of them had the same reaction as mine or Bai Hua's. The judges' reactions were measured, their critiques thorough but fair. Zhi Ruo's got a lukewarm reception, with the only comment being the pill's lack of purity. It wasn't until they reached the last remaining product, where they had a notable reaction. In a vial unlike my own, it boasted a bright purple hue.

"Jingyu Lian, among the contestants so far, yours is the only one to fit the recipe's name in its entirety. Do you know why?"

She nodded, stepping forward. "When female ginseng is used in combination with the processed wolfsbane, it will cause a reaction that amplifies each ingredient's effects, turning the mixture into a violet hue," she explained confidently. "The female ginseng enhances the restorative properties of the wolfsbane while also acting as a stabilizer for the volatile Bloodthorn Seeds."

*Ginseng? But I thought . . .*

The judges exchanged glances, their faces clearly showing approval and surprise. Elder Wei Lian, seizing the opportunity to criticize, leaned forward with a scrutinizing expression. "Your mixture may have the correct color and impressive synergy, but there are several aspects of your recipe that raise concerns. For instance, the female ginseng's interaction with wolfsbane might intensify the antidote's potency, but it also increases the risk of adverse effects if not precisely measured."

He paused, letting his words sink in before continuing. "Furthermore, your choice to use dried female ginseng instead of fresh may have compromised the overall efficacy of the antidote. Dried herbs lose some of their essential oils and active compounds, reducing their medicinal strength."

Jingyu Lian maintained her composure, though her eyes flickered with a hint of frustration. "The dried form was sufficient. A true alchemist adapts to the resources at hand."

Lei Ren intervened with a calm and authoritative tone. "Despite Elder Wei Lian's valid points, it is evident that you possess a well-rounded understanding of alchemy, Jingyu Lian. Your ability to balance the interactions between the ingredients and achieve the intended color demonstrates your skill."

He turned to address all the contestants. "This competition is not just about following a recipe; it is about understanding the principles behind each ingredient and anticipating their effects. Innovation and tradition must coexist harmoniously. Jingyu Lian, your antidote is impressive, but remember that even a slight miscalculation can have significant consequences."

I stood there, watching her as she returned back to the line with her head held high. If I had to guess, she had the best one yet. The judges' deliberations continued, their discussions growing more animated as they compared the various antidotes. I could see Elder Wei Lian point between my and Jingyu Lian's product. Lei Ren seemed unfazed, crossing his arms and talking quietly.

The minutes felt like hours, as they concluded their judgements. Ma Hualong came forward, looking off into the distance and inclining his head toward someone from the entrance. Two invigilators rushed out, carrying an item covered in fine purple silk. Once they arrived at the center, the man spoke in a booming voice.

"In this round of the Gauntlet, the judges have evaluated each antidote based on its adherence to the recipe, its effectiveness, and the alchemical skill demonstrated. The contestant who has shown the most promise and has crafted the most effective antidote is Jingyu Lian!"

A raucous round of applause resounded throughout the arena. She closed her eyes, almost sagging in relief.

# A Recipe for Retribution

I clapped along politely, biting down on the rush of disappointment and the slightest hint of regret.

But between the regret of losing honorably and winning disgracefully, I knew I'd choose the former a hundred times over.

Well, maybe ninety-nine times. Sometimes I got tempted by the easy way out.

Ma Hualong promptly removed the silk covering the mystery item, revealing what was hidden underneath.

A thin glass vial containing an intense violet color.

"Behold," Ma Hualong announced, "the original Violet Bloom Antidote. Made of wolfsbane, Bloodthorn seeds, activated charcoal made from lotus rhizomes and skullcap, distilled water, and one final key ingredient."

My heart quickened. Wolfsbane, Bloodthorn seeds, activated charcoal—these were all key ingredients that I had guessed correctly. It strengthened my case for making it to the final round, but I was inwardly curious about the last remaining ingredient. Could Jingyu Lian have been correct about the female ginseng?

"The last ingredient," he said, building suspense, "is angelica root, otherwise known as female ginseng."

I cursed silently, realizing my mistake. I had been peripherally aware of it, but more familiar with its other name as female ginseng. That explained why Ma Hualong had paused when I asked my question on whether or not ginseng was included in the recipe.

"Jingyu Lian," Ma Hualong said, turning toward her with a respectful nod, "you were the only contestant to correctly identify the final ingredient. Could you explain how you came to this conclusion?"

"While unrelated to ginseng, it's equally valuable, particularly in women's health for centuries. As a powerful blood tonic, it enhances the efficacy of wolfsbane, a key component of the antidote." She paused, her gaze sweeping over the judges. "Through extensive research and a fortunate familiarity with women's health practices, I was able to deduce its inclusion in this formula."

The judges nodded approvingly, impressed by her depth of knowledge and the grace with which she handled her victory. Elder Wei Lian clapped along politely, but his smile didn't reach his eyes.

I couldn't help but notice Jingyu Lian's reaction was subdued despite her triumph. She kept glancing at the latest addition among the judges, her gaze lingering with an indescribable emotion. Was it suspicion?

Lei Ren, maintaining his stoic demeanor, finally spoke. "Jingyu Lian, your understanding of the ingredients and their interactions is commendable. Your ability to draw connections from your research to this ancient recipe demonstrates both skill and insight. Alchemy is not just about knowledge but also about precision and adaptability. You have shown both today."

Jingyu Lian bowed slightly, acknowledging Lei Ren's words. "Thank you, Master Lei Ren. I will strive to continue learning and refining my skills."

The judges continued their deliberations, and the tension in the arena was palpable. Ma Hualong stepped forward again, his expression serious. "The contestants who have qualified for the final round, based on their skill, knowledge, and the effectiveness of their antidotes, are as follows."

He paused.

"Second place goes to Kai Liu."

I smiled as I stepped forward. I was only one ingredient short, but I had made it. The applause felt like a validation of my efforts.

Third and fourth place went to Tian Zhu and Fang Xiang, perennial high-performers since the first round. I eyed them, seeing their elation upon qualifying. The remaining contestants fidgeted, looking among each other for who would be selected. Bai Hua seemed resigned, closing his eyes with a sad smile on his face.

The final spot hung in the balance. Ma Hualong finally announced, "The fifth and last spot goes to . . . Zhi Ruo."

The librarian's eyes widened in surprise, and he stepped forward, bowing deeply to the judges.

Bai Hua, who stood just outside the qualified group, took his elimination with grace. He approached both me and Zhi Ruo, shaking our hands warmly.

"Congratulations to both of you," he said sincerely. "I wish you the best of luck in the final round. I'll be watching in the stands with Tao Ren."

He glanced over in the crowd. A certain loudmouthed blacksmith was whooping and hollering from the stands.

"Thank you, Bai Hua," I replied, shaking his hand firmly. "I'll win for you!"

Zhi Ruo added, "Yes, best of luck to you in your future endeavors."

Regardless of his loss, he certainly made his mark on the audience. The Summer Sun Cosmetics made their debut with a resounding impact here in the Gauntlet. Perhaps I could ask Bai Hua for a discount? I think everyone from back home would enjoy what he had to offer.

Ma Hualong addressed the qualified contestants once more. "You have all shown great promise and skill to reach this stage. However, the final round will be the most challenging yet. It will take place in three days, not only to give us time to prepare the Marble Jade Arena but also to ensure you are ready for what lies ahead."

He paused, his gaze intense. "Do not take these three days as an opportunity to relax. The final round will test you in ways you have not yet imagined. It will be both dangerous and intense. Prepare yourselves accordingly."

The warning sent a shiver down my spine, filling me with a mixture of nervousness and excitement. What could the final round possibly entail? I was dying to know!

*Maybe I should eavesdrop on Jingyu Lian and her father again . . . Ha!*

As we were dismissed, I couldn't help but ponder the upcoming challenge. I knew I had to make the most of these three days, studying and refining my skills to ensure I was ready for whatever the final round would demand.

I summoned the Heavenly Interface to look at the progress on my most recent quest.

*Quest: Mind Refinement (Breakthrough)*
*—Revise one hundred alchemical recipes and improve upon the processes within your Memory Palace. (36/100)*

I needed to complete this over the next few days. But revising alchemical recipes and improving them was difficult; most of them were already refined to their utmost limit. And even if they weren't, I wasn't at the level where I could spot the areas they could be improved.

But if there was a place where I could learn more recipes, as well as methods to improve them, there was only one in Crescent Bay City.

"Zhi Ruo, would you mind if I used that favor from the first round now?"

Gu Bei, a proud disciple of Narrow Stone Peak, stumbled through the maze-like alleys of Crescent Bay City. The city's labyrinthine layout, with its sudden turns and shadowed recesses, would have been disorienting even for a sober mind. But the trained cultivator was anything but sober.

"Blasted city!" He cursed, nearly tripping over a loose cobblestone. "Can't even walk straight in this maze!"

He hiccupped, a sour smell of cheap wine wafting from his breath.

The alcohol had dulled his senses, making him easy prey for the shadows that seemed to dance around every corner. The din of the night was filled with the chirping of crickets, but Gu Bei could swear he heard the faintest sound of wings flapping and a barely perceptible hiss cutting through the darkness.

"G-get away from me!" Gu Bei hissed, his eyes widening in fear. "Do you know who I am?!"

The paranoia was thick in the air, fueled by both the alcohol and what happened to the rest of the Five Fists.

He hunched over a wall, taking a few seconds to catch his breath. His eyes darted around the narrow alley, struggling to grasp what had just happened.

"What's going on?" he whispered to himself, his voice barely audible over the pounding of his heart. "Who's doing this to me?"

Just then, a streak of light plummeted from the sky, landing squarely on Gu Bei's shoulder. An oil lantern shattered, showering him in hot oil and igniting his robes.

"AIIIIEEE!" Gu Bei shrieked, flailing wildly. He ripped off his burning clothes, the flames licking at his skin as he rolled on the ground in a desperate attempt to extinguish them.

A strangled cry escaped his lips. The lantern's oil clung to his robes, turning them into a fiery shroud. Panic seized him as he clawed at the fabric, each tug met with the agonizing sting of burning flesh. He thrashed in the alley, his movements wild and uncoordinated, the flames casting grotesque shadows on the brick walls.

As he tumbled through the dirt, the sound of his own frantic breathing filled his ears. He finally managed to snuff out the fire, but not before singeing his hair and leaving angry red welts on his skin. Naked and humiliated, Gu Bei staggered to his feet, his eyes darting around the narrow alley.

He could hear the faint flapping of wings and the soft hiss again, making his paranoia spike. The alley opened into a crowded street, and as Gu Bei stumbled out, gasping and naked, the city folk erupted in laughter. Pointing fingers and mocking jeers surrounded him.

"Look at the drunkard!" someone shouted.

"Lost your clothes in a bet?" another mocked.

Gu Bei tried to cover himself with his hands, his face burning with shame. Just as he thought things couldn't get worse, a pair of city guards pushed their way through the crowd.

"Public indecency! You're under arrest!" one guard barked, grabbing Gu Bei roughly by the arm.

"No! You don't understand! I was being chased by—by spirits!" Gu Bei howled, struggling against the guards' grip. But his protests fell on deaf ears as they dragged him away.

High above, in the shadows of a rooftop, Tianyi and Windy watched the spectacle unfold. Tianyi's blue wings shimmered faintly in the moonlight as she communicated her satisfaction through a wave of triumphant feelings to her charge.

The young Wind Serpent, with his pure-white scales glistening, flicked his tail in approval.

Scattered throughout the streets of Crescent Bay City, the rest of the Five Fists shared similar fates. The first lay unconscious in an alley, a pile of heavy roof tiles scattered around him—a clear sign of an "accidental" fall. Farther along, the second disciple was found missing several teeth, trampled by a pair of spooked horses that were now running amok through the streets. A few blocks away, the third and fourth disciples lay buried under a pile of debris and rotting fruit, having crashed into a food stall and a cart full of miscellaneous goods.

Meanwhile, hidden in the shadows, Windy and Tianyi observed the unfolding chaos with a shared sense of satisfaction. It was their doing, of course. A well-placed strike from Windy had caused the scaffolding of the food stall to collapse, a well-timed gust of wind from Tianyi's wings to dislodge roof tiles, and then—instant karma.

The area looked like the aftermath of a drunken rampage. To the casual observer, it seemed like a group of inebriated cultivators had caused havoc, their actions resulting in a series of unfortunate accidents.

Windy raised his head and flicked his tongue into the air, navigating the city with grace and speed, followed by Tianyi from high above. This plan was only possible with the serpent's tracking skills, having an innate ability to find prey he's bitten. Eventually, they made their way back to the first disciple, groaning in a drunken stupor and hanging on to his last thread of consciousness on an empty street.

The serpent crawled over to the man's shaved head, coiling itself around his neck with instinctual precision. Disoriented and barely coherent, he felt the cold scales tightening around his throat. The disciple's eyes widened in terror as he struggled weakly, the grip slowly suffocating him and turning his face an alarming shade of blue.

Before Windy could tighten further, Tianyi flitted down and placed herself on the serpent's snout. She sent a wave of caution and restraint through their telepathic bond. The message was clear.

*It's enough. Let's go.*

Windy, ever the predator, narrowed his eyes in challenge. He could understand the intent, but something primal in him rebelled. Why leave them alive? Why not finish the job? This human was weak, pathetic. An easy kill.

Tianyi sensed his reluctance, a flicker of frustration passing between them. She fluttered in front of his snout, sending a telepathic message of assurance.

*Trust me.*

Windy's eyes flickered to the figure beneath him. He could sense the man's fear, the desperation in his shallow breaths.

A single thought passed through the serpent's mind.

*Why do I obey?*

He knew what he was. A snake. A predator. The natural order dictated that the strong devour the weak, that those who could not defend themselves were nothing more than prey. So why was he here, compliant, obeying a creature smaller and seemingly weaker than himself?

Memories came unbidden, flashing through his young mind like lightning. He remembered the first time he had seen Tianyi's power despite her small stature, rending scars on trees with her wings. It was she who had orchestrated and directed this intricate plan to avenge Kai, guiding him with a precision and foresight that defied her size and appearance.

Tianyi's insistence pushed through again, stronger this time. It resonated with a power that Windy couldn't deny, the pure, untainted energy of a being older and wiser than him. Reluctantly, he uncoiled himself, slithering away from the man's neck. A hiss of warning was his final act of defiance.

The butterfly fluttered ahead, leading the way back to their inn. Windy followed, a sense of unease lingering in his scales. He had conceded this time, but the question remained. Why show mercy to those who would harm them? He would wait, observe, learn. For now, he would trust Tianyi's judgment, but the predator in him was far from satisfied.

As the pair moved swiftly through the shadowed alleys of Crescent Bay City, Tianyi's sharp senses picked up a familiar figure approaching the inn. With a telepathic nudge, she urged Windy to increase his pace. The Wind Serpent, ever agile, scaled the inn's walls with ease, his body hugging the grooves and crevices.

In one fluid motion, the serpent flung open the window, allowing both him and Tianyi to slip inside. Just as they did, Feng Wu walked in, his presence calm and composed.

"I've brought you some food," Feng Wu said, his tone gentle. He poured Tianyi a bowl of sugar and honey water, his face apologetic. "I can't be seen purchasing alcohol as a Taoist, but I hope this will suffice."

Tianyi fluttered her wings appreciatively, the faint shimmer in her gossamer wings conveying her thanks. Windy, meanwhile, was presented with a bunch of rats, which he eagerly began to consume.

As the two Spirit Beasts dove into their respective meals, Feng Wu glanced around the room, his eyes landing on the open window.

"Huh. I guess I must've left it open."

# CHAPTER FORTY-EIGHT

# Study Buddies

As the towering trees of my mind's library shimmered, a wave of exhaustion washed over me. I emerged from my Memory Palace, blinking to the soft glow of sunlight peeking through the windows of the Million Books Pavilion. I glanced over to check at the progress of my quest.

> *Quest: Mind Refinement (Breakthrough)*
> *—Revise one hundred alchemical recipes and improve upon the*
> *processes within your Memory Palace. (55/100)*

Not bad for one night's work, I supposed.

Rubbing my temples, I stretched my stiff limbs and surveyed the scene around me. Dozens of open books lay scattered across the table, their pages filled with intricate recipes and alchemical diagrams.

Across from me, Zhi Ruo remained hunched over his own mountain of books. He hadn't even blinked, it seemed, since I'd last looked up.

The stack of books beside him had grown exponentially. In the time I'd spent within my Memory Palace, it seemed Zhi Ruo had traversed entire libraries. I couldn't help but feel a pang of admiration for his unwavering diligence. The man was a walking encyclopedia.

But something else struck me—the sheer speed at which he was consuming the information. It was like watching a whirlwind devour a scroll, each page a mere blur in his hands. He paused, tapping a finger against his temple as if committing a particularly elusive passage to memory, then resumed his relentless pace.

A thought sparked in my mind, a connection between his rapid reading and my own. *Could it be . . . ?*

"Zhi Ruo," I said, my voice a bit hoarse from disuse. I glanced over at my cup of tea that had gone cold long ago, and drank it to soothe my parched throat.

He startled, his head snapping up from the book. A lock of his unkempt hair fell across his forehead, partially obscuring his baggy eyes, evidence of the late-night cram session we'd both embarked upon.

"Ah, Kai," he replied, his voice raspy and a little bewildered. "Finished your meditation already?"

"Something like that." I chuckled, gesturing toward the mess of books around us. "Do you often pull all-nighters like this?"

He shook his head, a rueful smile touching his lips. "Only when I have to. My wife wouldn't be too happy if I spent all my time holed up in here."

"I can imagine," I said, nodding in sympathy. "But you seem to be making good progress."

A spark of pride flickered in his eyes. "I'm trying my best. This competition is no joke. The only reason I can keep up with the likes of you and the others is because I've been doing this."

He was right; comparing Zhi Ruo of the first round to the one who made the finals was like night and day. He was growing in real time, as his skills grew to match his well of knowledge.

"Indeed," I agreed. Then, taking a deep breath, I decided to broach the subject that had piqued my curiosity. "Zhi Ruo, do you have a skill called Accelerated Reading?"

He froze, his eyes widening slightly. The air crackled with a sudden tension. "What . . . what makes you ask that?"

"Because no one could possibly read this many books in such a short time without it. And, well, I have it too."

A long moment of silence passed. The only sound was the rustling of pages as Zhi Ruo slowly closed the book he was holding. He met my gaze, his eyes narrowed in contemplation.

"Kai," he finally said, his voice low and measured, "why would you think I possess such a skill? It's not exactly common knowledge."

"It's not common knowledge," I agreed, "but it makes perfect sense for someone like you, a librarian of the Million Books Pavilion. And besides," I added with a sly grin, "I'm pretty good at recognizing my own kind."

His lips twitched into a reluctant smile. "I see. Well, I suppose there's no point in denying it. Yes, Kai, I do have it."

I couldn't help but ponder his revelation. Zhi Ruo, a librarian with a hidden talent for Accelerated Reading. It made a strange sort of sense. But why would someone with such a gift choose to participate in the Grand Alchemy Gauntlet?

Leaning forward with genuine curiosity, I asked him a question. "If you don't mind me asking, what prompted you to enter the Gauntlet? Was it the fame? The recognition? The opportunity to showcase your alchemical prowess?"

He shook his head, his smile tinged with wistfulness. "Nothing so grand, I'm afraid. It's simply that . . . I want to provide a better life for my family."

My eyebrows rose in surprise. "Your family?"

"Yes," he replied, his gaze fixed on the worn pages of a book he had picked up. "My wife and children. They deserve more than the meager living I can provide as a librarian. The Gauntlet, with its potential rewards and recognition, offered a chance to change that."

"But surely there are other ways to earn money," I pointed out. "With your skill and knowledge . . ."

He chuckled dryly. "Not as quickly or as reliably as this, Kai. Alchemy is a lucrative profession, and the Gauntlet provides unparalleled exposure. Besides, I've already received offers from a few prominent clans to come under their wing and practice alchemy."

"That's incredible, Zhi! Congratulations."

"Thank you," he said, proud. "It would mean safety, security, and a future for my children. Generational wealth, even. But I know, realistically, I won't win against the likes of you and Jingyu Lian. However, a strong showing in this Gauntlet will give me leverage to negotiate even better offers."

His words resonated with a quiet resolve. He wasn't here for glory or fame; he was fighting for the future of his family. It was a motivation I could understand and respect.

"And you, Kai?" he asked. "What are your plans? With your talent, you'll have plenty of eyes on you, win or lose. Have you considered what you'll do with the attention?"

I hesitated, caught off guard by his question. "I . . . I haven't thought that far ahead," I admitted. "My main goal is to repay the Verdant Lotus Sect for their kindness and guidance. Another thing I had in mind was expanding my shop back home. How does Kai's Emporium sound?"

Zhi Ruo nodded thoughtfully, and he stifled a giggle at the thought of my Emporium. How rude!

"A noble goal," he said. "But life is rarely so simple, Kai. You're young, and you have a unique talent, a gift that could open doors you never imagined. Don't dismiss the opportunities that come your way."

He paused, his gaze unwavering. "If I were you, I'd seriously consider any offers from the Alchemy Association. With your performance here, you could very well end up serving directly under the elders, just as Ma Hualong did when he won the Gauntlet."

I stayed quiet for a moment. The idea of joining the Alchemy Association, growing under their tutelage . . . It would be a life-changer. I'd be set for life!

"Well, regardless of what happens"—I got up, dusting my maroon robes off as I did so—"I know we'll put up our best effort. Do you mind if I come back this evening to study again? Same time?"

"You know where to find me, Kai."

I bade him farewell, carefully putting all the books I read back in their place.

Opening the double-doors leading out of the pavilion, I was greeted with the crisp morning air. The sun, though still low in the sky, cast a golden glow over the city, its light reflecting off the frost that had formed overnight.

Despite the early hour, the streets were already bustling with activity. Merchants were setting up their stalls, hawkers were crying out their wares, and civilians were going about their daily business. As I made my way through the crowds, I couldn't help but overhear snippets of conversation.

"Crazy night, it was," a woman muttered to her companion, shaking her head in disbelief. "A bunch of cultivators, drunk as skunks, tearing up the streets."

"One of 'em got kicked in the face by Old Man Wowang's horses," a nearby man chimed in, chuckling. "Lost a few teeth, he did. Serves him right for being such a rowdy drunkard."

Another voice joined the chorus. "Cultivator or not, there's no training to strengthen your teeth against a horse's hoof . . ."

I stifled a laugh as I moved on. The events of the previous night seemed to have provided the city's gossipmongers with ample fodder for amusement.

As I walked, I noticed several areas where the streets were damaged—overturned carts, broken stalls, and scattered debris. It seemed the drunken rampage had been quite extensive. I shook my head, wondering what could have possessed a group of cultivators to behave in such a reckless manner.

Eventually, I made it back to the Jade Harmony Inn, my mind still buzzing with the events of the morning. The warm, inviting atmosphere of the inn was a welcome contrast to the cold, bustling streets. I knocked on the door leading to my room, and I heard a muffled voice from the other side.

It swung open to reveal Feng Wu, grinning at me.

"Well? How was your time at the Million Books Pavilion?"

"Excellent," I replied, returning Feng Wu's grin. "Zhi Ruo's an excellent study partner, though he sure can read through books fast." I paused for a beat. "Speaking of partners, how are Tianyi and Windy?"

I poked my head in to see Tianyi, who was perched delicately on the windowsill. Windy, coiled comfortably on a cushion, raised his head in greeting.

"They seem to have settled in well. I fed them yesterday, but they're always looking out the window for some reason. Perhaps they want to explore?"

"I have an idea," I said, a plan forming in my mind. "Why don't we all go out for breakfast? It's not good for them to be cooped up in here all the time."

He nodded in approval, and we set out as a group. As we walked, Feng Wu placed a comforting hand on my shoulder.

"I just wanted to say that I'm so proud of you, Kai," he said, his voice filled with warmth. "Your performance in the Gauntlet has been nothing short of extraordinary."

I felt guilt as he spoke. I hadn't told him about Elder Wei's interference or Jingyu Lian's involvement in getting Lei Ren added as a judge. It felt like a betrayal, keeping this from him when he had been nothing but supportive. But the situation seemed to have resolved itself, and I didn't want to cause any unnecessary worry.

"Speaking of the Gauntlet," he continued, "how interesting that Master Lei Ren was one of the judges for this round. I wonder how he ended up on the panel so late?"

I froze, my heart pounding in my chest. Did he know? Had he somehow figured out my involvement in Lei Ren's sudden appearance?

"I . . . I don't know," I stammered, trying to regain my composure. "It was a surprise to everyone, I think."

Feng Wu studied me for a moment, his eyes narrowed slightly. I felt my back dampen with sweat.

"Are you all right, Kai?" he asked, his voice laced with concern. "You seem a little on edge."

I forced a smile, hoping to dispel his suspicions. "Just tired, I guess. All that studying has taken its toll." I quickly changed the subject, gesturing toward a nearby food stall. "What do you think about that place? It looks quite good."

But Feng Wu wasn't so easily distracted. He placed a gentle hand on my arm, halting my progress. "Kai," he said, his voice low and serious, "did you have anything to do with Master Lei Ren's addition to the judges' panel?"

His words pierced through my carefully constructed facade. I opened my mouth to deny it, but the words caught in my throat.

"I . . ." I began, then hesitated.

Feng Wu's eyes softened, and he gave my arm a reassuring squeeze. "Kai," he said gently, "you can tell me anything. You know that, don't you?"

And that was all he needed to say before I cracked.


Elsewhere, in Crescent Bay City, a certain blue-eyed alchemist was sitting across a table beside an old man in pristine, silver robes.

Jingyu Lian spoke, her voice firm but respectful. "Thank you for taking the time to meet with me, Master Lei Ren. It's an honour."

"Spare me the formalities. What do you want?"

She remained in her seat, stiff as a rod. Jingyu Lian took a deep breath, her gaze unwavering as she looked directly into his eyes. "Master Lei Ren," she began, her voice steady, "I need to know the truth. Were you instated as a judge by my father to give me a favorable result?"

The question hung in the air, heavy with implication. The silence that followed was almost unbearable. Lei Ren's expression remained unreadable, his eyes locked onto hers, weighing her words.

# CHAPTER FORTY-NINE

# Wheels Within Wheels

W hy would you think that?" Lei Ren finally asked, leaning back in his chair.

Jingyu Lian met his gaze unflinchingly, her spine straight, her voice steady despite the turmoil of emotions within her. "Your late entry into the judging panel was highly unusual. And throughout the assessment, you consistently countered Elder Wei Lian's influence. It seemed deliberate. As if you were there to ensure fairness. As if you knew Elder Wei Lian would attempt to undermine my efforts."

"And so what if I was?" he challenged, leaning forward.

She bowed her head, her voice steady but laced with emotion. "Master Lei Ren, I respectfully ask you not to interfere. Although I appreciate your willingness to help, I have no desire to win unfairly. I want my victory to be earned through my own efforts, not through manipulation."

For a moment, silence stretched between them, tense and expectant. Then, unexpectedly, the older man burst out laughing, a deep, hearty laugh that echoed throughout the room.

Her head snapped up, her cheeks flushed with a mixture of anger and embarrassment. "What is so amusing?!"

Lei Ren raised a hand, still chuckling. "Forgive me, young alchemist," he said, wiping a tear from his eye. "Your earnestness is refreshing. But let me assure you, Jingyu Lian, your father did not orchestrate my involvement in the Gauntlet."

"Then why . . . ?"

Leaning forward, Lei Ren's eyes gleamed with a predatory intensity. "I was made aware of certain advantages hidden within your envelope. My task was to observe you. If you had succumbed to temptation and utilized those advantages, I would have exposed your dishonesty without hesitation. Your reputation, and that of your clan, would have been irreparably tarnished."

He paused, allowing his words to sink in. "But you didn't. You proved yourself to be a true alchemist, one of integrity and skill. Therefore, I judged your work impartially, as was my duty."

Her confusion only deepened. Jingyu Lian's mind reeled. Someone had gone to great lengths to ensure a fair trial for her. "Who orchestrated this?"

Lei Ren's expression softened slightly, a rare hint of warmth in his eyes. "I won't tell you who, but know this: It was someone with your best interests at heart. Someone who clearly had faith in your integrity and your skills."

Jingyu Lian's thoughts whirled. Someone believed in her so deeply that they went to such lengths to ensure her fair treatment. But who? She couldn't fathom who it might be, and Lei Ren's silence on the matter only added to the mystery.

"But in regards to your request, I'm glad to admit you won't have to worry about my, or anyone's, interference in the finals. I can say that, at least."

She looked at him, searching his face for any hint of deceit; but there was none to be found. She clasped her hands together and bowed deeply, a gesture of respect to the retired alchemist. "Thank you, Master Lei Ren."

"If only my son had your manners . . ." Lei Ren sighed, briefly transforming from a domineering authority figure to an exasperated father. "You are dismissed, Jingyu Lian. May you find success through your own merits."

She bowed once more, her mind a whirlwind of thoughts and emotions as she exited the room.

Who could have orchestrated such intricate measures for her benefit? The possibilities spun through her mind, each more baffling than the last.

As she stepped into the corridor, she was greeted by the familiar figure of her Senior Brother, Tian Zhan; the top genius of the Whispering Wind Sect. His eagle-like eyes scanned her for any signs of stress but were pleased to see her composed.

"Junior Sister," Tian Zhan greeted her. "How did the meeting go?"

Jingyu managed a small smile, though her thoughts were still tangled. "Unexpectedly well. Master Lei Ren assured me that it wasn't my father who arranged his involvement in the Gauntlet."

Tian Zhan frowned, his brow furrowing in confusion. "If not your father, then who? It doesn't make sense. He's the only one with a motive to see you succeed in the Gauntlet. Aside from us, of course. I'm cheering you on!"

She rolled her eyes at the second-class disciple who shot her a thumbs-up. Despite being distant cousins, she likened him to an older brother of sorts. The closest thing she had to a family.

She analyzed every option as they exited the inn.

Who had the motive to protect her from Elder Wei Lian but also expose her if she took her father's instructions and cheated?

*Someone with my best interests at heart . . . Someone who clearly had faith in my integrity and skill.*

Tao Ren? A fellow contestant, and one with a direct connection to Master Lei Ren. But she had never spoken to him throughout the entire competition. She dismissed it.

*Although, he was friends with . . .*

That was when another possibility struck her.

"Kai Liu . . . ?"


"You're really asking for it. One of these days, Kai . . ."

I squirmed in front of Feng Wu. I had told him everything. It was hard not to when he gave me that disappointed look. His face seemed to drain of color the more I told him about Jingyu Lian and her father's conversation.

"Sorry, Feng Wu. I know I should've consulted you, but I knew we were pressed for time. It was—"

He shook his head and poured me a cup of tea, the fragrant steam curling between us. We had chosen the Spirited Noodle, its usual clamor providing a convenient cover for our conversation. The chaotic noise around us was almost comforting. Windy slithered around my robe, his cool scales brushing against my skin as he coiled around my arm, occasionally flicking out his tongue. Tianyi, perched delicately in her cage, sipped sugar water from a small dish provided by the attentive staff who recognized us from previous visits.

"No need to explain, Kai." He sipped his own cup, looking at the center of the restaurant where two men brawled. "You're close friends with Tao Ren. Seeking out someone of authority like Lei Ren to deal with them . . . I can see why you'd do it."

As I breathed a sigh of relief, Feng Wu pierced me with his gaze.

"*But,*" he continued, "putting yourself in between Wei Lian and Lei Lian's schemes? If at any point it had gotten wrong, you would've been facing one or both their ire."

I paused for a moment, and realized that Lei Lian was Jingyu Lian's father in this context. I swallowed, knowing he was right.

"I know, that's why I tried my best to be subtle about it. I didn't confront him at the restaurant for that reason. Do I look like I want to be involved in an 'accident' after overhearing a scheme that could ruin the Lian clan's reputation?"

"Kai, I understand your intentions. Your heart was in the right place, and I can't fault you for wanting to do the right thing. But you must realize that the world of alchemy is fraught with political maneuvering and hidden dangers. One wrong step can cost you everything."

"She deserved a fair chance, just like everyone else."

He leaned back in his chair, studying me intently. "And what if your actions had been discovered? What if Wei Lian had found out about your involvement? He could have destroyed you, Kai. Your reputation, your future in alchemy— everything you've worked for could have been taken away in an instant."

"I didn't think about that at the time. I just wanted to do the right thing."

"What's done is done. But promise me, Kai. Promise me that you won't do something like this again without consulting me first. It's not just your future on the line. You represent the Verdant Lotus Sect, and your actions have consequences for all of us."

"Promise, Feng Wu."

He shook his head, a mixture of exasperation and affection in his eyes. "You did a good job considering the situation. But remember, you can't always do everything on your own. It hasn't been that long since the incident with the Silent Moon. You didn't forget that either, did you?"

Despite the urge to bury myself in a deep hole in the ground, I mustered out a small affirmation before putting my head down, playing with my food.

"So," he continued, leaning forward, "what are your plans for this afternoon?"

"Well, I'll have to go back to the Million Books Pavilion to work on my quest. I need to complete it if I want to stand a chance against Jingyu Lian in the finals. To be honest, she is superior to me in terms of alchemy and I need every advantage I can get."

Feng Wu raised an eyebrow. "What's this quest about again?"

I took a deep breath, thinking about the daunting task ahead. "To improve upon a hundred alchemical recipes within my Memory Palace. The problem is that most recipes are already refined to their utmost limit. And if they aren't, I might not even realize how to improve them. I'm not at the level where I can just make them better in an instant."

If I had a year to do it, then I wouldn't have had a problem. But I wanted to finish this quest before the finals. If my reward for completing my first Mind Refinement quest was the Memory Palace, then whatever it had in store for me would be crucial to defeating her.

"Well, what does the quest classify as an improvement?"

I paused. Checking the quest, it said nothing of what it considered as an improvement. Only to improve upon the processes of the recipe.

"I don't know, I just assumed it meant improving the effect of the end product," I replied. "But the quest doesn't specify any other criteria."

He nodded, a spark of an idea in his eyes. "What about reducing the cost of ingredients? Streamlining the preparation process? Making the recipe more accessible to less experienced alchemists? These are all ways to improve a recipe without changing the end result."

The simplicity and brilliance of his suggestions dawned on me. Why hadn't I thought about that?

"You're right. Those are improvements too. And the Million Books Pavilion must have countless forgotten recipes from different regions that might need those exact kinds of improvements."

Feng Wu smiled. "That's the power of having another mind to cooperate with. Remember, Kai, you're not alone in this. Use the resources and people around you. You'd be surprised at how much it can help."

"Thanks. Actually, I want to try it right now; see if your hypothesis is correct. Do you mind if I . . . ?"

He shook his head and shrugged. "By all means, go ahead. I'll catch any errant bowls flying at you while you're there."

I closed my eyes and did my best to block out the chaos within the restaurant.

The towering trees of my mind's library shimmered as I materialized within my Memory Palace. My focus sharpened, filtering through the vast array of recipes I'd encountered, many of which I had deemed impossible to improve upon regarding the end product. Yet, with Feng Wu's advice echoing in my mind, I began to consider a different approach: efficiency and accessibility.

One recipe caught my eye—a simple herbal remedy for common colds and fevers, often used in local villages. I remembered my initial dismissal of it, thinking there was little room for significant improvement. But now I approached it with a new perspective.

The original process involved multiple stages of preparation—soaking, boiling, and simmering the herbs at different intervals, which was both time-consuming and required constant supervision. As I reviewed the steps, I pinpointed an inefficiency: the soaking stage.

In the recipe, soaking the herbs for several hours was meant to soften them and extract their essence slowly. However, modern methods could accelerate this process. I imagined an infusion technique, using a gentle, continuous heat to expedite the extraction without losing potency. By adjusting the temperature and duration, the soaking and boiling stages could be merged, streamlining the entire preparation.

Satisfied with my improvement, I exited my Memory Palace. Opening my eyes, I saw Feng Wu watching me expectantly.

"Well?" he asked.

I checked the quest status.

> *Quest: Mind Refinement (Breakthrough)*
> *—Revise one hundred alchemical recipes and improve upon the*
> *processes within your Memory Palace. (56/100)*

Exhaling, a smile spread across my face. "It worked. Your idea worked. The Interface classified it as an improvement."

"See? Sometimes it's not about the obvious improvements. Efficiency, accessibility—those matter just as much."

I clasped my hands together and bowed deeply, my voice loud and clear despite the din of the restaurant. "This young master is eternally grateful for the wisdom imparted by Senior Feng Wu!"

The man chuckled, playing along with a mock-serious tone. We exchanged banter for several minutes, the weight of the earlier conversation lifting. With renewed purpose and a light heart, I felt ready to tackle my quest with fresh vigor.

# CHAPTER FIFTY

# Breakthrough

I moved on to the next recipe, letting it unfurl before me.

Entitled the "Sunfire Vitality Elixir," it detailed a concoction said to enhance a cultivator's inner fire and resilience. However, the process was convoluted, requiring precise timing and a complex sequence of heating and cooling cycles.

As I meticulously examined the steps, I kept in mind what I needed to do.

Although the Heavenly Interface didn't have a specific idea in mind for refinement, it seemed to have a quantitative threshold for what constituted an "improvement." Based on my experience with the other recipes, it appeared that a modification needed to enhance the recipe's effectiveness or efficiency by at least 10 percent to be recognized as a valid advancement.

With this in mind, I scrutinized the Sunfire Vitality Elixir recipe, searching for opportunities to optimize the process. The initial step involved simmering a mixture of Sunfire Blade Grass and Bamboo Viper Scale powder for three hours, a time-consuming process that could easily be disrupted by fluctuations in temperature.

Drawing upon my knowledge of modern techniques, I envisioned a modification: utilizing a pill furnace with precise temperature control to reduce the simmering time by half. Furthermore, the recipe called for a specific type of alchemical water, drawn from a secluded spring. While this water was said to enhance the elixir's fire-enhancing properties, it was an unnecessary extravagance. By carefully purifying and distilling ordinary water, I could achieve a similar effect.

I glanced at the quest log in my mind's eye, eager to see if the Heavenly Interface recognized my efforts.

---

*Quest: Mind Refinement (Breakthrough)*
*—Revise one hundred alchemical recipes and improve upon the*
*processes within your Memory Palace. (83/100)*

I couldn't hold back the smile forming on my face. At this rate, I'd be finished by tonight! With time to spare! If I were the sort to indulge, I would've kissed Feng Wu for that advice!

I dove into recipe after recipe, each one a puzzle waiting to be solved. I streamlined, substituted, innovated, and optimized, always with the goal of pushing the boundaries of efficiency and accessibility.

I reviewed the last recipe, the Jade Skin Preservation Pill, a concoction said to maintain a youthful complexion and radiant skin. This was a product within Bai Hua's purview.

However, the process was convoluted, requiring a multiday brewing process.

Armed with the wisdom of Feng Wu and the countless hours of study within my Memory Palace, I saw the recipe with fresh eyes. I identified bottlenecks in the process, unnecessary steps that could be consolidated, and substitutions for rare ingredients that would not compromise the elixir's efficacy.

With a final flourish, I completed my revision, my mind buzzing with the thrill of discovery. As I closed my eyes, the familiar chime of the Heavenly Interface resonated in my mind.

> *Quest: Mind Refinement (Breakthrough) has been completed.*
> *Due to your status as Interface Manipulator,*
> *your rewards will be adjusted accordingly.*

"WOO-HOO!"

Zhi Ruo jumped, almost collapsing a pile of books on top of himself. "*Kai*, please don't do that! You almost gave me a heart attack."

"Never mind that, Zhi! I finished my quest!"

His face changed from irritation to astonishment. "Already? But it's only been four hours!"

"I know, it's all because o—"

> *You feel a surge of clarity.*
> *The intricacies of the world unfold before your inner eye.*
> *Your Mind has advanced to Qi Initiation Stage—Rank 1.*

> *Your Mind is growing more powerful.*
> *You can now utilize the skill Refinement Simulation Technique.*

Like the first time I completed the Mind Refinement quest, I felt my mind expand, the complexities of the recipes and their interactions becoming clearer and more intuitive. I blinked to allow myself some time to readjust.

"I've reached a breakthrough!" I exclaimed, barely able to contain my excitement.

Zhi Ruo blinked, trying to process my sudden outburst. "A breakthrough? You mean—"

"Yes! My mind has advanced to the first rank of the Qi Initiation stage! And I've unlocked a new skill, the Refinement Simulation Technique."

His eyes widened in amazement. "That's incredible, Kai! What does the Refinement Simulation Technique do?"

> *Refinement Simulation Technique (Level 1):*
> *A technique that activates instinctively when refining*
> *begins and heightens awareness. It enables visualization*
> *of the refining process, allowing the alchemist to predict ingredient*
> *interactions and furnace reactions. This technique provides adjustments,*
> *enabling reflexive corrections to prevent instability,*
> *and grants unparalleled control over the refining process.*

"It allows me to simulate and test alchemical refinements mentally before I actually create them," I said, my voice brimming with enthusiasm. "I need to test it out. Is there a place where we can practice alchemy?"

Zhi Ruo frowned thoughtfully. "There is a building near the Alchemy Association, but it's closed right now."

Then a thought struck me. "Wait! What if I use recipes that don't require anything more than simple tools? We don't need a full alchemical lab for that, right?"

"If that's the case, we can use my study room. It has enough space and basic tools for simple alchemical practices. It's what I used to practice for the Gauntlet!"

"Perfect! Lead the way."

Zhi Ruo guided me to his study, a spacious room lined with bookshelves and alchemical tools neatly arranged on wooden tables.

"All right, let's see what this Refinement Simulation Technique can do," I said, taking a deep breath.

Looking at the available ingredients, I could only practice with the most basic of recipes. A certain one came to mind, triggering memories of my challenge against the Silent Moon Sect.

"I'll be making the Spirit Soothing Pill."

Zhi Ruo nodded, helping me collect the ingredients to create it.

As soon as I began, the Refinement Simulation Technique activated reflexively. I felt a heightened awareness of my surroundings, as if I could see an overlay of myself moving, preparing the ingredients, and placing them in the pill furnace. It was an almost surreal experience, like watching a premonition unfold.

In this mental simulation, I was drawn to a peculiar detail: the poor quality of the pill furnace. It made it harder to infuse qi and maintain a constant heat, causing fluctuations that could ruin the entire process. This realization struck me within a split-second, and I slowly came out of my trance.

"Zhi Ruo," I began, turning to him, "have you had difficulties maintaining the temperature of your pill furnace?"

He looked at me, surprised. "Yes, I have. It's because I couldn't afford a high-quality one for training and got this one at a discount. How did you know?"

I explained how the skill allowed me to predict mistakes before they happen.

"That's incredible, Kai," Zhi Ruo said, admiration in his voice. "I've never heard of such a technique before."

I smiled, feeling accomplished. "Let's see if my prediction is right."

I started the process, carefully preparing the ingredients and placing them into the furnace. I adjusted the temperature as needed, compensating for the furnace's flaws and the simple tools. The simulation had shown me the pitfalls, and I navigated around them with ease. As the ingredients began to combine, I felt the process flowing smoothly. The temperature remained stable, and the qi infusion was precise. It seemed that with my breakthrough, my qi manipulation abilities had only gotten sharper.

The furnace, despite its flaws, was no match for the clarity and control the technique provided.

Finally, the Spirit Soothing Pill was complete. I held it up. The pill radiated a soft, calming energy, its surface smooth and flawless.

He examined it, his eyes wide with amazement. "Kai, this is incredible. The quality is exceptional. Your new technique is truly powerful!"

I puffed up my chest, raising my sleeves with an exaggerated flourish. "Oh, this is just the beginning, Zhi Ruo! With this new technique, my alchemical prowess will reach unparalleled heights. Just imagine what I'll be able to achieve!"

Zhi Ruo grinned, catching on to my exaggerated tone. "Oh, do tell, Master Kai. Enlighten this humble scholar with your boundless wisdom."

"No furnace too flawed, no ingredient too stubborn! All will bend to my will!"

The man chuckled, playing along. "Truly, Master Kai, you are destined for greatness. Perhaps the next elixir should be one of immortality, so we can bask in your brilliance for all eternity!"

I laughed, the playful banter lifting the remaining tension from the room. "Indeed, my dear Zhi Ruo. But first, let us test the limits of this technique. What other recipes shall we conquer tonight?"

Zhi Ruo's eyes sparkled with excitement. "Oh, what if we try with . . ."

We spent the rest of the night testing various recipes, each one a new adventure. The Refinement Simulation Technique proved invaluable, turning even the most complex concoctions into manageable tasks. Our laughter and banter filled the study, making the hours fly by.

"Ugh, my head . . ." I moaned, nursing a light headache from all our shenanigans last night.

I sipped on tea, the last product of my Refinement Simulation Technique before we concluded our experiments. The blend of oolong and pu-erh served to keep me alert and energized, despite the lack of sleep. As I sipped, I took a moment to reflect on the discoveries we made with the Refinement Simulation Technique.

We spent most of the night documenting our findings. We realized the technique relies on my existing alchemical knowledge; if I didn't know a technique or ingredient, the simulation couldn't show the full picture. It only worked with what I already knew.

We compiled notes on the technique's workings, limitations, and the recipes we had successfully refined. I shared this knowledge freely with Zhi Ruo, grateful for his help and confident he wouldn't use it against me.

"You know," Zhi Ruo said as we finished writing, "since we share many similar skills, I might be able to trigger the same conditions which allowed for the quest upon reaching the same cultivation rank for my mind."

"You definitely should. Just after the Gauntlet, once I've already won. I don't need you making things more difficult for me."

We shared a laugh. I could hear the Million Books Pavilion slowly filling in with people. It was faint, however, as only scholars, scholar-officials, or students could access the Million Books Pavilion. It was only through sheer luck I managed to befriend Zhi Ruo and gain access to it.

The librarian looked at me, eyes bright with curiosity. "So, what are your plans for this afternoon, Kai?"

I stretched, feeling the fatigue in my muscles. "I'll take a quick nap to energize myself, then come back here to train and practice my new skill as much as I can. Since the Refinement Simulation Technique is limited by my knowledge, I need to understand it better. I'll take a break on the final day tomorrow to be ready for the finals."

He nodded in agreement, but then his expression shifted to one of concern. "Just make sure you don't oversleep and miss the meeting this afternoon at the Alchemy Association."

I frowned, my mind going blank for a moment. "What meeting?"

# CHAPTER FIFTY-ONE

# Tools of the Trade

You're lucky I reminded you," Zhi Ruo said, shaking his head.

As we made our way toward the Alchemy Association, I couldn't help but berate myself internally. Of course there would be a prize for making it to the finals! How could I have been so wrapped up in my own little world that I missed that crucial detail? I had been so consumed with my quest and the intrigue surrounding Jingyu Lian that I had completely overlooked it.

After a quick nap and a hearty breakfast—while he went home to visit his family—we met up again, ready to face the day. I had even picked up a small but elegant ink pot for Guowei Wang. It wouldn't hurt to bring him a gift.

The Alchemy Association building loomed ahead, its grandeur never failing to impress. It was almost dizzying despite having come here so many times already.

As we approached the entrance, I noticed the three other contestants who had made it to the finals. Among them was Jingyu Lian, who was staring at me with an intensity that gave me shivers down my spine.

Before I could muster the courage to ask her if she had a problem, Ma Hualong's booming voice greeted us.

"Welcome, finalists!"

I couldn't shake the feeling that there was something she wanted to say to me, but now wasn't the time to dwell on it.

We followed the coordinator past the familiar face of the clerk and down the grand staircase toward the vault. His presence here was unusual; usually, Guowei Wang handled the distribution of rewards.

"I trust you all have rested well?" Ma Hualong inquired, his eyes scanning our faces.

A chorus of affirmations rose from the group, but my own response was a bit delayed from lack of sleep.

"Good, I have a question for you all. Why do you think the Gauntlet operates on the model where after every round, those who qualify get prizes, and those who perform at the top of every round gain an advantage that helps them move on to the next round?"

Silence fell over the group as we pondered his question.

We passed through several heavily guarded doors without an answer. Finally, Ma Hualong broke the silence.

"In alchemy, as in cultivation," he began, his voice echoing in the corridor, "small successes build upon one another, creating momentum that propels the practitioner to greater heights. Energy and effort, once set in motion, tend to amplify over time."

His words resonated with me. Every small victory, every successful concoction, had fueled my confidence and drive to learn more. Each step forward had opened up new possibilities, leading me to where I was today.

"As you advance, the challenges grow steeper. The rewards and advantages are not just incentives but essential tools to help you climb higher."

We reached the final door, leading to where Guowei Wang was.

There, the vault-keeper sat with a small smile on his face.

"For the past four rounds, you've all had the honor of receiving one item from the vault of your choice. This time, however, instead of choosing an ingredient or product, you will each select a tool."

"A tool?" Tian Zhu asked, raising an eyebrow. "What kind of tool?"

"These tools are specially crafted, a collaboration between us and the finest artisans the province had to offer. They are designed to accelerate your growth and nurture the field of alchemy. The tools are also encouraged to be used in the final round."

Fang Xiang stepped forward, his voice dripping with eagerness. "So these tools are designed to give us an edge in the finals?"

"Exactly," the man confirmed. "Each tool has unique properties that can enhance your alchemical process and increase your chances of victory. Choose wisely, as the tool you select will assist you in the final round *and* be a valuable asset in your future endeavors."

Zhi Ruo, always the practical one, asked, "Are these tools tailored to our individual strengths and weaknesses?"

"Indeed. Each tool here is versatile, but they have features that cater to different alchemical styles and techniques. It's up to you to decide which one aligns best with your approach. You have all come this far by honing your skills and listening to your inner voice. Let that guide you in making your choice. Guowei Wang and I will be available for questions as you make your choice. Then, after, the final round will be explained in detail."

We followed them deeper into the vault. The air grew cooler, and the lighting dimmed as we ventured further. The walls, lined with shelves filled with rare ingredients and precious pills, seemed to pulse with an ancient energy. My heart raced with anticipation as we approached the back of the vault.

Guowei Wang stepped forward. With a swift motion, he retrieved a talisman from his robe and pressed it against a seemingly solid wall. The air shimmered, and an invisible door revealed itself, swinging open to expose a hidden chamber.

We stepped inside, and I couldn't help but gasp at the sight before me. A vast array of top-tier alchemical tools, each more magnificent than the last, was meticulously aligned before us.

Ma Hualong gestured for us to explore. "Take your time. Examine each tool carefully. This decision could very well influence the outcome of the final round."

He glanced over to Jingyu Lian, beckoning her over. "As the top performer in the last round, you will have the benefit of picking first."

She nodded and made a beeline toward a separate section of the vault dedicated to handheld tools.

Zhi Ruo and I gravitated toward the pill furnaces, their imposing forms dominating the center of the chamber. "Pill furnaces are the heart of any alchemist's workshop," the librarian murmured, his eyes scanning the array with scholarly intensity. "I'd wager these are the most sought-after prizes."

But as we delved deeper into the selection, I couldn't help but notice that Tian Zhu and Fang Xiang were conspicuously avoiding the pill furnaces, instead focusing on other, seemingly less-significant tools.

"Curious," I remarked to Zhi Ruo, a hint of puzzlement in my voice. "Why do you think they're ignoring the furnaces?"

Zhi Ruo shrugged, his brows furrowed in thought. "Perhaps they have a specific strategy in mind," he offered. "Or maybe . . ."

A voice chimed in from behind us, causing him to jump in surprise. Guowei Wang stood by with a smile on his face. "They already have their own pill furnaces. The children of wealthy clans often inherit centuries-old furnaces, imbued with the qi of countless refinements. These treasures are far more potent than anything we could offer here."

Realizing this was my chance, I pulled out the ink pot I had brought and held it out to him. "Before I forget, Guowei, I brought this for you as a token of appreciation. You've been crucial in helping me pick out the treasures I wanted from here."

Guowei Wang's eyes widened in surprise. He took the ink pot, examining it with a soft smile. "Thank you, Kai. This is a very thoughtful gift. An ink pot?"

I nodded. "I don't live here, so it'll be hard to keep in touch. I figured to buy you an ink pot so we can send letters back and forth!"

He bowed slightly, clearly touched by the gesture.

I nodded, feeling a sense of satisfaction. It was nice to see my small token of appreciation received so warmly. Guowei Wang continued his explanation, his tone warm and informative.

"Now, as I was saying, those who already have powerful pill furnaces see no need to select another. They prefer to choose tools that complement their existing equipment. For those of you who are . . ."

"Commoners?" Zhi Ruo said, seeing the older man struggle to find the appropriate words to describe us.

"Well, yes. Those who do not have a pill furnace to inherit would benefit the most from here."

I exchanged a glance with Zhi Ruo and couldn't help but chuckle. "Well, Zhi, it seems we're at a disadvantage without our own ancient, family-heirloom pill furnaces."

Zhi Ruo laughed, shaking his head. "Indeed, Kai. We mere commoners have to make do with what we can get."

"Kai Liu!" Ma Hualong said from the other end of the vault. "You're next! Take your pick."

Guowei Wang joined us as we began to peruse the pill furnaces. His deep knowledge of each one became evident as he guided us through the selection, stopping at each furnace to explain its unique properties and the styles they suited best.

"This one here," he said, pointing to a sleek, silver furnace with delicate engravings, "is ideal for those who focus on precision and control. The internal structure allows for fine adjustments to the temperature and qi infusion, making it perfect for refining delicate elixirs."

I nodded, taking in his words as we moved on to the next one. Each furnace had its own story, its own strengths and weaknesses. It was fascinating to see how varied they were, and how each was designed with a specific alchemical approach in mind.

Guowei Wang stopped in front of a larger, sturdier furnace, its exterior adorned with runes that seemed to pulse with latent energy. "This one is for those who deal with large batches or more robust concoctions. The reinforced structure and enhanced qi channels can handle higher volumes and more potent ingredients without compromising the stability of the process."

I could see the appeal of each one, but none of them felt quite right for me.

We continued down the line, and my eyes fell on a pill furnace at the very end.

It was much more complex than the rest, with a wide, round, vase-like appearance. The lid was styled like a pagoda roof with two-tiered levels and a finial knob at the very top. Intricate mechanisms adorned its sides, and I could see various controls that seemed almost overwhelming at first glance.

Guowei Wang noticed my interest and walked over. "Ah, this one. It's a complicated item with a dark past. It was created by an artisan who over-engineered it with the intent of making it a gift for an official's son to help him become an alchemist. Unfortunately, the pill furnace is ridiculously complicated, requiring fine controls along the sides to give the user unparalleled control over the process. Each layer of the roof can undertake a different alchemical process."

He paused, letting the weight of his words settle in. "The politician was angered by its complexity, leading to a feud with the artisan. The man ended up being hanged, and this pill furnace was his last remaining work."

I stared at the furnace, feeling a strange connection to it. Its complexity, its potential for precision and control—it felt tailor-made for my Refinement Simulation Technique. "Can you show me how the controls work?" I asked, my curiosity piqued.

Guowei Wang nodded, his eyes gleaming with approval. He showed us the basic controls but emphasized that there were more nuances to it that couldn't be shown in just one demonstration. Instead of discouraging me, it only served to motivate me even more. The more complex and demanding the furnace, the better it would synergize with my skills. This pill furnace, with its unparalleled control and multi-layered functionality, had the highest ceiling for long-term gains.

"I'll choose this one," I declared.

With my choice made, the rest of the selections followed quickly. Fang Xiang picked a brush designed to aid in the creation of alchemy arrays, its bristles made from the tail hairs of a spirit fox. Tian Zhu selected a pair of gloves that apparently enhanced one's dexterity. Zhi Ruo, after some contemplation, chose a simpler yet finely crafted pill furnace that matched his steady and methodical approach to alchemy.

As we all gathered back in line, I noticed Jingyu Lian holding a glass case containing a set of golden needles. The sight reminded me of Elder Zhu's acupuncture needles, and curiosity got the better of me.

"Jingyu Lian," I began, trying to sound casual, "why did you choose the golden acupuncture needles as your tools?"

She looked at me oddly, but there was no trace of arrogance or hostility in her eyes. Instead, she addressed me respectfully. "These needles allow me to infuse qi into my ingredients directly, bringing about new and various side-effects. Additionally, they can be used for acupuncture, which is a skill I've been honing for years."

Her answer was straightforward, and I found myself respecting her dedication. Before I could say anything else, Ma Hualong's voice cut through the room.

"Now that everyone has selected their tools, I will explain the final round: the Crucible of the Five Elements."

# CHAPTER FIFTY-TWO

# Allies and Adversaries

A whirlwind of information about the final round left my head spinning. The Crucible of the Five Elements . . . It sounded daunting, exciting, and a little bit terrifying. My gaze drifted to the ancient storage ring on my finger, a gift from Guowei Wang that held my prize, the Two-Star Pagoda Pill Furnace. It was hard to believe that such a massive tool was now mine.

I'd have to get as familiar with it before the round. There went my day off, I supposed.

"If I'd known Guowei Wang was so generous," Zhi Ruo grumbled beside me, "I would've gifted him a fine brush to complement that ink pot!"

A chuckle escaped my lips. "I got lucky," I admitted, remembering the near-humiliation of renting a wheelbarrow to transport my unwieldy prize. "Storage rings are a luxury for most, it seems."

Zhi Ruo shot me a wry look. "Tell me about it," he muttered, struggling to maneuver his chosen tool on the small cart provided by the Association. "Maybe an alchemist's salary will finally get me one."

"First thing on the shopping list," I agreed with a grin. "Unless you fancy lugging that contraption around everywhere."

Before he could retort, a voice called out from across the Marble Jade Arena. "Hey, you two!"

Tian Zhu and Fang Xiang stood there, leaning against the wall with uncharacteristic smiles on their faces. They weren't directly antagonistic toward me like Jian Duan, but they were far from friendly before this. My eyebrows furrowed. Their sudden affability felt . . . suspicious. I nudged Zhi Ruo, exchanging a questioning glance. What could these two want?

"Congratulations on making it this far," Tian Zhu began, his tone almost too friendly. "Especially given your backgrounds."

Fang Xiang nodded in agreement. "It's impressive. Most wouldn't have thought commoners could compete at this level."

I bristled at the word but kept my expression neutral. "Thanks. Hard work pays off, I suppose."

Fang Xiang's smile widened, though it didn't reach his eyes. "Indeed it does. But hard work alone won't be enough for the final round. The Crucible of the Five Elements is going to be a true test of our abilities."

Tian Zhu leaned in slightly, lowering his voice. "We were thinking . . . after Ma Hualong's explanation, it became clear that the final round will be incredibly challenging. It would be smart to eliminate the biggest threat among us."

I frowned, not liking where this was heading. "What are you trying to say?"

Fang Xiang glanced around, ensuring no one else was listening. "We're suggesting a temporary alliance. Jingyu Lian is the most formidable competitor and the favorite to win it all. If we work together, we can take her out first."

"You want us to collude to take out Jingyu Lian?" I asked, my voice rising slightly. "That's . . ."

Zhi Ruo stood by me, his face set with determination. "I'm not comfortable with this idea at all. We should compete on our merits, not through deceit."

Tian Zhu's smile faded, replaced by a look of irritation. "You two are missing the bigger picture. This is about strategy. She's the only one standing in the way of all of us having a real shot at winning."

I shook my head, my resolve firm. "If you're so weak that you have to gang up on a woman, maybe you should just quit. I'm here to compete, not to conspire."

His eyes flashed with anger, but he didn't respond. Fang Xiang opened his mouth to argue, but I cut him off. "I've crossed lines and broken rules before, but I can live with what's in my soul. I won't betray that for a cheap victory. Come on, Zhi. We don't need to listen to any more of this drivel."

I turned away and walked off, they said something as we departed, but I didn't care to listen.

The both of us were walking in silence, the tension from the confrontation still hanging in the air.

"Watch your back," Zhi Ruo said quietly. "They might not take kindly to our refusal."

"I know," I replied. "Be careful on your way home. I don't trust them not to try something underhanded."

He nodded, his expression serious. "What about you? What are you going to do?"

I hesitated, not wanting to reveal my true intentions. "Just need to get something. I'll meet up with you later."

The librarian gave me a skeptical look but didn't press further.

With a nod, I turned and retraced my steps, trying to remember the direction Jingyu Lian had taken after leaving the arena. The chilly afternoon air bit at my skin, and I pulled my robe tighter around me. The streets were filled with people dressed in thicker clothing, their breath visible in the cold.

"There she is," I muttered to myself.

I spotted a familiar hooded robe in the distance. Jingyu Lian's distinctive attire was hard to miss.

I quickened my pace, weaving through the crowd, but just as I was about to reach her, a hand like a steel vice clamped down on my arm. Pain flared through my shoulder as I was yanked backward and forced to my knees.

A cold voice cut through the din. "And where do you think you're going?"

I looked up, trying to see who had me in their grasp. The figure was cloaked, their face obscured by shadows. The strength in their grip told me they were no ordinary person. I tried to wrench myself free but to no avail.

"Tian Zhan! Let him go!"

Just like that, the pressure disappeared at her command. He drew back, almost gliding toward her but still facing between us in a protective manner. Jingyu Lian gazed at me with an intrigued look.

"Kai Liu? What do you want?"

My arm throbbed from the sudden release, but I pushed the pain aside, focusing on the opportunity to speak with her. "I wanted to talk to you about something important," I began, trying to keep my voice steady.

Her eyebrow arched, a slight frown marring her otherwise serene face. "Here in the middle of the street?"

"No," I mumbled, my gaze darting around at the curious onlookers. "Probably somewhere more discreet."

"Follow me." A curt nod was all she offered before turning on her heel and leading the way. We followed her through a labyrinth of narrow alleyways.

Before I knew it, we were in a quiet tea shop. The owner greeted her with a deep bow and led us to a private room with sliding doors. The atmosphere was calm and serene, as a musician played the lute outside, just faint enough to hear. She and her escort removed their hoods, revealing their faces fully.

The escort, Tian Zhan, had wild gray hair and piercing eyes that reminded me of Windy's. *Where have I . . . ?*

Recognition hit me like a ton of bricks. This was the same person I had seen at Spirited Noodle when I first came to Crescent Bay City all those months ago.

His eyes, sharp as a hawk's, remained fixed on me with undisguised suspicion.

Jingyu Lian, however, seemed more composed. She settled onto a cushion with the grace of a swan, her gaze unwavering.

"Well? What did you want to say?"

"Fang Xiang and Tian Zhu approached me and Zhi Ruo. They suggested we work together to eliminate you in the final round."

Taking her silence as a sign, I continued.

"I refused," I said firmly. "I don't believe in ganging up on someone. I just wanted to warn you."

Jingyu Lian went quiet, her gaze piercing through me. The silence stretched, and I felt a knot of nervousness tightening in my stomach. Finally, she spoke, her voice soft but demanding. "Why are you doing this? Why go so far to protect a stranger?"

I blinked, caught off guard. "What are you talking about? It's not about protection. I just have integrity. I don't want to cheat."

"Cheating, *yes*," she echoed, her voice laced with a hint of irony. Her eyes narrowed, a glint of suspicion in their depths. "You seem to have a knack for interfering in other people's affairs, don't you?"

My heart skipped a beat. Did she know? I feared the worst, wondering if she realized I had eavesdropped on her and her father at Cloudrift Pavilion. "I . . . I don't know what you're talking about."

But her gaze remained unwavering, piercing through my facade like a blade. "Master Lei Ren," she said softly, the name hanging in the air like a challenge. "You were the one who brought him into the Gauntlet, weren't you?"

*Shit.*

A cold dread washed over me. I had been discovered.

She continued to stare at me, her expression unreadable. I braced myself for accusations, for the icy disdain I was sure would follow.

But instead, her voice was surprisingly soft, almost curious. "Why didn't you leave things be?" she asked. "You could have had an easier path to winning the Gauntlet."

The question hung in the air, heavy with unspoken implications. My heart hammered in my chest, but my gaze didn't waver. "Winning by deceit isn't winning at all," I countered, my voice steadier than I felt. "I want to earn my victory, not steal it."

Unless you counted Jian Duan. Or Elder Jun. But they didn't count!

A faint smile tugged at the corner of her lips. "You're an unusual one, Kai Liu," she murmured.

Tian Zhan seemed to relax, his stern demeanor easing a bit. I breathed a sigh of relief. Having slitted eyes trained on you for several minutes was unnerving, to say the least.

"It seems you've found yourself a suitor, *Lady Lian*," he remarked with a slight smirk.

I felt my face flush with embarrassment. "It's not like that!" I protested, waving my hands in denial. "I just wanted to help."

"I jest," he said, bowing his head slightly. "Kai Liu, is it? I apologize for the earlier . . . enthusiasm. I owe you a debt of gratitude for looking out for my Junior Sister. Rest assured, we'll take your warning to heart."

"Thank you, Kai," she said softly, her tone carrying genuine gratitude as she looked into my eyes. "I won't forget this."

*Thud-thud!*

Her words, so simple yet so powerful, struck a chord within me. My heart pounded erratically in my chest, each beat louder than the last. I couldn't tell if it was the relief that she didn't press further about Master Lei Ren or something else entirely.

"No problem. Just doing what I should."

I took a deep breath, trying to still my thoughts. Something was wrong with me. Was this the onset of Qi Deviation? Poison? The erratic heartbeat and sudden rush of emotions certainly felt like it. I shook my head, trying to dispel the thought. Maybe it was just the sheer relief of not being exposed.

Lost in my head, I stood there for a moment as they left the private room, then groaned.

Feng Wu was going to kill me for pulling another stunt like this.

I knelt on the cold floor of the Jade Harmony Inn, my forehead pressed against the wooden boards. I truly lived up to my moniker as Kowtow Kai with this one.

"I'm sorry, Feng Wu! I'm really sorry! I just thought it was the right thing to do," I pleaded, my voice shaking with fear. "Please don't hurt me!"

Feng Wu stood in front of me, his hands clasped behind his back. The silence stretched, thick with unspoken disappointment, and I braced myself for the inevitable scolding.

"Get up, Kai," he said with a sigh, his tone surprisingly gentle. "You're not in trouble for antagonizing Fang Xiang and Tian Zhu."

"I'm not?" I asked, hesitantly rising to my feet.

"No. In fact, you might have just earned yourself a powerful ally in the process, far more powerful than those two combined."

"Jingyu Lian? Why would her favor be so important?"

I could see how her affiliations with the Whispering Wind Sect was crucial, but that didn't seem as big of a benefit he was making it out to be.

Feng Wu's eyes narrowed slightly as he studied me. "Not just her. Tian Zhan is no ordinary disciple. The Howling Wind. He's their rising star and rumored to be next in line to inherit their sect leader's position."

My jaw dropped. "There's no way . . ."

"Did he have gray hair and sharp eyes?" Feng Wu asked, his tone calm.

I nodded, still reeling from the revelation. "Yeah, he did. But . . . that was him?"

He nodded, a slight smile playing on his lips. "When we ran into him at the Spirited Noodle that one time, I had an inkling it was Tian Zhan, based on his appearance. But I didn't think he was acting as a personal escort for Jingyu Lian."

The tension that had been gripping me eased slightly as I realized I wasn't in as much trouble as I'd thought.

Feng Wu's smile vanished, replaced by a stern expression. "Don't get too comfortable," he warned, his voice taking on a chilly edge. "You are in trouble. Just not for the reason you think."

My heart sank. "But—you said—"

"You're in trouble for not listening to me and avoiding fights," Feng Wu interrupted, sounding as cold as the winter air outside. "I specifically told you to stay out of this political mess between the other clans and families. And what did you do? You jumped right into the middle of it."

His shadow seemed to loom over me, and I felt a chill run down my spine. "Feng Wu, wait! You can't hurt me! Are you really going to injure me before the finals? Hey, I'm not even an official disciple! You can't do this to a guest!"

Feng Wu's eyes were closed as he drew near. The temperature seemed to drop by several degrees. "Are you ready for your punishment, Kai?"

I looked over to my familiars in a panic, looking for support. Windy was resting peacefully, ignoring the trouble, and Tianyi seemed unwilling to make eye contact with me. Those no-good familiars! Ignoring me when I'm in peril!

My screams were heard throughout the Jade Harmony Inn and far beyond.

# CHAPTER FIFTY-THREE

# The Crucible Begins

The screams and shouts of the crowd could be heard from the contestant's lounge. I sighed, feeling too mentally tired to even get nervous. Zhi Ruo stared at me curiously, his pill furnace lying beside him on a cart.

"You're still not gonna tell me what Feng Wu did to you?"

I shivered, the memories of that night too harsh to remember. "If you three idiots getting me drunk last night didn't work. What makes you think I'd say it now?"

The second-class disciple hadn't laid a hand on me, but the mental scars I received that day . . . It was enough to prevent me from interfering in any politics anymore. Jian Duan could punch me in the face right now and I'd preach pacifism and non-violence to his face, so long as it prevented Feng Wu from punishing me again.

"You know you can tell us everything, right? We're sworn comrades! I wouldn't tell another soul about what happened!"

"It's not that. I—"

"Could you two be quiet?" a voice interrupted snidely from afar. I turned to see Tian Zhu, wearing the new gloves he got from the vault, turning around to look at us grouchily. "Some of us actually have important things to discuss."

"Oh, like your plans for a two-on-one ambush?" I retorted, a smirk playing on my lips. "Now, *that's* important."

Tian Zhu's face reddened, his fists clenching. "You—"

The rest of his words were cut short by the arrival of Jingyu Lian, who entered the lounge with her usual air of cool composure.

Tian Zhu, who had been on the verge of a retort, abruptly turned away, his anger seemingly evaporating under her gaze.

Fashionably late, as always.

I couldn't help but grin, all while trying to ignore the strange fluttery feeling in my stomach that popped up when I saw her.

She turned to me and Zhi Ruo, giving us both a nod of acknowledgment. I waved to her casually, and Zhi Ruo politely smiled back. It seemed she was warming up to us. Being in her good books would be a boon for the both of us, I suppose.

Not that I'd need it! *They'll look at this in the future and be glad they have a connection to me, the great Kai Liu!*

The door swung open to reveal an official; his tired eyes scanned over the room. "Please, follow me. The introductions will soon begin."

One by one, the contestants began to follow the official out of the lounge. As Tian Zhu and Fang Xiang walked past us, they shot us dirty looks. I shrugged it off, but couldn't help but notice Zhi Ruo's grip tightening on the handle of his cart as he maneuvered his pill furnace. We walked at the back, the heavy cart slowing him down.

"Guess we didn't get much sleep these past nights, huh?" Zhi Ruo said, his voice strained from the effort.

"Yeah," I replied, feeling the fatigue settling in my bones. "But we've made it this far. No point in complaining now."

Zhi Ruo chuckled. "True. Just promise me one thing, Kai."

"What's that?"

"Let's give it our all. No holding back, even if we're up against each other."

I smiled, appreciating his sportsmanship. "Agreed. Good luck, Zhi."

"Same to you."

We reached the edge of the arena, where the official stopped us. The air was thick with anticipation, the roar of the crowd just beyond. The official turned to Jingyu Lian, bowing slightly.

"Jingyu Lian, you'll be the first to enter the arena."

She nodded, stepping forward with her usual grace. As she walked into the open arena, the crowd erupted into thunderous applause and cheers.

Ma Hualong's voice boomed over the noise. "Hailing from the Whispering Wind Sect! The Lian clan's alchemical genius who stands as the favorite to win the title! JINGYU LIAN!"

He motioned to her, indicating the circular arena divided into five distinct areas, each representing one of the elements. Forming a pentagram around the circle, chains were tethered to the floor and raised all the way to the ceiling. From here, I could see a massive array of ingredients, and my mind was already whirling with potential recipes I could work with.

"Miss Jingyu, please choose the element you'd like to begin with."

I watched nervously as she surveyed the arena. I prayed silently, desperately hoping she wouldn't pick the one I had my eyes on. But to my dismay, she announced her choice with a confident smile.

"I will begin with the wood element."

She began to make her way to the green section of the arena, symbolizing wood. Just before stepping into her designated area, she turned and looked directly at me. Then, with a playful wink, she proceeded to her spot.

I cursed under my breath, unable to hide my annoyance. "Shouldn't have been so nice to her if she was gonna be like this," I muttered to Zhi Ruo, who laughed softly.

Before I could dwell on my frustration, the official called my name. My heart pounded as I stepped forward, the noise of the crowd now a distant hum in my ears. The bright lights of the arena blinded me for a moment, but I forced myself to focus.

"Representing the Verdant Lotus Sect, the young alchemist who revived the ancient Essence Extraction technique, once used by the legendary Master Li Tao to usher in a new era for alchemy! Kai Liu!"

A wave of dizziness washed over me. Why did my introduction feel ten times louder than Jingyu Lian's? My knees wobbled slightly, but I steadied myself, forcing a confident grin onto my face. From the stands, I heard two distinct voices cut through the roar.

"KAI! YOU'VE GOT THIS! I'VE BET THE HOUSE ON YOU!" Tao's boisterous cheer nearly knocked me off my feet.

"Don't let him down, Kai!" Bai Hua's voice, though quieter, was filled with warmth and encouragement. "I'm rooting for you, even if I *did* put my money on Jingyu Lian!"

I chuckled, shaking my head at their antics. A quick scan of the crowd revealed Feng Wu, his face beaming with pride, Tianyi perched on his shoulder, and a flash of white and blue from Windy tucked in his sleeve. A surge of warmth spread through my chest. I wasn't alone in this.

Ma Hualong's voice brought me back to the present. "Kai Liu, please choose your starting element."

With my ideal option taken, I had no choice but to go for the next best thing. "I'll choose water."

Settling down by the blue-themed section of the arena, I gave Jingyu Lian a small frown.

"Really? Choosing the wood element?"

"Weren't you the one talking about facing each other fairly? It wouldn't be a fair challenge if I let you get your specialty."

The others placed themselves among the other elements after they were introduced. Tian Zhu chose fire, Fang Xiang chose metal, and Zhi Ruo chose earth.

"Contestants will have thirty minutes on each section to create as many pills as they can, before moving clockwise to the next section!"

I glanced over. After water, I'd arrive at wood, fire, earth, and then metal. In my mind, the round had already begun, as I worked to analyze all the ingredients and plot out which ones to make, in what order, and how to incorporate them into my strategy for the rest of the round.

"This goes on until each contestant has had the opportunity to work at each elemental section once! There are only a limited amount of ingredients, so they must choose carefully! From there, the second phase begins!"

"Tidecaller Vine, Bubblebloom Algae . . ." I muttered to myself, seeing all the familiar ingredients from past rounds at our disposal.

"The second phase will be a battle royale! All contestants must compete to knock each other out of bounds, or render them unable to continue using the concoctions they've prepared! There will be absolutely no martial arts or cultivation techniques allowed during this trial!"

The crowd roared like thunder, and all I felt was a burning sense of determination. This was it. All my hours spent at the Million Books Pavilion, my tribulations at the Verdant Lotus Sect . . . They would all come to a conclusion right here.

"BEGIN!"

Using the storage ring, I spawned the Two-Star Pagoda Pill Furnace right beside me on the floor, because of its sheer size in comparison to regular pill furnaces, I couldn't place it on the table.

But because of that, it meant I could create larger batches of pills, and due to its special nature, I'd be able to start two different recipes at the same time!

Before the Pill Furnace even properly settled onto the ground, I was seizing ingredients I'd need.

The ones to begin with were Ice Obsidian, Purple Eel Venom, and mint. The first two were potent ingredients but also the hardest to prepare. I'd start with them. Like second nature, my Refinement Simulation Technique activated, showing me the most efficient way to my goal, telegraphing my future moves while being mindful of the time.

I immediately went to preparing them, crushing the obsidian into a fine dust, extracting the mint essence, and diluting the venom. The water element section was full of versatile ingredients.

Within minutes, I had the ingredients ready and placed them into the bottom layer of the pill furnace. My fingers danced over the intricate knobs and dials, adjusting the condensation valves and infusion conduits to ensure the perfect balance of qi flow. I thanked the heavens this pill furnace came with a manual, otherwise I never would've figured out how to use it.

With the lower chamber set, I quickly selected a second set of ingredients for the top layer: Lotus Nectar, Aqua Vine Essence, and Celestial Ice Crystal. The nectar and vine essence would form the base, providing a stable foundation.

Time was ticking, and the pressure was on. I imbued the furnace with my qi, kickstarting it to life.

Only simple recipes, cut down to the barest essentials, could be created within the thirty-minute limit, and even then, only two or three products at most. I needed to be efficient and precise.

Preparing the second set of ingredients, I was able to focus fully on the task, dependent on my Refinement Simulation Technique's ability to keep an accurate track of the time. The process was meticulous, requiring me to extract the nectar from the petals, concentrate the Aqua Vine Essence, and finely crush the ice crystals.

As I carefully placed the prepared ingredients into the top layer of the furnace, I assessed the progress of the first batch of ingredients.

Unlike the other rounds where quality and perfection was prioritized, efficiency and quantity was the name of the game. It didn't matter how our products were preserved if we were going to use them immediately.

Glancing around, I noticed the other contestants adopting a similar philosophy. Jingyu Lian moved with a fluid grace, her hands a blur as she handled the ingredients with practiced efficiency. Tian Zhu and Fang Xiang, though usually meticulous, were cutting corners wherever possible, their faces set in determined expressions. Even Zhi Ruo, usually methodical, was speeding through his preparations.

Steam began to escape from the holes throughout the furnace, signaling the start of the second recipe's transmutation process. My hands blurred as I managed both layers, adjusting the heat distribution and qi flow to maintain optimal conditions for both batches.

Minutes passed in a blur of concentrated effort. Finally, I removed the top layer, revealing a turquoise clumpy powder. It wasn't my best work, but it would serve its purpose as Serpent's Breath Smoke Bombs.

With those completed, I turned my attention back to the second recipe. When the mixture reached the right consistency, I extracted the potion and poured it into neat vials. This concoction would be an Elixir of Rapid Growth, designed to make plants sprout and grow instantly. I'd need to grab certain ingredients in the wood zone for this elixir to be of any use.

Seeing a bit of time left, I decided to prepare another useful concoction. I grabbed some Slickweed Kelp, its glossy leaves shimmering under the arena lights. I used my hand to draw out an orb of pure essence and transfer it into two vials. The distinct memory of using it to dissolve Jian Duan's Breath Gel was still fresh in my mind, and I knew it'd come in handy as a perfect counter to the other contestant's concoctions.

"Time's up! You have one minute to move to the next zone!"

Pressing the storage ring to my furnace, I drew it back into place before moving quickly into the wood section. I sighed, seeing how Jingyu Lian took the most valuable products already. But my strategy was adaptable, and I readjusted accordingly.

Wood was the most versatile among the elements, capable of poisons, healing elixirs, and even restrictive traps. It didn't matter what she took, I could make potent mixtures even with the most basic of ingredients here.

I grabbed the Sundew plant. Its vibrant crimson stalks and glistening, dewdrop covered leaves pulsed with a deceptive beauty. Its predatory nature was evident in the sticky droplets that adorned its foliage, each a tiny trap waiting to ensnare unsuspecting insects. I plucked a handful of the leaves, careful to avoid the delicate hairs that triggered them.

With practiced efficiency, I harvested the droplets, their viscous texture clinging to my fingers like honey. I then combined them with a mixture of crushed bark from the Ironwood tree, known for its sturdiness, and essence of the moonpetal flower, renowned for its binding properties. The resulting concoction swirled in my mortar, a mesmerizing blend of crimson, brown, and silvery-white hues.

I poured the mixture into several small vials, sealing them tightly. This concoction, while incomplete, would serve as the foundation for a powerful immobilizing agent. Once exposed to heat, the mixture would rapidly harden, encasing its target in a shell akin to stone, effectively restricting their movements. I'd need to find an appropriate ingredient to pair with this in the fire zone.

A sly grin spread across my face as I imagined the chaos this would cause in the arena. The thought of my rivals struggling to break free from my sticky, hardening concoction filled me with a sense of mischievous glee.

"Ten minutes left!" Ma Hualong's voice boomed through the arena, jolting me back to the present.

I quickly surveyed the remaining ingredients, my mind racing to devise additional concoctions to bolster my arsenal.

Among the remaining ingredients, one caught my eye—the Runny Nose Orchid. A grin tugged at my lips. This unassuming plant had a potent pollen that could send anyone into a sneezing fit.

Carefully, I harvested the pollen, using a delicate brush to collect the fine grains. The Runny Nose Orchid required gentle handling, as any rough movement could release the pollen prematurely. I carefully plucked the orchid's delicate stems, their faint floral scent tickling my nose. A sudden, uncontrollable urge to sneeze bubbled up within me. I froze, holding my breath, my eyes watering.

"Not now," I hissed under my breath, praying that the urge would subside.

I cautiously resumed my task, my movements slow and deliberate as I brushed the pollen grains into a small vial. The grains shimmered like golden dust, their potency almost palpable. With a sigh of relief, I sealed the vial, the urge to sneeze finally receding. With the pollen safely collected, I turned my attention to another key ingredient, the Horsetail Pine. Extracting its resin would provide the perfect binding agent for my concoction.

A thick, amber-colored resin slowly seeped out, filling the air with a pungent, piney aroma. The combination of the pollen and resin would create a powerful irritant.

The Tormenting Pollen Mist was my goal. It would diffuse into the air, creating a cloud of fine particles that would induce uncontrollable sneezing fits in anyone unfortunate enough to inhale it. Perfect for disrupting the concentration of my competitors.

Finally, the furnace signaled the completion of the process. I carefully removed the top layer, revealing a fine, golden powder. I quickly funneled it into small vials, sealing them tightly. The Tormenting Pollen Mist was ready.

"Oh, I almost forgot!"

I looked at the shelves, looking for any interesting ingredients to use with my Elixir of Rapid Growth. I seized a small bottle of Entangling Vine seeds.

"Time's up! Move to the next zone!" Ma Hualong's voice echoed.

My palms were sweaty as I hurriedly packed up my tools and ingredients, slipping the vials into my storage ring. The fire zone awaited, and I couldn't afford to waste a single moment.

CHAPTER FIFTY-FOUR

# Wit and Wuxing

I should have expected the scarcity of ingredients as we moved through the zones, but not to this extent. My frustration mounted as I glanced around the fire zone, struggling to think of useful combinations to make. The once plentiful and varied array of ingredients had been picked clean by the people before me, leaving behind only the most basic components.

"Come on, there has to be something," I muttered to myself, sifting through what little remained. Most of the potent fire-based ingredients like the Sunfire Blade Grass were gone.

I ended up only being able to make simple Ember Pills. They lacked the potency and versatility of the more advanced concoctions I had hoped to create; the fire zone had the most potential in regards to offense, after all. I hoped it would be enough to pair with the Sundew Sticky Bomb . . .

Optimistically, I figured the others were likely suffering from the same conundrum.

When Ma Hualong's voice echoed through the arena, signaling the time to move to the earth zone, I felt a mix of relief and trepidation. The earth zone, like the fire zone, had been thoroughly ransacked. Only the most mundane ingredients were left, the treasures of the earth long gone.

I rummaged through the remnants, pulling out what little I could find from the shelves. Activated Charcoal was plentiful, its dark, gritty texture a stark contrast to the vibrant, rare ingredients I had hoped for. With little choice, I decided to focus on detoxification pills. Though not flashy or overtly powerful, they could serve as a counter to the potential poisons my competitors might use.

As I ground the charcoal into a fine powder and began the refinement process, I couldn't help but think.

*This is it. The best I can do here is prepare for defense.*

The clock ticked mercilessly, each second a reminder of the time slipping away.

The process was monotonous, my hands moving on autopilot. Grinding, mixing, refining—a dance I knew all too well. Finally, the detoxification pills were complete, small black orbs that could neutralize toxins and poisons. They were functional, practical, but hardly the game-changers I needed.

"Time to move to the next zone!" Ma Hualong's voice cut through the air once more. I exhaled deeply, a mix of relief and anxiety. Gathering my tools and ingredients, I moved quickly to the final zone—metal.

To my surprise, the metal zone was relatively untouched compared to the others. I glanced around, my eyes widening at the sight of the various metallic ingredients still available. I grinned, seeing that I could work with a familiar ingredient—pyrite.

I grabbed it, along with bottles of liquid mercury.

Elder Wei Lian's demonstration during the pyrite round had been a masterclass in exploiting the unique properties of the metal, despite his unsavory reputation. His ability to harness the power of pyrite left a lasting impression on me. Pyrite, with its explosive potential, could be a game-changer if used correctly.

"All right," I muttered, my eyes gleaming with anticipation as I snatched a hefty chunk of pyrite from the table, its metallic surface glinting under the arena lights. "Let's see what kind of havoc we can unleash with this."

Beside the pyrite, I arranged a small mound of finely-ground iron ore powder, its dark hue starkly contrasting with the shimmering gold. Then, with a delicate touch, I lifted a vial of Oreweaver Spider Silk, its contents preserved in a viscous, silvery liquid. Spun from the metallic threads of a peculiar arachnid that thrived off metallic substances, it was renowned for its extraordinary strength and near-instantaneous hardening properties—the perfect complement to my volatile concoction.

The final touch, liquid mercury, would infuse the concoction with its transformative essence. Its fluidity and ability to bind with other metals held the key to the reaction I sought—a transmutation that would turn a simple thrown vial into a rapidly expanding, viscous trap, solidifying upon contact into a prison as unyielding as iron.

Unlike my Sundew Sticky Bomb, this metallic snare would resist ordinary solvents once the pyrite combusts and the liquid hardens. It was a risky gamble, a dance with the unpredictable nature of mercury and pyrite, but the potential reward was too great to ignore.

It was a risky, untested recipe, but my Refinement Simulation Technique would guide me, predicting the shortcomings and potential of the mixture.

With them placed before me, the technique worked reflexively. My mind's eye projected possible outcomes, guiding my hands as I worked.

"Here goes nothing," I whispered. "Let's start with *these*."

The chaotic noise of the arena faded into the background as I visualized the Two-Star Pagoda Pill Furnace in my mind. It became a dynamic, three-dimensional space where ingredients interacted, merged, and transformed.

The iron ore powder and liquid mercury were the first. I adjusted the temperature slightly to ensure the mercury remained in its liquid state, maximizing its bonding properties without risking vaporization.

Next, I added the pyrite. This was the most delicate part of the process. Pyrite's explosive nature introduced a volatile element to the mixture. I saw the concoction bubbling and threatening to destabilize in my simulation. With a quick move, I lowered the heat to a specific temperature that would prevent it from exploding.

To the crowd, it probably looked like I was methodically making the recipe, but in reality, every second was a battle against potential disaster. The pyrite slowly settled into the mixture, its energy contained but ready to be unleashed upon impact.

Finally, I introduced the Oreweaver Spider Silk. Due to its unique property, my Essence Extraction skill worked on it the same way it has with other metals. I pushed continuously, forcing the essence to bend under my will and extracted it slowly into the palm of my hand.

The simulation showed the essence weaving through the liquid. I adjusted the heat once more, ensuring the essence fully integrated with the mixture.

My hands moved with practiced precision, guided by the simulation. I could see the mixture was complete. It pulsed with a metallic sheen. I had to work fast to store them in the vials with an air-tight seal.

Upon feeling the bottles, still hot to the touch, I felt a surge of confidence. These would be a crucial item for the round.

"The first phase is OVER!" Ma Hualong shouted at the top of his lungs. "Look under your alchemical stations and you will find a leather belt with which you can secure all your concoctions with. Prepare yourselves!"

I hurriedly followed instructions, taking out the leather belt from where they said it would be. It had multiple pouches and mini-pockets, each perfectly designed for alchemical vials. I slipped my vials into the slots, appreciating how they clicked securely into place. The larger pouches held my sturdier creations, while the smaller ones snugly fit the more delicate concoctions.

Muscular men, each the same size as Ping Hai, began pulling on the chains throughout the arena. Their muscles bulged and veins popped as they pulled downward. The heavy clanking of metal echoed as the floor beneath us started to rise. The arena floor ascended high into the air, bringing us closer to the roaring crowd for a better view. I was now eye level with the crowd.

Ma Hualong, Elder Wei Lian, and Elder Mingmei stepped forward, slapping their palms down on the ground from three distinct points around the arena.

A translucent barrier encased the crowd, shimmering with protective energy. Ma Hualong's voice boomed, cutting through the excitement.

"The second stage is set! Contestants will lose if they are knocked out of bounds and fall off the stage, get knocked out, or are otherwise made unable to continue. Feel free to use the surroundings to your advantage! With that in mind, let the battle begin!"

The crowd's roar shook the Marble Jade Arena, the energy palpable. I tightened my grip on the newly prepared vials, feeling the weight of the moment settle on my shoulders as I offhandedly placed my pill furnace back in the ring.

I glanced left and right. To my left was Jingyu Lian. To my right was Fang Xiang. I stepped backward, allowing me to see both of them at once. My eyes snapped over to see Fang Xiang making his move.

But it wasn't toward me.

Like it was preplanned, Tian Zhu and Fang Xiang both struck at Zhi Ruo, throwing vials at him simultaneously. The man yelped and ducked for cover behind his pill furnace as fiery and icy explosions erupted around him. Tian Zhu's concoction created a blazing inferno, while Fang Xiang's released a burst of frost, the combination creating a volatile mix of steam and flame.

"Zhi Ruo!" I shouted, my heart racing as I saw him struggling to maintain his footing amid the chaos.

Without hesitation, I sprinted toward them, my mind racing to formulate a plan. I couldn't let them take my friend out so easily. As I closed the distance, Tian Zhu noticed me and sneered.

"Look who decided to play hero," He taunted, readying another vial.

Before he could throw it, a blast of icy mist struck him from the side, catching him off guard and freezing him in place momentarily. Jingyu Lian stepped forward, her presence commanding as she wielded her alchemical prowess with precision.

"You should watch your back," she said coldly, her eyes locked on him.

Fang Xiang called out in alarm, "Tian Zhu, fall back!"

Seizing the moment, I tossed my Serpent's Breath Smoke Bomb at Fang Xiang. The pill broke apart with ease, releasing a thick, turquoise smoke that quickly enveloped him. He staggered back, coughing and waving his arms to clear the air, but the hallucinogenic effects were already taking hold.

As he struggled to regain his composure, I turned to Zhi Ruo, who was emerging from behind his pill furnace, his face pale but determined.

"Did you really think that I wasn't prepared for you?" Tian Zhu said from afar, pouring a liquid that melted the frost covering his body. "It was your mistake for leaving the fire zone to *me*."

Flames licked at the translucent barrier protecting the crowd. Jingyu Lian's frown deepened as she stared at the wall of flames created by the man.

I turned to Zhi Ruo. "Go! Deal with Tian Zhu!"

I remembered Zhi Ruo's starting point. Earth. Each of the five elements reacted with each other in various ways, countering or strengthening one another. But one thing I knew for sure, was that earth smothered fire. Zhi Ruo was the perfect match against him.

Jingyu Lian began at wood, she was at a direct disadvantage with Tian Zhu.

As though he grasped my intentions, he nodded firmly and moved forward.

But then I saw Zhi Ruo freeze for a moment, his eyes darting between me, Tian Zhu, and Jingyu Lian. Instead of immediately engaging, he placed his heavy pill furnace back onto his cart and began lugging it toward the chaotic battle zone.

*Is he planning to make pills in the middle of a fight?* I wondered, momentarily confused by his actions.

However, my attention was quickly pulled back to Fang Xiang. Expecting him to be reeling from the hallucinogenic effects of my Serpent's Breath Smoke Bomb, I was shocked to see him seemingly unaffected.

"Did you think your petty tricks would work on me?" he taunted, his voice steady and clear. He held up a small, shimmering pill. "Antidote for your little smoke bomb. Purple Eel Venom? Nice try, though."

I should've known he prepared some sort of counter to hallucinogens. After all, he was . . . Well, he was a *finalist*. Of course he'd have one or two tricks up his sleeve.

"You seem surprised, did you honestly think I wouldn't be prepared for such a basic tactic?"

There was a long silence. He raised an eyebrow. "Honestly, Kai Liu, do you even know who you're dealing with? Have you even bothered to learn my name?"

I blinked, caught off guard by his sudden outburst. "Uh, yeah, you're Fang Xiang, right? You, er, made it into the top five during the second round. With the pyrite crystal that collects sunlight?"

He threw his hands up in exasperation. "That was Tian Zhu! Hold on a second! You barely even know who I am! We've been in this competition together for weeks, and you act like I'm some random passerby!"

I had to admit, I hadn't paid much attention to Fang Xiang throughout the competition. He had always been somewhat of a background figure, overshadowed by the more flamboyant personalities of the other contestants. I just grouped him up with Jian Duan and his ilk.

Speaking of, what happened to him?

Fang Xiang continued his rant while I spaced out. "Do I seem like some nameless extra to you? Some forgettable background character you can just throw a potion at and expect to win?"

"Look," I said, trying to appease him, "I didn't mean any disrespect—"

Fang Xiang cut me off with a dramatic sigh. "But let me tell you, Kai Liu, I'm not just some side character in your little story. I'm a force to be reckoned with! I'm Fang Xiang, a finalist in the Gauntlet, not some nameless lackey! I have a backstory, motivations, even a secret family recipe for candied ginger!"

"Listen," I said, trying to bring the focus back to the task at hand, "I'm not here to debate your role in some sort of story. I'm here to win."

"And you think you can win against me? A mere village herbalist who stumbled his way into the final round?" He flexed his hand, shattering the vial in his hand and allowing the mixture to cover his skin with liquid metal. "I'll show you the true power of a seasoned alchemist."

I dropped another Serpent's Breath Smoke Bomb, and he stayed in place.

"Fool! You think it'll work on me twice?"

I tossed the Entangling Vine seeds down on the ground, waiting for the perfect moment. As soon as I saw his silhouette in the smoke, I hurled my Elixir of Rapid Growth down. The seeds sprouted instantly, snaking all around Fang Xiang's body and immobilizing him. The thick vines wrapped around his limbs, tightening their grip with every passing second.

For a moment, I thought I had him. But Fang Xiang didn't remain idle. He used his fists, now covered in liquid metal, to grasp the thorny vines and rip them off with brute force. Despite his efforts, the vines continued to grow rapidly, regaining their grip as soon as he tore them away.

Seizing the opportunity while he was distracted, I threw a vial of Slickweed Kelp Essence at him. The liquid splashed over his metal-covered fists, breaking down the liquid metal rapidly and rendering his defensive tactic useless.

Fang Xiang retaliated with a large orb that he launched directly at me. The orb shattered midair, breaking into shrapnel that blew me backward and left multiple cuts on my body. The cuts stung with a familiar burn—poison.

Gritting my teeth against the pain, I immediately consumed one of my Charcoal Essence Detoxification Pills. The effects were almost immediate, the burning sensation dulling as the pill worked to neutralize the poison in my bloodstream. I watched as the alchemist continued ripping the vines off, albeit much slower with the pain of spiked vines piercing into his palms.

I hurled another potion while he was distracted, and the glass vial shattered into powder, releasing a warm yellow mist throughout.

"I don't know how many times I need to tell you, poison won't—"

Fang Xiang sneezed, his eyes watering as he fell victim to the Tormenting Pollen Mist. He doubled over, sneezing uncontrollably, his face contorted in irritation and discomfort.

"Unfortunately, it's not a poison," I said, a smirk tugging at the corner of my lips. "It's much worse."

Fang Xiang tried to throw something at me, but his constant sneezing affected his aim, and the vial fell to the side, shattering harmlessly on the ground. Seizing the moment, I pulled out another vial, the one I created in the metal zone. I hurled it at him with all my might.

The vial exploded on impact, and the liquid expanded, covering Fang Xiang and the vines that bound him. Within seconds, the substance solidified, rendering him immobile. He struggled against the hardened mass, but his efforts were in vain.

"Curse you, Kai Liu!" he yelled, his voice muffled by the sticky substance. "This isn't over!"

I couldn't help but grin, a surge of adrenaline coursing through my veins. "Sorry, Fang Xiang, but it seems your spotlight moment has come to an end. Try to be a bit less forgettable next time."

# CHAPTER FIFTY-FIVE

# Trial by Fire (and Water, Earth, Metal, and Wood)

I took a moment to catch my breath, wiping the sweat from my brow. Fang Xiang was securely immobilized, his sneezing and cursing fading into the background noise of the roaring crowd. I quickly took a mental inventory of the potions and items I had used in the battle against him.

I still had two Serpent's Breath Smoke Bombs left. The Entangling Vine seeds—those were all used up. Maybe I could find another plant or seed to pair with them in the wood zone.

"Two Slickweed Kelp Essence vials, three detoxification pills and one Tormenting Pollen Mist bomb left," I muttered quietly.

My concoction from the metal zone, which I'd call the Binding Snare Potion, worked beautifully. But I only had one left, so I had to use it at the most opportune moment.

All my Ember Pills and Sundew Sticky Bomb Elixirs were untouched.

Taking a deep breath, I scanned the arena.

The air crackled with elemental energy as Jingyu Lian and Tian Zhu clashed. Tremors rippled through the ground, followed by blasts of searing heat. She deftly wove through the chaos, throwing a volley of thorn-laden seedpods that sprouted into a thorny barricade to block the flames.

It would've been easy for me to intervene, but I wouldn't squander my resources in this chaotic melee.

No, I would observe, learn, and strike when the iron was hot—or rather, when the opponents were sufficiently weakened. This wasn't cheating, just playing smart!

Like a phantom, I retreated to the edge of the arena, taking cover at the edge of the water zone, behind the alchemical station. A makeshift bunker offering a vantage point to analyze the unfolding chaos.

Tian Zhu clearly targeted her, his advantage fueling his aggression. He bombarded her with fiery pills, each one exploding into a miniature inferno that scorched the earth and tested her defenses.

Seeing how liberal he was, I wondered just how much those gloves from the vault improved his dexterity by. He was clearly responsible for ransacking the fire zone! It seemed as though all the pills he made were from there.

"Running away?! I expected better from you, Jingyu Lian!" Tian Zhu's shout cut through the air.

My eyes were locked on Zhi Ruo, who had reached the battlefield, his pill furnace in tow. Instead of using it to make pills, he maneuvered it like a massive shield, its heavy metal surface deflecting Tian Zhu's explosive attacks. His cart rattled with every blow, threatening to break at any moment.

"That's cheating!" Tian Zhu bellowed, frustration clear in his voice. He threw another fiery pill at Zhi Ruo, but it exploded harmlessly against the sturdy furnace.

"Cheating?" the librarian called back. "It's part of the surroundings. Adapt or get left behind."

The both of them looked to Ma Hualong for confirmation, allowing for a pause in the battlefield. Caught off guard by their sudden attention, the man's voice rang out from where he was keeping the barrier activated.

"The equipment from the vault brought by contestants is considered part of the surroundings and can be used freely. Continue the battle!"

Tian Zhu's face twisted with anger, but he was forced to focus back on the fight. In his distraction, Jingyu Lian seized the opportunity. She hurled a vial to the ground, and from it, a dense cloud of silvery mist billowed out. He recoiled, coughing and spluttering as the mist enveloped him.

The sudden chill caused his flames to flicker and sputter, his movements slowing as a thin layer of frost began to form on his skin.

"Enough of this!"

I watched as the arrogant alchemist, trying to reignite his attacks, stepped out of the fire zone to escape the mist's area of effect.

Right into Zhi Ruo's path.

The librarian threw a vial with surprising accuracy, the glass shattering into harmless pieces against Tian Zhu's chest. A liquid covered him, and a faint hum filled the air. Zhi Ruo lifted his cart with all his strength, tipping the pill furnace over until it started to roll slowly onto the floor.

I watched as Tian Zhu began drinking what I assumed was a detoxifying elixir.

He smirked at Zhi Ruo. Throwing another pill that sent him rolling on the floor, close to the edge of the arena. He scrambled up to his feet, breathless and disheveled. His expression, however, looked far from defeated. "It's not a poison, if that's what you're thinking."

Tian Zhu's smirk faded. His clothes and body were being pulled toward the pill furnace, which was rolling faster than what should've been possible. "That elixir contained Lodestone Mushroom powder. A neat ingredient that attracts metals toward itself."

His panic was palpable as he realized he couldn't outrun it, no matter how hard he tried. Desperation set in, and Tian Zhu began to run, but his movements were futile. It was as if he was running in place, his legs churning but not gaining any ground.

The pill furnace, now a relentless iron juggernaut, rolled faster and faster, drawing him inexorably closer. Tian Zhu threw his several explosive pills at it in a last-ditch effort to stop its advance. The pills detonated in a series of fiery blasts, but the furnace remained unscathed, its thick iron shell impervious to his attacks.

His panic turned to sheer terror as the furnace closed in.

*"AIIIEEEEE!"*

With a final, desperate scream, Tian Zhu tried to leap out of the way, but it was too late. The pill furnace collided with him with a sickening crunch, knocking the alchemist out cold and sending the rest of his pills flying out of his belt. His limp body was dragged along the ground, finally coming to rest as the furnace rolled to a stop.

. . . Was he dead?

A small, pitiful moan from underneath the pill furnace confirmed he wasn't.

I pumped my fist, a surge of adrenaline coursing through me. He had done it!

As I prepared to join the fray, something caught my eye.

The mist from Jingyu Lian's attack hadn't dispersed. It was *spreading*.

Zhi Ruo stood frozen in place, his smirk still plastered on his face but his eyes wide with alarm. His limbs were locked in place, as if an invisible force held him captive. A faint, sickly sweet scent wafted through the air, barely noticeable amid the lingering smoke and the metallic tang of the arena.

Poison!

My mind screamed the warning, but it was too late. I'd already taken a breath, the cloying sweetness coating the back of my throat. My muscles stiffened, my movements slowing as the poison's insidious tendrils snaked through my body.

Just then, a blur of white erupted from the cloud of smoke. Jingyu Lian, her face a mask of cold determination, walked toward my paralyzed friend.

"I apologize," she said. "But only one of us can move forward to be the victor." She shoved him out of bounds with a light push.

My heart pounded in my chest as I watched Zhi Ruo tumble over the edge. Without thinking, I ran forward, desperate to save him. He wouldn't be able to soften his fall!

But my body didn't cooperate. The poison coursing through my veins slowed my movements to a crawl.

Gritting my teeth, I took another detoxification pill, feeling its effects battle the poison's grip. I reached the edge just in time to see one of the many muscular cultivators stationed below catch Zhi Ruo. Relief washed over me, but it was short-lived. I turned to her, my anger barely contained. After all we'd done, and she ambushed him like that!

"That was a low blow, even for you."

A flicker of remorse crossed her face, but it was quickly masked by her usual icy composure. "Don't mistake my intentions, Kai Liu," she said, her voice cold and sharp. "I do not enjoy underhanded tactics. But I will not hesitate to use them if necessary. Especially when so much is at stake."

Even though she was right, a part of me rebelled against her pragmatism. "I understand," I managed to rasp out, my voice thick with the lingering effects of the poison. "But don't expect me to go easy on you."

A spark of challenge ignited in her eyes, a flicker of respect replacing the icy facade. "I wouldn't have it any other way," she retorted, her voice ringing with conviction. "Prove your worth, Kai Liu. Fight me with everything you have."

The crowd's roar echoed around the Marble Jade Arena, amplifying the tension between us. As the mist began to clear, revealing the battlefield, I tightened my grip on the vials in my hand. This was it. The final showdown.

I drew another breath, steadying myself. The chaotic sounds of the arena faded into the background as I focused on the task ahead.

Forget Zhi Ruo.

My friend, who had fought bravely and smartly, was now out of the competition. The unfairness of it gnawed at me, but I couldn't afford to dwell on it.

Forget her, and all the complex feelings I've built up over time.

Jingyu Lian, with her cold determination and fierce resolve. There was a part of me that admired her, even respected her. But admiration had no place here.

Forget the guilt.

The guilt of wanting to win, of pushing past friends and foes alike. The nagging voice that told me I should fight fair, that I should be the hero. Heroes had no place in this arena.

I shed the weight of empathy, of righteousness. These were luxuries I couldn't afford.

I was not a hero here, not a savior. I was an alchemist, a competitor determined to prove I'm the best. My opponent demanded my full attention, nothing less.

The muscular cultivators leapt onto the edge of the ring, their powerful frames easily lifting Fang Xiang free from his bindings with a liquid that dissolved the hardened mixture. He was still sneezing and cursing, his voice a hoarse rasp from the ordeal. Another cultivator tried to peel Tian Zhu off the pill furnace, but after a few failed attempts, he gave up and simply picked up both Tian Zhu and the pill furnace together, carrying the unconscious alchemist off the stage.

Ma Hualong's voice boomed out, cutting through the noise of the crowd. "Only two remain! Kai Liu and Jingyu Lian! Prepare to fight for the title of Grand Alchemy Gauntlet Champion!"

Without another word, we both sprang into action. I threw a Serpent's Breath Smoke Bomb, the vial arcing through the air before shattering at her feet. Thick, turquoise smoke billowed out, enveloping her in its hallucinogenic haze. My eyes darted around, searching for an opening. My gaze landed on a pile of discarded branches, remnants of Jingyu Lian's earlier attacks against Tian Zhu. A plan formed in my mind.

I whipped out the vial containing my last Elixir of Rapid Growth and hurled it toward the pile. The elixir shattered upon impact, the golden liquid seeping into the withered plants. Almost instantly, they began to writhe and twist, growing at an unnatural rate.

The smoke began to dissipate. The branches, now thick and gnarled, had formed a dense, impenetrable barrier around her, their thorns reaching out like hungry claws.

Jingyu Lian, however, was not one to be easily ensnared. With a fluid motion, she tossed a vial at the base of the vines. The glass shattered, releasing a pungent, earthy aroma. Almost immediately, the once-thriving vines began to wither and decay, their growth stunted by the potent concoction.

In the next instant, a glint of gold caught my eye. Her golden needles, glowing with a soft, ethereal light, flew through the air toward me. My heart leaped into my throat as I realized her intent. Was she trying to poke me full of holes?! Weren't we forbidden from using techniques directly against one another?!

But instead of me, the needles struck with pinpoint accuracy piercing a vial on my belt.

The warmth of the Sundew Sticky Bomb Elixir spread across my lower body, the viscous liquid rapidly expanding, trapping my legs and making it incredibly difficult to move.

"Shit!"

Panic clawed at my throat. I was trapped, a sitting duck for her next attack. No time to panic, I reminded myself, my mind racing through the possibilities. *Think, Kai, think!*

I glanced around frantically, my eyes scanning the arena for anything, anything at all, that could help me. And then I saw it: a scattered pile of red and orange pills by the Earth zone. Tian Zhu's concoctions, no doubt, spilled when he was dragged into the pill furnace.

A desperate plan sparked in my mind.

With a grunt of effort, I lurched forward, my trapped legs dragging behind me like anchors.

I was not going down without a fight.

Ignoring the searing pain in my legs, I took the last remaining Ember Pill I had. With a surge of adrenaline, I flung the pill toward the pile lying precariously on the floor, praying my aim was true.

The pill arced through the air. It landed amid the pile, making a small burst of flames, causing a chain reaction.

A wave of heat washed over me as the fire spread, engulfing even the shelves of ingredients nearby.

Jingyu Lian stumbled back, her eyes widening in surprise. The sudden inferno created a barrier between us, buying me precious seconds. I seized the opportunity, channeling my qi into my legs, desperate to break free from the sticky prison.

My lower body strained against the now hardened sticky substance, but it was no use. Every punch, every desperate attempt to free myself only resulted in more frustration. My mind rushed through the available options.

Slickweed Kelp Essence? No, it was elementally incompatible with the Sundew Sticky Bomb. This was one of the few times the potent solvent wouldn't have worked.

An idea sparked in my mind. With a deep breath, I reached into my storage ring and summoned my pill furnace. I hoped Ma Hualong wouldn't call foul on this. He did say we were free to use our tools in the final round.

The pill furnace materialized above the ground, dropping with a heavy thud. It landed precisely where the Sundew Sticky Bomb had gone off, the hardened elixir turning brittle from the sudden impact. The furnace shattered it into pieces, setting my legs free.

I staggered forward, the relief of movement surging through me.

With a roar of defiance, I launched myself forward, adrenaline pumping through my veins. She was distracted, her attention momentarily drawn to the raging inferno I had ignited. This was my chance.

I circled around the chaos, keeping to the shadows as I stalked toward her flank. I reached into my pouch, my fingers closing around the vial of Tormenting Pollen Mist. This was a gamble, but I had to take it.

With a swift underhand throw, the vial arced through the air, shattering against the ground near Jingyu Lian's feet. The golden mist erupted, its particles swirling around her like a swarm of angry bees. She reacted instantly, covering her mouth and nose with her sleeve, but her eyes remained exposed.

A moment later, her eyes began to water, a telltale sign that the pollen was taking effect. She pressed on, her movements faltering slightly, but a sudden, uncontrollable sneeze ripped through her, and she doubled over. The vial she had been about to throw clattered harmlessly to the ground.

This was my opening. I lunged forward, my remaining Binding Snare Potion held high. I hurled it at her, the metallic liquid splattering across her robes and the stone floor.

Her eyes widened in alarm as she felt the concoction begin to harden. She tried to break free, but the mercury-infused mixture was too fast, too strong. Within seconds, both legs and one arm were encased in a solid metal shell, her movements restricted.

Her head was bowed, and her shoulders were slumped with what I could only assume was exhaustion.

My eyes darted to the fallen vial Jingyu had dropped earlier. If I could reach it, I might be able to use its contents against her and win this.

But just as I was about to close in, she moved. In one swift, fluid motion, her free hand flicked out, sending a single golden needle flying straight toward me.

I barely had time to react. The needle struck me in the sternum, a sharp pain radiating through my chest.

I gasped, the impact sending me reeling backward. My muscles seized in place, and I could hardly breathe.

Was this the precise strike of an acupoint, or had she laced the needle with a swift-acting poison?

A sharp, localized pain radiated from the impact site, intensifying with every attempted breath. No burning sensation, no spreading numbness that might signal a toxin invading my system.

A desperate gasp tore from my lungs as pain radiated through my chest. I tried to move, to raise a hand, to throw another vial, but my body was a puppet with its strings cut. Helpless, I watched Jingyu Lian writhe against the metallic snare.

Hope flickered within me as I saw her struggles falter. We both ran out of concoctions, and she had nothing to break herself free from my trap with.

*Just a little longer*, I thought, a desperate prayer echoing in my mind. *Just a little longer until this paralysis wears off, and victory would be mine.*

With a determined glint in her eye, she whipped her free hand out, a golden needle gleaming in the sunlight. It struck the fallen vial between us with a sharp ting, shattering the glass and releasing its contents into the air.

A pungent, acrid scent filled my nostrils, and a wave of dizziness washed over me.

My lungs burned as the toxin invaded, every muscle screaming in protest. But beneath the pain, a primal fury ignited.

*No!*

The word clawed its way up my throat, a silent roar of defiance.

*I won't lose! Not like this! Not after everything—*

Images flashed through my mind: Elder Ming's smile, Feng Wu's patient guidance, Li Na and Han Wei's unwavering support. The faces of the people back home, their hopeful eyes filled with pride.

*I can't fail them.*

*I won't fail them.*

The world narrowed, a tunnel of fading light. I saw Jingyu Lian's eyes, a flicker of something like regret in their depths. But it wasn't enough. It would never be enough to extinguish the fire burning within me.

*I have to win.*

*For them.*

*For me.*

The last vestiges of consciousness flickered and died, the world consumed by darkness. But even as I succumbed to the poison's embrace, a single, unyielding thought echoed in the void:

*I will not lose.*

# CHAPTER FIFTY-SIX

# A New Champion, a New Threat

With a quick flick of my wrist, I sent a golden needle toward the fallen vial. The glass shattered, releasing Ghost Willow extract into the air. I covered my mouth and nose, but Kai, paralyzed and unable to react in time, inhaled the potent toxin.

His bloodshot eyes widened in desperation as he struggled against the effects of the Ghost Willow. His breath came in ragged gasps, and I could see the intense effort he was putting into staying conscious. My heart hammered a rhythm of guilt and admiration. He had his reasons for wanting this, I knew. Reasons as strong as my own.

Then, with a final shudder, Kai's eyes rolled back. His body went limp, collapsing like a puppet with its strings cut. A wave of respect, bitter and pure, washed over me. He was a warrior, this boy I'd foolishly underestimated. He'd saved my pride, ensured a fair fight . . . but I couldn't return the favor. Not today. Too much hung in the balance.

Ma Hualong's voice thundered through the arena, shattering the tense silence. "Jingyu Lian, victor of the Grand Alchemy Gauntlet!"

The crowd's roar was a distant hum in my ears as I stood there, still trapped in the concoction he had made, with all but one limb free to move. My hair was a wild tangle, my lungs burned, my body ached. This victory had been ripped from the jaws of defeat, ugly and hard-won. But it was mine.

My gaze fell to Kai, a storm of emotions raging within. We had both given our all. Only one of us could stand at the end, and that one was me.

The weight of it settled heavily on my shoulders, a hollow victory. This was what I'd sacrificed for, fought tooth and nail to achieve. Yet, the taste in my mouth was ash, not honey.

Several invigilators converged on me, pouring a solvent over my bindings, their touch brisk and impersonal.

They moved with a practiced efficiency, their faces impassive. One of them turned to me, offering a hand to guide me to the medical wing.

I shook my head, denying their help. "I'm fine," I said, my voice steady despite the exhaustion clawing at me. "Take care of him first."

They nodded in unison, disappearing with Kai into the tunnel. I watched them go, then turned toward the stands. My father's silhouette stood out, a question mark etched on his face. The memory of his whispered urgings to cheat clawed at my throat.

A wave of defiance surged through me, a mix of pride and bitterness. I proved myself today, I thought fiercely.

Not just to the sect, but to him.

I squared my shoulders, lifting my chin like a banner. The crowd's cheers washed over me, a distant tide. As I made my way out, Elder Wei Lian materialized from the throng, a serpent in silken robes.

"Congratulations, Jingyu," he purred, the venom barely masked. "Fortune, it seems, favored you today."

"Thank you, Uncle," I returned, my voice glacial. "Let this victory solidify my claim to the Alchemy Pavilion."

A flicker of anger crossed his face, swiftly concealed. "We shall see," he replied, each word a carefully placed stone in a wall of doubt.

This was merely a battle won, not the war. Many trials lay ahead, but today had proven one thing: I would face him on my terms, unyielding and unbroken.

As I trudged to the medical hall, one of the invigilators accompanied me. My legs felt like lead, my body battered from the grueling round. The man opened the door for me, revealing the other contestants.

Tian Zhu lay unconscious on a bed, his face bruised and swollen. Fang Xiang sat upright, unable to see with his puffy eyes. Kai Liu was being attended to by a physician, battered and unconscious. Across the room, Zhi Ruo was awake and animated, discussing something with the healer tending to him.

The invigilator guided me to a corner of the room, where a screen provided a modicum of privacy. I changed into a fresh set of clothes, each movement sending jolts of pain through my weary body. Once dressed, I downed multiple potions, their bitter taste a small price to pay for relief. The physician attending to me was efficient, her touch gentle yet firm.

"Minor injuries," she diagnosed, her voice calm. "But you're running low on qi. You should rest before the formal announcement."

I nodded, grateful for the care but eager to be alone with my thoughts. Silence settled over the room, a heavy blanket that muffled the outside world's noise. I glanced at Zhi Ruo, who had settled at his bedside with a look of calm on his face.

Always, it had been so easy to step over the fallen, the loser, to see them as mere stepping stones on my path to greatness. But seeing him and Kai Liu . . . this was different.

As I drew near, the memory of my ploy against him—swift, opportunistic—stung with a fresh guilt. He had defied Tian Zhu and Fang Xiang, just like Kai. A flurry of justifications for what I did sprang to my lips, but all that emerged were two words.

"I'm sorry."

His head lifted, surprise momentarily washing over his face. "If that's for the unceremonious shove out of bounds, apology accepted," he said, a wry twist to his lips. "I thought I was going to die for a second."

His easy forgiveness threw me off balance. "Aren't you . . . angry?"

A knowing gleam entered his eyes as his smile widened. "I'm not Kai, Jingyu. I understand ambition, the hunger for victory. A competition is a competition, after all." He leaned back with a sigh, a contented warrior sheathing his sword. "I came further than I ever dreamed, and I had no doubt I'd lose to you or Kai, one way or another. My goal was just to catch the eye of a sect or clan. Maybe with this showing, I'll finally be recruited as an alchemist and provide a better life for my family."

His words, though meant to be comforting, only stirred the turmoil within me. Had I become so accustomed to viewing others as mere obstacles that I'd forgotten their humanity? A vision of my childhood flashed before my eyes, a memory I'd long buried beneath layers of ambition and self-preservation.

I saw myself as a young girl, clinging to my father's robes as we navigated the bustling streets of Jianghu. He'd always warned me to be wary of strangers, to never let my guard down. The world, he'd said, was full of wolves disguised as sheep, eager to prey on the naive and trusting.

His words had become my mantra, a shield I held up against the world. I had learned to navigate the treacherous currents of court politics, to decipher the hidden meanings behind honeyed words and false smiles. I had become adept at building walls around my heart, allowing only a select few to glimpse the vulnerable core beneath.

Tian Zhan, my cousin and closest friend, was one of those few. He had been my constant companion, my confidant, the one person I could truly trust. His unwavering loyalty and genuine affection had been a beacon of light in my often dark and lonely path.

But even with him, there was a part of me that remained guarded, a part that feared betrayal and the pain it inevitably brought. This fear had driven me to excel, to become the best alchemist I could be, to prove my worth and secure my position in the world.

And yet, here I was, feeling a pang of remorse for my actions against Zhi and Kai. Their unwavering spirit, their refusal to resort to underhanded tactics, had shaken the foundations of my carefully constructed worldview.

The path ahead seemed uncertain, but one thing was clear: I could no longer walk it with a closed heart. The time had come to open myself to the possibility of trust, to embrace the vulnerability that came with genuine connection.

"Have you received any offers so far?"

He seemed surprised by my question and hesitated for just a moment.

"Yes, I have. From the East River Sect and the Sun Clan. Why?"

I mulled over his options. The East River was a middling sect, trying to bolster their weak pavilion with a promising alchemist. The Sun Clan have a reputation for using their alchemists as little more than tools. Given Zhi Ruo's talent, both offers seemed like they were undervaluing him, likely due to his status and not coming from a famous family. He deserved better, and I could help with that.

"Zhi Ruo," I began, my voice steady, "how would you feel about joining the Whispering Wind Sect's Alchemy Pavilion? I can ensure that whatever offer you get, it will be double than what the others are offering."

He looked at me, stunned. "Are you joking?"

"I'm not," I replied firmly. "Your talent is undeniable, and I know the Whispering Wind Sect would benefit greatly from someone of your caliber. I can ensure you and your family are taken care of."

He studied me for a moment, his expression thoughtful. "I . . . I'll need to consider it," he said finally. "I'll let you know once I get the remaining offers. But thank you. Thank you so much."

"It's the least I can do."

Just then, an invigilator called my name, signaling it was time to return. I gave him a final nod and left the room, my mind a whirlwind of emotions.

I reached the arena, the noise of the crowd washing over me like a tidal wave. I stood tall, lifting my chin as I stepped into the spotlight.

Ma Hualong stepped forward, his presence commanding attention as the crowd's cheers began to die down. He raised his hand, and the arena fell into a respectful silence. His voice, deep and resonant, filled the space as he spoke.

"Jingyu Lian, by the authority vested in me by the Alchemy Association, I hereby crown you as the Grand Alchemy Gauntlet Champion. As the victor, you have earned the right to be mentored by the legends of the Alchemy Association."

He placed a hand on my shoulder, a symbolic gesture of recognition. I swallowed hard, the weight of this opportunity settling on me. This was a once-in-a-lifetime chance, not only to progress my skills but also to forge connections with the most powerful people in the province. It was a path to solidifying my future and the future of the Whispering Wind Sect's Alchemy Pavilion.

But as the cheers gradually subsided, an unexpected figure stepped forward, causing a ripple of murmurs to spread through the audience. Ma Hualong's face twisted in confusion and a hint of anger.

A man clad in black and blue robes, recognizable as the Silent Moon Sect, approached with a confident stride. Four men flanked him, their gazes indifferent. But they emitted a certain pressure. One that I only felt from the likes of our Sect Leader.

What was going on?

The man pardoned himself for the intrusion, bowing slightly before addressing the crowd. "I apologize for the interruption, but I couldn't miss the opportunity to personally congratulate Jingyu Lian on her astounding victory."

Ma Hualong's face flushed with anger, his voice sharp. "Elder Jun, you cannot—"

He raised a hand, cutting him off. "Ah, but I am no longer 'Elder' Jun," he corrected with a smile that didn't reach his eyes. "I am the Sect Leader of the Silent Moon Sect."

Gasps echoed through the arena as Elder Jun's words sunk in. He extended his hand, revealing a storage ring that glinted in the light. "As the new Sect Leader, I wish to present Jingyu Lian with a gift, a token of our appreciation and admiration for her skills."

With a flick of his wrist, piles of rare ingredients and artifacts poured out, forming a small mountain of treasures at my feet. I narrowed my eyes.

This wasn't just a congratulatory gesture; it was a blatant display of the Silent Moon Sect's wealth and power. This "gift" was a statement, a reminder of their influence.

Elder Jun's smile remained fixed as he continued, "I hope this suffices to show our admiration for your talents, Jingyu Lian."

Ma Hualong's face twisted with barely suppressed rage, but Elder Jun pivoted smoothly, not allowing him the chance to interrupt. "What a fortunate coincidence it is," he said, his voice carrying effortlessly over the hushed crowd, "that the final results of the Gauntlet coincide with my appointment as Sect Leader. It feels like the stars themselves have aligned."

He gestured to the men standing beside him, their expressions unreadable. "Allow me to introduce the newly instated elders of the Silent Moon Sect. This is Elder Cheng, Elder Wei, Elder Xun, and Elder Fang."

I scanned their faces, trying to place their names, but they were unfamiliar. Each of them exuded an aura of power and authority, their presence almost overwhelming.

As I turned to look at the crowd, I caught sight of my father. His face had gone deathly pale, as if he had seen a ghost. His eyes were wide with a mixture of shock and something else I couldn't quite identify—fear?

"Elder Jun," I began, choosing my next words carefully, "I am honored by your generous gift. The Silent Moon Sect's recognition is . . . unexpected but appreciated."

His smile remained fixed, but there was a predatory gleam in his eyes. "We believe in recognizing true potential. The future of the alchemical arts depends on talents like *yours*."

As he spoke, I couldn't shake the feeling that this "gift" was more than it seemed—a calculated move in a larger game. My father's pallor, the unfamiliar elders, and Sect Leader Jun . . . It all pointed to something much bigger and more dangerous.

The tension in the air was palpable as Ma Hualong stepped forward, clearly struggling to maintain his composure. "This ceremony is about the achievements of our contestants," he said, his voice tight. "Let us not overshadow their hard work with politics."

Elder Jun's eyes flickered with amusement, but he nodded. "Of course, Ma Hualong. Today is indeed about celebrating talent and perseverance. Let us honor Jingyu Lian and all the participants."

As the crowd resumed their applause, I glanced once more at my father. His fear mirrored my own growing dread.

This victory, it seemed, was only the beginning of a much more treacherous journey.

# Acknowledgments

Time flies when you're writing another volume. Too fast, honestly. Once again, I'd like to give my thanks to all the people who supported me thus far.

To my beautiful girlfriend, Amanda, who's kept me accountable and kept me company in cafés throughout Downtown Toronto whenever I needed to hunker down and write.

To my physiotherapist, Jonah, for curing me of my tendonitis. I need to make an appointment with you again. It's flaring back up.

To my friends and family, who've been nothing but supportive.

To my supporters on Patreon and RoyalRoad, interacting with me, giving their support and feedback. As the famous basketball player Kevin Durant once said, "You the real MVP."

# About the Author

Carlos Calma is a Canadian author who has been captivated by LitRPG and progression fantasy since he was young. He began reading these genres as a child and started writing his own stories while in high school. This passion has continued into his adult life. Calma resides in Toronto, Ontario.

# RESPAWN YOUR CURIOSITY

*follow us on our socials*

 podiumentertainment.com

 @podiumentertainment

 /podiumentertainment

 @podium_ent

 @podiumentertainment

9 781039 488571